F
G12   Gainham, Sarah.
             Private worlds.

PRIVATE WORLDS

By Sarah Gainham

SARAH GAINHAM

PRIVATE

WORLDS

HOLT, RINEHART AND WINSTON

NEW YORK   CHICAGO   SAN FRANCISCO

F
G12

Designer: Ernst Reichl
SBN: 03-085062-2
Printed in the United States of America

80-49   9-26-11   255   695/560

THIS BOOK IS FOR SONJA WESTLING-PECK

On March 11th 1938 German troops crossed the borders of Austria and two days later the absorption of German-Austria into Greater Germany was formally announced by a jubilant Adolf Hitler. This event, then or eighteen months later when the Second World War began, affected the life of every one of the population.

As to almost everyone in Vienna, the long-expected *Anschluss* came as a shock when it actually happened, to the company of the Burgtheater. Most artists, however public their lives, care little for political affairs and Julia Homburg, one of the best-loved classical actresses of the famous theatre, was no exception. But her husband, Franz Wedeker, was a Socialist and a Jew. If he fell into the hands of the Nazis, he was doomed. After an unavailing attempt to leave the country, he returned, a terrified fugitive to his own home. For a time the family of his housekeeper provided a refuge in their Alpine village, but in the mobilisation that preceded the outbreak of War, even the high hills offered no safety and once more he went back to the city and to the security that only the personal devotion of his wife and their servant could provide. Too late now to find false papers and leave the country; they must hide him in their home. Only because Julia was well-known and clever enough to use her position was even this fragile barrier against the world possible.

The unknown presence in her home, the unsleeping effort to maintain the fiction of Franz's departure into exile, gradually enmeshed Julia in a complex web of intrigue and lying; deceptions which constantly, inevitably, led to further deceptions. Some comfort in the dreadful burden of fear she could take from the gay and easy-going Nando, met with as an opponent in a moment of danger when anxiety and strain had already emptied her marriage of all inner reality except the reality of duty and the constant threat of discovery. Discovery would mean death, for Franz at once and for the two women slowly from starvation and forced labour in prison. Even to her lover Julia must lie; only one man knew the secret, an old friend, Georg Kerenyi. With the closing of Austria's borders to Jugoslavia, yet another danger arose. A niece of Franz Wedeker's was living with Julia's mother in their country house almost on the frontier, where she could not remain once the district became a military area. Unable to leave Vienna herself, Julia persuaded the only person whose knowledge could not endanger them all, to offer the friendless girl a home and the frightened Ruth found a protector in Georg Kerenyi. In the great round-up of October 1941 in Vienna, Ruth and her unborn child disappeared forever, leaving Kerenyi with a bitter grief and rage against the world and against his own failure to save his child and its mother. In the faint hope of finding her still alive in Poland, Kerenyi volunteered for the *Wehrmacht*, leaving Julia without an ally in her desperate battle. He did not find Ruth, and in despair enlisted himself among those determined opponents of the Nazis who tried several times to assassinate Hitler.

Julia managed for a time to avoid joining one of the theatre tours which played to the troops in forward areas but sooner or later she would have to go or risk being noticeable as unfriendly to those in power. Nando was going to Krakov as a civil service representative on a Court of Enquiry and they arranged to be in Poland at the same time; as they thought, a lucky chance. It did not prove fortunate, however, for what was happening at that time in Poland proved so shocking that Nando could no longer remain in the Nazi civil service and transferred to the Army as a lesser evil.

Except for the housekeeper, Fina, Julia was then quite alone, at war with the whole world; her own people, even her own friends and colleagues were as much her opponents as those outward enemies who bombed Vienna, wrecked its beautiful palaces and its great theatres, and whose armies crept ever closer with the threat of a terrible revenge for Hitler's mad crimes. Her sad husband was imprisoned in the one small room which could be kept secret, his health wrecked by confinement and an illness which could not be properly treated, his only comfort and salvation being his work which issued as a treatise on political theory: *Thoughts on the Control of Power*. This book was, of course, secret. To save it both from the Nazis and from the approaching Soviet armies, it was entrusted to former colleagues of Georg Kerenyi's who could get it to the safety of Switzerland, and once again this effort to save what was valuable cost lives and burdened even further already overloaded consciences.

By then even the ignorant knew that the War was lost. Europe was about to be engulfed by total war. All sanity had long since disappeared from all the combatants; nothing that could be encompassed by fiction could even approach the devastation and moral degradation of what really happened in Europe during and just after that War. In the mindless uproar of its end the innocent were as guilty as the criminal and those who had from the first fought the madness of their world went under in the tempest of hatred and revenge together with their oppressors. Among them, Franz and Fina died and Julia was seriously injured.

The thirty years' civil war in Europe was over. Conflict had spread to the entire globe, and in the ruins of the civilised world were buried uncountable treasure and something like fifty million human beings; something like that number, for they were never counted in full. The catastrophe was so great that its extent is still not grasped, a generation later; at the time it was clearer than it is today, for smashed cities, starving survivors and disease were visible symbols of the inner, moral breakdown of reason and civilised restraints which had made the disaster possible.

The whole of Europe with the only exceptions of Switzerland, Sweden and the Iberian peninsula, was to greater or lesser extent occupied by foreign armies. The classic lands of the renaissance and the enlightenment presented spectacles of brutal depravity that marked even mere onlookers for life; nobody who saw Greece, France, Italy and the great cities of central Europe in the years immediately following the War can ever forget the terrible impressions of guilt and remorse, and sheer incredulity, produced by the results of our European downfall.

In those areas which were formally, so to speak, as well as actually occupied, the populations were totally impotent. In some countries even the framework of local administration had to be replaced by the occupiers; it had disappeared altogether. This was not true of Austria where a particularly sound system of communal life somehow survived from its codification in the 18th century, and where the administrative machinery of society continued to maintain order, keep records and hold the survivors together in some kind of coherent community. Yet anything that could be done was done only by permission of the real authority, the conquering armies.

The tattered and shell-shocked living were seen then, and saw themselves, through the eyes of strangers and enemies. One of these was Robert Inglis, a British officer whose job was to examine the records of those among the hordes of wandering men who happened, by some circumstance, to come to the notice of the occupying armies. Among these wrecked lives was Georg Kerenyi, who was of interest as having been involved in the conspiracy against Hitler's life in 1944. To escape the vengeance of the Gestapo after the failure of the plot, Kerenyi had bargained for his life with SS-General Tenius whose marriage to a Viennese actress brought him into the circle of Kerenyi's acquaintance. Subsequently captured as a prisoner of war, Kerenyi returned in the belief, shared by everyone he knew, that Tenius was dead in the ruined city of Breslau where he held the office of Chief of Police, and which held out as an isolated fortress encircled by the Red Army until after the end of the War. At the time this seemed of minor significance, and Kerenyi's immediate preoccupation was to find his former friends, in the first place Julia Homburg.

He saw her again embittered and morbidly resentful, at odds with friends and colleagues and suspected by the occupying Allies. The wartime intrigues had come home to roost; in particular that Julia had been obliged, by the fear of becoming conspicuously hostile to the Nazis, to go through a form of divorce from her husband. This event shocked, among others, a former journalist friend, Colton Barber, who returned to Vienna after the war. Just because she was hiding Franz Wedeker in their home, just because she had refused to abandon him, the outward sign of abandonment was forced upon her. This was something very easily misunderstood by those who had not lived under a police terror, and it is clear that a woman capable of undertaking a seven-year long and single-handed struggle for the life of one man must be a human being of intransigent stubborness, pride and courage. These are not qualities that make people easy to get along with and the priceless value of an unyielding spirit is not obvious except at those times when it is irreplaceable. That the battle was, at its very end lost, increased Julia's bitterness to an obsession.

Still, since she was alive, life must go on, and she retired to the half-ruined house in the country left empty by the death of her mother, and occupied her energies with putting the house into some sort of order and providing a home in it for the sister of her dead lover, a refugee from the Russian-occupied Zone of Austria, and incidentally for Kerenyi. Kerenyi in turn brought Robert Inglis to the place in the country and the lonely, reserved and perhaps rather humourless young Englishman became a devoted friend of Julia's and then of her ward Lali's, whom he eventually married. To provide Lali's fatherless child with a background, Julia adopted him as her heir, and towards the end of 1951 in spite of interruptions and problems, it began to seem possible that there was a future for them all. Only slowly, and with much difficulty, however, could Julia overcome the barriers she had herself built up against the future, and three months before the opening of this stage of her story she at last agreed to marry Kerenyi. They travelled away together for a summer in the Greek islands, and with the return from this journey, the reader meets them again.

It is perhaps necessary to add that, although both the physical surroundings of this story and its historical framework are real, the persons and their actions are all fictional. The correctness of the background and the credibility of the actions of these imaginary people have been confirmed many times by those fitted to know, that is by Viennese who lived through the years of German occupation, war and Allied occupation. More than a few such readers have said to the writer that she should really recognize them on meeting them, for the story is their story. This is a source of humility, gratitude and great pride to the inventor of Julia Homburg, Franz Wedeker and Georg Kerenyi.

VIENNA
August 1970

BOOK ONE

I

'A note from Robert to welcome us home. He really has, Robert, a high sense of occasion, don't you agree?' With the words Julia Homburg-Kerenyi laid down the letter she held and turned slightly, indicating it to her husband.

'Certainly, he always had. Though I seem to recall you often referring to that quality in him as "being stuffy".' Kerenyi, hands in pockets in the very state of one returning after a long absence, a long journey, of not being quite there yet, moved slowly over and picked up the letter. There were many other letters awaiting them on the table, but up to now only this one had been opened. It was not franked by the Post, but in the lower left-hand corner was the formal advice '*en ville*'.

' "We wanted to be the first to greet you on your return to Vienna, to confirm again what you already know from my telegram",' he read aloud. ' "This is really from Lali, or at the very least from us both, but I am spoiling her still and write it for her. The daughter will, of course, be named for her mother, that is Lali's mother, and then for Julia, I shan't be able to see you since I am going back at once; had to come up for two days but want to be sure she doesn't exert herself too quickly. So I return today to Styria and am sure you will be far from missing my presence. We made, by the way, and it coincided, our first major sale last week. The foal of the Slovenian mare. So in every way all is well. Tom Wallingham writes from Ireland, suggesting a permanent partnership and this shows how splendidly everything is going, the Irish being as they are—mad but not foolish. . . ." '

Georg put down the sheet of paper and said with curiosity, 'I thought Robert had a whole month's leave? Why was he in Vienna?'

'Oh, I expect there are always things,' she said vaguely, and looking through envelopes. 'Those military mysteries.' Of Robert's service duties she spoke, as always, with a joking respect as of sibylline rites perfectly incomprehensible to the uninitiated. 'Here's a letter from Friedland. At least, that's what the postmark says.'

3

'Friedland? Who on earth could be writing to you from there? Well, have a look, you incurious creature.'

'Not me. It's for you. I don't think I knew there was such a place. I connect it with Wallenstein, not with nowadays.' She handed the thin, yellowish envelope to him and he took it with a puzzled frown that held some reserve, a slight reluctance.

'It's an east-west exchange point now,' he said. 'Appropriately enough, come to think of it. One could make a literary point of that; from the first Thirty Years' War to the second.'

He hardly heard some smiling rejoinder from Julia. She moved to the window, examining in the diffused lighting the finish of the brand-new paintwork with satisfaction.

'Well! Here's a rum go,' he exclaimed in English as he read.

'Odd expression. One of Robert's, I suppose?'

'Of course,' he agreed absently, his attention now wholly on the message in his hand.

The idea of an English phrase introduced into their normal speech brought a dim shadow of memory back from somewhere. The connection was unclear but it brought a taste of unease, or increased the slight rejection she felt at the mention of an east-west barrier and the still almost contemporary condition of warfare. The name of a village over the Danube, well out of the city, came into her mind. Stockerau, a restaurant, and she knew now why the phrase, the quite different but similar English phrase, disturbed her. It was there that Franz spent a haunted day on his return from the abortive attempt to cross the Czech frontier in March, 1938. As she thought to herself, you are being morbid, Georg handed her the mean little sheet of paper, covered in *Sütterlin* script.

'Heavens, I can't read that at this time of night.' But she figured out at least the ending and signature, enough to understand the change in Georg's face.

'Here's a pretty kettle of fish,' she commented, the long-remembered phrase forcing itself out with undesired certainty.

'That's not one of Robert's. Much too old-fashioned.'

'Tenius.' Her tone was astounded almost to disbelief. 'How can it be—Tenius? Isn't he dead?'

'Evidently not.'

'No but seriously. Hella will go off her head. But why should he write to you?'

'Just what I'm wondering.' Georg turned uneasily. The habit

of being a guest in this place still strong in his consciousness, he behaved like a visitor, as if forgetting in the shock of the letter that he now belonged here. 'How about a drink?' He lifted his big, rather ugly nose and jerked his head at the glass-fronted rococo cupboard that always held the drinks, and as he could see, continued to hold them after the rebuilding as before.

'Oh yes, do. But wine for me. D'you mind, there will be a bottle in the refrigerator . . . ?' She was so used to being waited on that the designed absence of the servant made no difference to the assumption that someone other than herself fetched wine.

'Ah, that's good,' said Julia as he poured wine for her; for himself he brought ice and mixed whisky and water. 'The Greek wines are very good, but one's own are better. Lighter, anyway.'

'This is better than Ouzo, too,' he said. Then, abruptly, 'What d'you think he wants, Tenius? I've been taking it for granted for five years that he was disposed of.'

'It was never officially confirmed, it's true. But all those stories . . . everyone assumed that he'd gone under in Breslau. Either suicide, or killed in the last corner of the last street. We all thought the reason for never hearing was that Breslau held out long after the capitulation. Even Hella believed that, she always thought her efforts to get him officially declared dead were simply formalities.'

'Now she'll be forced to divorce him and put up with the publicity.'

'I remember in Warsaw when she just cleared off to get married to Tenius and left us to fill the breach at the theatre. . . . "*Teatr Polski.*" You could still see it on the pediment. It comes back as if it were yesterday. God, how she has regretted that marriage.'

'Serves her right,' he said harshly. 'She shouldn't have connected herself with filth like Tenius.'

'She's always sworn she didn't know. . . .'

'Rubbish. She knew he was a General of police troops. But, of course, a potentate at the time. . . .' They were silent for a moment, contemplating with bleak alarm all the possible confusions, the manifold implications of a return from the dead of this man, hardly known, who once played an indirect part in their lives almost as significant as the part he had played directly for Julia's colleague. The return to memory of that obscure and now ruined country tavern where in a dead past they and their friends were accustomed to take outings from the city, for a change of air and atmosphere, was only the beginning. By chance they never went there together and for Georg the place existed no longer in memory any more than it still stood in reality; but just as the modest provision of countrified cooking and local wine—she seemed to recall roast pheasant with lentils—was stranded for Julia into the long-ago shock of her former husband's mentioning it on his fugitive and hunted return to his home, so there were other and more immediate concerns for Georg in this letter. It brought for him no ghost, however bewildering and painful; it was not a healed wound that throbbed but a sharply urgent spike of a question that prodded his wits into defence. The fortunes of war had not disposed of that ruse of war practised on Tenius when both he and Kerenyi were in danger. Not only the man returned from the dead; among his non-existent baggage were secrets thought safe by all who had once known him. His survival was like an unsuspected, rusted and unexploded shell-case, encrusted with the menacing leakage of its contents, turned up by a spade with frightening suddenness in the rebuilding operation of their lives.

This was no moment to point out to Julia that the shell-case was still explosive; first he must think it out for himself. In this silent decision his wife was only too glad to acquiesce; she no more wished to examine her own memories of Tenius than Kerenyi wished to stir them up further. There was an obvious means to their common purpose, and taking it Julia looked about her at the long room, now so different and yet so incurably the same.

'You haven't said if you like the new decorations?'

'I've hardly taken them in. It's very changed. White paint, the wall there gone, like a new place altogether, and yet not.'

'Yes, it's vast now, all one great long room. He did it very well I expect.' She referred to the designer, commissioned to rebuild the apartment in their absence. 'We must inspect it all—in the morning.'

'The kitchen seemed much bigger, when I was getting the wine,' he said, 'though I'm not sure I remember how it was before, at that.'

'There were three rooms on that corridor,' she reminded him, 'and they've been knocked into just two.'

There was a tiny pause, 'Well, two and a small bathroom for Frau Lisl.'

'Ah. Quite rebuilt,' he said.

'Yes,' she said, facing his meaning with a touch of high scorn for her own nervousness. 'We didn't need a boxroom there. People don't keep odd bits and pieces as they used to do.'

There was something unutterably wrong and quite uncorrectible in her choice of words.

'Yes, I remember now, we agreed on that,' he accepted his share of the responsibility for getting rid of the so unwanted little space in the back corridor. Julia moved down the room, and stopped before a painting between two of the long casements. 'I don't care for that. One of the architect's friends, I suppose. I think we might go in rather for a couple of the new realists. I don't much like abstracts.'

'No, you never took much stock in the abstract. It's quite good, though.'

'Oh, if it pleases you. . . .' She was easy, largely unconcerned; a return to an old indifference that did not please him although it usually issued, in personal relations, as kindness. It took them back to a state of tension that, in Greece, for the last two months had altogether been lacking. A thread of connection, far from happy, and existing long before even he had been aware of one of its sources as—then—forbidden desire.

'I once stood in here,' Julia said suddenly, 'years ago, after some quarrelsome discussion we had, and thought, or felt, how it might be if you put your arms round me and I could relax. An absolute *feel*, it was; it's familiar enough now, of course, but then impossible.'

'It would have been incest then.'

'Did you feel it too?'

'Not then, no. . . . I remember the occasion, but not then. The first time was later, at that incredibly vulgar, overdone luncheon party outside Warsaw.'

'I suppose,' she said slowly, and poured out more wine into the commonplace glass. 'I suppose we shall live it down? The past?'

'We shall have to live it into ourselves.'

'I've felt we have done that in outside things. But in our own relationship?'

'Relationships,' he said thoughtfully. 'Best leave them to find themselves like rivers, in channels where they can flow.' He turned over the letter from the transit camp for returned prisoners of war with one long finger, as if reluctant to touch it again. The obsolete script was now facing downwards where they could not see it.

7

'We don't need even to unpack our overnight bags,' she said with an effect of changing the subject. 'I wrote to Frau Lisl to leave everything ready until she arrives tomorrow. Shall we look round the new apartment now, after all?'

'The drawing room and study have disappeared altogether,' he said after a strolling few moments. 'I didn't notice before, but we entered the living room at a different angle from the old one—entrance, I mean.'

'Yes, he moved the long room up as it were, up the length of the frontage. Fortunately there were no walls that simply couldn't be disposed of or turned into wide arches. We had to compensate the people upstairs for their loss of chimneys by installing heating for them, but that was minor compared with . . . Here, you see, is the new bedroom, at the end, and he made a combined dressing room and bathroom next to it; that had to stay, the bathroom, because of the plumbing. The old toilet remains the same, or rather in the same place, for the same reason, and the hall one, too. Frau Lisl's bath is connected with the kitchen plumbing. Ingenious, isn't it? Hansi Ostrovsky said he was the best man in Vienna and I think he really is—he did the old Czernin palace afresh from top to bottom.'

'I remember reading, yes.'

'I didn't leave it to the designer to get rid of the big crystal in the drawing room, as it then was, nor the appliqués; they were dismounted before we left—the two days you had to go to Graz—and auctioned at the Dorotheum. Very good prices, they were sold at once. I didn't even know it, but they were good, it seems. Fortunately the dealers didn't know either—that I didn't know, I mean.'

'Graz,' he said with a disquiet quite out of proportion. 'What on earth was I doing in Graz?' It was, after all, over two months ago.

'You were writing something. Wasn't it about the renovations in the Armoury that you so disapproved of?'

'Not the theatre? I just don't recall. Funny, I just don't remember what the devil I was doing in Graz, two months ago.'

'Perhaps,' she was forced to say, against her will, 'you are confusing it with what you were doing in Graz ten years ago?'

'Your memory is so much better than mine.'

'And my connection with Graz much older.'

'Of course, the house. And you were at school near there . . .'

'The house. Though it's nowhere near Graz. But the memories of the house belong to you now as much as to me.'

'Ah, no,' he said. 'I approached it for the first time since the War from quite a different direction. Graz was an outpost—hardly existed.'

'I suppose so,' she agreed quietly. 'But I always seem to have gone to the house, and before that, to school, from Graz Station.'

'School came first then?' He tried with an idle tone to remove the conversation further into the past.

'Well, yes. The Convent—I went there awfully young.' She drew breath. 'Being got rid of, you know? But the house came a bit later—summer of 1919 it must have been. I remember that clearly. . . .'

They were back now in the living room, and he poured her another glass of wine, refilling his own whisky or, as he would say in the idiom he picked up from American friends, freshening it up.

'What you say about forgetting just what you were in Graz for —it's not quite true that my memory is better. I get this place mixed up—always did—with my parents' apartment in the IIIrd District. The knucklebone tiles in the bathroom, the fishbone parquet. Not the ornamental inlay work in the, in what was, the drawing room—there was nothing as elaborate as that in my own home. They went in, in every respect, for that inverted snobbery of being totally conventional, never overdoing anything. Except, of course, the loyalty to the Monarchy. They overdid that all right.'

'How do you mean, overdid it—he was a civil servant, your father, wasn't he?'

'Yes, of course, I didn't mean in the—what would you say? The moral meaning of loyalty. I only meant, they didn't really have to change all their property, even my mother's little scraps, into war bonds and State investments so that they were *absolutely* penniless.'

'I've wondered about that. Do you realise I know nothing of your childhood? But your mother married again quite soon?'

'Hence the house in Styria,' she agreed. 'But do you *want* to know about my childhood? I never even think of you being a child —in fact I can't imagine you as a child.' She laughed at the incongruity. 'I think you were born, if at all, as a fully-grown man.'

'Certainly I want to know. I want to know everything about you. Male possessiveness, no doubt.'

'Possess my childhood? Well, that at any rate would be something new for me—nobody else ever did.'

'Except yourself,' he pointed out.

'And later,' she pressed him. 'You want to know about my teens? Adolescence—all that?'

'Everything,' he said, staking a comprehensive claim. 'I shall probably even seek out the earliest photographs of you in the archives at the theatre, to place you finally, immovably.'

'Hmm,' she said, pulling down the corners of her mouth rather comically, 'funny hairdo and all?'

'Absolutely, funny hairdo and all.'

'Odd you didn't think of this in Greece—all those islands, all that time we had . . .'

'Islands, you see, are not at all to do with you in the past. Greece is so very physical—don't you agree? In spite of all the classical treasures and pre-history and democracy and cradles of civilisation?' This last in palpable inverted commas, to make her laugh. Which she very agreeably did and for the moment—he was again aware that she agreed in this—they were away from the more recent past into safer waters. Waters whose currents must bring them eventually back towards the last few years and the realities of the place in which they so comfortably found themselves. But, of that, in their momentary relief, they neither of them thought. Because it was relief; there was a quality of apprehension in their situation, by no means only caused by the letter from Tenius, being just as they were and just where they were.

'You mean, we enjoyed the immediate there—the sea with its immense density, everything so brilliant, actual. It's the light, you think?'

'So they say. Certainly not the people—surly lot.'

'Not surly—quarrelsome, rather. But listen, you knew me when I wore pre-war clothes that would look funny now. Why the photographs?'

'I don't know. To place something. I mean—to replace something.' He stopped to think. 'But the earliest photographs must belong to a time I didn't know you, in any case.'

'Do you know, I don't remember when we first met? You just came to be there.'

It was the fact that it had been he who introduced her, as a journalist who knew all the Burgtheater people, to her first husband, that closed once again by common consent, that avenue and they talked instead of Greece. For it was that introduction that blotted him, Kerenyi, out of her consciousness in the early years of their acquaintance. It was as friend of her lover and husband that he so gradually 'came to be there'. And these realities existed for them both as living shadows while his own former loves were almost unimportant; not because the new wife, the former widow of his friend, lacked a vivid jealousy but because his past was in the past and hers was in the present.

Yet there was an element of danger in the idea of recalling the past that stimulated both of them; perhaps just the possibility of danger made the idea of research attractive. For what neither of them lacked, most conspicuously did not lack, was courage. And it would be the 'three o'clock in the morning' kind of courage that would be needed for exploration of what they must, what it was essential that they should, bring alive into their present. Whether or not either of them was conscious of this at that moment is doubtful. They were very conscious people, both of them, but the feeling of that moment was more superficial, more concerned with the manifold complexities of adjusting their immediate living, in Julia's apartment in Julia's house which she had inherited from her murdered husband. That many-layered complexity was present now in all its threatening unease.

'Well, we shall have time to explore all that,' she said lightly and held out her glass for refilling. 'I can begin now, if you like. The first thing I remember. . . .' She paused theatrically, going back with a histrionic air she would never have used professionally, but was meant as a private joke for Georg, to the distant and safe past. Nearer memories would, with time, with their professional lives and possibly with boredom at the theme, take care of themselves by growing dim.

'You aren't tired?'

'Rather the other way about—jumpy from all that sitting still. But, are you?'

'Me? I'm never tired, you know that.'

'Well, then, the first thing I remember. . . . Good heavens, what is the first thing I remember . . . ?'

The small girl stood, very aware of her demurely formal attire, the gathered white silk of her dress and the black stockings, black patent-leather party shoes, the band over her dark hair which lay straight down her back—it was usually plaited and showed the wavy marks of that—in brushed primness that could quickly become unordered natural curves. That she stood was the mark of the occasion; she waited until her starched-aproned nurse, frozen to a frontage of sternness, pushed her forward to go up to her mother. She had never been up so late before, it was after nine o'clock. The room, cleared of its central objects for many guests, seemed even larger, higher, than to a child's eye view it always was, and it seemed to gleam in every particular. There were a number of people present, all above her, immensely taller than herself and all of them in rustling silk, whispering over the floor with movement, or with rising long upward legs cut off by evening coats or—more sharply—military tunics. Above her eye level by miles, medals and orders clinked against each other; there were one or two great glittering badges which she thought of as brooches, with wide crossed silk bands under them, at the join of legs and evening coats, but even then she noticed that the straight-across tunics were not ornamented with such badges. They, on the other hand, gave off a slight jingling from dress-spurs and these she could easily see because she must constantly look down to make sure where she was going and to avoid the trailing ruffling of silks and at a higher level the action of fans, gloves, scarves and the slender scabbards of ceremonial swords which had the attribute of moving unexpectedly —to her unexpectedly—as they were manipulated by sinewy male hands just at her eyes' height.

'Enchanting little creature,' said a feminine voice of a quality she was many times later to encounter. 'She does you endless credit, my dear Sonja.' Sonja, she knew, of course, was her mother whom she was almost sightlessly now approaching by what must have been instinct. The scents were so various she could only take them as a cloud, and it may have been those odours of luxury that made her slightly dizzy. It was the small pressure of her mother's hand, often rehearsed, that told her when she must make the deep curtsey and she achieved it creditably, not raising her eyes until the quite minor royal personage spoke directly to her in a tone she recognised as especially for children.

Her mother's hand was touching her shoulder with small tapering fingers which she did not need to look at to see exactly as flashing with rings; which, indeed, she must not look at. This told her that she must now reply to the remark made to her but above her, even though he bent down. She made the trained reply, the touch on her shoulder withdrew her, a froth of feminine lace enveloped her head for a moment as lips pressed against her forehead and she was moved away from hand to hand, rustle to rustle, clink to clink of spurs and medals, to make the round of the salon. This took the prescribed time almost exactly and she could see in the distance at the open double doors, her nurse with hands folded at her waist, reappear to claim her. It was time to withdraw and she withdrew, neither with haste nor relief for this was, quite simply, what one did.

She was not sure whether it was an anniversary or a promotion of her father's. Both were recently much spoken of and they were now confused in her mind, but of course that did not matter because she knew exactly what was expected of her.

Pressed, in the nursery, all she found to say about the tall moustached personage bending over her was that he smelled of brandy, an odour she recognised because her nurse was accustomed to take a glass of hot water with brandy before going to bed in her next-door 'cabinet'; she always came past the bed to make sure that her charge was fast asleep, thus often waking her. This offended her nurse, she did not understand at all why it should but accepted this too, as in the order of things.

But she quickly realised, it may even have been the following morning when coming in from her walk she was in the kitchen where she was sometimes taken illicitly by her nurse, that she must say more than that—that about the brandy smell. So she quite naturally embroidered a little her impression, and found herself bouncing slightly, on a long, sinewed thigh, very hard, while hands touched and cuddled her and a voice asked, brushing her cheek with moustaches just like the royal person's, if she liked to be tickled.

'You leave the child alone!' said her nurse's voice, outraged, above her head; she was aware without registering it, that there was fear as well as anger in the voice suddenly rough and speaking in dialect.

She never saw the coachman or whatever he was about the place again, and was not in doubt that her nurse had complained of him and he was instantly dismissed. The next time one of the men touched her she knew enough to move away quickly. That is, she knew this was something not expected of her, to sit on anyone's knee except her nurse's. For that she would be scolded. But she recalled, too, some while after, when it was snowing and she was being led through a door where her dancing class was, the same voice of a man, speaking to her nurse with reproach and her nurse replying in a softened voice. That was the first time, then when her nurse explained it to the man with moustaches which imitated royalty, that she heard of the change. And, sure enough, a few weeks later the nurse was gone to a new post and the governess arrived in her stead. When she asked her mother where nurse was, she was told that a new baby in a new place in Bohemia had claimed this expert attention and moreover, nurse was about to be married. When she asked whether the man was at the place in Bohemia too, her mother replied with amused curiosity, yes, but how on earth did she know? Oh, she said, putting her head on one side as the ladies in silks rustling over the floor did, I guessed. But it never did occur to her that her mother didn't understand that she meant *that* man. He is going into the Army, said her mother, and sighed, sorry for nurse. The child was sorry only for herself, for nurse was round and soft and the new governess not only insisted on her learning her own speech but complained constantly of the unbelievable cruelty and mischance of her being here in Vienna, abandoned among the enemy by that brute of a foreigner. . . . The child, however, thought that by foreigner she herself and her mother were meant and though she very quickly spoke French idiomatically it remained like a stone in her shoe that the bitterness of Mademoiselle (who was really Madame) put her and her whole surroundings into a different category of being, rejected by Mademoiselle for some other, unknown, state of affairs to which she was—that is, Mademoiselle was—unable to revert by reason of some brute of a man, a foreigner; to which category she herself was understood to belong.

But in fact she did not at all understand, for almost everyone whom she yet knew was from somewhere else than Vienna but was still not foreign. Including her mother, who came from romantic mountains and rolling hills to which she was always going to be taken again if it were only not for this dreadful war. Once she had been there, she knew from the telling, but remembered nothing and this gave her a feeling of wrongness when it was mentioned. She ought to remember. But this was nothing at all like the sensation of utter differentness that Mademoiselle was clearly talking so often about. That differentness, of Mademoiselle's, was evidently a hostile barrier; something the child thought of as tangible, yet which she could not encompass in her small stock of knowledge. But something that definitely did not belong among the things she knew to be expected of her. Since she could not put this into words she did not ask her mother about it. Foreignness, from Mademoiselle's monologue, became unFrenchness; but it was all unclear for in Vienna, or rather in the surroundings the child was familiar with, foreignness hardly existed as a separateness, only as something so accepted that it had never been—and never was to be—explained to her. And it was unclear too, whether it was only they—her family—who were foreigners, or whether, as sometimes seemed to appear through Mademoiselle's talk, the label belonged to others as well. And if so, foreign from what? But gradually, over months, it came out that it was only non-Frenchness that was foreign. This satisfied, for a time, the puzzlement. It was clear that Frenchness was one thing and everything else was foreign—but exactly why foreignness should be something to be ashamed of, that the child did not quite absorb. The riddle began again when she heard one of the servants say 'that foreign female', unmistakably meaning Mademoiselle because he shook a fist at her back. So she, then, was foreign?

She confused, too, the matter of foreignness with the mysterious condition, which for a time she thought of as an object of some unknown kind, of War. Not only Mademoiselle talked constantly of War, the servants did too; and in a quite different fashion, so did her father. Only her mother rarely used the word. Apparently this War had been there for a long time. She was not aware of there having ever been any other state, since her consciousness dawned when the War was already in being. She only gathered that from the concept of War, which acquired blackness from a number of figures about her beginning always to wear clothing of that hue, often being mentioned in connection with its opposite, a word that as yet had no meaning.

And here began in the child's mind the feeling of something being or becoming wrong with everything; with the entire enfolding and encompassing fluidity in which she existed. Her father having always been a background presence, she was not aware of him consciously, but he here appeared in a conjunction with this subaqueous tremor of the atmosphere, or ruffle in the flowing or enclosing state of being. As nearly always with the changes of awareness in children, it was a conjunction she was not supposed to know about.

It had been forgotten, or was simply not known by her father, that the child was in the neighbouring room, having been bidden to appear at a certain hour for some ladies expected to coffee. Neither these guests, nor yet her mother, were there; the child did not now know what was expected of her and so she seated herself with an aspect of primness in the chair her mother usually occupied and established herself with small gestures and movements in imitation of the scene she expected shortly to take place, as if the ladies and her mother were really there. But she did this silently and made the remarks she knew would be expected of her—she could easily replace those made by the ladies since they were almost always the same ones—without speaking aloud. The very fact that the double doors to the adjoining room were open, as they usually were in the afternoon, to her father's study proved to her by habit that he was not there; and indeed he never was there in the afternoon. That had never happened. Even when an unusually sharp rap at the corridor door could be heard, it did not occur to the child that the room was occupied by its owner. Only when, in the rustle of skirts his voice sounded with an effect of abruptness and dryness, did his presence with a slight shock dawn on her.

'Ah, there you are, Madame,' his voice said with an emphasis which, as she knew his tone, accused the person entering of being late.

'I am sorry, I was a little delayed,' replied her governess in French.

'I prefer to speak my own language if you have no objection. You are, after all, an Austrian citizen, Madame. And it is on that subject I have, regrettably, to speak. It has come to my ears, to come directly to the point, that you talk to my daughter . . .'

'Ah!' cried the governess in her accented German, 'the servants again. They hate me, as you know, Monsieur. . . .' Her tone was of a high irritation the child was quite used to, but on this occasion underlaid by an almost servile nervousness which the speaker tried to cover by her aggressive manner which was certainly, as it always was, accompanied by a toss of the head.

The child now half-rose, with a sensation of embarrassment at doing something which was definitely not expected of her, that was near terror. Her respect for her father approached fear. As the notion of being where she should, inexplicably to herself, obviously not be, came to her it was at once replaced by the decision not to give her presence away. She drew back, trembling a little, into the chair, whose back she supposed would hide her even if one of the two persons talking should move so as to see into this room. And with the cunning of children, she raised her feet quickly to the seat of the chair where there was plenty of space for them, if she sat with her arms folded round her knees.

'I do not listen to servants' talk, Madame. And if you will be so good as to address me by my correct title, I shall be grateful to you. To continue: the conversation was heard by myself. If one can call it conversation; I should rather call it a diatribe. Although my duties take up more than enough of my time, I am not quite so unconcerned with the existence of my only child as never to go near her schoolroom. . . .' Here a weary note made itself felt in her father's voice and the child could imagine him pressing a hand to his forehead with a patience that complained of his almost constant headache.

There was silence, and then the stiff rustle of papers being moved about. 'It is possible that you are not aware, Madame Zilchek, that your husband has deserted his regiment, his colours, his oath . . .' Here her father's voice rose as she had never yet heard it rise, into what was almost a shriek. 'And that this fact places you, as a former French citizen, in a most equivocal situation. In all the circumstances of which you informed my wife at the time of your coming to us, I hesitate to draw the obvious and immediate consequences of what I myself heard you saying to my daughter. That is to say, I *did* hesitate.'

'I am alone in the . . .'

'One moment, if you please. I knew of this disgraceful conduct of the man who is your lawful husband—I would remind you— some days ago. Indeed, I was on my way to you, to try with what tact I could, in spite of my own anger, and indeed horror, at his behaviour, to tell you of it when I heard you addressing my daughter as a "*sale Boche*".'

'I wasn't—no, no, I didn't mean . . .'

'Apparently this man Zilchek thinks of himself as something he calls, I have no doubt, a Czech citizen. We have recently heard this expression once or twice.' A sound of almost feminine sarcasm crept into the voice, which became again controlled by an effort that could be heard in its coldness and unevenness.

'As you may judge by the lapse of three days between that time and this afternoon, I have thought very earnestly about the matter and I am well aware of the seriousness for one in your position and a dependant of mine, of any hasty action on my part. But, having considered the matter from every point of view, I have come to the conclusion that just as your *husband* has renounced his allegiance, so have you, Madame, betrayed the trust placed in yourself in respect of my daughter.'

There was the sound of a confused movement, loud gasps, and then a wail and sobs muffled into a handkerchief.

'But, *Herr Sektionschef*, you cannot turn me out into . . .' the voice tailed off into choking tears and sobs.

There was the sound of a chair being pushed back as her father, evidently, rose from his desk.

'You should have thought of that, Madame, before,' said his voice with concise vindictiveness. 'Your personal situation contained an element of what one may now see as danger, from the very start. Did it not? A person of discretion would have recognised that fact, even if decent feeling for those who provide your board and lodging and pay you a reasonable salary—not to mention the feelings of a mere child—had not dictated a different conduct from you.'

There was a waiting pause which was, however, filled only by increasingly desperate weeping so that the child herself began to weep in sympathy and fear, stifling any sounds she made in her skirts, fortunately as it now turned out, already muffling her face by her knees being drawn up close.

'This is a revolting scene!' cried her father, and his voice broke, filling the child with a lost and increasing terror. 'Control yourself!'

There were sounds of rustling and movement mingled with the sobs: what could be happening?

'What are you thinking of?' his voice almost screamed. 'What use is it to fling yourself about now? You must leave at once! I should be afraid of your approaching my child again. You are obviously not normal—not able to—'

Hasty steps and the door slammed to the corridor, but the sobs continued so that the child knew it was her father who had decamped.

The cowering child hardly found time to cast about frantically for what she should do, when the outside bell rang, and there inter-

vened a great bustle of steps running down the stairs, of loud talk
and even cries, of steps rising again on the so familiar treads of
stone which with unnatural clearness could be heard ringing in the
gripping, frosty cold of outside air. Without waiting to think how or
why, the child fled from the terrifying piling of emotions, through
the next, the large salon, through a service room that ad-
joined it and out into a passage from which she could run down the
back stairs to the servants' quarters.

'Nurse!' she screamed wildly, 'nurse! Where is nurse?'

She tumbled into a fat bosom, huge fullness of stomach, enfolding arms of vital energy and a curiously hoarse, but soft voice
that spoke in dialect, saying 'what now, what is it, come along then,
don't cry now, nobody's going to hurt you' and the like in a continuous stream of comfort. The smell was of pastry and heat, and
sweat and a breath of garlic; it was cook, familiar, known, but
never before touched. Trying already to control herself, the child
stammered something about Mademoiselle, she hardly knew what,
and the cook replied with easy scorn 'oh, Gawd, that foreigner
again,' and took the child into her little narrow room where there
was a huge fat feather-bed rising like the bread-dough she had sometimes seen in her illicit visits to the kitchen with nurse in the past.

'You're shivering, poor little mite,' said cook, and lifted her into
the odorous bed, under the soft down mountain, where all was cosy
and lit by a flicker of the soft candle-flame, though the room itself
was chill enough for her to be glad of the quilt. And presently, just
as cook was beginning to glance at the total dark out of the window,
by which she knew she must begin to get dinner ready, the child
slept, catching breath now and then in a late sob.

It must have been, probably, that same evening but much later
that she heard the voices of her parents together, above her; this
fact of their being together without other people present stuck in
her mind.

'But she can't remain here,' objected her father's voice, outraged. 'It's not suitable. Probably not healthy, either.'

'Don't be absurd,' replied her mother with a sharply ironical
sound that belonged to her voice when speaking to her husband.
'The child's fast asleep for one thing. And you eat cook's food every
day—what's wrong with the child sharing her bed for one night?
Better, anyway, than waking her and taking her back to that ter-
magant upstairs. And what on earth you can have said to her to get

her into such a state, I should like to know. Or perhaps, I mean I'd much rather not know.'

'You left it to me to get rid of her!' came the voice-sound to which only years later a name could be put, of hysteria.

'Quite the contrary,' said her mother dryly. 'You wished to do it yourself, and asked me *how* you should best do it. I told you to tell her simply that we could no longer afford to keep her and that we would pay her fare to Zürich, where she could get her papers in order again and go back to France. But what do you do? You make some immense, emotional scene of patriotism, you bring in all sorts of details that precisely in the circumstances should *not* have been mentioned. And then you wonder at it that you have a fearful scene on your hands. You wanted a scene. You stayed away from the office so that you could *have* a scene, and you got a scene. I've no doubt at all that you depended upon me coming in and rescuing the situation before it got totally out of hand; but how could you— or I—know that I should get held up by this ridiculous riot? But I did, and you had better learn from it that times have changed.'

The child, half-awake, was even so aware that there was something wrong with the acerbity of this answer, not in its sharpness for that was frequently to be heard between her parents, but in something else, an assertiveness that her mother did not usually find necessary.

'I had no idea at all that you would be out there in Mariannengasse', he protested, lost in her mother's cleverness.

'Of course you had,' she replied brusquely, 'I told you I was going to the dressmaker before collecting Marie and the cousins for coffee.'

'You didn't say a word . . .' He began, his voice trembling with anger and nervousness.

'Be quiet. She's awake. Come along and leave her here for tonight. Tomorrow that harridan will be gone, bungled as you've arranged it. I've no doubt we shall have other—official consequences too—of her ever being here. Married to a Czech nationalist—why did you never tell me, for Heaven's sake? Just because she was cheap!'

'The child had to have a governess,' he muttered, his voice lowered in case the child should hear, which she did.

'If there is any question, we shall have to say you didn't know. She lied about her husband—common enough among that sort of people! And this time, for everybody's sake, take my advice for once and don't let's have any more heroics.' And then, the Hungarian hardness of voice even more pronounced, 'Even if you can't endure to admit you didn't know something!'

After that night there was no more governess, and no new one came, so that the child was a good deal more with her mother than formerly; or else, she was with the cook. For it now seemed as if suddenly, most of the servants were gone too. At first it was the two menservants who disappeared, and one of these, who had been in the household since before the child was born, seemed to her so old that she could hardly believe that he, too, was gone to be a soldier. In those days it was still the custom for men, at any rate, to look older than they were, for the accent of social atmosphere was on stability, continuity, reliability and it was not until she heard her mother talking of the departure of this man that she became aware that he was about forty. This circumstance stuck in her mind for two reasons; first it seemed to the child that forty was an immense age and since her mother used the phrase 'only about forty' in answer to a question of one of the female cousins who came regularly in and out, she acquired a notion from the expression of this elderly cousin's face that age and comparisons of age were something to be cautious about. The second reason was that her father and mother were heard to agree with the cousin, in the undertones which were all that were ever used to speak of any unpleasant aspect of War, that if men of forty were already—this word was slightly emphasised—being sent to the armies eastwards, then some unhappy state of affairs obtained in this vague eastern region where the fighting was. One was evidently not supposed to take this unease into account, not in even so private a way as a fragmentary discussion within a family circle. The feeling that anything of this kind —and it was nebulous to a degree—should not be mentioned was as strong as that absolute ban on some other matters of a most personal nature which were never mentioned; and yet it was of a quite different order. This was made clear by the tone of her father's voice, not her mother's, which remained its normal one of ironical and sometimes almost acid amusement. Her father's voice took on, whenever such an aspect of the War was even hinted at, and it was hardly more than hinted at, a ceremonious and respectful note almost like the sound of anything to do with Church. Not that such moments were frequent, quite the contrary; almost always when the War, or the Army, was mentioned it was in connection with victories and heroism and patriotism, none of which was clearly understandable to the child. The more often such nouns were defined to her by her father, though never by her mother, the less she understood them; for his voice when he spoke of such things took on just that tremor of febrile emotion that she connected with the afternoon of Mademoiselle's sudden departure and all the strange and terrifying details of that scene which were inextricably mixed with a sensation of her own wrongness in knowing of it at all, and with 'foreignness' which she previously thought to have understood as non-Frenchness but which then suddenly somersaulted into another kind of foreignness; her father's concept of that state. So that victories and heroism and patriotism took on the subtone of something other than their public, as it were, splendour.

At this time too, two of the cousins, who were her aunts but not her mother's relatives, went away as well, leaving only the quite elderly one who did not, when alone bring with her the familiar scent of violets she connected with 'the cousins'. It was understood that the two younger cousins were also heroic, for they were going to a place called a base hospital and this place, too, was somewhere 'eastwards'. They were heroic, but here too the confusion entered because they were also, according to her mother's tone, somehow improper; only the most extreme necessity could excuse one going to a base hospital, it seemed, and yet there was no extremity but on the contrary, there were victories and noble sacrifices. Neither could the child understand, between what was said and the various tones it was said in, how it came about that the two younger cousins were away, and apparently for a long time, alone together when it was known that they had hardly even gone out of their house before unless accompanied either by their much elder sister, or by a female servant who smelled sour. From now on she was required to say 'Aunt' when she spoke to the elder of the cousins; while the much younger and prettier cousins were there—that is, always—the word was discouraged. It dawned only very slowly on the child that her father and the elder aunt, and the two young girls, were of different generations and by some complicated continuous conversation or carried-over references of speech, that her own mother belonged rather with them than with Aunt or her father. The child was by no means clear as to how it penetrated her consciousness that the scorn in her mother's voice when she spoke of the cousins going to the base hospital had less to do with the paraded social impropriety of this unknown place or institution—which was not clear, either—than with a wish on her mother's part that she might have gone there too.

The shaft of this understanding came about through another visitor, already quite familiar but of late coming not only more often to see them, but coming in the day-time, by himself and when her mother was alone. She herself was not counted as a rule, as being there. On a number of occasions when the outer bell rang, she was told to go down and talk to cook; but by now the reality of what was expected of the child had been worn somewhat fine by changes and sometimes she did not go down to cook when she was told, but retired to her schoolroom to read or play with dolls and a doll's house. During this period the weather was increasingly hot and humid, and the evenings so long that it was rather hard to sleep, and still harder to concentrate on the lessons her father set for her. Occasionally she even wandered about the rooms and corridors alone, wishing she might be allowed to join the grown-up conversation going on in the small salon; but nowadays those doors were often closed and, naturally, were not to be opened. Not that she did not enjoy cook's company. Cook was always great fun and had many stories and rhymes to tell her, which she repeated with the understanding that her father was not to know about them. This was because nursery rhymes and dialect stories were childish and incorrect behaviour; but enjoyable. But cook, too, was sometimes difficult to understand when she spoke of 'my man' who was far, far away somewhere fighting and in speaking of whom a very strong emotional anger and resentment was to be felt in cook which did not at all fit with the way her father spoke of heroes and armies.

Sometimes, when she was with cook and her father's friend was above stairs, cook would shake her head and say in her soft but coarse and rumbling voice that 'it's all very well, but them as stays at home don't know what they suffer'. Once the child asked cook whether she meant her mother who stayed at home in contrast to the time when she was almost always out except when guests were there, and cook replied with that tone of resentment already familiar, no, she meant men who didn't go to the war. 'They don't give you talk about heroes,' said cook, jerking her head, 'ask *him* upstairs, and he won't give you no stuff about flags and victories.' But when the child pressed her, the woman was reluctant to talk more, only muttering something as she pulled softly at the pastry-dough stretched out over the table, about 'he knows better—months flat on his back, as he was'. But on the other hand, the child was allowed to cut off the thicker edges of the finished pastry, before it was rolled up, as long as she was very careful to get the shape quite even and not leave any thickened pieces to spoil the symmetry of the finished sweetmeat when it was triumphantly rolled with its filling that smelled so good of apple and spices, better almost than the delicious lost smell of violets that the cousins once brought with them.

And, called to say good evening, the child noticed for the first time that her father's friend limped heavily and used a thick stick with a curious handle to it, when he walked. He wore uniform, though, so was clearly a hero.

One day when this friend was leaving, he stopped to talk to the maid who preceded him to the front door to open it for him. This was the same servant who now took care of the child's room and clothing, and whom the child connected closely with herself for various reasons, not the least of which was that they were both christened Felicitas Julia; but the servant was addressed as Julie, a familiar form never allowed for the child herself. Julie began to weep when addressed by the disabled officer, picking up the corner of her apron to hide as well as wipe away, her tears.

'I still haven't heard,' she replied to the question put to her in a voice of real sympathy. 'But it's very kind of the *Herr Oberst* to take so much interest . . .'

'Give me his regimental number and so on,' said the visitor and turned with an apologetic little shrug to the child's mother who stood there in the hall with them. 'Unless Florian has already tried to discover . . . ?'

'Florian?' said her mother. And then in French, 'as if he would ever think of such a thing!'

'Have all the details written down for me, Julie,' said the Colonel quietly. 'I shall be here tomorrow probably. I'll do what I can, at any rate.' And as the girl caught his hand to kiss it, he disengaged himself gently and spoke to the child's mother. 'I may as well get some good of this horrible office stool I occupy.' And the child recognised in his voice a sound she was used to with her mother, a tone of scorn that covered some stronger feeling.

It was perhaps a week later that the servant began to weep frequently, in bursts of painful suddenness. She would lean against a door, or a cupboard, in the middle of some piece of work, and wail pitifully, at which the child always began to cry with her, touched with a grief she could not understand. Two or three times in the next week or so, it must have been, she asked the child to go into her father's study and look at his diary to make sure of the date which appeared to be of great concern to her. Without anyone telling her to keep quiet, the child mentioned this to no one, not even cook to whom one might say anything. But it appeared, cook knew about the dates for one early evening when she was straining the soup she spoke through the fragrant cloud of steam.

'Still nothing, Julie?'

'Not a thing. I'll have to say something to *gnae' Frau* soon.'

'Leave it for a bit. I've known it stop for months and months just out of shock. You can't be sure, a delicate little thing like you. Why, I could snap you in two with my hands, so thin you are. Now, now, don't start crying again, for Heaven's sake. Here, there's some coffee left from upstairs . . .' Then, as she set aside the metal strainer with a clang, 'I suppose you are *sure* of the date?'

The girl sat sideways at the scrubbed kitchen table and the child could see her hand rubbing slowly and rhythmically up and round one ankle as if it hurt her, this ankle supported on the cross bar between the legs of the solid kitchen chair.

'No,' she said slowly, and stopped crying. 'I *know*.'

'I know about the date,' said the child proudly. 'I went to look myself. And I'm sure I counted right.'

'Jesus, Maria and Josef,' cried cook. 'The things that child understands!' But they did not tell her not to say anything 'upstairs' for they knew without discussion that she would not do that. And in some mysterious way, the child did understand, not what the dates actually signified, but what the problem was. For it is by no means true that children are by nature ignorant of such matters; on the contrary, they know of them by instinct without knowing what they know and only not asking questions because they do already know enough to be aware that this is something they are not supposed to understand. For in those days girl-children were intended to be in total ignorance of all the bodily processes and by some trick of deliberate forgetfulness of their own childhood, adult people agreed to believe that this was so, although they knew very well from their own pasts that only in a very few girls did the ignorance exist.

25

II

'Are these really the first things you remember?' asked Georg.

'I'm not sure. Nor of the sequence of the memories. But the first thing that came into my mind when you asked me, that really was the reception. Whether all the other things came afterwards as I've put them, I don't really know. I've no doubt some of them came before—the sitting on the man's knee, for instance. Because my nurse must have left fairly soon after that evening party—that was my father's promotion to *Sektionschef*, of course. Since he was in the Interior Ministry, it was an important post.'

'Especially at that time. And that must have been 1915, I suppose.'

'I think it may have been 1916, but I'm not sure. I have a feeling that the scene over the French governess was rather later—she was there quite a long time, I think. Yes, because she was with us at Ischl the summer before the old Emperor died. We saw him one day at Ischl—did I say we went there for the summers? Mademoiselle said he would die soon from the look on him, and I remembered that when he did die.'

'Now wait. She must have been there quite a year, because you've never lost your perfect French accent, and at that age languages don't stick in the mind unless they become subconscious.'

'I don't think as long as a year. . . . there was a French nun at school, in any case, for French. It's very difficult to place things. For instance, I have the feeling that this sitting on the man's knee may have happened several times.'

'Clearly your nurse, if she were in love with this man, would have noticed nothing suspicious about him fondling you just once.'

'I know now that she was jealous, naturally. But she may have been warned, too, without my knowing of it. But I don't feel sure about it—people of peasant stock are often much more physically tender with children, just as they are much more brutal, than people like us. It may have meant nothing. Certainly I was not frightened—or pleased; until I heard her voice I took no notice. It's the voice I remember, really, and the voice brings back the feel of his hard leg in leather breeches and him tickling me. Or starting to. And then, perhaps I just remember it because nobody else except my nurse, ever did cuddle me. They both came from the Brunn neighbourhood. All the servants did, because father owned a sawmill near there and knew people. That was the only thing he didn't turn into worthless stocks and shares, because a sawmill was useful to the war effort.'

'You can't have known that at the time!'

'Oh yes. It was one of the things mother would twit him with in her own way—pretending to make jokes but meaning it. She never did that, afterwards. That special voice disappeared for good, even before he died, I think.'

'With the advent of the friend, perhaps?'

'Naturally. But it wasn't an advent. He and my father had known each other for years. It was a return.'

'For your mother as well as your father?'

'I rather think not. She may have met him before he went into the artillery, but only as one of numbers of people, from the way they talked afterwards.'

'Curious situation,' he mused, pushing out his underlip and narrowing his eyes as if to see so far back. 'In those days, very curious. Women in your mother's position didn't have affairs.'

'It must have been the War, you see. Life before must have been so public; servants, relatives, entertaining. And those clothes that took hours, and the hairdressing every morning and evening. There was always the personal maid, as well as half a dozen servants in the house, going about. And one couldn't go somewhere else, either. The danger of being recognised. And the personal maid when one got back, noticing details we should never think of in our clothes; things like petticoats, for instance. I remember my mother being dressed, often. And there might be several petticoats in the evening, and the ribbons in the bodices that might get snapped if you didn't have somebody to tie them in bows. And how would anybody get in and out of those corsets, and the hobble skirts—impossible. . . .'

They began to laugh at the visions of inextricable drapery this brought up. 'I don't get it about the petticoats, though,' he brought out between bursts of laughter.

'Well, they all had different lace on them and the maid would know which one went on first but I doubt if the woman being dressed would. I'm sure I don't sometimes when I'm being got into some terrific costume.' Julia stopped to laugh again and then, in a quite different voice, she said, 'But you'll see that now. Now you'll come and see me in the dressing-room. Just wait until you see me being dressed for "Olympia"!'

'But that was much earlier than your mother's clothes in the first War!' he protested, still laughing.

'Not essentially different, I don't think. Really, what changed was the outline made by the corsets. Nothing much else. Well, by the time hobble skirts came in, petticoats changed, I suppose.'

'Do you remember them?'

'Oh no, I don't think so. But I'm pretty much of an expert on period costume, after all.' She stopped to think for a moment and looked about the 'new' room, now part of an open flight with the dining section forming what had once been the living room full of books, up to about half its original length. Where they now sat was the middle section of the street-front, formerly the almost unused drawing room. Further along, the far wall was entirely closed, from floor to ceiling with white bookshelves, springing out with no visible supports across the whole width. Georg, following her eyes round the area lit by standing and table lamps—overhead lights had quite disappeared in favour of expanses of clear ceiling—reflected that the designer possessed not only considerable talents but must also be a man of tact. For the book-wall made an end in more than one sense, to the section of the apartment where anyone but themselves should be. Behind it and reached by an entrance in the passage, were the dressing-room, bathroom and their new bedroom where once the spare room stood always empty. The guest room now occupied what had once been a dining room, looking over an inside court.

The deliberate cutting up of the frontage and its termination in a wall of books mostly brought from his own former flat, now appeared so considered that Georg wondered whether Julia had suggested it to the designer, and if she did, how she expressed her wish. But no, he thought as she began to speak again, the designer knew the story as everyone in Vienna did. He would not need to be instructed, but would himself have suggested that break.

'What I do remember was my mother's hair being suddenly quite different. She began to wear it in a simple knot—she had a lot of hair—low on the back of her head. That was when her own maid went, obviously.'

'As the men went, so the women, left with soldiers' pay, went into factories to earn higher wages. It must have been one of the greatest of the social changes. Of course, they weren't really better off; it only seemed as if they would be. And the thin girl, the one with the baby . . . ?'

'Ah, that was a watershed. That was the first time I heard my mother openly defy my father. And they quarrelled publicly, in front of me and cook.'

'But why cook?'

'It was she who came to tell my mother about the girl's trouble. By then, they must have known the boy was killed.

'It may have been some days or even weeks later, one evening my mother asked cook to come upstairs. I know now that she expected cook's presence to force my father to accept the situation. Since I was down in the kitchen with cook, I came up with her and none of them noticed me. I can see her setting her hair to rights and putting her cap back on. She was grey already, then. Then she tied on a fresh apron—I wonder now whether my mother had prepared her in some way? She had one of those wide faces with a snub nose and big mouth, the sort of face that looks pugnacious somehow, even when it isn't. If she went upstairs she stepped in a special way, and walked round the carpets. But this time she didn't do that, and walked with her natural tread, heavy and deliberate like a man. Her ankle boots made quite a tramping for she was a big, tall woman. She was almost as tall as my father and fat, enormously fat. My mother looked like a doll beside her, and I could easily hide behind her skirts.

'Of course, I'd known ever since the business with the calendar. And after cook told my mother we all spoke openly about it together in the kitchen, it could hardly be avoided because the poor girl was constantly sick—fear, I suppose, and grief. My father was the only one who didn't know, though he could have seen by then, if he'd ever looked at her.'

That it was a terrible misfortune was clear, but this misfortune was concerned with the death in battle of the peasant boy, who was not, in the kitchen, called a hero, but a poor boy. It now appeared with a clap of moral thunder that it was not a misfortune but a disgrace, a matter for horror and rage. It was much worse, evidently, than doing something that was not expected of you; it came into the category of unmentionables, far worse than bursting into tears when scolded over lessons, which was about the worst thing one could do and was punished by a particular tone of patient coldness as one was instructed to go to one's room and do the lesson again until one could conduct oneself correctly. In such moments the child was addressed as 'the child' as if she were not there. But this was even more terrible for her father's voice shook and rose shrilly almost as if he were afraid, except of course, he couldn't be. It was even worse than whatever it was the foreigner had done who deserted Mademoiselle—worse than being a Czech citizen. God kept coming into it, as well, and this was incomprehensible for the child knew about God, whose stern loving-kindness was kept well in hand by gentle Jesus provided one was good or tried to be. But perhaps this was another God? God with loving-kindness (which was interpreted as necessary discipline) replaced by revenge and punishment . . . And all the time cook, who addressed her father when spoken to with customary respect, kept looking straight at his face which in itself constituted defiance and rebellion, without any expression on her kind, ugly face at all.

Abruptly, the child's mother spoke in a voice the child had not heard before, without any irony or jokingness but with the sharp coldness which the jokes were meant both to express and hide. A naked coldness.

'The girl stays here. I will not have her put out. She has nowhere to go.'

The child did not hear at all what her father now said, for she pushed her face into the thick folds of cook's skirts which smelled of bacon fat for some reason.

But she did hear her mother say, 'Most certainly not. She is not in the house this evening and I won't have her bullied. She has quite enough to suffer, as it is, poor little thing. Once and for all, she stays here.'

Here cook turned to go without being told she might, and in panic the child clutched her skirts to stay in hiding. But she need not have feared, for the thick strong hand held her shoulder and the high bulk shielded her so that she was hardly visible even if her father were looking. If she had dared turn round she would have seen that he leaned with one hand on the high back of his study chair, his head turned to stare out of the window of which the cur-

30

tains had not been drawn although it was dark. His high, thin shoulders were bent. As the door closed on their relief, cook and the child, they heard his overpitched voice.

'The whole world seems to be going mad!'

The girl stayed, true. But after a few weeks, cook went and this was a terrible loss to the child so that they both wept bitterly as cook packed her basket. A new cook came, a sly-faced woman who stole the provisions out of the store room and gave them to a man very small and meagre with a dark, narrow face who came to the kitchen door in the evenings. The child's mother did not check the stores any more, neither did the child go to the kitchen much except when sent with a message. Gradually, there were less and less stores to check, and the new cook did not care about her work. A slatternly old female came to help with the cleaning, and when winter came the place was cold for it needed several servants to stoke the tall stoves with sweet-smelling wood blocks.

Then, without warning, the child was bought new clothing of a particular design and dark colour and two days later her mother took her in the hired carriage to the railway station, and from there a long journey in a dirty and rattling train. She was never so long in a train before. When they left the train it was almost dark; the sombre uniform of the man who took off his hat and spoke to her mother was almost frightening, both it and his voice were so solemn.

Her mother was very silent on the journey, seated most of the time with her face averted, a look of such weary sadness on her face as she stared out at the wheeling landscape and the swooping telegraph lines, that the child did not like to interrupt her reverie. It was fun, though, to eat out of a covered basket, spreading napkins on their knees. The child did not feel much natural excitement at the lights and bustle of the station, intimidated by her mother's depression. The ride in the swaying carriage was not long and everything outside was by now quite invisible until she was led up low steps and into a lighted hallway where nuns greeted them and one nun took her hand to lead her away. At this she cried out and her mother spoke quietly, putting out a hand to pull her back and embrace her.

'Don't worry, my baby. I shall be back in a few minutes. Just go with Sister Bonifacia like a good girl.'

She never remembered her mother addressing her as my baby; it warned her that something unpleasant was about to take place. But Sister Bonifacia was a round-faced and jolly girl who smiled at her and led her by the hand. She stayed with the child in the room with two beds where they were to sleep, and employed the time with unpacking the child's clothing and instructing her exactly how and where it was all to be kept. The small bag her mother brought with her was left untouched. Presently another nun came in and then they all went through long corridors that resounded at her own steps, for the nuns moved silently, and crossed a large hall and down another corridor, everything distempered a yellowish white which made the lights, in reality quite dim, seem glaring. They were in a rather small room now, where a very old lady was seated behind a large desk at the side of which her mother, too, sat. This old lady, who wore different robes and head gear addressed her as 'my child' but did not say much, murmuring most of the time with her mother while the two young nuns stood by the door with their heads lowered and the child seemed to be very alone in the centre of the room.

Later, dazed with sleepiness, they were in a large chapel where there were many other girls, all bigger and older than herself. Then a small tray of simple food was brought to the room and the child drank her milk and was asleep before her mother could undress her.

In the grey morning it was cold. For the first time the child grasped that she was to be left here by her mother. This filled her with such desolate fear that she did not cry at all and Sister Bonifacia whispered approvingly that she was a good, brave, child when, after kissing her once more in the outside hall, her mother went down the low steps with her quick, graceful step and little head in its tilted hat as high and proud as always on the slender neck. The child was led away then, before she had time to see the carriage move or know whether her mother leaned out of the window to wave to her.

'Poor little scrap,' said Georg, as if of a real child in the present. 'I suppose nowadays people tell children more what is happening to them? One forgets that they can't possibly know .... almost like being a prisoner of war.'

This last memory, of his own life, brought them abruptly into the present and Georg looked at his wristwatch.

'Good heavens, it's three o'clock in the morning!' They both rose and Julia, without moving her arms, stretched herself upward to relax all the muscles unconsciously held tense.

'It's Sunday tomorrow, fortunately,' she said, and turned with a movement of unsureness which was probably simply tiredness but was so untypical of her that it was noticeable.

This was the first time they had ever slept together in this house, and the undoubted fact that their being together was sanctioned not only by long and deep emotional ties but by both profane and sacred authority did nothing to change the suspect air it wore and which they recognised tacitly by moving in and out of corridor and bathroom, in and out of their bedroom, separately, as if in an hotel. But the moment came when they must face each other in the new room with its new furniture set in new ways at new angles; the different colours seeming now a deliberate disguise, just as the carpet stretched from wall to wall in a way then almost unknown in central Europe gave the room an air of somehow improper luxuriousness. Especially its colour now appeared illicit, for it was a deep rose-red, the colour essentially appropriate to Julia's person but one which with a shocking suddenness reminded her of a velvet dressing gown of just that rose-red which carried memories of old fear and personal humiliation.

'I think we have to get him to change this carpet,' she said, not remembering that Georg could not know what she referred to.

'It seems rather beautiful to me,' he said, and then was late-struck by her tone of voice which contained an inner vibration whose mysterious context was only too well-known to him; he no longer needed any explanation. And this solved the immediate question for he knew instantly that he must now act, even if with a certain brutality. They were still both standing and he took her now in his arms, bent his head and kissed her with tenderness and passion. But he moved his hand to hold her upper right arm fast, so that she could not raise it except against his greater strength. Their communion was so close that he knew she must recognise this grasp and its reason.

On the night of their wedding, before they left for Greece, they spent the curiously isolated interim between being lovers and being married and travelling away together, at an hotel. His own small apartment was already sold and hers was being dismantled by armies of workmen who had so signally failed, it now seemed, to rip the past to pieces as they ripped the old structure of domestic life to pieces.

On that occasion, Julia, knowingly or unknowingly, gripped his wounded arm at just the point where nerve ends irreparably torn

33

could, and frequently did, cause him stabs of intense pain. The quality of combat in their relationship warned him then that she did this on purpose; and she might well do it again now. A slight pressure in that part of his arm could cause a sensual half-pain, like the pleasurable ebbing of a bad toothache; strong pressure as she used it on that night, produced a shot of brilliant agony that for a space of time could disable him, making it difficult even to breathe and during which he must keep completely still in order not to scream with pain.

The grasp on her arm was the signal that Georg was, sooner or later, determined to be master of his and her situation. Julia was instantly aware of this and even as he kissed her the intractable and fierce side of her nature warned her that battle as well as love was joined. Without intending to, she withdrew, very slightly, in his embrace. Georg instantly released her, raised his healthy left arm and hit her quite hard with the flat of his hand on the side of her face and head presented to him.

Her hands half raised as they were when he released her, Julia swayed slightly with the blow, and then remained rigidly still, an expression of stupefied disbelief stamped on her features as if she were frozen into stone by incredulity; there was no sensation of pain. They remained perfectly still for a long moment, their eyes on each other's faces, breath held, as if waiting for a crucial signal. As their breath together ran out in a mutual gasp of recognition, they began to laugh together with a delicious sensuality and absurdity at the expression of her face, which he saw and she felt.

They both knew that it was not the blow that represented brutality, but Georg's intention. The blow was love; the intention, battle.

III

'Strange being in the town in August,' said Julia at breakfast two days later. 'I'm glad we have this theatrical history project to do; it would be too boring to do nothing for the rest of the month. Though we didn't enjoy being photographed yesterday among the ruins and rebuilding of the Burg. That was uncanny—you know? Ah, I almost forgot. These German art historians want to go to a Heurigen, and Hansi was asking if you could come too, on Friday? Out to Gumpoldskirchen.'

'Friday?' he asked absently, giving a dish of cold ham an uncertain look as if he did not know whether he wanted more to eat. He then picked up a slice of the ham on a fork and laid it on his plate, still with the air of being in two minds about it. 'Wasn't I supposed to do something on Friday afternoon? Yes, it was Friday that Tenius wanted to meet me.'

'Tenius?' She looked startled and hostile, so that he wondered if she might have been deceiving herself into thinking that they need hear nothing more about the unwanted return. 'I really don't see why you have to see him. We don't at all want to go back to that wartime feeling. And incidentally, I meant to ask you . . . How is it Tenius is here at all? He's a German. Why wasn't he repatriated to wherever he came from?'

'I don't think I could have refused to see him.' Georgy hesitated. 'As to him being in Vienna, it can only be that he claimed a domicile here because he is still married to a Viennese, after all, and owns a house here. If he went home he'd be arrested at once, I imagine.'

'Arrested!' She stared. 'Good God. I hadn't thought of that. But of course, you're right. But isn't he in more danger in Austria than Germany? We still have the Occupation, after all?'

'Well yes. But the warrant that almost certainly exists for his arrest would be in Germany.'

'Then the best advice you can give him is to go to South America as fast as he can,' Julia said decisively. 'He must know by now that Hella Schneider-Tenius is hardly going to welcome him with open arms. I saw old Frau Schneider yesterday and she was saying that Hella was delighted to be able to serve divorce papers on Tenius at last. Of course, that was an exaggeration, but she obviously will grab at the opportunity, with relief if not with delight. Since Tenius had the bad taste not to die, at least Hella can get her hands on him now.'

Georg stared blankly at his wife for a moment, and then laughed explosively, a bark of recognition at the unmistakable stamp of Hella Schneider's thought processes.

'Of course! It didn't occur to me before, but I bet she's found out what time his train arrives so that the lawyer's clerk can be on the station platform.'

But Julia was still considering the mention of arrest, and now she pushed her coffee cup away from her sharply, crumpling the bright linen tablecloth. A sharp, once-familiar frown appeared between her brows.

'Georgy, listen,' she said, apprehension making her sound angry, 'Tenius coming back from Siberia is going to bring up all sorts of half-forgotten secrets. Not only Hella's. I remember he was concerned—forgive me speaking of it—with the round-up here in 1941. And you had some dealings with him later, after the attempt on Hitler's life. Didn't you? Have you considered that if he is arrested, if there is a trial, we may be involved?'

'Of course, my dear. It's for that reason I need to see Tenius. We must know what he intends.'

'I've never quite known what went on between you two in 1944. But it must have been something serious for you. You wouldn't have badgered me at that time to help you for any trivial reason.'

He stared at her, startled. 'Didn't I ever tell you? Somehow I assumed you knew . . . . We made a bargain. I'll tell you exactly. You know I was used by the conspirators of the 20th July plot as a message carrier? It was my job to move about all the time and, what was important in that kind of clandestine activity, on official business but in directions and at times quite different from military movements as such. Now, I suspected from experience that not all the men who knew of the plot—and by July '44 there were a lot of them—were as careful about secrecy as they might be. From the nature of a courier's function I went to people I hardly knew or they came to me, with coded messages of various kinds. Sometimes even written schedules of troop movements and that sort of thing. Not because large bodies of troops were concerned in the conspiracy; as you know, they weren't. But the officers involved were frequently re-posted, the fronts were in constant movement, and it was essential for the leaders of the plot to keep in touch with their friends. In the last stages these messages went through me mainly by telephone, and that again involved a whole lot of people knowing things that they might—if they knew other details or if they cared to investigate—put together and come up with the right answer. *Which was treason.*

'I could be betrayed by some unknown *Wehrmacht* telephone girl chatting over coffee to some other unknown who already knew another detail, and who could therefore be struck by the number of calls I made that were nothing to do with the reporting I was doing officially. I was stretching the latitude of my ostensible function to its limits and beyond, and on one occasion I nearly was caught by crossing the wires of some stupid black-market racket that the security police were watching.

'When the Plot failed it was clear that practically nothing and nobody with any connection to it could escape investigation. I had to cover myself if I wanted to survive. The obvious way was to get posted. That was easy, I could and did arrange it myself. The other essential thing was to have some good reason for all my activities if they came out, as they were pretty well bound to do. That's where Tenius came in. I chose him because I knew where I could get hold of him privately and because I knew he was already worried about what went on in his police area. He'd already written one very cautious report trying to disclaim responsibility for matters he was officially in charge of since the whole area was his concern, but which —to do him justice—he had no genuine control over at all. On the other hand, there were enough things he really had done against the rules of war, to make him pretty frightened about the future. I suggested to him that he should give me a copy of his report on Auschwitz which had been pushed into a pigeon-hole and ignored. I could get it into the hands of friends and he could use it as whitewash if he needed to—that is, if the War went wrong. He knew even better than I did that the War was long since lost, of course. In return he agreed to signal Gestapo HQ in Berlin to lay off me on the ground that I had been secretly reporting to him for a couple of years. He made his whole career as an opponent of the Army, you know, it was well-known that he was one of the most active allies Himmler had in the Party rivalry with the Army. As it turned out, he'd written a second report, and actually had it with him to deliver personally—it was clear he was going to make sure this time that it couldn't 'get lost'. He got me a copy and I took it with me to Agram.

'I've never believed that Tenius kept his side of the bargain. And if he did signal the Prinz Albrechtstrasse, the evidence was destroyed with everything else when Gestapo headquarters was bombed. I was transferred again, with suspicious suddenness from Agram to the Front in Transylvania, as you know, and captured.'

'But why do you believe that Tenius never sent his signal to Berlin? I mean, you could have been sent to Rumania by pure chance.'

'I was interrogated quite thoroughly by the British—by Robert in fact, when I was repatriated. If there were any evidence of a contact from me to the Gestapo or the security police—Tenius' lot—they would have treated me very differently. Even after I told Robert about it, my version was accepted as true, which it was.'

'Yes, but . . . I'm obviously missing some essential detail. I don't see why the British should have known what, if anything, remained in the ruins of Berlin. Berlin was taken by the Russians, not the British.'

'True, but in the few weeks the Soviets held Berlin alone they had no time to do any serious searching for documents in the ruins of the city. In fact, a British historian in a book about Hitler's death in the Bunker, says that the Russians did not even find the diary he left, and it was simply lying on his chair for anyone to pick up. Certainly we don't know what, if anything, the Russians have. But most of the researching was done by the western Allies and though I hear they are cautious about allowing anyone to see their records, I think they would have come across anything to do with men in any public kind of function by now. I don't think I would have got my editorial licence renewed if there was anything of that kind in the files.'

'But if Tenius himself kept a copy of his message to the Prinz Albrechtstrasse? I mean, if he sent one, he could have a copy there, in Hella's house.'

'If he ever sent a signal, and if it or a copy of it still exists, then

38

I could be accused now of having betrayed the 20th July conspiracy to the Gestapo.'

Kerenyi said this in a curiously flat, quiet tone, looking directly at Julia the while. Julia held his look steadily, taking in the reason for his long and somewhat formal account in all its unhappy implications, but she made no reply and none was needed.

'That's the blackest prospect and I only tell you about it just in case the worst should happen. But really I think it much more likely that Tenius won't try to involve me. Even if he does, his lawyers would advise against such a dubious argument.'

'You mean, neither the Allies nor the Germans really likes the idea of the officers' plot?'

'In the present mythology about the War, it's required to approve of trying to remove Hitler, so that if the plot were in evidence at a trial it would be better for Tenius to have been on the side of the conspirators. But that attitude is far removed from reality, especially for the German authorities. They're trying to restore the rule of law, not to recall conditions in which men are forced to try such desperate remedies for their problems.'

'The question is, does Tenius realise that?'

'I don't see why it should bulk very large in his mind, do you? But it's precisely that that I have to find out. He may not even realise that he is in danger of arrest and trial. He may never have heard of "automatic arrest categories".'

It was just this not knowing that brought up in their minds the atmosphere of the past, in which for years every action and every conversation must be weighed, and weighed against knowledge in other, unknown, people that they could not be aware of. It was the nebulous disquiet of an *unknown* menace that echoed like a knell into the different life they were engaged in laboriously constructing from wreckage.

Julia looked about her with the strange sensation that she saw the long, light, sun-filled room, its windows open to the sounds of the day four floors below them in the street, imposed on the picture of the rooms as they were before. It was entirely different in every possible aspect except its location in that house and in that street of that city, from what it had been thirteen years before. Yet even the moist pink slices of unevenly cut ham, in some vagrant reproduction of another, forgotten scene, brought back the past. The table spread with coloured linen for breakfast, the brilliantly painted

39

china dishes, above all the light that filled once shadowed rooms and the pale paintwork and walls replacing dark panelling, dark window framings, were different. Quite different. But in her own being, the other rooms lay behind the shapes and colours of this day, ineffaceable as the events they represented were ineffaceable.

She rose from the table and crossed to the window, her long dressing-gown of blue silk—that colour, too, was different—making no sound on the thick carpet. There was no net curtain to be drawn aside; the windows stood open and uncovered to the sunshine. The warm little breeze of a perfect summer day stirred the dark hair, tickling her brow. Just so, in that so different room had she often stood in the dark and watched the man now seated behind her as he crossed the street going away from the house so that, by unspoken agreement, she could make sure he was neither followed nor accosted as he left.

'Back where we started, in a way,' she said abruptly. 'Exiles, refugees, possible threats.' She turned back into the room and added with an effect of irritation, 'Of course, all this light paintwork, pale carpets and curtains, will take much more keeping clean . . .'

Her husband rose to meet her as she came back to the table. He took the long hand which wore his rings, feeling its delicate, nervous, feminine muscularity which to him was intensely erotic, raised it and laid it against his own cheek, which in contrast appeared leathern, even saturnine.

'I never get used to the whiteness of your skin,' he said as if reading her own impression of contrast, as he moved her hand to kiss it and saw it lying in his own sinewy grasp. 'With your dark hair and eyes you might be expected to have a quite different complexion. I'm desperately sorry about this Tenius business, involving you again with such things . . . .'

'Come to think of it,' said Julia, 'you always preferred dark-skinned women.' She disliked the sensation of jealousy so much a part of her feeling for Georg; although it was preferable at the moment to consider something so personal rather than what he had told her. Jealousy reduced her own sovereignty and she was not used to that. A vagrant thought came into her mind that she had, in the past, chosen her men and chosen them because they could not or did not want to dominate her. In this most difficult of all relationships not only had Georg chosen her and insisted on formalising their relationship against her own wishes; he was too, a man accustomed to dominate and who had never lived with a woman as an equal. It struck her then as strange that she had not clearly seen this fact before; but, of course, it was the acceptance of it which made her reluctant to marry him. Almost with dismay she considered the prospect of a continuing and continuous tension of emotion which was, both by their attainments and the nature of their different work, bound to be the object of curious attention from many people known to them—and unknown, the public. She retreated at once into professionalism.

'I've got to be at the Hofburg at ten,' she said, glancing sideways at the watch already on Georg's wrist. 'I'm learning a terrific lot from all this "history of the theatre" stuff. Jesuits and all sorts of things. I suppose I must once have known it—d'you think? You do, of course; they brought you up, the Jesuits.'

'Somewhat different ones, probably.' He was amused in spite of the nature of their conversation, at her vagueness. He knew quite well what the current of her thought was, but unlike Julia, he enjoyed the hidden duel of their new life. He had the great advantage over his opponent, for that is what she was, that the situation was clear to him from the start so that he was prepared for it and knew it for what it was, a struggle in which she must accept defeat and he must enforce it, if she were to win. 'I'd better shower first, though. It's editorial meeting-day and I've hardly read a word we've printed for the last three months.'

'Don't forget to tell Frau Lisl whether you will be back in time for dinner,' Julia called after his back. Then she followed him, as if drawn by his own movement. 'Three months? We were only away for seven weeks?'

'I didn't have my mind on my work just before we left,' he called back; the rest of his reply was lost in the sudden burst of water against the shower curtain. Pulling suits and dresses about to see what she should wear, Julia was filled with unwilling joy that he admitted this.

She was, also, late for her appointment for the first time her colleagues remembered and there was some teasing on the subject of newly-married couples that struck her as ridiculous as well as suggestive, in a way her friends did not show before when they all knew perfectly well that Georgy was her lover. Now, evidently, the regularised liaison was in more than one sense, public property. Just as the 'affair' was a private matter and covered by the complex and unformulated rules of self-protection they all observed because they were a group of people who lived in public, so now the marriage made possible a certain air of curiosity; it was an open fact which they were entitled to take into account just as Julia was obliged to take it into account. And not only with professional friends—and enemies. The delay was caused by Frau Lisl waylaying Julia as she was about to leave the house, and enquiring with a conspiratorial air what Julia's new husband would like for dinner. Quite unused to such domestic questions, Julia had left exactly enough time for her to reach the Hofburg.

'I don't know,' she replied to Frau Lisl's question. 'You always do the menus; just decide yourself what we should eat.'

'Yes, but Dr. Kerenyi,' insisted the housekeeper archly. 'He must have his own favourite dishes.'

'If he has, he will let you know about them,' said Julia, looking at her watch. 'Why don't you ask him?'

'Oh, but I couldn't bother *him*,' said Frau Lisl.

'Of course you can ask him. His time is far less rigidly ruled than mine is and you'll probably see more of him at home than you've ever seen me. But you don't need to worry much about his food preferences. I don't think he was ever fussy over food, except that he doesn't like anything artificial or elaborate. And in any case, you've known him as long as you've worked for me. . . .'

This short exchange was just enough, together with an unusual wait for a taxi on the corner of the street, to make Julia late. As she escaped, and waited for a cab, Julia was struck by the puzzlement her answers evidently caused Frau Lisl. And as she showed conventional amusement at her friends' teasing remarks and reacted to them with jokes, she found herself adding this new exposure of her private life to the questioning looks of her housekeeper. Frau Lisl had worked for Julia by now for more than three years; never before was there any question about Frau Lisl's absolute rule in the household. She was a well-trained housekeeper taking care of the domestic life of another professional who might equally well have been a man. Or so Julia had always thought of the matter; evidently she was now expected to become a housewife. This struck her as funny until someone, suggesting a break for the midday meal, remarked that she, no doubt would be expected at home for luncheon.

'Oh no,' she said. 'Georgy has a meeting of his editorial board today and it will probably go on for hours and hours. I don't suppose we shall eat together much in the day-time anyway.'

Again there were surprised looks and smiles and Julia felt irritation at the complicity of her companions in their agreed little joke which she suddenly felt to be not only rather vulgarly insinuating, but in addition, to imply that she was being shut out of their community in some way. She told herself she was being absurd; except for the team from Munich who were compiling a history of the German theatre and who intended to go off together, everyone present was intimately friendly with her and they had worked together since their teens. It was ridiculous to think of Ostrovsky, established as an ally of hers in the eyes of all their circle for fifteen years and more, as wishing to exclude her from his intimacy. The two of them were almost twin beings in the theatrical world, he as producer and she as his favourite performer. And Walter Harich with his handsome and imposing presence which was now just beginning to become florid, had supported and helped her when she was a lanky slip of a girl and he just famous. Just as she herself helped Anita Silovsky as a young girl beginning her career during the War. She was ashamed of her thought still more on hearing Mundel's voice; if she had protected him from the results of his formerly undisciplined drinking, he had done at least as much for her when she desperately needed help and rest. They had even lived in the same rooms after the War and after Mundel's house was burned down, with an extraordinary harmony for several years; there were not many actors capable of that kind of tact and restraint in personal relationships.

And yet she could not rid herself of that inward quaver of anxiety. They were transferring her, certainly without knowing it, back to her long-distant former marriage when she always ate lunch at home. It was the continuance of this fixed custom when she was ostensibly living alone—she knew that afterwards—which gradually induced in her immediate circle the suspicion that the marriage was not ended, that Franz Wedeker was still there; that she, Julia, was hiding her outlawed and divorced husband. It was only after his death at the end of the War that she first began to eat her midday meal in the canteens and black-market restaurants of the 'hunger time'; previously their meeting times were the evenings after

43

the theatre. Luncheon was private then and it was by carrying-over of their memories into the new situation that made them evidently expect the old custom to be revived.

There was a little silence between them, as they stood, grouped among the shadowy magnificences of an ancient and hallowed place. The survival of the chapel they were facing here in a court-yard of the old Palace which literally encompassed their common history, was what provided their unconscious assumption of the two opposites of that history. That it survived and would continue to do so into the future, and that all political and temporal arrangements were transitory, including the occupation of their city by foreign armies. But in their silence a past nearer and more personal was also contained and in the pause something was resolved about that past and about the present.

'Good, let's eat on the Wall,' said Hansi Ostrovsky as if they had been discussing where they should go, and they all moved away towards the waiting car. 'Willy! We're off!'

'Coming,' called Mundel, left the group he was talking to and ducked his massive head to enter the car where the others already sat, somewhat crowded even without the addition of his bulk.

'Good thing you're so slender, Anita,' said Ostrovsky. 'Willy's taking up far more than his share of the seat.'

'Can I help it if I'm broad built?' complained Mundel. 'That bloody course of gymnastics you made me take has made me even heavier.'

'But much tauter,' countered Julia, half turning to laugh at him. 'You've lost your paunch. And years in looks, you old boozer.'

Driving, Harich spoke indistinctly round a cigarette. 'I had a call from Hella yesterday. Apparently she'll be coming here tomorrow for some business thing, she said, and I asked her to join us at the *Heurigen*. She mentioned it, so it's clear she knew we were having a party and I couldn't get out of it.'

'That's the second time Hella's made a rush visit in the last few days,' Anita said, breaking her normal quietness. 'I wonder what she's up to?' From her tone it was clear that they all took it for granted that Hella Schneider must, as always, be 'up to' something.

The car threaded its way cautiously through the archway and narrow corners of the old Imperial stables, now being gradually added to and rebuilt as a trade-fair complex. Harich stopped it under a blank wall providing shade and they all emerged into hot sunlight, increased in force by the narrow and high walls. As Willy Mundel took her arm to walk up the sloping pathway, once part of the city walls and now overgrown with rank bushes and scented trees, Julia answered Anita's question reluctantly.

'You don't know what she's up to, then? It's Tenius. He's reappeared.'

'Tenius?' they all echoed the name in varying tones of unbelief.

'He wrote to Georgy from Friedland,' she added, knowing it would be impossible to hide the fact for long.

'But he's dead!' objected Harich, stopping at the rustic gate of the little garden-tavern.

'He's come back from the dead, then,' Mundel answered. They ducked their heads under the screening vines that scrambled all over the place and arranged themselves round the only empty table. 'I see foreign tourists are beginning to discover this place,' he added with a disapproval that somehow extended itself to the subject of their astonishment. None of them made any attempt at a conventional pretence of being glad to hear this news.

'I suppose he's afraid to go back to West Germany,' Hansi Ostrovsky interjected into their discussion of what they would eat. The question was not difficult to settle, the bill of fare having only half a dozen dishes on it. 'These war-criminal prisoners are only released on condition that they should be tried in the German courts.'

'One has the impression that they are released separately or in small batches to keep the war-crimes trials on the boil.'

'Of course,' agreed Harich. 'No wine, thanks, I'll drink mineral water.' Except for Willy Mundel, the whole company agreed on this abstention, for they all had work to do in the afternoon.

'It seems so weird working in the day-time—I mean, all day,' sighed Anita. 'How I'd love a beer.' She glanced enviously as the fat woman in a *Dirndl* carried past them a tray filled with tall glasses of foaming beer.

'Well, have one then,' said Mundel, 'one should never suffer unnecessarily.'

'I'd better not. Won't Tenius be tried here, then?'

'I don't know,' Hansi answered her. 'But I suppose there will be a demand for his extradition.'

'And that will give him the chance to get away, during the delay?'

45

'That's what I said to Georgy,' said Julia. 'I mean, that he'd better clear out to South America as fast as he can.'

'Let us hope he does. He'll probably go through Bolzano. Jochen was telling me the other day the town is full of ex-SS men. He thinks they run their mutual aid society at least partly from there.'

'Does that really exist?' asked Anita doubtfully. 'Jochen does have an absolute complex about Nazis. . . .'

'Well, poor old Thorn, he always feels embarrassed at having been born a German,' Harich finished his food with the slight gloom of a man who never allows himself to eat as much as he wants.

'If I order pancakes, will you share with me, Anita?' asked Hansi.

'You lucky thin beasts,' grumbled Harich. 'Of course, the SS-society does exist. How else did all these people just disappear? They can't all have been killed. Nobody believes that.'

'Perhaps they will gradually all reappear from prisoner of war camps,' suggested Mundel gloomily. 'Like this brute Tenius.'

'A merry prospect. I can see us being pestered for the next twenty years and the tax-payer having to keep the swine in idleness in prison for the rest of their lives.'

'My father always said we should invoke the death-penalty more often for war crimes,' said Anita. 'You know, he nearly joined the Party once. What a bit of luck he didn't!'

'I thought he did,' Julia raised her head with the effect of suddenness, and the sharp frown appeared between her brows. 'I remember you saying he was going to join—when was it? A rehearsal, wasn't it, when you were still new?'

The two women, across the table and the difference in ages, frowned in an effort to recall, and then Julia's eyes widened and instantly Anita dropped her glance in tact and said something about coffee.

'Must have been during my banishment, then,' said Mundel, finishing his glass of wine. 'I thought your Papa was too busy making money during the War to bother with politics.' The immense fortune made by Anita Silovsky's father out of war contracts was one of their constant jokes; a joke they sometimes embroidered with macabre and cynical details in which the fortunate daughter joined with a half-affectionate contempt for her parents, one of the recurring characteristics of people who grew up in that War already fading into history—for the young.

'Your self-banishment,' corrected Hansi. And as if driven to say it, he went on slowly. 'I remember that day now. That was the day when Jochen Thorn, Wally and myself all realised that each of us knew . . . about Franz.'

There was a stillness, the breeze rustled the hot vine-leaves in the now almost empty garden.

'Did you discuss it?' asked Julia at last, very quietly.

'Not a word. Neither then nor any other time. We just knew.'

'I suppose I was the only one of us who didn't know—until afterwards,' said Mundel. They all sat motionless as if to move would break some tabu and their voices were low as voices are that speak of forbidden things.

'I behaved badly after the War,' said Julia abruptly. 'I was a bit unhinged for a time, I think.'

'None of us behaved too well at that time,' said Hansi, passing an ascetic hand over his almost bald head.

'I don't think you behaved badly,' Anita half-whispered, playing with the tiny spoon in the saucer of her coffee cup. 'I absolutely agreed with you that you couldn't bear people to talk about it. I mean, of course, I have no right to say anything—I can't imagine ever having the courage to hide somebody from the police myself—but I thought at the time of all that fuss, that I'd feel the same, as if some man one didn't like were pawing one. . . .'

They sat there, all of them except Anita remembering the dead man and filled with the wretched sensation of waste at his death and the guilt of their own survival. Presently they began to rise and sort out money for the modest bill. Strolling down back to where the car was parked, they began gradually to talk again of work.

IV

'I must admit I feel very uneasy about seeing him,' Georgy said. 'I don't mean about the possible complications—though they're bad enough. I mean an irrational disquiet.'

'Yes. The thing is, he brings everything back. We even spoke of it at lunch today.'

'Tenius, you mean?'

'Well, the past. It's never been mentioned openly before, always indirectly if at all. It was rather strange, starting with the question of whether I was coming back to lunch at home—as I always used to do. Then Tenius, as if it were all planned. Uncanny, almost.'

'That's the feeling I have. As if he were casting his shadow before him and that shadow is the War and the past. Somehow we forget it most of the time; but it's always there. Even the Occupation we forget or ignore.'

'We've got used to it. And it hardly interferes with ordinary life any more. Come to look at it seriously, I suppose the Occupation could go on for ever . . . ?'

'Nothing goes on for ever. Politically, I mean. But it's hard to imagine any possible end to it. It's thirteen years since 1938. And the two power-blocks are face to face here. Neither is likely to give way. . . . one can't even hope they should because we should then be exposed at once to pressure from the Communist block. But it does produce an unfortunate irresponsibility in our public life. We were talking about that again today in the editorial conference. Every few months it comes up, when we have to worry about funds —nearly always over money. The only possible responsibility we can assume is in the Press; and the Press is financially in the hands of either the Parties or the Occupiers. Apart from one or two local newspapers, there isn't a free discussion forum in the country because you can't count papers heavily influenced by the Church either—the Church having entered politics between the Wars to such a disastrous extent. We are practically the only really independent periodical in existence—and our existence is threatened every few months by lack of money. Both the French and the Americans offer us subsidies and it's hard to go on refusing them— chaps fear for their jobs, naturally. . . .'

'Couldn't you talk the British into offering a subsidy as well? Then you could accept a sort of arrangement of an equal amount from each?'

'Oh, my dear, we've considered that a hundred times. But that would make it automatically an affair of the Control Council and the Russians would insist on having a share. That would be the end of us—Four-Power Control. We need that like a bullet in the brain.'

'And the money earned by Franz's book?'

'It's all mortgaged—was before we knew how much it would be.'

'I still wish you would accept a partnership in Franz's estate. . . .' This came hesitantly.

'You know that's impossible. If I weren't editor, it would be different. But how can I profit from his death like that?'

'It's not you; it's the cause of free speech, as you clever people would say. And you wouldn't profit, it would be an investment in the editorial foundation.'

Georg laughed at that argument, his own turned against him.

'Who would believe that? I wouldn't myself. No, we just have to reconcile ourselves to being poor. We're lucky if we get away with our attempt on those terms.'

'Of course,' Julia said thoughtfully, 'it would be a bad investment—about as sensible as some of my father's. . . .'

'Practical creature,' he said with the indulgence of one who cared little for security, perhaps because he did not believe in its existence. This disbelief was real and not feigned and so natural to Georg Kerenyi that he never understood that other people did not and could not credit its sincerity. Free men are rare for freedom is only another word for aloneness and defencelessness. 'But speaking of your father, you were going to. . . .' He broke off with a word half smothered as he rose to answer the telephone which spread its gasping shrill through the long room. 'Excuse me,' he added, meaning as much for his bad language as for going away.

'Kerenyi,' he said into the receiver. Then, 'Who? I'm sorry, I didn't quite get . . . . Mm? Luders? Never heard of him. Never mind, connect us. . . .' In the clickings and rattling of the pause in the long-

49

distance connection, he said aloud to Julia, 'She calls him *Herr General-Direktor*. Who can it be?'

'Yes, this is Kerenyi. Who is this, please? Who? What! Berthold! My dear fellow, are you still among the living? This is getting to be a habit. Yes, I gathered you were speaking from Hamburg from the operator. So you got away in one piece? Me? Not quite. But I came back in December '46 so I belong to the fortunate. How are you? Rich—I'm glad to hear it. You would make money, it's in your nature. I'm well, and what's more I'm happy. Oh, of course quarrelling with everybody. That's my nature as yours is not to quarrel.... Why happy? I've just married again. You drove her once, in Warsaw. Beautiful as ever, yes, if not more so. I'm sure she remembers you; I recall her complaining of your impudence. Of course we must meet—when do you arrive? Friday will be difficult. I'm already booked for Gumpoldskirchen in the evening and the afternoon is devoted, if that's the word, to a most painful interview with our old friend Tenius. I take it, he is the cause of your telephoning me? I thought so. We are meeting at the Café Herrenhof at three-thirty. Good. You can come on to the Heurigen with me if you have time? Naturally you are welcome. We shall try to wean you from your North-German habits of privacy. Yes, I have a car. Good. Then, three-thirty on Friday. *Servus.*'

'Well!' he said, putting down the new white receiver and turning to Julia, 'what d'you think of that? You remember Corporal Luders, don't you, he drove your car on that dreary tour to Warsaw in 1942?'

'Odd he knew where to find you,' she said and he wondered for the thousandth time at the practical way her mind moved.

'He must have called the office, where the answering service would give him this number.'

'And I wonder how long this assembling of old contacts by Tenius was going on, before we returned. We've been away for weeks, after all. It now occurs to me that Hella and various other people may have known about his imminent return for some time....'

'Various other people? Are you thinking of the war-crimes investigators perhaps?'

'Yes. I am, and I don't care for it. Not a bit, I don't. Was the envelope of his note to you thrown away? There's no date on the note itself, I noticed.' Georg cast only a perfunctory glance at the

50

waste-paper basket; it was, as always, cleared of even that morning's detritus.

'Well,' he answered, jumping as she knew he would, at once to her meaning, 'Robert is no longer concerned with returning prisoners. They can't get involved.'

'No. But Robert had a whole month's leave and I just wonder. . . . could this have anything to do with his having been to Vienna?'

'Oh, surely not. Just some detail of his present job, don't you think?' He was prowling to and fro as he often did; indeed this habit was one of the considerations that led to the decision to make the whole flight of rooms on the front of the apartment into one long extension.

'I wouldn't want them and the children to be in any way touched by Tenius.'

'That won't happen,' he replied with sharp determination. 'I shall see to that. Tenius stays outside, where he belongs.'

'Outside, yes, outside. But sometimes the outside comes in. I remember that thought years ago. Silence came in from outside the night Hitler came to Vienna. And, you might say, silence was the last thing that belonged to that night. But here it was silent, as if the stillness of being cut off from the real world crept into the house here. Fanciful, isn't it? Not like me at all, to think in that way. But I notice it more and more, as we talk to each other—how detached my thoughts become from the obvious, from what just clearly is happening.'

'Not detached,' he said quietly, 'rather, an introspection you have never allowed yourself. Or never had time to give yourself to. But something that belongs to an exploration we make with each other. For instance—several times in the last couple of days you've mentioned money in connection with your father. That's not like you. Shrewd, yes, that you've always been. But you never cared for money. Not for itself.'

'And I don't care for money now. But—' she stopped and turned with a feline movement on him. 'You ought to know what it is. I expect you to know everything. I'm worried about the fortune I inherited from Franz. I don't like it and I don't like the way I care about it. Or am I just impressed by having so much money? The indemnity paid in this last year is so large—far too much. Of course, I know, I inherit everything as next-of-kin. From Franz, from his great-uncle, from *Tante Ilse* or whatever her name was—you see, I don't even know her name—in Cologne. They are all dead. And I inherit. They're nothing to do with me, but I inherit.'

'But the children will get it,' he pointed out patiently, 'Lali's and Robert's children; and Nando.'

'Yes, but through me. And I have no real right to it. It bothers me, and it gets mixed up in my mind with the way my father wasted —yes, wasted—my mother's small fortune. It gets mixed up, ridiculous though it is. Why should I inherit money that can't by any stretch of the imagination be said to belong to me, when my mother lost every penny she had. . . . And in the end was shot like a criminal?'

'You seem to have forgotten,' he said with stringent coldness, 'that you protected Franz for years—seven years to be exact, almost to the day. Why doesn't that give you a right to his family's money?'

'But you feel it yourself,' Julia accused him. 'You refuse a subsidy from this money—which he would have given you and you'd have taken. If he—they—had lived to give it to you.'

'That is a matter of the outside world. I can't allow it to be said that I accepted funds from your former husband. But for you —can't you simply agree that you had the luck to be left?'

'I notice you don't say "survive",' she said.

'You might just as well have been killed. Or taken your own life, as Ida Orloff did.'

'Ida Orloff,' she said, returning to quietness and thoughtfulness, 'I remember seeing her as a girl. Mother took me, it was one of the first times I went to the theatre, I suppose. She was a *cause célèbre*, still. Everybody knew about her and Hauptmann, though it was years past already, then.'

'Yes, the Hauptmanns took care of that with their philistine secrecy.'

'Philistine!' she sounded shocked. 'Don't you think of him as a great writer, then?'

'Good God, no. He was a splendid theatre man, but no poetic writer. Never that. And inside him was a little lower-middle-class family man. He would never have made all that discreet fuss about his love affairs if he weren't.'

She laughed at this typically inverted example of his unremittingly critical intelligence.

'I remember exactly the first time I went to the theatre,' he said. 'In Budapest. Standing room, of course, for *William Tell*. D'you remember?'

'Certainly. I was taken to one act of *Romeo and Juliet* when I was six,' she answered immediately. 'I distinctly remember being taken home again and leaving my parents in the box.'

'You've been told that and only think you remember.'

She thought about this, frowning in concentration.

'No,' she havered, bringing it out very slowly, 'I do remember, but not directly. I recall it through something else. Wait a moment and I'll get it back. . . .' Then, with a little cry of triumph and amusement, 'It must have been the very day I arrived in the convent. The very day—no, I mean the day after, when I went into the schoolroom. All the others were about nine or ten, I suppose and all day-girls, from the neighbourhood. I was by far the youngest boarder. Oh, by years. That bit I know from later. But the thing about the names, you see. It wasn't Sister Bonifacia, she taught mathematics. I can't bring back the name of the Sister, but I do see it as if it were now, her calling out for Felicitas von Homburg. Well, the "von" was wrong to start with, my father wasn't a "von" but you know how it was, then. Everybody put up your rank almost automatically and he was a *Sektionschef.* . . . I suppose he'd have got the "von" if the Emperor hadn't. . . . And most of the girls seemed to have titles anyway. There was a silence, we were always very quiet. Then all the girls began to turn round and stir, looking at me stealthily, which worried me. I didn't know until later that we were not supposed to turn about and fidget during classes. I feel how much bigger they all were than me, and how vast and light the room seemed. *They* knew, of course, that I was meant since I was the only stranger there—but it didn't seem like that at the time. . . . Then the nun came towards me, it took ages, and called me "my child". That reminded me of my father who always said "the child" and I was so worried I began to cry. I suppose, the changes and strangeness. I simply didn't know what it was all about but there was the feeling that I was doing something I wasn't supposed to do —that was a fearful menace long before I really remember anything. When she got up to me she crouched down by me—I know now she was sorry for me—and asked if I didn't recognise my own name. They wore black bands across their foreheads under their caps and hers made a sort of ridge when she raised her eyebrows.

53

'It sounded so loud when I said "but my name's *Julia* Homburg"
that I swear I could hear an echo—anyway, there is an echo there.
This Sister was frowning, because Julia is a secular name and I
ought to have been called by my Saint's name. She didn't say any
more but just gave me my exercise book and pencil and set me a
writing task and patted my shoulder. Later there was a lot of discussion and I was taken into the room where the Mother Superior
sat and she questioned me—very remote and gentle. The lay sisters
were often rough and even some of the nuns, but she was always
gentle though her quietness was more frightening than when the
lay sisters pushed our shoulders—they weren't supposed to touch
us, I suppose you know? Nobody was supposed to touch anybody,
if it comes to that. I don't remember what I said, but I must have
insisted on keeping my lay name, because when my mother came—
oh, ages later—she asked me why I told the Mother Superior I was
named after Juliet in Shakespeare? She was amused, I couldn't
think why. She told me later when I was a grown girl that it was
true; they went to *Romeo and Juliet* a few weeks after they were
married and she felt sick and knew she must be pregnant and how
she hated the thought of having a baby. That made me feel very
grown up, she came nearer to me. I knew she was asking me to forgive her for not having loved me much as a child. She couldn't help
it; she was very unhappy. I always knew that.'

'Always?'

'Oh yes, that was a state of being. Do you suppose that was the
root of my becoming an actress? I was sure I would be; no I mean I
wanted to be and thought I couldn't possibly be. Father would never
have allowed it, I knew that.'

'It's a bit self-consciously Freudian,' he said dubiously, 'and it
must have come years later.'

'It was certainly the moment when I became Julia, at any rate.
Why I was so sure I couldn't be Felicitas I don't know, but I was
sure I was nothing but Julia. Up to then, I suppose, I'd been simply
"the child". I got very spoilt; all the older girls petted me and called
me baby and sweetie. Nobody did that at home, so I played up
like mad and at the same time I felt it was all rather common of
them. Most of them, in fact, were superior in rank to us. But I
see now I got then a sort of feeling of some advantage—some
privileged position. . . . ? I'm not sure how to say it, but it must
have confirmed in my child's mind what my father planted there,

54

the feeling of being a special person from whom much was expected and who was therefore entitled to consideration.'

'Ghastly little prig you must have been. . . . No, perhaps not. I see what you mean. You continued to be "the child" but from then on from a favourable instead of an unfavourable standpoint. Not something in the way, or there to be trained as a grown-up, but as baby and sweetie.'

'And yet I never lost—haven't now—the feeling that much is expected of me.'

'That's not unique, of course. That's the training of the old world which is gone. That rights and duties absolutely belong together, an indissoluble bond.'

'But you don't have it, that feeling . . . ?'

'No. I rejected it. And consciously. But—in my own defence— I must point out that I accepted other duties.'

'I didn't mean it as a criticism,' she said hastily, almost humbly.

'You might well do. The duties I took—take—upon myself are those I want anyway. Those I did not want I managed to shed with ease, without even knowing it.'

Julia knew to what he referred, but said nothing. She felt a rising thread of irritation, of resentment at what she thought of as Georg's male, arrogant assumption that it was he and he alone who abandoned her former husband's niece to her death. It never came into his mind, apparently, that it was she, Julia, who pushed the girl into his care and therefore into his bed simply because at the time she could not deal with a second, and an officially registered Jew of her husband's family, in her own apartment or even among her own professional contacts. He assumed an absolute blame for what was at least as much her responsibility as his.

'People did just get rounded up,' she said at last, elliptically. 'Probably Franz would have been if he'd ever gone out of this apartment. Has that never occurred to you?'

'Of course it has. That's not why I blame myself. What I do blame myself for, and it gets stronger lately, is that I thought of her as an object. I know now, and it horrifies me, disgusts me, that if you had been threatened I would have acted. Yes, I know now that even then I put you in a different category. I assumed you could deal with your difficulties as a man would do and I would at once have come to your help if you'd been in danger, as I would for a man, a friend. But I didn't think of her like that at all. When it came to the showdown, I thought not of her, even then, but of the unborn child. That, you know, is profoundly disgusting.'

'It isn't,' she insisted. 'Ruth was an object, you didn't make her into one. Nearly all women are objects. You are falling for this legend that because she was Jewish you had some special duty to her, more than you would have for any of your other girls. Maris, for instance. You actually blackmailed her and you don't seem to feel any guilt for that though you might easily have caused her arrest. Just the fact that you compare Ruth's situation with mine proves it. You think of me as able to deal with the world; I wasn't. I went blindly from one day to the next, driven by necessity and helped by somebody as defenceless as Ruth—if not more so. Fina. You forget her, the eternal servant. I was conscious the entire time that I *couldn't* get out of the spiral of secrecy; Fina never wanted to. She was quite willing, never questioned the matter, to sacrifice herself, body and soul and money too—and that must have mattered to Fina, a peasant after all. She would have gone on for ever, never doubting that it was worth it. No, don't deceive yourself Georgy, Fina was the victim. The final victim. You never went to bed with Fina; that's the real difference in your mind. Because you and Ruth lived together, out of masculine sexual possessiveness, you now feel guilt.'

'No,' he said quietly, 'it was the child. The unborn child.'

Suddenly they were in the centre of a terrible, a heart-tearing scene where jagged spikes of the past like splinters of glassy rock pierced their innermost beings.

'You will reproach me with that too, in time,' she said in a low, shaking voice. He stared at her taut, pale-skinned, finely outlined face with a stare the objectiveness of which could not be disguised by his own inner passion.

'You're jealous!' he accused her, with a savage accent of satisfaction.

'Yes,' she almost screamed, and then immediately modulated her voice and certainly not out of concern that the housekeeper might hear them, but out of habitual care for her throat. 'I'm jealous, jealous, jealous!' The change in the pitch of her wonderful, plangent voice gave the word a sinister eloquence which struck a deep chord in him; of the joy of combat with her, with the past, with the fate they carried like burdens on their backs that showed the outer world no compliant bending no matter what wounds, inner or outward, might be dealt them.

'I'm jealous because you talk of her as if I were not alone then, more alone than she was. You say if I'd needed help, you'd have hurried to my aid. You lie. Where were you when the Russians came? You let yourself be fooled by this criminal swine Tenius. You were far away then, when it came to the point. Now, once again, you worry about him, about what happens in the outer world. Just as you did then. If you really cared about me, what happened to Ruth—and that was years past so you'd had plenty of time to digest the lesson—would have made you stay with me. But no, you went soldiering when I needed you. . . . off over the hills and far away with your chums, the sergeants, like this Berthold Luders —yes, I remember him! A fiddler, a spiv, in Warsaw. Taking care of himself. . . .'

Georg interrupted without raising his voice, with a coldness that stopped her rage in its volcanic flood.

'I'd just like to have seen your face, then in 1944, if I'd even hinted at staying here. You'd have called me a coward then as you do now. Then you saw your defence as the line of the Army. I remember it, if you don't. You condemned the conspiracy against Hitler. It opened the lines of your defence. You condemned me for travelling to Agram instead of to the East where the fighting was. But, don't forget, I got there soon enough. Soon enough to bring back wounds that you can torture me with; by pressing your feminine strong hands on my arm whenever you feel like doing so. Especially in those moments when you fear I might force you to give yourself finally—not to me, not into my power—but give yourself away.'

'How can you say that,' she cried, deflected from rage into grief. 'How can you say that when you know you possess me totally? Think of Greece, the incredible nights, full of that brilliance that's more lucent that daylight anywhere else. . . .'

'No,' said Georg with the cunning of Odysseus, 'there is something in you that never gives itself. You possess me, I never possess you.'

'I never think of possession,' she cried with disgust, 'only men think like that!'

'Yes, and you think of me—you feel me, as a man. Not as me.'

He stopped and something occurred to him that he could use. 'Just as you were "the child" so I am now "the man".'

'Oh yes,' she agreed trying to match his cleverness. 'You're right there. You are "the man". The only and absolute male being, the single irreplaceable phallic male.'

'Literary rubbish,' he was derisive. 'You've been reading Lawrence, I suppose?'

'Lawrence? That cracked English poet we were all so mad about in the thirties? Why, I haven't even thought of him for years!'

'No, but you can dredge up his phrases still when you need to. Don't you see how false your position is, how unreal? You wouldn't need such fustian if you weren't threatened, if your unreality weren't exposed. You try to use life and other people as barriers to shelter your damned egotism. And with me, because I don't accept your barriers, you have to rationalise me as an intellectual notion. You turn sensuality into talk because you can't stand the real thing.'

'Intellectual? Barriers? I just don't know what you mean!'

'No, you won't know, you'll do anything to prevent yourself knowing. I can even put my finger on what it is in you that you reserve to yourself; what you never gave Franz and certainly not Nando. The reason perhaps, that you never had children.'

He waited a moment, but not for a reply. He waited coldly, watching her with a look she would have named vindictive if she were not so lost in her anger and confusion that words only had meaning if they could wound him or herself; she hardly knew which.

'I dare say Nando never missed it, he was a humble and simple man who accepted with gratitude what you were pleased to give him. But I wonder now if Franz didn't feel it. I think he must have done. Perhaps, even, that was part of the strain that . . . .'

'You are going too far,' she warned, horrified and breathless at what terrible supposition he might be going to feed into her resistant mind, which she might never again be able to dislodge. 'Is there nothing you won't say?'

'Nothing that I might not say, driven to it. I felt the gap in your consciousness the moment we returned to Vienna, even though you aren't yet working. You began to think of your work and dropped me with half your self, relegated me to a certain place in your life. It is work you keep something in your vitality apart for, some part of you that nobody is ever allowed to trespass upon.

There is a door in yourself that never opens, and behind it is the final energy of your nature, which is reserved for work.'

'You may be right,' Julia returned, showing him a high front of pride. 'That was what you always respected in me. But now you want to take it away from me, like a small boy with a new watch, you must take it to pieces even if you destroy it. But you shan't destroy me!'

'Destroy you?' he said, incredulously. Then, quietly, 'Is that what you believe of me?' And without more ado, he left her alone.

Left alone, in itself an injury, she put her hands up to her forehead to push away her hair with a desperate gesture. She thought over and over again, why did I ever marry again, I must have been mad. Mad. Her gripping fingers came upon the thin, delicate mark at the side of her brow that was all she retained of physical injury. Her hands sprang away from her face as if stung and she turned, clenching her fists, turned blindly to escape from herself, towards the open window from which she stared down into the empty street. The night was overcast, the warmth both sticky and dusty as it is in late summer. Far below her, hardly to be seen, a short stocky figure left the cellar tavern next door—that place too was inescapably part of memory—and crossed the street. As he came under the street lamp, she saw that he staggered and heard faintly that he sang an old song tunelessly as he wavered homeward. The intense, comical humanness of the unknown man, drunk and blissful, broke her anger and she began to weep and laugh together.

V

Because of the photographers who must do their posing before the familiar corner of the old city was filled with its normal affairs and populous with citizens and visitors, Julia was obliged to go out very early the following morning.

This was unusual, but not so strange as to account for the unease that accompanied her through a long morning's work with the strangers. Never did the history of the German-language theatre seem so threadbare an interest; it was incredible that such a thin, wearisome, academic concern could absorb the energies of grown men. In the grip of the tenacious and demanding vigour of the technicians from Germany, the minute preoccupation with detail of the historians, she began once again, as in the past, to feel an hostility towards them, a resistance to their hard seriousness which was so innately German. These individual men deserved nothing of the kind and Julia was aware of the injustice which she called in her mind a fit of cantankerousness; she caught herself classing these inoffensive professionals with Tenius, though she tried self-consciously to be co-operative with them and with her own colleagues. But the work was awkward and strained, and not only because the visitors were thinking in a different idiom, a different shape of thought from her own so that they interfered with the deep-lying communication between herself and her intimate friends. These latter would agree, she knew, that it was this unwelcome strangeness that caused their jerkiness but Julia knew with all her strong professional ties that the fault lay in herself. Her anxiety kept breaking the thick, well-tried, thread of common understanding. It was like a rope that tugged and got stuck instead of running smoothly through the loops of their acquired 'instinct' of consciousness. The sensation of being out of touch was enough to add irritation to her personal concern and although she could not accept what Georg said in the perjorative sense he gave it during their quarrel, she felt a fear that the powerful, even savage, emotions of her new life would fail to resolve themselves into harmony; that they would erupt into what

Georg quite truly called her reserved vitality. Somewhere the nerve-memories were already being interrupted and this was obvious to those who knew her well.

They worked straight through until after two in the afternoon and when Julia arrived at home, tired out, the apartment was quite empty and silent, as she expected to be. Eating something without tasting it, she was struck by a new thought. The breakdown of professional communication was new; it never happened even in the worst days of the War. Indeed, the theatre was then a refuge, the only part of living that remained under orderly control. Only after the theatres were officially closed did the boredom of unnecessary and unfamiliar other work bring with it the disorder of the world in which she had no escape from her desperate responsibility for Franz and Fina.

But the calm, fresh neatness of her rooms reassured her; she slept for an hour and awoke with the refreshed nerves of a sound constitution. She had never been ill in her life, and even the ailments of childhood touched her schooldays more like inoculations than illnesses. When, later, she suffered physical weariness and wounds inflicted by outward brutality she recovered with a completeness that astounded less stoutly built natures. The only remaining sign of injury was the thin line of the surgeon's art over her left temple; and that would have faded to invisibility if the deep and crumpled scar it replaced had not been left so long before it was removed. By the time she was due to be collected for the expedition to the vintner's garden, she felt quite recovered.

Since their route lay through Rodaun, they talked in the car of Hofmannsthal, the period of whose work the historians would be concerned with in the next few days. Presently they were out in open hillsides; from woods and meadows the change was sudden to the sweep of unchanging and therefore comforting lines of vines, gravid with bunches of grapes full grown but not yet ripe.

These long lines ran sloping over the low roll of land, towards them as if advancing on the dusty road and flowing past down its far side. They did not show the curving parallels of ploughland caused by the movements of horses, for by the infinite patience of human hands they were set straight in the earth; as straight as stripes in coloured linen and as neatly parallel as railway lines, the gaps between the stocks and the space between their rows always the same. The distances were laid down from time immemorial by customs more rigid than written law. The vines, cultivated as they now were since Roman times, wore the aspect of infinity, perhaps from the repetition of straight lines, and nature submitted itself to human wishes so completely that it no longer seemed enforced.

'Reminds me of the Yorkshire moors,' said one of the men who had spent several years in England as a prisoner. 'Except for the vines, of course.'

'But the moors aren't cultivated, are they?' asked another softly, his voice flattened by the surrounding peaceful warm space.

'They ploughed them up a lot in the War,' replied the former prisoner. 'That's a view! It's dark even when the sun shines there, and that's rare enough.'

'Shines here all right. Even with the windows down it's burning hot.'

They drew up at last outside one of the secretive massive double gates. The houses were low-built, the small windows sunk into deep walls, roofs coming down as if the houses crouched. There were few people about, the local people were working in the vineyards away out of the little town. Strangers were few here for they were in the Russian-occupied Zone and the quiet of late afternoon was almost oppressive in the heat. A child crossed the little street, if it could be called a street, and in contrast to the city there were no foreign cars here. A thick-set woman in her middle years now opened the side gate and the Germans filed in, answering her greetings in their strange voices.

'I can hardly understand what she says,' muttered one of them a little resentfully as they crossed the cobbled yard past the house, stables, a dark barn, a closed stall where a horse stamped and the smell was strong, ammoniac.

At the bare, unscrubbed wooden tables a few people sat, bent towards each other, speaking quietly. It was so quiet that the rustle of the big plane tree could be heard as they walked under it out into the orchard. The cool of the yard gave way again to heat, and Julia ducked under the low branch of an apple tree, smelling the fallers in the rank grass.

'Ah!' said the voice of one of the men behind her, and that was all.

Through the apple trees heavy with fruit pocked and yellow from the age of the trees and lack of care, and the already harvested cherry trees with darkly metallic trunks, a long low vista of vines spread out before them that seemed to go on to the horizon, sloping very gently. They did not see the table at which the rest of the party already sat until they were on it and heard voices.

There must have been a bustle of greetings and everyone moving to greet them and make room for them, and indeed Julia heard her own voice. But that was all nothing and could just as well have been silence for she felt and saw only Georg staring up at her as he very slowly rose in his uneven fashion, fixing her eyes with his hard, secretive, almost brutally searching gaze.

The pang of excitement was so violent that she feared, a moment later, that everyone else must have felt it transfix her.

She was brought to herself by someone asking, evidently not for the first time, where she wished to sit, and felt dazed at being still there among a crowd.

'Oh, sorry. Anywhere,' she said hastily. 'Here.' And she slid along the low bench so that she was opposite Georg. The men dispersed themselves among their feminine companions with a good deal of laughter and discussion; only Kerenyi remained standing where he was until Julia was seated and then sat down again without moving for the others or even saying anything. After a noticeable pause, he turned to Anita Silovsky beside him and asked her if she approved the special wine served to them in thick glass mugs with handles like straight-sided beer mugs.

'You're looking pale, Julie,' said Hella Schneider. 'Working too hard?'

'You aren't,' replied Julia, and indeed Hella was like a splendid tea-rose in her tanned, blonde beauty shown off to perfection by a white dress. Hella looked across at Georg and then back at Julia with a questioning smile. They had not seen her since their marriage; the curiosity everyone must feel was undisguised in Hella's face. Not discreet and congratulatory as it could be felt in the others but with a slight greed, an envy in it, which with the openness of an egocentric, she proceeded to express.

'Or is Georgy wearing you out? I always heard he was a monster to live with and it's obvious from the way you look at each other that you're eating each other alive.'

'Really, Hella, you are the absolute end of everything,' Jochen Thorn beside her shouted with delighted laughter.

'But, why?' she cried, laughing herself and showing perfect

teeth. 'You don't expect me to pick and choose my words, when we've all known each other for twenty years, do you?' She looked round the table, dazzling everyone with her vigour and fair prettiness. 'Well, almost all of us,' she added with a sudden change to false modesty. The man on her other side, whom Julia saw now to be a stranger, said something in an undertone that made Hella laugh again.

'Oh, that's an open secret, I've been meaning to have an affair with Georgy for ages. Just, somehow I never got around to it. And now I suppose it's too late . . . . eh, Georgy?'

'I'm afraid it is,' Kerenyi bowed towards her mockingly. 'You should have made your wishes known before, my love.'

'Oh, but I did, often. But either the one or the other of us was always entangled. Dear me, it's a good thing we're all bad at counting.'

'Where you're concerned memory has only one side,' said Thorn, pretending gallantry and raising his eyebrows humourously at his wife at the other end of the table.

'To know about you, Jochen, I need only count to two,' she called back, smacking her dark, small hand warningly on the table. There was a shout of laughter at this, for all but the newcomers knew that Jochen Thorn and Hella enjoyed a brief and stormy passage of arms when he first came to Vienna from Germany just after the War began.

'But of course, I recognise you now. You're Berthold Luders, aren't you? You look so different. . . .' Julia shook her head in wonderment at her own failure to recall the man next to Hella.

'It's nearly ten years ago,' said the man, 'I wonder you know me again at all.'

He had just the same air of cheerful unconcern, but it was disguised now at any rate at first glance, by the air of decision, prosperity and well-being that clung to him like the aroma of good brandy. He inclined his head to catch what Hella said as if privately to him, and Julia saw a jewel flash in his cufflink as he raised his glass to drink.

The woman from the house now clumped up to the table, laden with a huge tray on which reposed a stack of thick stoneware plates and a dish piled up with small roasted chickens. The photographer with the Berlin accent moved quickly to allow her access to the table.

'Aha,' he cried in his strange voice, 'the hunger years are here again!'

'Recurring fate,' said Georgy, speared a chicken on one of the thin, tinny forks and slid it on to a plate which he passed over the table to Julia. 'Like Styria, Julie, isn't it—roast chickens?'

'Don't tell me you ever roasted chickens, Julie?' cried Thorn's wife, 'I just can't imagine it!'

'When I couldn't find anybody else to do it for me,' agreed Julia, pulling off one leg and sinking her teeth into its flesh. 'Of course I had some advice from my various menfolk. . . .' She stopped to swallow and added, 'I was extremely domesticated for a couple of months. You should have seen my hands!'

She could not tell by his tone whether Georgy meant to remind her of a happy or miserable occasion; possibly both she thought wryly. Like most of their memories. As Hella laughed, Julia looked up at the end of the table where Luders bent towards her again in some joke and heard herself almost audibly, saying terrible things to Georgy last night. She pushed her mind quickly to Luders; of course, he *was* a spiv, a black-marketeer—how else could he have made a fortune in five years? She glanced back at her husband, but he was describing something with outlining gestures of a drumstick in his fingers, to Anita who listened with her rather long, not pretty, pale face very seriously turned to him, her soft hair falling forward as usual. There was now such a general noise of talk and laughter that Julia could not hear properly what Georgy was telling Anita, only words and scraps of words. He was absorbed apparently in what he was saying, and did not look at her. She could not prevent herself trying to hear, and between remorse at the cruelty of last night's quarrel and a ridiculous feeling that Georgy was trying to punish her by not looking at her again after what might well have been a sarcastically intended reminder of his return to real life from prison, she felt a twinge of bitterness and fear. She was behaving like a fool; first in wounding him at his most vulnerable point, and then showing that she feared his anger. Anita's quietness and attentiveness pointed out better than any attempt to flirt with him, what in a woman must appeal to Georg. The childish absurdity of thinking, even for an instant, that Georgy would stoop to such a trick as pretending to shut her out of his conversation, showed how near a state of emotional panic she was; she told herself that.

65

Instantly her furious mockery of last night, pretending to reassure him of his male supremacy while meaning a denial of his power to control their situation, came back. She felt miserably not only the shocking vulgarity of such affectation but her words came back as a frightening truth. He was indeed the one and only man, and solely as a woman could she keep him. Neither beauty nor recognised talent would count in the real issue between them; she had become accustomed to a supremacy in her own world which quite simply didn't count. It depended on a personal isolation that continued for years, for nearly five years, until that night in the house in Styria when with sovereign confidence and in almost total silence Kerenyi took possession of what was his. The silence was dictated by the house being full of people, naturally that was all, but it struck her now as almost sinister. He did not need words then and did not need them now; she forced words on him and when he accused her of keeping him at some inward distance not measurable in the physical world, he was right. And the danger was that she would not be able to change herself; her pride would bore him and he would return to his former life. For the very circumstance that so increased her secure pride in the years after the War—namely that he was unwillingly celibate because he desired only herself— was now a thing of the past. To put it coarsely, and she put it very coarsely to herself, he had her where he wanted her now; if she denied him the reality of his conquest he would, with the hard realism she knew so well, shrug his shoulders and relinquish his demand for a real relationship. He would call it a last foolish belief in romance and she could positively hear the contempt with which he would imbue that word. Not that it would ever be said aloud.

That was what was so strange about the duel of their fierce pride; what really happened, happened in silence. Just as Georgy had never once spoken to her or touched her with the least sensuality during the time they lived so close together, in the privations of that winter after the War, so he would at some moment in the future, simply turn away from her inwardly. Her house gave him a refuge then, ill, injured and alienated from the world, as they both were. It was a refuge for both of them, and belonged no more to herself than to him, or to Robert and Lali or to the other British officers Robert brought with him; one or two of them had actually lost their names for her. They, like the time when they knew her, existed no more. She, like themselves, returned to the real and postwar world, but different worlds. Only Robert retained his permanence, through marrying into her world, hers and Georgy's. . . . With frightful clearness she saw that 'the young people' would silently—there was that word, again—take Georgy's part and blame her for failing him. The unthinking supremacy she took for granted in her affection for Robert and Lali, almost that of a patroness she thought now with self-disgust, would disappear. They would, out of their own innocent harmony from which human relations must appear so simple, judge her. She would be forced to defend herself and she knew herself too well to think she could ever do that. Just as her pride had allowed no defence to the accusations of the ignorant that she had selfishly divorced her outlawed husband at the orders of the Party during the War, so she would be silent under more real reproaches if she let her second marriage fail. She was in a trap and marriage had sprung the jaws of the trap together.

During this time Julia ate chicken and fresh tomatoes with the aromatic scent of just having been plucked; she drank wine and made disjointed fragments of answer to remarks made on all sides. They would all *know*, she thought, replying to some silly joke over her shoulder in answer to the greetings of Hansi Ostrovsky and Mundel who now came up full of apologies for their late arrival. Hansi, for the second time, brought his dark, slender new girl with him and from Hella's mustering look Julia saw that Hansi seemed ridiculous in his overwhelming, nervous infatuation with a girl young enough to be his daughter. Middle-aged love, she thought; yes, what could be more absurd? And to fail at it the final absurdity.

'Move up,' said Hansi, 'we want to sit next to you.'

Julia obediently moved up and both her old friend and his charming young lover stepped over the bench and seated themselves. The girl did this quite unself-consciously, a movement graceful and unemphasised; it was just to her the simplest way to get to her seat without making everybody shuffle about, but it made Julia feel suddenly old, for it was something that no woman brought up before the War would have done. Monika's face, too, in the clear, rosy light of evening, had the soft, almost liquid quality of the very young, the skin fresh as the faint breeze now becoming deliciously cooled as the heat of the sun was withdrawn. No experience had yet formed those features, either for good or ill, with whatever character they would eventually achieve. Not War nor its aftermath touched her; she was a newborn creature, the postwar girl who came to the city from a small western town untouched by the grinding anguish of recent history and did not even know yet that she would become impatient over the obsession with the past of the people about her.

Fresh food was brought, and fresh wine, for the newcomers. With the arrival of Ostrovsky the conversation inevitably fixed itself upon the theatre, for—his new girl apart—he never thought or talked of anything else.

Because they had been travelling most of the summer Julia was in the dark as to the final plans for the season starting on September the first. She heard now, in the course of the conversation which took it for granted that the subject was as familiar to her as to the others who were in Vienna up to the close of the former season at the end of June, that no Greek classical trilogy was planned for the coming year. Indeed, no Greek plays at all. It was clear, as she allowed the others to inform her without giving away to them the central fact that she was unaware of the decisions, that her own suggestions of that spring had been entirely ignored. And from Hansi Ostrovsky's lack of embarrassment it became clear, too, that they were so completely ignored as to be by now forgotten. Just as from Hansi's obliviousness, which he was incapable of pretending to if it were not real, so it also became clear from a subtle undertone of triumph from Hella that she did remember the earlier discussions and herself was one of the people influential in overthrowing them.

The new members of the company were discussed as they all, years before, discussed Anita now completely part of their lives. Two plays were examined, one French and one English, planned for the smaller house of the Burgtheater and they agreed without any of them being able to suggest either a reason or a cure, that both these plays were superficial and seemed curiously old-fashioned.

'We have to go back to the old, great writers, the classic theatre, to find material that has any meaning for us today,' said Hansi. 'That's why I am so glad we shall do *Macbeth* and *Antony and Cleopatra* next winter. There's something the public can recognise in these plays of passion and rage. Neither comedy of manners nor the secure assumptions of Goethe and company mean anything today.'

'Blood guilt is nearer to us, you mean,' said one of the camera men. 'But doesn't the public want a relief—just amusement?'

'No,' put in Kerenyi, 'it doesn't. Light plays are praised by the critics, but the audiences fill the theatre for serious stuff. Look at Csokor's *November 3rd 1918....* It's full of faults and I said myself it was hopelessly out of date. But there is something in it of reality, of naked passion, that the public feels. Often enough, the very people who make fun of it are those who go back to see it again. As if they were trying to understand something....'

'That isn't true, Georgy,' argued Hella, concerned as always with her own affairs. 'I'm playing to full houses everywhere I take Maugham's *Jane* and what could be more a comedy of manners than that?'

'Wrong again. They go to see *you*, because they've seen you in films.' Mundel waved his arm as he spoke to attract the attention of the bearer of wine. She did not see his signal and he clicked his tongue in annoyance.

'What difference does that make?' argued Hella, crossly but reasonably. 'They go for amusement, whether to see me or the play doesn't matter to the argument.'

'You can't draw conclusions from summer tours in any case,' said Harich. 'The audience is different. Now, if you'd got the point of Maugham's story the right way round, that might prove something because then the audience could be said to be going to see a highly moral tale about telling the truth instead of society lies....'

'I see you've come round to Robert's view of *Jane*,' said Julia with some amusement. 'He said that from the first, that we'd got the story on its head.'

'Robert?' Harich was puzzled at the name of an outsider. 'Ah, yes, that nice English boy of yours!'

'He didn't say any such thing the evening we discussed it!' cried Hella as if accusing the absent man of some fault.

'He was too shy, in public,' said Georgy. 'He explained it afterwards to us in his serious way. But by then the production was almost finished and there wasn't much point trying to change it— you wouldn't have listened in any case.'

'True,' said Hella, complacently, 'the play is a great success as it is.'

Almost in an undertone, Anita murmured a question as to how

Hella could suppose for a moment that her ridiculous production was a success?

'She's too young still for the part in any case.' She added, 'Even if she didn't make herself appear younger; the whole point of the youth of the husband is lost.'

'You've seen it then?' Georg asked idly and as she was replying yes, she was at the dress rehearsal, Kerenyi's attention wandered with a depressing sensation of the unutterable triviality of what they were saying, the waste of time. . . . He raised his eyes above the level of the now only half to be seen foliage of the fruit trees to the translucent darkening purple of the skies, luminous still with a long afterlight, a band of pale, pale green still visible westward. He recalled instantaneously and together the livid pallor of skies in the extreme north in which that blaze of ice-green meant unlimited cold in the few instants it showed almost like a flash; and just such a band of light at dusk in some old painting. What was it, where had he seen it, with little hills below, a kneeling figure against pallid rocks in subtly blended robes of lavender and blue . . . ? St. Anthony in the desert, was it, a desert far from either aridity or desertion, translated into the semblance of the hills about Florence by a painter who never saw a desert whether of sandy heat or arctic snows? But it did not matter where, or what figure by what painter; that it existed was enough.

Gradually Kerenyi became aware that Ostrovsky was saying, or repeating, with astonishment the rhetorical question of who else but Julia would play Cleopatra? But of course she must have known, there was never any question. . . . And in the assertion was the doubt; it carried the statement with it that Julia was now ripe for Cleopatra in her forties, and that implication contained the inner implication that time in her life as an actress was at the flood and was about to become *time passing*. You clown, he said to himself, you egotist. That is what she is fighting, whether she knows it or not. Not you, homunculus, but Time. That is why she fell so easily into the memories of childhood, not to describe to you but to herself, the swinging loop of time.

So the waste of the evening is no waste and nothing is wasted; and with an effect of sudden energy, he plunged with a sharp and acerbic irony back into the superficialities that expressed obliquely what could not be said.

Hella Schneider was talking of money to Berthold Luders. Just as it should be, and it was already clear that she saw the visitor as a possible financier of new projects for new tours with old, faded and popular productions intended—without Hella knowing it or dreaming of it—to flatter audiences into the belief that they enjoyed what they would call culture. What a whore she is, Kerenyi thought and could have laughed aloud at the imitation of interest Luders offered to Hella's cupidity. With his cheerful and prosperous unconcern Luders produced a miniature of the gullible rich male dazzled by fame and beauty; he's a born actor thought Kerenyi with immense enjoyment.

'No, I certainly do not agree,' he said when appealed to confirm a particularly crass piece of vulgarity from Hella. 'Ostrovksy is right.' He used Hansi's surname, in case Luders might not know to whom he referred if he used the Christian one. 'If nobody ever told simple people that Mozart is great art, they would enjoy his music as easily as they do popular songs. The public accepts the best there is in the theatre if only it is offered to them without the stinking intellectual snobbery which is the greatest fault of the German-speaking world. Hella just uses the philistine snobbery to pass off rubbish on the ignorant with a sauce of names the public has been taught to respect. That's the worst sort of counterfeiting.'

In the laughter, and the half-angry protests from Hella, Kerenyi watched Luders glancing with interested blandness from one to the other of them, picking up with native quickness the threads of a world strange to him but worth studying. He was no more impressed with their fame than they were themselves, but watched them as experts in their own profession from whom he could learn something. Why did he concentrate on making money, Kerenyi wondered; that seemed to him the stupidest way of spending one's energies, yet Luders was anything but stupid. The ludicrous yet menacing interview that afternoon would have proved it, if Kerenyi did not already know it.

That wreck of a man, his creased clothes of an old cut and packed for years, hastily resumed and looking again like civilian clothes worn by one normally in uniform, hanging on his huge bones like the rags of a scarecrow. The skin once filled and more than filled with fleshly abundance now flopped empty from jowls and neck, dried juiceless, bloodless and meagre, in collar, wrists and stomach of clothing once taut and stretched by his exuberant stoutness. Tenius, with his attempted condescension, the General consorting with sergeants; as out of date, as ludicrous, as the clothes and the loss of flesh. The broken teeth, the broken nose, the collapse into self-pity. And Luders, no more impressed with the pitiful leftover before him than he was years before by the man in the prime of power; neither respect nor pity, then or now. Watchful interest and concentration. Kerenyi was sure that the concentration had a meaning, it was not for nothing. Even supposing that a man with multifarious business affairs would come to Vienna from Hamburg, across Europe, to inspect this spectre from the past; the contained attention Luders paid Tenius would have told Kerenyi differently.

Yet he gave nothing away. The words and movements that showed what he wished to be seen, were not expressions of what Luders felt and thought. And, not in the sense of which it is true of everyone, that what they say means something different to the hearer from its meaning by the speaker. And not in the sense that everyone colours what he says to put his own view of himself in the best light possible whether consciously or unconsciously. No, Luders deliberately and naturally hid his real feelings, thoughts, purposes. That was why he was such a good conspirator, thought Kerenyi watching his old wartime friend—was he a friend? That was why he never got caught nor even suspected. He was not obliged as Kerenyi himself, he was well aware, was obliged to dissemble by will-power, so that to an acute understanding his insincerity must be detectable.

VI

'This place is really the end of the line, lovely though it is. One has the feeling in Vienna of a dead end. Both literally with the iron curtain on the Danube, and historically, psychologically.'

'Yet it's a lot more civilised than any place in Germany,' Thorn, who was originally German himself, countered the opinion of one of his compatriots, now in the city for the first time in his life. 'A much easier place to live.'

'Yes, living in retirement. Berlin may be harsher, cruder; it certainly is and West Germany even more so. But the Germans are facing both the past and the future. This place is living in its past and that's going to become kitsch, like anything that's put in a frame and contemplated with the sort of sublime self-satisfaction the Austrians attach to their past. Already one sees it in the way things are arranged for tourists. Even this history we are doing; it's really becoming an exercise in nostalgia, nothing more.'

'Oh, he's quite right, Jochen,' said Julia, only pretending to agree. 'The last trace of the old Austria disappeared in 1938 and what we've now gone back to is something that never really existed. We've invented it ourselves. . . .'

She would have said more, but was stopped by the half-laughing outcry from the others, all but the photographer who spoke originally.

'Yes, but you're not *coping* with your problems,' argued that man stubbornly, determined to maintain his point in spite of its tactlessness.

'How can we?' asked Georgy reasonably. 'Between the four occupation forces and their enforced coalition government, we are condemned to impotence. It seems to be the penalty of unity. Germany is split up but shows at least some dynamism; we are a nation perhaps for the first time, at the price of inertia. Do you want us to start fighting amongst ourselves again, as we did before the War, just to show we are alive?'

'You have a point, there,' said the German gloomily and sub-sided with his half-full glass of wine.

'Kerenyi is probably right about the four allies together,' of-fered Luders, for a moment serious. 'In Hamburg the British were so busy enjoying the life of conquerors they didn't interfere with us at all in business—but they would have done if there'd been rivals there. Have to, for political reasons.'

'D'you think the Occupation will go on forever here?' Hella suggested, pretending an interest she did not feel.

'Can't see any reason why it shouldn't,' said Thorn moodily. He was more patriotic towards his adopted country than many na-tives.

'Self-perpetuating, like the coalition, or earthworms,' sug-gested Kerenyi.

'When every damned smallest thing has to be agreed on at the level of the lowest common denominator, the result is inevitably corruption and the loss of standards.' Hansi Ostrovsky glanced up at the branches of the tree above their heads as an electric lamp came alight there. It was almost dark now. 'Look at us—we've twice as many employees or more, than we had before the War but nobody could maintain that we're as good as we were then.'

'It's the lack of new theatrical writers,' said Julia suddenly. 'More than anything.'

'If there were any we shouldn't produce them. They'd go to Munich or Hamburg where they don't have to fight the political double-apparatus over every detail.'

'Don't be ungrateful, Hansi,' Georgy laughed at his angry look. 'We've survived, almost intact after all.'

'Intact!' protested Anita, 'when the Burg is still in ruins?'

There was the silence of depression for a moment and then they all began to chatter at once about other things, as they always did when the theatre, their home, was mentioned.

'Just the same, it's true,' said Harich later. 'If we can survive and bridge over something of the past into the next years that will be quite an achievement for our generation. After that, it's up to the young, the new people.'

'And suppose we don't want your past?' asked Monika, speak-ing as it were publicly, for the first time.

'You will,' he said confidently. 'It gives you something to dis-mantle, to change.'

'You must have something to argue with, after all,' Hansi told her lovingly. And he turned to Julia and began to discuss the new production of *Antony and Cleopatra.*

By the time they left the orchard it was too late for Kerenyi and Luders to discuss their private business. Julia hardly noticed that he proposed himself for a visit on the following morning, for she was already deep in the problems of a role she had never yet played.

And when Luders was announced at noon on Saturday she was listening to Ostrovsky on the telephone, as he discussed with obsessive concern his views of the play she was re-reading. Their professional communion was too old, too habitual for the overt suggestion to need making that the Queen of Egypt was at the time of her famous love affair, already ageing; that was a concept so much a part of their consideration of the play that it was taken for granted.

Julia greeted the guest with an abstracted nod from the telephone, but she saw him with a reserve more complex than his connection to Tenius. He was younger than herself and Georg, not much more than thirty-two, she guessed, although he had little of youth about him; the thought of his age as about the same as Robert's was hardly possible. The threat of ageing implicit in Hansi's concept of Cleopatra was a statement about herself and was mixed with other threatening possibilities. Tenius, coming from the past, could jeopardise the future and the future itself was shrinking from an unconsidered wealth of time to a nearly measureable span. Luders was a physical bond with the actual past in which a younger Julia saw Tenius for the first time as dangerous and clownish at once. He was also a reminder that his younger life was moving as hers once moved, towards the future, never catching up with those who were older, always less old. She, Julia was now *older*; in accepting Cleopatra's being no longer young she accepted her own place in a procession in which Luders would not overtake her until after she was. . . . On the surface of her mind she recalled that she had no reason to like Luders.

Yet she could not deny that he was candidly and refreshingly amusing and attentive when he arrived promptly at noon, with a small and inexpensive bouquet of scented pinks bought from a street-seller and a compact recording gadget.

'I thought you might find something of this sort useful in rehearsing. Perhaps you won't want to use it. If you don't nothing is lost, but I know a film chap in Hamburg who finds it helpful to be able to gauge exactly what he sounds like. It's quite a new idea— very simple to work, you see?' He showed her with a typical economy of fuss how to use the little recorder. 'Of course, the voices have no tone quality, but you can hear exactly the differences of emphasis and expression. This is our newest refinement of the type. The faults of the older models have been corrected—I hope.'

'You make them, then?' asked Georgy.

'Them and other things,' he said. 'This is one of my companies. The microphone is one we use ourselves for board meetings and so on—a whole group can be heard on it.'

'Fascinating thing,' said Kerenyi, viewing the microphone with his customary wariness towards anything requiring manual skill. Julia herself understood at once how to work the device and suggested they should switch it on so that she could form an opinion as to whether it might be useful to her as a self-critic.

'I heard,' she said, 'that some people in Munich were using an American idea for training; they see themselves on a closed-circuit television.'

'Yes, we make those too,' he answered agreeably, but Julia had a fleeting impression of something not entirely welcome to him from his voice. And then, sarcastically, 'The *Amis* are making use of a lot of former German patents in this field.'

'Got them the same way you did, I expect,' said Georgy. 'Which brings us to the less amusing aspect of your being here. Julie knows my connection with Tenius. You'd better tell her about yours. You can trust her not to talk about your business affairs and she ought to know.'

Berthold Luders waited for Julia to seat herself and then himself took a chair on the other side of the table on which the many-faced microphone stood, looking disproportionately large for its compact recorder.

'I'll demonstrate afterwards how you scrub the wire,' he said, glancing at the thing. 'I don't want to have a recording of this chat lying about anywhere.'

Julia was surprised by this remark, but her curiosity soon satisfied.

'It's quite simple,' Luders said in a new tone, soft and deliberate, his business voice. 'This device and various other electronic jobs of the same general kind were originally *Wehrmacht* patents. I acquired them at the end of the war. In other words, since we are among friends—I stole them. I also managed to rescue a quantity of smallish weapons from the same place and sold them in 1946 to what was then Palestine for use in the Israeli guerilla war against the British.

'So that you understand this, I'd better give you some background. Just before the Warsaw uprising I thought it wise to get myself posted. I went to Breslau where some chums of mine were on Tenius' staff. Technical boys; they worked at a high-security unit. This little outfit was engaged on interrogation of captured Russian scientists and technicians. . . . It's all right, *gnaedige Frau*, no need to wince. There were no horrors there, these people were too valuable to be—damaged. Things like this, VHF, closed-circuit television . . .' he indicated the microphone with a well-cared for hand . . . 'were used to listen and look in on these prisoners who were otherwise comparatively free to move about inside the prison and talk together. They were no use to my friends if they didn't talk, you see. I got myself posted to this unit as supply sergeant, at the time thinking of it just as a pretty soft job, which it was. Up to the middle of February, when Breslau was surrounded by Soviet tanks. They already maintained bridgeheads over the Oder at Frankfurt and Küstrin. That meant if anyone was to escape from Breslau they must move fast and move east and then south-east, where the country was wilder, between the industrial area and Krakov, over to the hilly country. Get it?

'We held a council of war some time in the first week of February. I don't recall exactly when, everything at that time runs into everything else but it was the first week, because I do remember the 8th of February. On the night of the 8th our friend Tenius appeared with his senior staff. Our orders were to get the prisoners out to Southern Bavaria. This suited us very well; we could clear off with the prisoners officially and get lost somewhere on the way. Our orders were to do almost what we had planned for ourselves, which just shows how good our staff work was. We were to leave the next day. The only snag was that General of the SS bloody Tenius —excuse me—was to accompany us. *He* said, to supervise the valuable chaps we were escorting. In fact, to save his own skin. Not that I'm suggesting Tenius was a coward, any more than my own friends were. We were in a situation where caution, let alone cow-

77

ardice, no longer had any point. There was literally, as I don't have to tell you, no place in Germany that offered any safety. Tenius chose, as we had already chosen, to flee forward rather than remain in the trap.

'Well, compared with the Red Army Tenius was a small danger. We were left no time to make a new plan and we didn't need to. Without a word we all understood that Tenius would have to be chucked out or shot at some point of our journey. The prototypes of this recorder and several other things we actually packed into the boot of his staff car. The stack of weapons was laid out over the floors of our three trucks and covered with rations cartons on which we and the prisoners lay or sat. Our official weapons we carried with us.

'We had a lot of luck. I always was lucky. The staff car as well as ourselves, carried a radio receiver and we could test out whether there were Russian-speaking troops sending messages in our vicinity as we moved. The crunch came when Tenius picked up an order to report to Berlin. I shall never forget that moment. The sun shone and there was no snow. We were in a country lane just about to eat, well sheltered by fir trees and hilly ground on all sides. I went over to the staff car to speak to the driver and heard the radio, turned low of course, repeating "Attention, here is the Fuehrer's Headquarters" and a list of officers who were to report at once. I can see it now. Tenius turned that big dog-head of his and stared at the radio, his mouth, full of canned meat, half open. His driver looked at me. If he left us we lost our prototypes—there would be no chance to unload them from his command car without his seeing, in broad daylight.

'The driver said quietly, behind his back to me, "Shall I knock him off?" I thought for a minute. Then I muttered, "No, give him a swipe over the ear with the butt of your machine-pistol and drive off fast. I'll get the others into the trucks and follow within five minutes. Keep the radio on to check the surroundings. You know the frequency. Don't go off this lane unless you must. Clear?"

'Some of the men and the prisoners were off in the bushes—you know? I rounded them up so fast they had no time to think—and if they did they would think the enemy was nearby. So we left Tenius there, somewhere in the Bohemian Forest. I don't know why I didn't let the driver finish him. I may have worried about the noise of shots—or maybe we'd had enough of killing. A couple of hours later, I took over the staff car. In those circumstances I couldn't trust the driver since he knew the value of what was in its boot.'

'What became of him?' asked Julia.

'He's the works manager,' replied Luders laconically. 'At one of my plants.' He looked across at Kerenyi, his eyes narrowed speculatively. 'I suppose that's why Tenius is a bit deaf in his right ear, nowadays. The driver clipped him a hefty crack over the nut.'

'I don't quite see why you make a point of these weapons you—er—liberated?' Georgy wanted to know. Luders shook his head pityingly at his unpractical friend.

'I sold them for cigarettes as soon as I got over to Hamburg—oh yes, we got there almost intact at last. The cigarettes bought the workshop which is now five biggish factories. Yes, in those days you had to think and act quickly. You never got the chance of a second run-up!'

'But why does Tenius constitute a danger to you?' Julia persisted. 'He can't—what's it called—put you on a charge for desertion now?'

'As I ran off to the trucks, I heard him yelling after me, just before the car motor drowned his voice. He was shouting "I know what you're up to, you sons of bitches. D'you think I don't know what's in the boot of my own car?" Then he gave a sort of yelp as the driver hit him from behind.'

'Served him right,' said Julia with satisfaction.

'And your prisoners?'

'We delivered them to the British at Hamelin. Of course, without escort or transport. Just left them on the doorstep. Foundlings, as you might say.'

'Can he do anything to you—now?'

'I don't know,' replied Luders, still in that soft, moderate voice. 'But I'm not going to risk it, any more than you will.'

She said, startled, 'You don't mean to do anything . . . ?'

'Won't be necessary. There's been a warrant out for his arrest since 1946. I kept an eye on that, you can imagine.'

'But he'll talk in Court!'

'Well,' said Luders slowly, and reached in his jacket pocket for cigarettes, 'that's what we have to discuss, isn't it?'

Frau Lisl, the housekeeper, came in at that moment to tell Julia that the midday meal was served. The two men rose to let her go before them to the table. Luders slid his unlit cigarette back into its packet; evidently his prosperity has not yet quite taken over from postwar cigarette currency, thought Julia as she moved.

Because of Frau Lisl going to and fro they did not talk of their main preoccupation during luncheon. They addressed themselves at last to a bowl of fresh peaches in the centre of the table and Luders spoke in his business tone.

'What d'you think, Kerenyi?'

Georgy pushed peach skins to the side of his plate with his fruit knife.

'As long as Tenius is on trial or in danger of retrial. . . . That's the doorbell. Are you expecting somebody, Julie?'

She did not even bother to answer; they stared at the door as if they knew who must be at its other side, and as Frau Lisl opened it to announce something, she was pushed away and the gaunt, tall, ruined figure of Tenius could be seen entering.

As that big frame advanced towards the table, carrying with it a shadow in its way of moving, of its former portentous size and self-importance, Julia laid her hands on the table-napkin on her lap. She did this with the perfect naturalness of an accomplished woman used all her life to social behaviour, but yet made it clear that she did it deliberately so that her long hands, now just under the rim of the round dining table, were not available to be taken in greeting, or, still less, to be kissed. At the same instant she turned her head very slightly and as it were instinctively, to look at her husband's eyes. And he understood this look and moved too, very slightly, so that his rather high square shoulder was a little interposed between the woman at the table and the man who approached her.

Tenius, trained by the intuitions of prison life perhaps, recognised some constellation in these tiny movements and stopped his forward progress. He betrayed for an instant in his fallen, ugly face, which yet contained some dignity acquired by suffering not understood, a confusion. He did not know what he should now do, since the obvious move to introduce himself anew to someone not seen for years, was interrupted. It was a moment of crucial importance for him, too. He saw that he was not welcome, that matters were radically changed since he was a master in this place. But neither Julia nor Kerenyi was concerned with him as a human being at all; only with the realisation that this was the very first time that she asked and received protection, as a woman, from her husband.

Yet Tenius, no matter how brutal his understanding, was not a really stupid man, but an accomplished career-builder. Every perception in him including his accepted social and political attitudes was held in abeyance, encapsulated in his distant 'black' prison camp which contained only senior SS officers; in a moment he felt the attacking uncertainty that the behaviour proper to his kind, to himself, was anachronous in the late summer of 1951. And especially in this place which he never trusted or liked, and where he smarted already from a suspicion that the absence of anyone to greet him on his arrival was not by chance—he had been able to persuade himself for twenty-four hours that it was—of a message gone astray. A further inner collapse of artificially retained confidence was visible in the downward lines of former fat in his face.

The silence of the three people at the table, none of whom made any pretence of rising at his entrance, turned them suddenly into a bench of judges. Tenius had thought much of his trial at which he was to sound a clarion of resistance. He knew that a trial was certain, but thought of it as the confrontation of legalists bought by the occupiers, with one who had not surrendered. This was, and he now recognised it, an unreal notion bred in captivity by endless discussion between convinced National Socialists. In a trice the situation was changed; a bluff call to loyalty was out of place here and now. Tenius saw that this was not the way to achieve anything but in the suddenness of the insight he could not think what was. For the moment he simply stood there, his heavy bones drooping and the jacket made to fit a figure twice his present girth hanging from his shoulder blades like the baggy garment of a clown.

He was ridiculous, and in the moment of ridicule they were sorry for him.

Somehow he was seated and the coffee tray that appeared carried a cup for him, too. He was reassured by the behaviour of the truly civilised, as those who only attain the trappings of civilised behaviour often are. So at once, Tenius began to bluster.

'Well, you two, you've done rather well for yourselves, eh? But what are we going to do about my little business, that's the problem. . . .'

'Little business is good,' said Luders in his soft, business voice. His moral brutality matched anything of a more ostentatious kind that Tenius could produce. And this for the good reason that Tenius and his kind had taught Luders the defences appropriate in their nihilist world. The difference lay in the purposes for which Luders was prepared to use the methods learned in a sinister and secret warfare now, in defence of a reconstruction of the world destroyed by Tenius and his fellows, a re-establishment still provisional and without sound foundations.

'But there's no problem. There are ways of getting you out to Argentina in a week or so. You must lie low. Nobody must know you were here. You should leave here tonight, by the night train south.'

'But Hella—my wife?' objected Tenius. 'I haven't even seen her yet!'

His three interlocutors exchanged glances: was it possible that he still did not know?

'Have you not heard from Hella?' asked Kerenyi.

'There's hardly been time yet,' Tenius tried to sound confident. 'Nobody knew I was to be released.'

'You mean I was the only person you wrote to?' Kerenyi was incredulous.

'We could only send one card,' muttered Tenius, pushing with his spatulate fingers at the creased cloth hanging over his knee and keeping his head lowered to see, apparently, what he was doing. It was not easy to understand what he said, for he had lost teeth and mumbled through the broken remains in a voice always deep and thick. 'Wanted to get myself sorted out a bit, before. . . .'

The ludicrous contrast between Tenius as he now was and the triumphantly handsome, luxurious and self-confident woman of last night was so immeasurable to the three people watching his attempted self-deception—and even in his still alienated state it was not successful—that they all looked away from him with helpless embarrassment.

Kerenyi, as always, restless, rose from his chair and walked down the long room. Julia looked after him, knowing that he was the only one of the three of them who could understand from his own experience how to penetrate Tenius. Revolting as he was physically and morally, brutal and criminal as she knew him to be, he was also infinitely pathetic and she could not think of him as dangerous.

But he was dangerous in his primitive cunning.

'How did you know I was here?' he swung his lowered head at Luders although hardly glancing at him. 'Did he let you know?'

Luders took his time, thinking through the implications of the questions before he answered. He decided on the truth as a short cut through misunderstanding.

'No,' he enunciated concisely and deliberately. 'I watch the lists of prisoners returned through the Red Cross. I constantly need workpeople, mechanics, electricians, skilled men of all kinds.'

'And my name just happened to strike you?' Tenius continued with an effort at a sneer.

'No. I watched for you, too.'

'Wise of you. And do I get my fair share?'

'Of what?'

'Of your thefts, of course.'

'Let us be clear,' said Luders calmly. 'In the first place there are no fair shares in this hard world. In the second, if you have in mind reporting me for abstracting valuable patented equipment—which you clearly have—you will not find much sympathy either among the Allies or among the Germans. The Allies have done too much of that kind of thing themselves to care for publicity; and in Germany half the business world is based on some such loot from the breakdown of 1945.'

'But these electronic devices were removed from Breslau. And Breslau is now controlled by Poland—that is, by Russia. Had you thought of that?'

'Of course. And that you would have told the Russians anything you could about them. But you are unaware that these devices, as you call them, have implications for the future which make them the object of great interest to the Americans. They are not likely to co-operate in returning any information about them to the Soviets. In fact, they made efforts to buy or steal them for themselves. Successfully, naturally, and expensively. That is how I have learned, by trial and error, that nobody can legally touch my—our —possession of the patents. You see, the technicians who used these machines could have copied them. And they all work for me, now as then.'

'I certainly shan't take your word for that.'

'By all means don't. Ask others. Ask whom you will. They will all tell you the same thing. The old patents are completely covered by new and legal patents.'

Kerenyi made a movement from his vantage point by one of the windows, which made Luders turn his head.

'Of course,' he answered the unasked question quietly. 'That was the first thing I took care of.'

Tenius turned his heavy, ragged head from one to the other of them with a bewildered lostness. He had thought no further than this. For years his thoughts had hugged this secret means of blackmail but it had not occurred to him that it could be resisted. Prison for six and a half years trained Tenius for a jungle peopled by jackals; he thought of Germany as an extension of that jungle but the world in which Luders had taken his place as if by right was no jungle. The means by which Luders started his postwar career were the means of 1945—the jungle Tenius still thought about. The means by which he was keeping and extending his wealth and influence were the means of the established stolid burgers of Hamburg whose business ethics are as high as any in the world. There were many there, including the old patrician families in some cases, who restarted their lives on foundations as strange and dubious as Luders' beginnings; but those times were already gone and nobody knew better than Luders that his world showed an increasingly solid front to any threat from the past.

The silence in the room drew out, backed by the grinding ring of a tram from the next street corner, the vague and confused sounds of traffic and by a whipping breeze coming in at the open windows which had started in an instant from a hot calm. A door slammed somewhere and Julia looked round to make sure the windows were all securely held open.

'It's our Danube wind,' she explained to Luders, 'comes from nowhere and goes again.'

'Are you in touch with the SS self-help organisation?' asked Kerenyi with an effect of suddenness.

'Of course we are in touch with each other,' said Tenius, frowning awkwardly in an effort to understand what Kerenyi meant by his question.

'Go to them,' advised Georgy brusquely. 'They'll explain to you what you won't believe from us. They can give you a lot of help. Get you new clothes, send you to a good dentist. Take care of you. And get you out of here before the police catch up with you.'

'Ach, I'm not afraid of the Austrian police. I know them. They couldn't catch a ten-year-old boy pinching apples in the market if he had red hair and a hump back!' Tenius threw himself back in his chair with a wide gesture of the arm. 'We always had to act without them in everything. Hopeless lot, I can deal with them in my sleep.'

Luders gave a shocked gasp of laughter at this, at once such an unbelievable piece of arrogant tactlessness for one in the position Tenius was in, and so much just what he had read from Kerenyi's pen when, in the last years, the editor cursed the corruption of Vienna. But as his look jumped from Julia to Georgy he changed his expression instantaneously, so that at any rate Julia never saw the change for her eyes were fixed in such rage and hatred on Tenius that Luders was horrified at the change in her face.

'Oh, you could, could you,' she raged, looking for an incredible moment like one of the market women Tenius had just conjured up. 'Then let me tell you something, you great stupid lump! I remember you in your splendid uniform, surrounded by your crawling *aides-de-camp*, for years on end while I deceived *you*. I remember the first time I heard your name. It took a whole staff of you to drive a bunch of helpless senile patients from the Old People's Home and a few wailing girls that you could have picked up in one hand, into a train here to transport them. That you were very good at, that you could do better, far better than the Austrian police. And I smiled and chattered at you, you poor fool, and you never had the least idea of what I was doing, right here in this room you're sitting in now. Nor did you ever know what Georgy was up to, clever as you were. Everybody here knew, only the Germans didn't have a notion of what was going on. Even your precious Hella never told you—did she? Did she?'

'Hella?' said Tenius, struggling to his unwieldy feet. 'What do you mean, Hella?'

'Hella knew at the latest in July 1944 that I was hiding Franz here, and she must really have known long before that. It was an open secret.'

'Franz?' mumbled Tenius, never having heard Wedeker's name in his far imprisonment. But the implication, if slowly, sank in and as it sank in, he let himself sink with it, back into the chair from which he had half risen and stared at Julia with incredulous eyes, his mouth slightly open.

'Hella?'

'Of course, Hella,' she cried impatiently. 'And Georgy and half Vienna, including at least two civil servants in the Ministry of Interior.'

Kerenyi was still leaning on the window ledge, his long legs stuck out in front of him, hands in pockets. He pushed himself upright now and came over to Julia, to stand beside her as she leaned forward as if to threaten the astounded Tenius.

'You see, you shouldn't have mentioned the market,' he explained, as if being only reasonable. 'This household has bad memories of the SS in markets. Of the SS altogether. . . .'

'But Hella,' Tenius almost begged them. 'She was—she helped me with my report that summer. . . .' He swung his big head to and fro from Kerenyi to Luders and the thought of the report he so carefully altered in July 1944 brought back some of his lost subjective superiority so that he straightened himself and stood up and his ruined face changed. He now, for the first time, faintly resembled the man he formerly was, at least in expression.

'Now, let's get down to cases,' he said in a barrack-room tone, as of one delivering a carefully memorised brief.

'The report I wrote to SS *Reichsfuehrer* Himmler in the summer of 1944 clears me of any implication in the mass-pogroms. I was clearly against the whole process of the Final Solution. You, Kerenyi, took a copy of that report to your treasonable friends, but you can't prove that I gave it to you. You could easily have stolen it. You're sitting here in this very room now with a thief of State property, equipment that was top secret and essential to the German war effort. That throws doubt on your honesty as well as his. Moreover, the message I sent to my immediate superior officer in Berlin at that time said nothing of my report. It said simply that Sergeant Kerenyi had complained to me of enquiries by security service officers in connection with the traitorous attack on the life of the Fuehrer but that I personally had ordered Kerenyi to keep in touch with the conspirators so that he could inform me. Kerenyi was therefore to be handled as an agent of the security service in this investigation and further enquiries were to be referred to myself. That's as clear as daylight and don't make the mistake of thinking all policemen are dumb. The way the War ended turns that protection into evidence that you betrayed the conspiracy to me—a General of the security service. And as for Luders, he may have new patents from the occupying forces and if unchallenged they may be valid in the law of the Federal Republic of Germany. But the electronic devices stolen by Luders were the property of the German State and belong now to the legal heirs of that State, which is the Federal Republic. Alternatively, they belong to the heirs of the territory where they were last legally installed and that's Poland. We had lawyers in prison camp, high-ranking ones too. I know what I'm talking about. I can ruin you both. We still have our ways and means, in spite of defeat and treachery, and someone will be found to claim these patents for the German people. As for Kerenyi, he will be hounded out of public life. Those who were in favour of the conspiracy against the Fuehrer and all the millions who recognised it for the dastardly stab in the back that it was, will alike hold him in contempt. Your only alternative is to give me the help I have a right to.'

Tenius paused triumphantly, but to his astounded disbelief, neither of the two men he so confidently threatened showed any sign of fear.

'You can't really believe that your stupid report could help you now?' demanded Luders scornfully, and laughed furiously. 'Yes, of course I know about it, absurd story. Kerenyi told me yesterday. Don't you see, if you even mention it, it makes your position worse? It proves—if it could ever be found—that you knew what was going on. And even worse, that you knew you had to try to hide your own part in the camps. . . . You've completely lost touch with reality. Wake up, man, you've got to understand that times have changed.'

'But times have not really changed,' interrupted Kerenyi, coming to lean with his slightly crooked stance by one elbow on the back of the chair from which his wife had risen to attack Tenius. 'You knew damned well, *Herr Polizeigeneral*, in 1944, that you would be called to account for your career in the War. One might well say that you'd paid that bill, but don't you believe it! Your jailers delivered you back to Germany on condition that you should be tried. And you will be tried unless you come to your senses and clear out of Europe. We don't want you here any more than we ever did, and neither does your former wife want you here and you'd better understand that.'

From his attackers and from his crumbling fortress of ignorance, Tenius retreated, physically by moving haltingly backwards towards the door, and psychologically by putting on a pathetic, an almost tearful tone.

'But you're a German,' he appealed to Luders. 'These people here, they're all half-castes in a way. But you, you must have some feeling of patriotism, you must know. . . .'

'Don't talk to me of patriotism,' shouted Luders, losing at the word his careful and studied self-command. 'It's just as a German that I hate you. You destroyed us, inwardly and outwardly, you bunch of street-corner louts. Now we're all tarred with your brush, the whole world thinks of all of us as *your* kind. Every time I see the scaffolding and rebuilding in Hamburg I curse you. Every time some foreigner with not half my guts and brains condescends to me, I curse you. Every time I go to Berlin and see the Asians you brought into Germany I hate you more, and as a German, a German, you hear me?'

'Wait, Berthold,' said Kerenyi, 'we are not being sensible. The important point is to persuade him, not to indulge our own anger. He's got to understand that if he stays in Vienna he will be handed over to the Poles and shot. If he goes to Germany, he will be tried in a civil court and spend the rest of his life in gaol. He can hardly get less than life. That is the point he has to grasp.'

'Your name alone,' Julia spoke directly to Tenius, but without looking into his face. 'You might get away with it. The courts must be still overworked and they are not all that keen on actually looking for war crimes trials. That is, you might if your name were Schultze. But Tenius—it's an unusual name.'

'Schultze,' said Tenius blankly, 'I used to know a man called Schultze. . . .'

'Your comrades had him shot,' said Luders crisply. 'I knew him well in Warsaw.'

'A traitor,' Tenius growled, but he seemed now himself to know that his simple concepts were insufficient.

'A lot of us were that,' agreed Luders, 'but he was a fool, too. He let himself be used.'

'As we are being used now,' said Julia.

'Used?' Luders asked her sharply.

'We're going to help him to escape, aren't we? If we were logical, we should shoot him.'

'There's nothing on earth so dangerous as an honest woman,' said Kerenyi. And to his wife, 'Don't bring morals into this.'

'I just want us to be clear about it,' she said, as if flippantly. 'And what's more, we have to be quick about it. Speaking of poor Schultze reminds me that Malczewska is in Vienna, and she would recognise him.' She indicated with a lift of her chin the object of their discussion.

'Malczewska! That scorpion? But why should she ever see him?'

'Because she is working for Hella. You know she was originally a stage producer. She does Hella's adaptations for these commercial ventures of hers.'

'That's all we needed,' groaned Luders. 'A nationalist Pole from the Home Army intimate with his wife. . . . But what an extraordinary coincidence, that Malczewska should be actually working for Hella Schneider-Tenius!'

'Not so strange, really. She left Warsaw in the winter of 1944–1945 as you know, I suppose?' This to Luders, who nodded assent, not without a testing glance at Tenius. But that worthy seemed to be preoccupied with his own bewildered consideration of the changes he was now forced to confront and took no interest in what they were saying.

'Like yourself, she naturally travelled south-east, and I saw her for a moment on the day of the great air-raid, when the Opera was hit. She had been trekking across Europe for months then, injured and ill. She finished up in Graz just after the War ended and was employed there by the British occupation authorities—she speaks every European language well. She was kind once to Lali at that time—it seems to have been the only occasion Malczewska ever showed any sort of ordinary human feeling. And, granted her history, we can hardly hold that against her. So when these friends of ours, Lali and Robert, heard from Hella that she was looking for a cheap but experienced dramaturgist, they naturally suggested Malczewska. Who equally naturally accepted the chance to return to her own kind of work. I don't find anything strange in the story. It's just the way things happen. . . .'

'If Malczewska sees Tenius, he's a lost man. The Erinnyes are babes in arms to her longing for vengeance.'

'Or even hears he has returned,' pointed out Luders. 'Which she is more likely to do.' He screwed up his eyes slightly, rubbing at his blankly shaved chin with a thoughtful look into space while his thumb made not the slightest rustle over the smooth surface of his jaw. He turned his gaze on the silent Tenius, frowning as Tenius himself was frowning, in concentration.

'I don't want to be drawn into his trial,' he said slowly, working it out aloud as if Tenius were not present. 'It would take up a lot of time and money, possibly lead to lawsuits with the original inventors of these patents. There might even be something in what Tenius claims about the government. It would also be bad business publicity. But that is the extent of my own involvement. Malczewska changes the whole picture, really, d'you see? If someone near enough to hear of Tenius and his renewed disappearance is going to make a big fuss, then it might be better for him to be turned over to the police right away. I'd rather appear in a war crimes trial than be branded as a man who has so much to hide that he does business with Odessa over a swine like this one here. . . .'

'Odessa?' asked Julia, puzzled by the name of the Russian port.

'It's the initials of the SS self-help organisation,' explained Luders abstractedly. 'It's a problem, now, where it seemed quite simple before.'

'On the other hand,' said Kerenyi as he moved away to the window again with his limping sway, 'a trial with a lot of publicity would ruin me. I should have to resign my editorship. Any trial would be bad enough, but one with Malczewska and her friends as witnesses is bound to be so distorting of the facts that I should never survive it.'

'The key to this situation seems to be Hella Schneider,' pointed out Julia softly. The two men turned to look at her, and slowly, as if returning from far away, Tenius too raised his ruined head and stared at her. She returned the look of Luders and her husband, perhaps somewhat defiantly, but did not look at their victim. There was a long silence in the room as the three men about her caught up with her jump of perception by mental processes.

'But you can't turn me over to the police,' muttered Tenius at last, hoarsely stating as a possibility what he intended as a pleading denial.

'We should not have to do that,' said Luders quietly, having arrived at Julia's conclusion. 'I think perhaps we don't have to do anything at all . . . ?'

'You still have the alternative open to you,' pointed out Julia in a dry, objective tone and now looking straight at Tenius. 'You can leave today for some place where these Odessa people can help you more easily than here in Vienna where there are occupation troops and policemen about. I have no doubt Mr. Luders will be able to give you some advice as to where you might go.'

'I must think,' he mumbled desperately, turning his head to and fro.

'Yes,' she said, 'I remember very well that sensation. And it was you and your kind that made me feel it—for years on end.'

At this, as if he had at last perceived an absolute message of rejection, as if he had at last understood, Tenius went, without excusing himself or taking his leave, for the years of imprisonment had removed as if they never existed those surface smoothnesses of behaviour acquired during the steep rise of his career which never had time to take root so that they might cover—as they do for thousands of ambitious people—the bottomless crudity and harshness of the world he inhabited.

VII

Berthold Luders rose as soon as Tenius was gone, made his fare-wells and promised to inform Julia, if he might, of his return to Vienna which he confidently expected, as he said.

'What is he going to do?' Julia asked when they were left alone.

'Probably remind Tenius of Malczewska's part in the Warsaw Home Army, the uprising there. It was clear that Tenius did not recognise the name, didn't you think?'

'I dare say he never heard of her by name at all. She would just be one of a faceless multitude for him. Was he in Warsaw during the uprising?'

'Yes—called in when the forces stationed there were not able to put it down at once. It was partly under his orders that the city was destroyed and when the last remnants of the rebels fled into the only part of Warsaw still in existence—that is, the under-ground passages of the post and sewage works—it was he who thought of that and literally winkled them out almost to the last man.'

The thought of dark underground passages, of memories that were never allowed into her mind, made Julia shudder as if the warm afternoon were night, and cold. Tenius was already destined to be the personification of that time; it was from him as he was during the war, him personally, that Franz was hidden and pro-tected. He it already was, in person, who turned Kerenyi's hair grey, emptied his soul for years of anything but hatred, and re-moved as if by a lobotomy the power to create, turned him into a homeless wanderer who was capable of observing the world about him and putting his observation into words but no longer capable of original work. It was Tenius who, in a sinister conjuring trick, removed instantaneously, silently, the mother of Kerenyi's unborn child. It was by his action that a number of others who formerly lived in the world with her and were seen and felt as human beings every day and night, were removed as unburied rubbish, strewn over distant landscapes, and sinking into strange soils where some day mechanised ploughshares could turn up a button, the buckle of a uniform belt, the twisted and shattered scrap of a weapon long dropped in death. Tenius it was who ordered up the fearsome wave of reactive hatred that swept herself into a dungeon where Franz disappeared, wiped from a black slate and she was carried out like a broken lay-figure. The physical scars were smoothed away in what, in that moment, seemed nothing but the final hypocrisy, the crafty and deceitful removal of evidence of foul deeds done under cover of darkness which the world conspired to pretend had never happened. It was Tenius who set her down in a part of the room she now stood in, already a little unclear in its former being; already overlaid by the palimpsest of its new form which was her own act as an accessory in the conspiracy against the past. Just where Franz's desk had once stood massively was no longer certain, and the desk itself was chopped up and burned in the heating stoves of a neighbour in the house—she could not sell it with the rest of the former furnishings—but the moments when she sat at that empty desk over five years ago and faced in despair the fact of her own continued life, they still existed.

'Just the same, he ought to be tried,' she said, in a harsh, domineering tone which, too, belonged to that time as they both well remembered. With the phrase that conditioned her statement she was aware of condoning the escape of Tenius from justice. No: not justice for that could hardly exist for such acts, but revenge.

'What good would it do? Much harm, but what good? He's too broken to do more evil. I doubt if he has long to live. He's a gibbering ghost, really. There ought to be an island where his kind could be confined together, to live out their insanity where they can't infect other people without the living having to soil their hands on them.'

The thought of a fresh swing of the pendulum of hatred reminded Julia.

'When I said the whole thing turned on Hella, I meant only that she would chuck Tenius out with such speed and energy that he would agree to leave at once,' she said hesitantly. 'You don't suppose Luders understood it as a hint . . . ?'

'A hint—at what?' The sharp question proved an unease in Kerenyi as well as herself.

'If he spoke to Malczewska, or even failed to warn Hella not to do so . . . . She is perfectly capable of killing him, or of suggesting to her Polish friends. . . .'

'From my long knowledge of Hella Schneider, I should think it most unlikely for her ever to mention her "former" husband to anybody at all.'

'Unless Luders put it into her head that—that what? A mysterious stabbing in a sordid little hotel in the Leopoldstadt? Something of that sort would be even more final than a divorce and a ticket to Buenos Aires.'

'You think her capable of that?'

She turned from an idle contemplation of the traffic winding foreshortened through the sunny street beneath them and looked at her husband with a serious, level look.

'Don't you?' she asked simply.

'You realise that we have both had this idea ourselves? So far we do not know it has come into anybody else's mind. If we act on it, in no matter how negative and warning a way, then we make ourselves responsible for giving the idea to someone who could assess it positively.'

'You're using extraordinarily roundabout language,' she said fretfully. 'Not like you at all!'

'Besides,' she continued slowly, 'we have already put it into Luders' mind. Haven't we?'

'So we ought to try to undo that possible impression, you think?'

'Of course we ought to, although Luders is obviously not the man to miss the implications of his actions. He showed quite clearly in his comments on the men who helped him to "liberate" this equipment at the end of the War that he is conscious of mutual dependencies and obligations. I doubt he would consider having anything to do with the emigré Poles who hang about the IInd District, once he made Malczewska's acquaintance again. He would see at once that these are the sort of people who would find it an additional flavour to their revenge to involve Luders and ourselves in it. But by then it would be too late.'

'Yes, they are notorious for taking the law into their own hands. . . . But you misjudge Luders a little, I think. He wouldn't care if Tenius disappeared, that is true. But he would care if he involved Malczewska and even her dubious Polish friends, most of whom are really crooks who evade the controls of the police by claiming to be our victims—in fact by appealing to the Allies over the heads of the police. There are a lot of things Berthold Luders would not do. He knew Poland before the War and I know he risked his neck for Polish friends during it. And if he had the sense to know then that Malczewska is an hysteric to be avoided, he must know it even better now.'

'So you don't think he would—how would one put it? Take a short way out?'

'Not through Malczewska,' Georgy was careful to commit himself no further. 'What I am afraid of is that Tenius will force himself on Hella in some public way such as going to the rehearsal rooms where she works while she is in Vienna. Then Malczewska could easily simply see him and that would be enough.'

'And really,' said Julia slowly, 'when you think that respectable citizens, absolute pillars of society like ourselves, are quite prepared to cheat the law over Tenius, you really can't blame Malczewska.'

'I don't know that I have much confidence in the law as dispenser of Justice. Nor do I see the reality of justice in trying a man like Tenius by the process of penal law for actions committed under military law, *now*. It's getting too long after the War. And civil crime—that would have to be murder. It's not so easy, in a properly run court as it was at Nuremberg; you can't invent some vague concept like "crimes against humanity." It has to be the murder of an identified man by a murderer who can be proved to have killed him. If the 1941 round-up here is used for evidence—that's the easiest one to get at, probably—then murder is hardly provable because in the confusion at Lodz and Lublin that train was never traced, for certain.'

'It's all so irrational,' Julia said helplessly.

'But we are irrational. Luders used to say, during the War, that the Germans unconsciously invented the whole complex of the massacres in eastern Europe to even up the odds, give themselves a handicap to balance the decimation of the Red Army officer corps in the purges. He used to say there was no other explanation for doing something so contrary to their own interests as to use transport and manpower for so pointless an enterprise—and directly across the supply lines to the eastern fronts.'

'He has a singularly cold-blooded sense of humor, your Luders.'

'It wasn't humour. He was trying to express in his practical fashion what we all felt—that it was all happening in some pattern we had no key to. That what seemed to be happening was superficially imposed on some meaning we couldn't grasp.'

'Ah, one has that feeling sometimes with plays. All the conscious work with words and movements produces something quite different from what it seems to be.'

Frau Lisl coming at that moment, Julia lost the thread of her thought for she was never skilled at putting invisible concepts into words. She wanted to communicate some essential factor of her work to Georgy, knowing that he had long since understood it, but was glad to be interrupted, too. It was dangerous to talk of such things; discussion frayed them out and made them too fragile to form a sound warp for the real business of acting. Energy was wasted, as time was being squandered now on Tenius when she needed both to study the play that lived, still largely unknown, in the background of her consciousness.

She walked down the room and back again to where Georg was standing watching her. She felt the irritable boredom known only to creative natures, of being prevented by some outside contingency from getting down to an exciting task.

'Just at the time when you need all your energy and mind for the new part,' he said. 'It's too bad this disgusting business of Tenius should interfere.'

'Hansi always says at the beginning of every new production, that it's a good thing to have a certain amount of pressure, something to worry about unconnected with work. He accuses me of thinking too much and says I need to be distracted from it.'

'A little distraction, perhaps,' replied Georgy, remembering how her acting had suffered during the War. 'But nothing serious.'

'Then Tenius must be prevented from becoming serious,' she said, waved a hand with bravura as if to whisk the intruder out of existence.

'I think,' Georgy said uneasily, 'I'd better go and see what has happened to Tenius and Luders. Perhaps I can succeed, without saying anything, in discovering what Tenius means to do. If he is, indeed, able to form any coherent plans. . . .'

'If he hasn't already done something disastrous,' she agreed.

'I don't even know if he knows where Hella is working on her new project. But he certainly knows where her house is. He bought it for her and lived in it with her.'

'I thought Hella would be leaving again at once, to rejoin her tour?' asked Julia.

'I rather think she just said so to cover her reason for staying in Vienna for a few days. She is sharing the tour with two other plays and that could give her several days' freedom to deal with her divorce affairs without it being noticeable.'

'I didn't know that. A good idea, to spread the risk of losing on the tour. . . .'

Kerenyi came close to Julia and she put up her hands and caught his shoulders as if grasping at a support. He felt no fear now that she would deliberately use the embrace as an attack; for the first time in all their knowledge of each other he felt her as needing emotional help that he could give her and as being willing to accept it from him. For all the hundreds of times he had helped her professionally and in practical ways supported her long intrigue— their common intrigue—to protect her first husband, this was a quite new sensation. A sensation of painful sweetness that pierced his whole being, moved him so deeply that for a moment he would have been unable to speak. But he did not need to speak; they stood quite still, holding each other, their eyes closed. Then Kerenyi kissed her hand in the palm, and went out.

Julia had a powerful impulse to go to the tall window and watch him go away. She was obliged to force herself not to do so, for the urge was not the desire to catch a glimpse of one loved; it was the return of the nausea of strain, fear and disgust from the past when Georg's presence in that house always contained the threat of danger.

Instead of going to the window, Julia moved right down the long room to the wall of books where a pile of commentaries and historical reference books lay ready, the white tabs of paper marking passages she needed to read before beginning the actual study of her new part. But first she picked up her own copy of the play itself, just to feel it as being real. The stout paper covers and the printed lines gave off a slight odour of new print and paper; the familiar binding, the particular quality of the pages, was intensely actual, reassuring. Stroking the script affectionately she put it back and took up the topmost of the commentaries. It, too, was familiar, one of a series bound in dark green and heavy to hold, its old-fashioned, embossed gilded lettering and the painted library number, the close-printed pages smelling of bookish mustiness, the type set in the old style so much slower to read than modern typefaces and lettering. Many hands had held it, many minds studied it, the minute and copious footnotes added to by written cross-references to further interpretations, different views of the play, in the cramped hand of some former librarian, with the numbers of the books referred to. There were, as well, many pencilled marginalia, carefully rubbed out but still showing. It was courteously, constantly and unsuccessfully requested by the librarian that theatre members using library books should not make notes in them, but should use separate notebooks which could be obtained from the library on request....

Julia began to read with a concentration intensified by the absolute need to get away from the moral squalor which was the native element of Tenius.

VIII

Kerenyi found his quarry at once, as he knew he would. It would be the obvious thing to do for Luders to catch up Tenius on the pavement and go with him to the little basement wineshop next door, and that was just what he had done.

The old owner having died a few months before, his daughter-in-law and heiress had somewhat modernised the familiar place. The hot cooking-range with its coal fire was gone from the dark corner and the simple cooking was now done in a back room, but was still visible through the open doorway. The rough tables were covered by coloured plastic material of a 'contemporary' pattern that faded the traditional country design of the curtains at the low windows. There was a steamy haze of tobacco, wine and beer of generations past, a permanent smell of cooking leeks and celery for tomorrow's soup—for some reason this place always smelled of that and not of the equally frequent goulash. In its bad taste and simple workaday candour of being there for poor people, the little tavern was kind and comfortable for all comers.

Kerenyi lifted a hand to the two men sitting by the small window and went to greet the woman who owned the place, leaning his tall head in at the kitchen door and talking to her in her own dialect, giving the cropped hair of her small son a friendly tug as he asked after the boy's school work. Getting only a shuffling mutter in answer to this question, Kerenyi laughed as the child's mother urged him roughly to speak properly to the *Herr Doktor*.

The woman followed him to the corner table, serving cloth in hand, with the beer he asked for. Although still young, she was already showing the stolid gait and loose fat of her kind. She'll be the image of her mother-in-law in a few years, thought Kerenyi, recalling the hugely obese amazon who once reigned here.

'You came, then,' stated Luders calmly, and the woman glanced with a slight disfavour at him, at the sharp Hamburg voice in so notable a contrast to those she was used to. But she registered in the automatic way of publicans that the stranger used the familiar form of address to the *Herr Doktor* while the other, sick man was addressed formally.

'I am trying to persuade him to let me go and see his wife before he does,' explained Luders as Kerenyi lit one of the thin, black cigars he had lately taken to smoking. 'But he won't believe me that it would be wise to prepare her for a visit.' He turned his measuring eyes from Tenius who stared gloomily at the table, to Kerenyi and added with cheerful brutality. 'He doesn't understand the impression he makes.'

'It would be wiser still to give up the whole idea of seeing Hella,' said Georg with no less cruelty and directly to Tenius, 'She will keep you in the house just long enough to get her lawyers over to serve you with a petition for divorce. But her place is always full of friends and colleagues and you know how actors talk. . . .'

This frontal attack affected Tenius like a heavy blow and he sank down further on his hard bench seat, his hanging shoulders drooping still more and his head sinking down until it was almost between them. His head really is like a dog's somehow, thought Kerenyi; how perceptive Berthold is. But Tenius still said nothing; nor did he drink his beer. He was stunned by the complete reversal from dreams hugged in secret during years of hunger and isolation.

'Hella has made at least two attempts to have you officially declared dead,' Georg went on. 'After the German Red Cross reported someone saying he'd seen you alive in 1946 she was in a rage for weeks. And what is more, nobody in a place like this would recognise you, but if you go anywhere where Hella is likely to be, you are almost certain to be seen by people who would.'

He did not say that Hella herself was likely to inform the German—not the Austrian—police of her husband's presence and thus force them to demand his extradition to be tried in his home town which was small and far away where publicity was less to be feared.

There was a pause while the two of them drank their beer and Tenius sat slumped in the corner of the high-backed bench. He swung his head once or twice from side to side, but not as if searching for some way out of his dilemma; rather as if in some physical discomfort such as an earache. He began to breathe unevenly. At last he asked in his low, mumbling voice where the washroom was and Kerenyi indicated the direction with a jerk of his head. The big frame shambled across the small space slowly and disappeared behind the frieze curtain covering the short passage to the lavatories and the inner courtyard.

'Why couldn't the bastards keep him a few months longer?' muttered Luders. 'He wouldn't have survived another winter.'

'I doubt if he will in any case,' replied Kerenyi.

'He's taking a long time to think it over,' said Luders presently, glancing at his opulent gold watch. To do this he made a flicking gesture, shooting forward his wrist to pull back the gleaming shirt-cuff and turning the wrist-face towards himself briskly. Then he rose to his feet.

'Of course, he's cleared off,' he said.

There was no obvious way out of the tiny and crowded court, but Tenius had not been a policeman for years without learning of unorthodox back exits of all kinds nor how to recognise the one useful doorway from ones that led only to storerooms.

'He'll have gone to Hella's house,' he said. 'I'd better telephone her and warn her.'

'Did you know Tenius was about?' he asked when at last Hella came to the telephone.

'How did you know that?' demanded her voice with characteristic suspicion.

'He came to see me, of course. I think he's on his way to you now.'

'Good,' she said with satisfaction. 'I'll get the lawyer's clerk over straight away.' She cut off without thanking him, sure that his thought was only for her interest, and he went back to Luders laughing to himself.

'Look here,' he said, picking up his half-finished beer, 'it was a good idea of yours to whisk Tenius out of here before he could do any damage. But we had better admit right now that it isn't going to work. As Julia said, it's Hella's affair, and she is more capable of getting rid of him than anybody I know. You came to Vienna on business and it was the purest chance that Tenius followed up his Red Cross message to me by coming to see me while you were lunching with us. We neither of us know or care anything about his wartime career, and any ranting he may indulge in to the Public Prosecutor or his defence counsel, or the police or the Court in the last resort, is just the nonsense of a man unhinged by his sufferings.'

'Two objections,' replied Luders at once. 'First I have no business affairs here. Second, we still don't know whether he can prove anything.'

'Business you can find. The other we have to risk. Any other course will only get us into something serious and I have no right to involve Julia in further trouble. If it comes out about that report I shall have to take the consequences. I shall resign my editorship and offer the paper to my co-workers to run as a co-operative.'

'You talk about business as women do,' Luders shook his head, smiling. 'There's practically nothing in Austria of my sort of manufacturing. And certainly not in Vienna, where designs would be in the hands of Communist workpeople within a week. No thanks. I know what's happening here in the oil industry from friends of mine and that's enough for me. Not a pfennig of my capital goes into industry here. I'll have to think of something—wait a moment. I think I have an idea. . . .' He considered his friend with his bland, cool look. 'It's the obvious thing. Have you got time to take me over to your office and show me your accounts?'

'My accounts?' Kerenyi was blank with astonishment.

'Of course, man! You need an investment, don't you? Come along, let's go.' He was already waving a banknote to pay for the beer.

'But my dear chap, I've just told you I may have to resign. . . .' protested Kerenyi, already being towed to the door by a hand on his elbow. 'Although that prospect may be an inducement to you, of course.'

'You're not resigning anything. We're going to fight this thing out—and in the open. So far from hiding anything, we shall tell the truth. In print.' Luders was up the low steps to the street and snapping his fingers at the large and new limousine and its patient driver still waiting for him outside the next house.

'Tell him where to go,' he commanded, bundling the still arguing Kerenyi into the back of the hired Mercedes.

It is possible to walk, or to thread a way, through the centre of Vienna without ever walking along a street but only, from time to time, crossing one. Courtyards lead into alleys and back again through courts, many of which carry notices on their tall gates denying entry to pedestrians except to go to someone in the house. Tenius went up worn stone steps to a scratched and paintless doorway in the air shaft behind the tavern and found himself in such a courtyard. There was an errand boy with a large basket strolling along, whistling and clearly knowing what he was about. This boy led him for some way before disappearing into a basement entry. The fugitive blundered ahead, not sure what he sought, wanting only to get away from his tormentors. His head rang with their unfeeling advice as if he could still hear their voices and this made his head hum with a cloudy, spinning sensation. He supposed vaguely that he meant to go out to Hietzing in which case a taxi was a reasonable objective; but if what that scoundrel Kerenyi had said was correct and from some store of memory Tenius drew the impression that Kerenyi would be likely to know what he was talking about, he would do well to think the matter over before risking a cabman's scrutiny. If only he could think, his head buzzing and congested as it was, in the heat. In the last day or so he had eaten a good deal for the first time for years, and the food now seemed to be stuffed into his chest, all of its bulk. He was in a tiny, cobbled lane, tall and dark buildings on either hand, almost literally on either hand for they leaned so oppressively over Tenius that he felt he could touch their walls both at once. An invisible machine in a workshop clattered deafeningly as he passed its open door, turning to seek some indication of his whereabouts so that he presented his good ear. A girl swung a delivery bicycle across his path, the wheels silent but the big square container in front bouncing and bumping on the ancient stones, on which his own feet were slipping as if they moved under him.

With appalling suddenness a great clangour of bells rocked wildly through his head from so far above him that the brazen-tongued booming seemed to be falling upon him, and at once a diffused rattling of wings and a swift rising rush enveloped him as every pigeon, starling and sparrow in the city, from the sound, took to the air. A memory from boyhood communicated the neighbourhood of a great Church but he could see neither the squat dome of the Minster of his home, nor any other Church towers, nor any cloud of birds. The recorded sensation was of anger, hostility and a bewilderment no longer connected to the time of the twenties when, a gangling youngster, fatherless from the War, he left school to lounge on street corners with no prospect of work or training, with no money either, for the worthless dirty paper must be counted in millions to buy anything. Even bread, which was all he ate except when he stole, or except when he wangled something out of one of the political groups that indiscriminately offered an activity for which there was payment in a meal. He found some safety then, from the black magic of money and the infuriating contrast of utter pointlessness of what was said in the Church where his mother still tried to induce him to attend the canting services; a group that needed him. They lived a long way from his home, and both the Church and his hostility were forgotten in training and being a member of a secret organisation of which they enjoyed the secrecy, never claiming membership in the real, the admired, the disgracefully misused Army. But from this companionship too he was separated. The group was disbanded and he drifted back to the empty factory gates, the long streets of meagre hunger and threadbare old clothes that no longer fitted his fast-growing limbs.

That was before his liberation, before explanations that fitted into his experience were offered him and won his unconditional loyalty by giving him not only a coherent answer to bewilderment, but a job, a uniform and an attachment. The sound of the huge bronze bells was the sound of existence that first turned into living at the stroke of a pen giving him a numbered membership in the movement that was going to change all that.

The Fuehrer himself suffered in this place, where one could not even call a cab without wondering where the driver came from and from what sort of a foreign mixture he might be formed. The Fuehrer overcame its sentence of rejection, and he too would yet overcome. But just as Tenius felt this return of purpose, a group of people emerged from a dark doorway and jostled around him talking in incomprehensible dialect so that for a moment he was back in a nearer past where only the unknown tongue of Russian was heard; he felt a dreadful sensation that made his heart give a lurching bound of terror. It weakened him, making his limbs shake as if out of his control. His knees would buckle under him if he didn't get some air, it was impossible to breathe in this tunnel-like alley. He stumbled and the forward movement pulled him to an unsteady run into a deep gateway through which he could at last see sunlight. The effort of a few more steps and with a burst of relief he was out in the open space of a large square where a massive bulk of darkness threw a deep shade that made the light where he stood brighter, hotter. Too bright, it dazed him. He lumbered into the roadway, towards the inviting cool of the purple shadow where great towers loomed over him, from which the bells still hummed a trembling long note into quiet. A motor screeched, but he reached the shade of the Cathedral and leaned gratefully against aged stone, a bronze rail and a small jar of faded flowers which he did not connect with the sculpture protected by the railing. He could catch a deep breath and the restriction in his chest would relax. No sooner did he lean his head downwards, close his eyes and haul air into unwilling lungs, than he was surrounded by a crowd of chattering females in fantastically coloured hats that flickered around the level of his half-opened eyes unrelated to anything he could attach them to. He could hear an intoning voice but did not understand the foreign words; the women's voices jabbered and cackled, they waved their arms, pointing out something upwards that he could not see. The noises rushed over him in a torrent, unintelligible, and without meaning to he fled again. At the moment Tenius shambled into the street the traffic was released and a crescendo of shrieks behind him only drove him faster instead of warning him in the meaningless language. Engines roared like a tank squadron, the thick air split into a million splinters of light and sound, baffling noises and the stink of petrol fumes crowded him, he must tear open his chest to get air. A black, dully shining surface leaned up towards him, as he reeled, groaning for breath and a shrill whistle pierced his deaf ear like a physical blow. A hot dark rushed into his head and chest, a pounding thrum filled him from the inside, he would die if he could not get his breath. He was dying. The black enveloped him.

Returned prisoners were a familiar enough sight in the towns of Europe for there to be no doubt in anybody's mind as to what had happened. The police reported on Tenius even before his papers were officially checked, and the doctors who examined his human wreckage scarcely needed to diagnose his ills for there was little in the scale of diseases of strain and privation not present in his ruined constitution. It was, they said, a most extraordinary thing that Tenius should have survived so long and a prognosis was hardly worth attempting. A man who took care of himself might recover from years of Siberia, but Tenius was overtaxing a large frame and greedy appetites for years before the War started, and his physical strength was not founded in a healthy and well-fed childhood.

He shot into an exuberant and forceful manhood from the hungry years of Weimar working-class life only when the Party began to feed and exercise his frame.

The verdict of the hospital authorities, like that of the police when his identity was established, could be summarised in a shrug. But this notional shrug was not reflected in any report and was, naturally, not known to any of the people affected by the return of Tenius to the land of the living. As far as his acquaintances were concerned, Tenius remained an object of fear or hatred as if he could still affect their lives, or in the case of his former comrades the object of sympathy and loyalty which they were well able to translate into action.

During this time Kerenyi and Berthold Luders sat in the small and crowded editorial offices of Kerenyi's monthly review, conducting a mutually satisfactory but mutually misunderstood discussion. Luders began by addressing a few brusque questions to a crony of his in the newspaper world of Hamburg. He was twice cut off in the middle of this enquiry but refrained from complaining to his new colleague—he was quite decided on that point from the start—about the dreadful telephone system in Vienna. Luders then talked about management contracts and the need to increase circulation to an economic level in order to attract quality advertising, and the like. It would have bored Kerenyi had he listened but he did not listen, and spent the time planning the series of analytical articles forming in his mind from the inspired flight of fancy of his friend.

He kept repeating phrases, such as 'Oh yes,' and, 'Sure, my dear fellow,' and, 'Just a moment while I make a note,' while Luders scribbled figures, groaned over the accounts books and bank statements, and made incredibly rapid calculations in dollars which he said, to Kerenyi's disbelief, was easier than transferring marks into schillings. He was quite aware that Georg was not attending to him and when he really needed to know something he asked the typist who knew much more about the monthly review than its editor and was, to Luders' mind, more sensible.

'It's a marvel to me that you didn't go bankrupt at least a year ago,' he said at one point.

'I thought we were,' replied Georg absently and could not understand why this made Luders laugh.

Presently Luders began, with the help of the typist who stayed late out of curiosity, to put together various papers, contracts, the lease of the office and a number of back editions of the review.

The girl made a parcel of them and was instructed to get them sent over to the hotel without being told which hotel. The request was made with such an air of its being obvious what was meant that the girl hardly dared ask for the name but went into the only other room of the office and closed the door to telephone the biggest hotels to find out.

'That's how staff get trained,' said Berthold, hearing her voice through the door. 'Now, tomorrow we'll see your lawyers and the accountants and you can give me powers. I must get back tomorrow so we'd better start early. The 'plane goes just after two o'clock. It will take a week or so, because I have a number of other irons in the fire at the moment. But don't worry, my poor old mutton-head, we'll have you on your feet in no time.' He spoke as if Georgy suffered from some comical ailment such as lumbago, and his eyes strayed with affectionate derision over the jumble of papers and books heaped on desks, chairs and the floor. 'I'm going to have a lot of fun with this,' he said. 'I shall be able to swank about my intellectual interests in the service of democracy to all sorts of old buffers who still think me a spiv.'

'Isn't it the wrong country's democracy, for that purpose?' asked Georg mildly.

'Well, same language, that's enough for the moment,' Berthold disclaimed with his cheerful confidence in the feasibility of all his undertakings. But Kerenyi's stupidity stopped, with great definiteness, at the border of any subject he did not want to understand, such as finance.

'Berthold,' he said, 'if you have any notion of allying my paper to a German group or anything of that nature, you can forget it and we'll drop the whole thing.'

'Not for a moment,' Berthold assured him, 'quite the contrary. I'm going to expand you, first into Switzerland and then into the Federal Republic.' He said the name of the West German state with a double irony; of something new, untried and possibly transitory and of political arrangements in general which he thought of as being for his use rather than as using him. 'Don't worry. You won't be interfered with. You will gradually write for a larger public, but what you write remains your business. Of course, you'll want to expand your international eye, as it were, but you must want to do that in any case, don't you?'

'You're a shrewd devil,' said Kerenyi and laughed with appreciation.

'I suppose you won't credit it, but I believe in freedom. I do, really. It's the only way to get things done.'

'You know,' said his friend thoughtfully, looking at Luders with a speculative frown, 'when Julie gets used to you, I rather think you two will get on like a house afire. Which reminds me. We've forgotten Tenius.'

Kerenyi turned to his telephone and as if the movement were a signal, it buzzed. Hella Schneider wanted, with asperity, to know what had become of her expected visitor: the lawyer's clerk was sitting waiting.

'I don't know,' answered Georg. 'Perhaps he's walking over to Hietzing?'

'I bet he's lost himself,' said Luders behind him.

'It's quite simple,' Georg interrupted Hella's reproach. 'The clerk can go to where Tenius is staying.' And he gave her the address of the small hotel over the Danube canal where Tenius could be found.

'It will have to be put off until tomorrow, now,' she objected to this and was not pacified until Kerenyi suggested that the early morning was the most certain time to find someone in his hotel, in any case. As he put back the receiver, Kerenyi swung his chair round to Luders again and asked the question that was really occupying his mind.

'But how d'you know that the review is any good? How d'you know you will want to invest in it? You may think it damned bad or too highbrow.'

'I read it sometimes. Don't you know I'm on your subscription list? God, your business methods are absolutely non-existent.'

'Tell me, Berthold—do you keep in touch with all your old contacts?' Georg asked him thoughtfully.

'Of course. Those that are of any interest.' Luders shot his cuff again and glanced at the time. 'I must go.'

IX

Julia looked up from her history books as Georgy came in. She was sitting by the window near the wall of books so that she saw clearly into his face and its look of puzzlement, irresolution, gave her a swift impression that something unsatisfactory about his purpose in following Luders and Tenius early in the afternoon must have occurred. In reality, just as up to that moment, she was completely absorbed in her work so was Kerenyi so much preoccupied with the odd turn Luders had introduced into his professional affairs, that he had almost forgotten his original intention in following his friend. Julia did not want to think about Tenius again, indeed she wanted quite strongly to pretend that he formed no personal connection with herself and was only a peripheral concern by reason of his claims on Kerenyi. And although her perception at that moment was mistaken, her attitude was logical and sound and in maintaining this posture, as far as she was able, she would in the end force Tenius out of her life again.

'This historical background is frightfully interesting, Georgy,' she said without further ado, as he came up to her. 'It seems to have been a bit like our times. Realms and dynasties falling to pieces, confusion and change everywhere. Wars and treachery, alliances changing. I had no idea. . . .'

Kerenyi picked up the book she laid aside.

'A long time since I read Plutarch,' he said. 'But it was the time of the rise of Rome. The dynasties, the changes, almost all fell into the power of Rome.'

She considered this thought. Then she said, frowning, 'But the Roman Empire was a step forward in civilisation . . .?'

'Probably. But how do we know what the alternatives might have produced? Certainly not Greece, then and now the Greeks lack the capacity to hold together in trouble—the first necessity of any State aspiring to greatness. And if the new domination of Europe succeeds, history will be written by the victors again, so nobody will consider in the year 2000 whether Europe might have been better off in other circumstances.'

'You don't believe that yourself, Georgy. The Third Rome—oh, I see your logic—but they or their rulers can only export their own misery. They have nothing else to offer. However firm their hold may seem now, it can't last. No doubt the Romans weren't what their historians have made them seem; but they founded their colonies on order, law, the idea of service to the State, personal honour.'

'So do the Soviets—except the last.'

'No. Order, certainly. But law is chancy, different for different people. How do you say it?'

'Arbitrary,' he supplied.

She hesitated, but he did not help her, so she went on. 'And the narrowness of their order must inhibit all the thousands of ideas and changes and adaptations that make up the complexity of life.'

'And what about—let's see—the Turkish Empire? That lasted for centuries without the least concern for anything but the personal power of the rulers?'

'You shouldn't have chosen that example,' she countered, laughing now. 'That I know about from *Thoughts on the Control of Power*. As soon as Turkey was exposed, however slightly, to the need to maintain its power by modern forms of organisation and communication, the Ottoman Empire began to collapse from inside.'

'Almost a direct quote. I'm very much flattered. Tell me, when did you begin to think in this frighteningly theoretical fashion? You've always been so scornful of political thinking.'

'Yes, and what's more, your point about the Greeks and their failure of solidarity. The Soviet State can't support itself on any real loyalty of citizens to each other or to itself. Everybody distrusts everybody, the idea of a *personal* loyalty is high treason. Fragmentation, you used to call it. . . .'

'Well, well. I shall have to look to my laurels.'

'You will,' she agreed, enjoying herself. 'I've only just started. For years now I've been thinking about the things that happened to us all. Now there's somebody for me to talk to, I shall become as theoretical as you are—you'll see!'

'For Heaven's sake,' he cried in mock alarm. 'Don't do that. And, to distract you, I want to talk about something practical. Luders wants to invest money in the review. What d'you think of that?'

She stared in astonishment at so outlandish an idea.

'I think it's suspicious,' she said at last with disfavour. 'If he's serious, he'll try to interfere.'

'Well, I dare say he will. But if we draw up what Berthold calls a management contract, and draw it up carefully, I don't see how he can. You shall study the contract yourself and change it if you're not satisfied. But if it works out, it might prove the answer to my financial troubles.'

'But why should he think it a good investment—it certainly is not?'

'He says the circulation can be greatly expanded if he spends some money on it. The whole German-language area—you see?'

'But it would cease to be Austrian.'

'It would cease to be parochial. But the only valid concept of Austria was non-national, or multinational. So why not?'

'I'm not sure. It's so sudden. You were always against nationalism, I know, but I'm a nationalist, I think.'

'A patriot. To be a nationalist you'd have to change your nature. Not to mention your ancestry. Your maternal grandfather was Rumanian, his wife a German in Transylvania. On your father's side, his mother was born in Slovenia and the Lord only knows what *her* family did before they got their title. Didn't they come from Serbia, originally?'

'Well, Bosnia.'

'And your first husband was a Jew whose grandfather came to Vienna from Lemberg—illicitly. I remember Franz telling me that the old man had endless difficulty getting his papers in order before he could build this property we're sitting in now. And *his* father was a refugee from inside the Russian Pale. Your second husband is half German and half Magyar. My father's mother came from Slovakia and I rather fancy, had some Jewish blood.'

'I've always thought my mother had, too. Certainly, she could have been partly gypsy. She had those brilliant, quick black eyes and ivory skin, absolutely what one thinks of as a gypsy type. Dark, small, quick, finedrawn. And tough as a horse. For a couple of years she practically ran the farm and land in Styria, after she married again. My stepfather had to have several operations before his wounds finally cleared up and I remember there was very little help about when I first used to go to Steffelsgut as a child, from the Convent.'

'What was her mother-tongue?'

'She was bilingual. German-Hungarian.'

'Like me, then.'

'But she had a slight accent in German. Not quite an accent, a kind of intonation. You know that clipped fashion of speaking that Hungarians have—you have it a little.'

'Was she beautiful? A thousand pities all the photographs disappeared. I should love to know how she looked.'

'I think she may have been what we'd call sexy nowadays. Something bird-like about her . . . a quick, small, pretty way of moving, and her head always tilted upwards. I suppose that was because she had to look up to almost everyone she spoke to. I was bigger and taller than she was long before I stopped growing. Her bones were tiny, so that her hands were narrow and thin—like a bird, again. And a waist like this.' With an encircling gesture of her two hands. 'I remember when I noticed how small she was and how much I was growing. I was back from the Convent. Let me see—it must have been while the Convent was closed just after the War ended. Yes, it was certainly not an ordinary holiday. That would be in January, 1919, wouldn't it? There was the Abdication and the nuns talked about a revolution like the one in Russia, but they were talking like that for ages. When we were all sent home, that was the revolution. It was terribly cold at home, and dark, with the shutters mostly closed to keep the cold out. Only one room was heated, and the small dining table, the round one, was pushed into what used to be the little drawing room. My bedroom was arctic and the big salon hadn't been used for a couple of years, I think, at least. It was all locked up and shadowy, the chandeliers bundled up in ghostly sheets and when I heard shots I ran in there and pushed open the shutters and windows to see—you could see best into the street from there. Our footsteps echoed because the furniture was all heaped together to be covered and the place sounded empty. My father followed me in to see the revolution. I was sure it was that. We'd never had riots in our district before so it must be. There were soldiers on horseback down in the street, firing on the crowd. I suppose, really, it was a food riot. We jumped back from the window at the shots and his face looked strange, blank, stunned. As if he wasn't there any more. I ran.

'I suppose he went back to bed; he was in bed most of the time and he wept a lot. He died soon after; a broken heart though it was called influenza. At any rate, he didn't follow me into the room where the stove burned. Mother was in there, though, sitting by the round table with dishes still on it. The cook went out into the street to see the riot and we didn't know it but she was shot, we didn't know until the police came. But there was nobody left to do anything, and Mother asked me to get a tray for the dishes. When I came back upstairs, my father's friend, the wounded Colonel who came to see Mother, was there. I hesitated—you know how it is, I wasn't sure whether I should go in or not which proves that I knew there was something going on.

'Mother was saying something about Florian—that was my father. And when he answered her, he used the intimate form calling her *"du"*. I hadn't heard that before. He said Father was always hopelessly neurotic and I hadn't heard that before, either. Mother answered, and called him "Toni"—that was new to me, too. Her voice was quite different speaking to him when they were alone. I noticed that, but that wasn't new, I knew that already. I just remember it on that day because the whole feeling in the room and between them was much more definite. Much stronger, as if they'd come out in the open about something.

'He said then, "It's called neurasthenia." I looked up both words in the dictionary. I had to go into my father's study to get it and I didn't like that. I wasn't really allowed to go in there. But of course, I must have realised that everything was changed by then.'

'That was the time when all the rules fell to bits.'

'Then my mother saw me in the door and said in an affected, laughing voice something about her big girl being a help to her and I came in with the tray and they said *"Sie"* to each other again. As I stood by the table I watched my mother's face. It was then I noticed, really, how tiny she was. I remember saying something about why didn't we cook the little we did have to eat on the fire in the serving room on that floor; there was no need to use the kitchen for our scraps, it only made more work.

' "What a practical child she is," said the Colonel. He sounded nervous and false and of course, I couldn't explain that they didn't have to hide anything from me—I was relieved and comforted at the sensation of some genuine emotion in all this strangeness and coldness. And perhaps they understood that because it seems to me that we all said *"du"* to each other after that.'

'Did you go to the funeral? When your father died?'

'No, I was back at the Convent by then. My mother didn't write to the Mother Superior to tell her—or me—that she was married again. That was frightfully shocking, only a week or so after Father was buried. I began to get food parcels and they read me a letter that I was to be sent to the house in the country at the end of term. I never saw the old apartment again. You know—I don't even know its exact address?'

'I suppose you wouldn't,' he said thoughtfully.

'I remember it with perfect clarity, but it disappeared. Everything that I knew before was broken off with a clean break without my even knowing of it.'

'Then there was the Convent and the house in Styria, Steffelsgut?'

'Gut Schwering, it was then. His name was von Schwering—Toni's.'

'Very German, that name.'

'He was German. His family came from Saxony in Napoleon's time as Imperial Army officers and bought the property.'

'Imperial? You mean Habsburg, of course?'

'Well, of course,' said Julia, surprised. 'What else?'

They contemplated for a little while the implications of this remark and then Julia laughed.

'You see, I am a nationalist, after all.'

'Yes,' he said. 'A European nationalist, no less.'

'Cleopatra seems to have been mixed in her ancestry, too. Did you know she was really a Macedonian—or rather, her family came from there?'

'I've always had a theory that she was what would now be called a gypsy. And not from Shakespeare's comment, either. She must have been a woman of such extraordinary strength and intelligence that I can't believe she came from the inbred dynasty that was her official parentage. It's easy to imagine that her mother used some musician-slave during a great orgy, for her pleasure, and got a child by him.'

'What a splendid thought! She really must have been unique. D'you suppose she was beautiful? Women of great character are often magnetic to men in spite of their physical appearance rather than because of it—I've noticed that.'

'Difficult to say, because women who become legendary affect ideas of what feminine beauty is. So that people equate their famed faces with an ideal beauty. A flat, gawky lamp post of a woman like Garbo forms a whole generation of clothes and manners not really through classic features or charms at all, but by expressing something archetypal of which both she and her admirers may be quite unconscious. But the type then becomes beauty through her fame.'

'What is not yet clear to me is whether she was sensual to look at, or in her manner and movement? I rather think, not. She begins to form an effect of quick-wittedness, ambition, consciousness of power, a refusal to be relegated to femaleness. Domineering, perhaps, and cunning. She would use her feminine lures as weapons when she needed to but not be herself the captive of her own lusts. And then use them aggressively, openly, a female rapist dealing with male flesh as men usually expect to deal with female flesh.'

'You don't feel that she met her match in Antony?'

'Possibly. Probably, yes. But he was the tool of her imperial ambition, too—don't you think? That would explain why she insisted on being present at the sea-battle of Actium. She was keeping an eye on her general, and meaning to claim a personal victory for herself as Egypt. That would explain her insistence on fighting a naval battle—on land Antony would be paramount and no fame of victory could be attributed to Cleopatra. So when the battle turned against them, she fled to save her own fleet for another day. Don't you think that only when he threw away his male honour by following her and abandoning his comrades to their fate, only then did he become a human being to her?'

'Shakespeare's onlookers, if I remember aright, characterise her as lustful, though. Physically as much dependant on Antony's body as he on hers. I've always interpreted the guile she displayed in holding his love as coming out of real jealousy and need. Where is it? "See where he is . . ." something . . . "I did not send you: if you find him sad, say I am dancing; if in mirth, report that I am sudden sick. . . ." '

'Well, if you read it in a different tone, it looks simply like cunning. She is sometimes scornful of him. "A Roman thought has struck him" sounds almost like contempt.'

Julia considered Kerenyi's view, more conventional than her own and then with a shake of her head, rejected it.

'No, only towards the inevitable end did Cleopatra understand that she couldn't live without him. Then it must have occurred to her that she could use her knowledge of poisons and make good the threats of suicide she used formerly as blackmail on Antony. The notion that Cleopatra learned about poisons because she had suicidal tendencies is awfully strained. Like all rulers, she needed to get rid of enemies sometimes and being a woman, couldn't use a sword.'

'A good deal depends on the Antony you get. Do you know yet who is to play him?'

'Of course Hansi proposed Wally Harich but I don't like that. He's too much identified with the sentimental 19th-century attitude to Shakespeare. He'll play the heroic, romantic tone indistinguishable from his famous Egmont. As a matter of fact, Wally has altogether got stuck in one attitude. I'm for Thorn, or a complete stranger. . . . Look, Antony must have been more like an American General of the last War than a mooning lady's man. Or one of those splendid French soldiers with lots of dash and covered in scars, fighting their own government and the Nazis, intriguing with everybody and quarrelling with them at the same time. He must have been bewildered by Cleo's hold over him: there were a lot of women in his life before her, and none dominated him until he met her.'

Kerenyi leafed through a few pages of the script, thoughtfully.

'I've always found it one of the greatest of the plays. Much finer than *Romeo*. Stupid hypocrisy of our moralities that the very reality of their love—its illicitness and impropriety—has always made it a bit hot to handle. . . .'

'There you are,' she cried triumphantly, 'you agree with me!'

'It's terrifically erotic. Scares people, I guess.'

'Even Hansi is a bit scared of it. He's startled at his own courage, and rather wants to play it down now, I suspect.'

'Probably doesn't understand it. He's stayed a boy in some ways, a philandering boy who never married. Tell me something—there were stories at one time. Did you ever go to bed with Hansi?'

'Your memory!' she protested. 'That was a lifetime ago. Yes, I did, a few times.'

'And it came to nothing? Was it no good?'

'It wasn't real, just proximity and curiosity I expect. But it stopped, really. . . .'

'Well?'

'You introduced me to Franz.'

X

The silence which came both before Julia answered and which followed her reply had a quality both of shock and of weariness about it. To have stumbled once again upon this central fact of the past without being aware of even approaching it, showed a lack of foresight, of forgetfulness on Kerenyi's part and this in turn evidenced his lack of control over the situation. A situation he himself had insisted on bringing into being by regularising their relationship. They were able, before the intractable and mysterious fact of marriage took place, to ignore the former marriage to a large extent. But just as being married and no longer lovers gave outsiders a means of intervention, if only as comment, in their private lives, so it introduced a fresh factor into their own consciousness of themselves. It added a stake in the success of their venture as having publicly registered a confidence in their ability to carry off their victory over the past to those emotional and sensual stakes that could have been kept private but for this publishing of their victory long before it actually existed.

The fact of marrying not only brought to light the still unachieved nature of the victory over the past; it made its achievement a necessity for their outer as well as their inner world. They must not only succeed, but be seen to succeed. And the very passion on both sides which made a formal union seem inevitable was what interfered with their behaving rationally now that the union existed. Since neither of them could attach physical love to such chance objects as happened to come in their way, they had piled up a store of such explosive emotion and physical longing in the years just passed that the violence of their relation to each other could better have been resolved on a deserted island in the Greek archipelago —where it had seemed perfectly possible—than before a large and curious audience for which they were objects of envy and even dislike, as well as admiration.

The public aspect of their private concern with each other was underlined by an appointment for that evening at which they were now almost due and which was an invitation from the very person who was the cause of their long, charged silence. They remembered in the same instant and looked at their wrist-watches together, that they were to dine with Hans-Joachim Ostrovsky and that if Julia was going to change her dress she must do so at once.

And as if to make an explicit point of the stranded connections between the past and the present, they found on arriving at Ostrovsky's small bachelor flat that he was in the act of ordering a table for them at the very restaurant where he often took Julia to dinner during the years of her spurious solitude.

'They've rebuilt and just reopened,' he explained as he put down the telephone. 'I thought it would be entertaining to see how they've done the place up.'

He added as an afterthought, 'Kiki's never seen it.' Kiki was Monika, and the young girl, the only one of the quartet who might be expected not to know of any connection the ruined and rebuilt restaurant could have for her companions, was the only one who showed a slight impatience at the choice. She would have preferred to go to a fashionable place which she could use in the rivalries of her fellow students for the small prestiges so important to the young in normal times when they do not need to concern themselves with issues of life and death. And, with a good fortune they usually resent, times when the young do not even know that such issues can exist as matters of instant and constant personal decision; for normality reigned again on the surface of Monika's world so that she was unable to apprehend the unspoken but immanent anxieties of the people she met through her otherwise almost infinitely valuable adorer. Kiki's charm for Ostrovsky was precisely that she knew nothing of reality, that her mental and psychic landscape was as deliciously empty and innocent as her body was candidly fresh and smooth. The blank space in her upbringing which was all that the War represented in her being, the deprivation of religious and social training, was much more positively present than exposure to 'bad' influences could have been. If she were only a few years older Monika would have been affected by the presence in her provincial home of foreign and native young men already touched by war, famine and nihilism and would have learned inhibition by immediate experience. She missed that experience and through her father's absence and her mother's preoccupation with enforced work during her schooldays, she missed as well the oblique training of warning, exhortation and example in artificial inhibition. She was thus of an extreme innocence and reacted without calculation to the influence and glamour of her much older lover—without knowing that this was his attraction for her—as she did not do to the boys of her own age she met as a student. Monika's sexuality was genuinely stimulated by the fame of the people Hansi Ostrovsky was able to introduce her to, and would have felt an equal concupiscence for Kerenyi if he had wished her to, or a lesbian attachment to Julia. She was in love with fame, the theatre and the ease of what she was still unaware was money.

She felt, certainly, that such people should go, and should take her with them, to public places on a level with their prestige and could not understand Ostrovsky's preference for a restaurant in a back street she had never heard of. She was not even aware by an inherited perception that this preference came from a long tradition that to be ostentatious was anything but a sign of prestige and was left to those who were not instantly recognisable as superior. For Monika's inherited perceptions were interrupted, and this interruption was the only harm the war had done her.

The evening was intended as an opportunity to discuss the production of *Antony and Cleopatra*, a laying of foundations for an undertaking as subtly complex as the lacquered Chinese cabinet in Julia's living room. Hansi Ostrovsky must first acquaint himself with all the considerations and intuitions present in the mind of the central figure of this project before he could even embark upon the interleaving, interconnecting construction. He must know, not only Julia's concept of the play and her part in it, but what relationships she conceived of between the other figures of the play and the real-life persons who should represent them; not only all the balances of personality contained in the play, but of the actors as well, the designers, the as yet unknown composer who was to invent music to match them all. And above all, he must discover how far Julia herself intended to impose her own conception on his and the others' activity.

He could not achieve this end by direct questions for he knew Julia would at once protect her own perceptions by retreating into generalities if he did so. All the opaqueness of Ostrovsky's outward personality which was notorious and which, among a thousand other things, led him to choose a place for this reconnoitre unwelcome to two of the persons present, was in fact the protective cover for preoccupations and understandings of the only reality in his life. What often seemed stupidity or tactlessness was his genius which ignored everything not concerned with the theatre. He demonstrated this by speaking hardly a word to Kerenyi or Monika and concentrating all his formidable will and mind upon the person through whom his obsession was at that time operating.

Monika would have been very ready to interrupt and draw some of Hansi's concentration to herself, but was deflected from this impulse by Kerenyi who addressed himself with such attention to her small but self-confident store of opinion that she felt herself much flattered by his interest and confirmed in her notion of her own intelligence. Of Julia she remained slightly afraid and found herself, by the time sweetmeats of luscious delicacy were offered to them, wondering how this fascinating ugly man could waste himself on an almost tough professional with so little time to spare for him. Kerenyi seemed to Monika old but this only increased the powerful and vigorous charm that emanated from him. It had worked with many women before her and induced an almost palpable sensation of his masculinity; a sensation so strong that it took on a soft, delicious excitement and she could picture erotic encounters vividly to herself in which the partner of Kerenyi's own erotic imagination was eliminated triumphantly.

So in spite of its unpropitious beginning, the evening was a great success for all four people present. This lasted until the four of them removed to the redesigned apartment in the Schellinggasse which neither Ostrovsky nor Monika had yet seen.

'But it's marvellous!' Hansi was enthusiastic. 'That designer's a genius! He's used the space for the first time as it should be used. And, my dear, the carpets! They must have cost a fortune. He's kept all the best pieces, I see. Just got rid of the ugly things. And no overhead lights—it's perfectly splendid. The blending of modern and antique. . . . I say, Julie, I've never seen that cabinet before. The Chinese one? Did he find it for you?' And Hansi went over to examine the elaborately decorated lacquer, passing his fingers gently over the surface without looking, to feel the quality of the work. 'Genuine. There's no over-painting. It's the original lacquer, isn't it?'

Fascinated to the exclusion of the others, Ostrovsky switched on a floor lamp standing near, the better to examine the intricate interior of the cabinet.

'It was always here,' said Julia, laughing at his excitement. 'In what was the drawing room, but nobody ever noticed it much. The room was too crowded and badly lit. Now that it stands against the plain light wall, you can see it properly for the first time.'

'What a miracle it survived,' he said, almost with awe. 'I'm livid with envy!'

'Even the dear little marble pillars inside are intact,' cried Monika, bending forward, hands on knees, to see into the obscure depth. 'It seems to go on forever. . . .'

'Jade,' Hansi corrected her lovingly in an undertone so that the others should not hear.

'The designer says it's Dresden work,' Julia said, 'one of the early pieces of the Chinese period. He said it's certainly original, made by a Chinese.'

'I thought it was only porcelain designs they did at that time,' hazarded Monika.

'So did I. But apparently there were a few Chinese artists brought over who made these things as well.'

'I wonder what became of them . . . the Chinese, I mean?'

'It must be almost unique,' said Kerenyi, 'how can they tell it wasn't brought from China?'

'Oh, the woods are quite different, and the colours slightly but definitely, too.'

'I can imagine a solemn small Chinese grumbling at the materials he is supposed to work with, saying not like we have at home. . . .'

'And turning up his nose at everything in Europe!'

Laughing, they drifted to chairs, leaving Monika still peeping into the inner depths of the mysterious little reflected ornamentations until she heard them talking again about their boring play and turned, feeling rather slighted and foolish.

'Won't the central heating damage it?' she asked, but Hansi put out a hand to her without interrupting himself, so that she should come and sit next to him.

'Anita will play Charmian,' he was saying, 'but we need a physical contrast both to you and Anita for Iras. I'm not quite sure. . . .'

'Will you let me sit in with the stage designing, Hansi?' asked Kiki. 'I'll learn far more from him than all this art history stuff. It's dry as dust.' She pouted a wheedling mouth at him, pushing out her lower lip which was full and soft.

'Of course, darling,' said Hansi absently, still not looking at her, but putting out a hand to stroke her bare arm. Then he caught up with what she said and remembered that the 'him' was a bold and good-looking boy twenty-five years his junior. 'I'll see if I can arrange it. The Union, you know?'

He misunderstood her interest, but Monika did not recognise that and to her it seemed like a refusal on second thoughts, for her only concern with the young designer was to learn from him and at the same time be able to condescend to him as Hansi Ostrovsky's special girl. Without being aware that she was annoyed, Monika turned towards Julia.

'I can't understand you wanting to play Cleopatra, anyway,' she said innocently. 'Wasn't she quite old?'

This was so out of context with the discussion and so very much in context with Julia's deeper preoccupations, that it achieved the desired effect in a somewhat too noticeable way. Hansi gave a positive start, and Julia looked at Monika, her great eyes rather wide and blank, staring at something in the girl's face that Monika was unaware of betraying. She was not even aware that there was anything she could betray in her face for she was still quite innocent of her own motives.

'Cleopatra was only thirty-nine when she died,' said Kerenyi with his way of seeming to laugh at something, and his vibrating voice pierced into Kiki with a return of the amorous consciousness she felt in the restaurant. She was sure now that he wanted to make love to her and would have been humiliated if she could have known how obvious this thought was to her companions and how little it was present as a possible purpose, in Kerenyi's own mind.

'Of course, that was old in those days,' said Julia thoughtfully, not denying the implication. But the apparent simplicity of her reply, taking the remark about age as a coherent part of their conversation, made its intentional tactlessness clear to Monika in some way she did not comprehend and she felt sharp resentment as if at a rebuke.

The other three dropped their concern with professional matters and began to talk amusingly about theatrical gossip in general, so that Monika, in being amused was treated as a child and was more offended than ever. By addressing comments to her and telling her anecdotes they set up moving fences to her advance into their intimacy by drawing her into it—but as one who could be entertained by matters they had known since childhood and took, among themselves, for granted.

When they separated for the night the two men said precisely the same thing to their companions, Kerenyi to Julia and Hansi to Monika.

'You've made an enemy of her.'

'I think I meant to,' replied Julia, smiling.

'She's a nubile little piece,' Georgy teased her. 'Makes one want to crunch her slender little bones.'

'Except that she's darker, she reminds me of Anita as a girl when she was in love with Hella.'

This oblique remark made him laugh aloud as he asked if she ever had an affair with another woman.

'No, never. As Hella always says of you, I somehow never got around to it.'

'I should think it would be rather delicious.'

'Yes, evidently you do think so.'

'Oh, I meant as another woman,' he disclaimed. 'But would you mind? If I did?'

'Try it,' she offered gently, 'and find out.'

'That would be a frightfully boring waste of time. I only wanted to make you say you'd stab me if I did. If you won't do that, I shall drop the subject.'

'Certainly I shouldn't stab you. I should call you out and we'd have a duel. It would be the first male-female duel—with pistols, I mean—in history.'

'I don't advise that,' he said seriously, shaking his head. 'I've never seen you shoot, but Robert will tell you what a cracking good shot *I* am, if you don't know it.'

'I really can't say I care for your boastful tone. Can't you pretend at least a slight modesty?'

'Unreasonable creature! How can I be modest when the entire world knows I go to bed with you?'

'I remember the time when you were a bit scared of me.'

He stared, startled out of play-acting. 'How the hell did you know that?'

'Guessed.'

'My God, in that case perhaps I ought still to be scared of you?'

'Perhaps you ought. Remember that, if you're ever tempted with Kiki, won't you?'

'It would be almost worth it, just to see you in a temper. You look splendid when you're being savage. Like some great, dark, legendary bird of prey. I thought that this afternoon, when you flew at Tenius, as if you'd shrivel him up in your flaming plumage.'

'I don't think I like that. Like that thing that pecked out somebody's vitals and never stopped.'

'You're getting your legendary birds mixed up. I was speaking of the Phoenix, not some nasty liver-eating crow. . . .'

Later she said, leaning up on one elbow, 'I thought I heard the telephone.'

'I'm wide awake. Are you?'

'Yes. Let's get up and drink the rest of the wine.'

'Don't prowl about like that,' she said, giving him a glass. He stopped his movement to and fro, his hands pushing down the pockets of his dressing gown, and she saw as he pulled out his right hand that it was clenched into a fist.

'Why are you so uneasy?'

He half-smiled at her with his secretive eyes, and took the glass.

'There is something strange in the atmosphere—don't you feel it?'

'It's the heat,' she answered, 'there's going to be a storm.' Then, suddenly, 'It *was* the telephone ringing—before, wasn't it?'

'Probably downstairs, somebody calling the doctor out of bed.'

'Dreadful to be a doctor,' she said absently, and drank while he leaned over the table and picked up one of his thin cigars. As he shook out the match, the telephone began again to ring. 'Horrible invention,' he muttered.

'Georgy,' she said. 'Don't answer it.'

He looked at his wrist, but his watch lay on the bed-table. As he reached the door, he turned and saw her eyes on him, wide and deep.

'At least it's not the midnight ring at the door.'

Julia shuddered and turned away.

'Well?' she asked, when he returned.

'Luders. Sorry to disturb us at this uncivilised hour. He thought he'd better let us know that Tenius was picked up by the ambulance service a couple of hours ago, after having what seems to have been a heart attack in the street. Anyway, he collapsed and has been taken to the General Hospital.'

'That means a police report.'

'Of course.'

'And to cover themselves with the Allies, as soon as they've identified Tenius, the police will make a Press release?'

'I suppose so. They usually do.'

'Malczewska. Just what we feared. If she doesn't see it herself, somebody will tell her.'

'I wish' he said tautly, 'you would pronounce it properly. It's Malchevska, not Maltsevska.'

'Well, how could I know with that spelling! I get so mixed up.'

'It's not the spelling. You've never seen her name spelled out. You just want to reject her. You don't want to admit she exists as a human being, so you mispronounce her name. . . .'

They stood, staring into each other's eyes for what seemed a long time; it was Julia who gave way and they both took silent note of that.

'You're quite right,' Julia admitted at last. 'I've never forgotten the things she said to me after the great air-raid in 1945.'

'I can understand that. Yet Malczewska has suffered at least as much as either of us. But where we have recovered at least our external position, she remains a penniless refugee doing menial work instead of what she is trained for and capable of. She's lost her son, her home, her language and her profession. And God knows what besides.'

Julia thought about this while she sat down by a table on which she could set her wine glass. The familiar frown of concentration appeared between her brows.

'It's the meanest reason for rejecting somebody, that she is poor and shabby. But I'm not quite as poor-spirited as that. The prejudice really does come from that moment, when we could both have used some kindness. . . .'

'You must lose the illusion that suffering ennobles human beings. I'm not being cynical, you know, it's just true. Suffering can only ennoble those who have nobility in them. Or who have the character to force themselves to live up to their own high idea of themselves.'

'Ah, I catch your drift,' she said, slowly working it out. 'I am in the second category? Just as Franz and Lali, for instance, belong to the first with no streak of meanness or guile in them. We are very lucky, I suppose, to have known two people in our lives of whom one can say that. . . .'

'While, on the other hand,' he put in shrewdly, 'both of them need the hardness and guile of people like us to help them in a crisis. . . .'

'Perhaps. It's a comforting thought. But to return to Mal-czewska. I begin to see what you really mean. There cannot be any question of choice between her and Tenius? We can't for our own convenience take the part of what Tenius represents against what —however distantly and, to me, personally unpleasing—Malczew-ska represents?'

He sat down on the chair opposite hers.

'I knew you'd come through with the right answer, once it was clear to you.'

She smiled at his didactic tone. 'I dare say I would have come through with it, as you put it, before if I had not been thinking of something else all evening. . . .'

'The play?'

'Not quite. Not quite the play. Something in Hansi's manner. . . . No, not anything to do with his being in love.' She shook her head. 'No, either Hansi really has reservations about *A. and C.* or else there is some intrigue going on, something he has half-forgotten, just remembered.'

'But you discussed nothing else all through dinner. He seemed immersed in the whole project. And surely, much of the planning is already put in hand? That means a lot of money has already been —potentially—spent. Contracts signed—the designers, for instance. They evidently are budgeted for, otherwise Monika wouldn't be pressing yet to be allowed to look on?'

'Oh yes. Last week, and the starting conference of the designer, the composer, the costume people—all that, you know—is set for Wednesday. Still, there is something holding Hansi back. He hasn't got his heart in it.'

'I wish now I'd listened more at dinner,' Georgy frowned at Julia.

'Perhaps I'm being fanciful,' she said slowly but shook her head, half-denying what she suggested and half puzzled at the slightness of her own suspicions.

'I doubt that, but perhaps it is just the last trace in Hansi of the old moralistic attitude to the play? Nearly all the commentaries you've been studying are about seventy years old, after all, and based on much older things. . . .'

'It may be,' Julia wagged her head from side to side with a slight comical grimace. 'Erotic and illicit love. He'd rather do *Romeo*, I've no doubt. That will be the next thing and I shall play Nurse for the first time. . . .'

'Ah, that's who you were impersonating just now?' Kerenyi wagged his head in imitation, making a lascivious, familiar-servile grin. 'I don't quite see how your thoughts jumped to *Romeo*—nobody mentioned it, did they, this evening?'

'No. It's just that *they* were married, you see. Ridiculous, but these conventions go very deep, and unconventional people are unaware of them in themselves since they are convinced of their own unconventionality. Like Hansi. . . .'

Georgy laughed aloud, pleased with this notion of Hansi. As Julia picked up her glass to drink the wine, with the implied air of now it was time to get some sleep, she glanced up at her husband.

'We mustn't worry too much about Tenius. It's all not really very important.'

'Compared with the theater?' he asked slyly. They neither of them mentioned again the remark about playing Juliet's Nurse and perhaps they did not think of it. Or perhaps they silently compacted with each other to face that watershed of the admission of age when it became inevitable, and not before.

XI

'To tell the truth—always unwise, I suppose—I'd forgotten about Tenius since yesterday.'

'Easy enough here,' agreed Luders. 'Vienna and Tenius just don't go together. He's quite the wrong sort of intriguer—fixer—for the atmosphere of this city.'

'Atmosphere?' Julia laughed. 'There's no atmosphere left here. You should have known Vienna years ago. . . .'

'No, no. You can't destroy a thousand years in thirty. This city has its own atmosphere that you could cut with a knife. Anyway, I feel it enough to have made up my mind to leave these people who are coming entirely to you two. I shall follow your lead.'

'But why is the General Director here?' Hella wanted to know quite bluntly, having wasted only a moment on greetings.

'Mr. Luders knew Malczewska in Warsaw during the war and feels an interest in her.' Kerenyi indicated a chair to the actress, but she did not take it, preferring to cross to the open windows and occupy her irritable nervousness by pretending to watch the life going on in the street below.

'I see. That could be a good thing, perhaps. She's being very tiresome. And so are the doctors. They insist that Tenius is not fit to see my lawyers or accept these documents for at least three or four days. If all goes well, as they say.'

Julia glanced at her watch without commenting.

'She's late, too,' Hella Schneider-Tenius said in answer to this gesture and with a positive scowl of generalised anger against the world that refused for once to do as she wished.

'You shouldn't have left her to find her own way on the tram, then,' replied Julia unsympathetically. 'Why didn't you pick her up in your car and bring her with you?'

Hella looked startled at this suggestion. Considering the comfort of her employees, even in her own interests, was not a habit of hers as Julia and Kerenyi perfectly well knew.

'Oh, she was going to this *therapist* or something before she came here,' she complained defensively. 'She insists on going every morning. As if anything could be done about that arm of hers after all this time. There's the bell now. I suppose there's one good thing about the intolerable mess I'm in, and that is I shan't have to see the brute, now he's ill.'

A haggard-faced and very dark woman now entered the room and Kerenyi rose and went to meet her, taking from her her handbag and a bundle of papers in a folder to put them down on a table by the chair to which he led her.

'You look tired,' said Julia, feeling a sympathy never before felt for Malczewska. She nodded at the housekeeper still standing in the open door. 'Yes, coffee please, Frau Lisl.'

'I am tired,' answered Malczewska very quietly, and without the tone of aggressive hostility she normally used to Julia and indeed to almost everyone. 'I've hardly slept for days.'

'But did you know before, then? About Tenius being released?' Hella sounded almost frightened.

'No, I didn't know until yesterday evening when I heard on the news that former SS-General Tenius had been taken to hospital with a heart attack only two days after his release from prison camp.' She turned in her chair to speak to Kerenyi. 'They say police are watching at his bedside for him to regain consciousness. Does that mean he'll be arrested?'

'I think it does, yes.'

'He can only get life in a German Court,' Malczewska said bitterly. 'And if this heart attack is a serious one they may never even try him.'

She lifted her narrow head to strain her chin as if her neck ached; an expression of fateful suffering crossed the sallow, gypsy-like face, heavily lined and leathern and for an instant she closed her black eyes with the yellowed whites of chronic insomnia. There was a power in her of an implacable monomania that was very strongly to be felt at that moment, just because it was overlaid by some other passion.

'But Tenius only makes matters worse. Brings everything back.' She leaned sideways left, to grasp for cigarettes and lighter from her shabby handbag, failed to reach them at the first try and then moved her inert right arm to a better position with the left hand so that she could lean across it more easily.

'I'll move the table,' said Kerenyi in a suppressed tone and moving quickly. But she waved him impatiently away.

129

'It's all right. I can manage. The doctors got the new x-rays last week.' The cigarette was alight by now, and Malczewska held it in her fingers as she picked up the lame arm and let it fall again with a curiously derisive effect of its not belonging to her. 'There's some bone disease. Incurable, they say.'

'It may not be incurable,' said Luders abruptly. 'We'll get another opinion for you.'

She looked up at him and her gaze focussed; she recognised him.

'Luders! I thought you were dead. What are you doing here?'

'Same thing you are. Discussing Tenius.'

'Christ,' she said with an almost masculine, familiar crudeness. 'Fancy you being still around. . . .'

She looked from one to the other of them.

'I suppose you are really here to persuade me to keep quiet about Tenius,' she guessed. 'But since the police are already on to him, it's all rather taken out of your hands, isn't it?'

'Not at all,' Hella intervened brusquely. But whatever her argument was to have been, it remained undeveloped.

'You haven't got my message, Frau Schneider-Tenius. This thing I've got is very bad so they say. Apparently it spreads fast once it's got a hold. Oh yes, I made them tell me the truth though they tried to protect me from myself as I've no doubt they think of it. So I'm not interested in Tenius living as an official invalid for another twenty years in some sanatorium with every comfort, and a dozen doctors to say he's too ill to be tried.'

'That was not at all our idea,' said Luders. 'I wanted to get him away to South America where he'd have to cope with the world on his own.'

'With all the other SS-men to help him, I've no doubt. Don't be a fool, Luders. You never were a fool so don't start now. You know I won't fall for that.'

'He won't live long in any case,' said Kerenyi in a tone of anger with himself at being a part of this immoral and inhuman discussion. 'He's a total wreck.'

'A bit of wreckage, eh? Like me. But he's going to die on a Polish gallows and with the maximum publicity. I'd gladly kill him myself, but I shan't need to.'

'You said yourself the police are already watching him,' Hella tried again. 'That means he'll be extradited to Germany and not given up to the Poles.'

'As to that, we shall see,' Malczewska waved away the cup of coffee that was being offered to her. 'Your Odessa friends aren't the only ones who remove bodies, law or no law.'

'I don't think we should continue to talk about this,' said Julia suddenly. 'And I, for one, don't intend to do so.'

'But Julie! My divorce! And think of the consequences for us all if he's tried. For Georgy too, don't forget that. . . .' Hella was almost wailing with her helpless anger. 'We must persuade her, induce her. . . .'

'This is really monstrous,' Kerenyi limped forward so that he shielded Malczewska from Hella. 'I absolutely refuse to be used as a weapon against a helpless human being. You'll be suggesting having Malczewska arrested next. You really are an abominable woman, Hella. I would never have believed it of you, egotist though you are. . . .'

Hella interrupted him with a cry of genuine outrage for she could see nothing of impropriety in her position.

'There's nothing any of us can do now, anyway,' stated Luders flatly. 'Matters will take their course, one way or the other. It's perfectly obvious that the Polish underground must already know about Tenius being here. Either they'll get him or the police will keep him. And that's that.' He stopped and looked at Malczewska who watched them all with a savage but weary scorn. 'And I'm not sure I don't hope the Poles *will* get him.'

'Better from your point of view if the Poles do get him,' said Malczewska. 'Whatever he said in Court in Warsaw would be automatically disbelieved in the western world.'

'How do you know I'm concerned about what Tenius could say in Court?'

'Why else would you be here?'

The simple answer created a silence until Malczewska went on speaking after a long pause.

'Or you? Or you?' She nodded at Kerenyi and then at Hella. 'Oh, not you!' Julia was brushed aside with a left-handed gesture. 'You've just got yourself stuck with another difficult husband. Seems to be your fate. I think you must be a bad picker of men.'

'You see,' said Malczewska, and she seemed almost to be enjoying her anger. 'You never had a son. I had. One. He was just sixteen when he escaped from the Germans in the Warsaw uprising. He crossed the river to Praga—that's a suburb of Warsaw, in case your knowledge of the city doesn't go that far—and the Russians beat him to death in a cellar there. You don't like the word "cellar", do you? Neither do I. I've hidden in enough of them, God knows. I managed to get away myself—just. It would have been easier to walk into the German guns. But I had a reason for living. I wanted to avenge my boy. I killed a couple of Russians before my ammunition ran out. And now I'm going to kill Tenius and he completes the circle. The Poles are going to hang Tenius like the low criminal he is, and the fact that they'll do it under Russian orders only makes it more satisfactory.'

'The ingratitude of it! When I gave you a job and helped you!'

'You expected gratitude from me?' Malczewska asked softly of Hella. 'Rather typical of you. I suppose you thought just because I always said "Yes, ma'am. No, ma'am" that I was taken in by you? You are quite wrong. Every time I look at your face I think of you rutting in bed with Tenius. Every time you make one of your stagey movements I think of his huge, hairy paws crawling over your body and you shivering with delight. You did shiver with delight, didn't you? Ah yes, you look horrified, I'm being very improper. And doing it inartistically, as well. I'm sure either of you two expert ladies would conduct a scene with infinitely more artistry than I do. The difference is—I happen to mean it.'

'You've done enough stage work to be able to stage it very well, though,' cried Hella with sincere and self-righteous anger. 'I believe you only agreed to come here today to make your precious scene!'

'Of course. Has that only just occurred to you?'

'Well, one thing I can tell you. You'd better start looking for another job.' Hella took her white handbag and made for the door without further ado. Holding its edge, she thought of another shaft. 'And you certainly won't get one from any friend of mine!'

'You won't have any friends in a week from now,' replied Malczewska. 'So you'll find it as hard to get another dramaturgist as I shall to get another patron.'

The flick of a blue linen skirt was the only reply to this as Hella left the room and a moment later the sound of the outer door thudded closed. The four of them remaining in the long room contemplated in silence the bitter aftertaste of what had been said and done there.

'A good thing we made other plans,' said Luders at last.

'You know, I really am hating every moment of this.' Julia rose and walked to a large white table scattered with books and papers. She picked up one of the commentaries on Shakespeare, held it for a moment with an expression of disgust as if she could throw it on the floor to relieve her feelings, and laid it down again carefully.

'We've all behaved abominably,' she said, almost with a sigh.

'If you don't mind me saying so *gnaedige Frau*, you are a bit too sensitive to your inner censor.' Luders slid his strong white hands into the side pockets of his perfectly cut jacket and strolled over to a window to copy Hella in watching the street. 'We were bound to try this gambit. It didn't come off. My old friend here has neatly caught us in our own trap. Or rather, Tenius himself did, by having his long-overdue collapse just where it could do the most harm to everybody else concerned. Rather typical of the brute, come to think of it.'

'So we shall have to face it out,' said Kerenyi. 'Though I agree with you, Julie. I feel pretty shabby at this moment.'

'Bear it out until the edge of doom,' said Malczewska suddenly in a quite new voice. 'Except that doomsday is behind us. Or behind you three, at any rate. This swine Tenius is only a fading echo of doom. You'll all recover from it. I suppose that is why I hate you all. . . .'

When she was gone Luders said angrily, 'If she just didn't have to hate everybody all the time.'

'She hasn't changed much, has she?' agreed Kerenyi. 'But what a fate. . . . Did you know that story about the boy?'

'No. I lost sight of her at the start of the Uprising. Worse than her husband. He was transported with his whole unit when the Soviets entered eastern Poland in 1939 and never seen again.'

'You know, Malczewska is really Poland in person,' said Julia. 'All anger and bitterness, desperation, hopelessness.'

'Kill and be killed. It's shudderingly logical, dreadful.'

'She could never recover from her fearful life, of course. Maimed, inwardly and outwardly. Though I don't believe this illness is fatal, do you Kerenyi?'

'How can one tell? We don't even know what it is. But it would somehow be appropriate to Malczewska, if it were.'

Luders made his already familiar movement of shooting his cuff to see the time by his watch. 'I don't know why I'm worrying about the time,' he said. 'Having stopped another day to talk to Malczewska, I'm stuck here now until tomorrow with nothing at all to do. The first time that's happened to me since I was a boy, I think. . . .'

'There will be an uncomfortable waiting period for all of us until something happens.'

'In a sense, we're all at this horrible man's mercy almost as much as during the War.' Julia picked up the same book again and this time opened it at a place marked by a slip of paper before she laid it down. 'We're quite helpless.'

'At least he can't have us shot now,' Luders laughed suddenly.

'But you must often have had nothing to do in the Army?' asked Julia, abruptly reverting to his former remark.

'Absolutely not. Never so busy in my life. Mostly with unofficial business, naturally. Even when I wasn't up to something actually contrary to orders.'

'Yes, I remember the impression you gave then, of being always up to something.'

'Lucky for me my superiors weren't as perceptive as you.'

'Perhaps they had good reasons for not wanting to be,' she said dryly.

Luders shot her a sharply enquiring look. 'Very likely,' he agreed easily but neither then or at any future time did he take this subject further in Julia's hearing.

'Even if we have nothing at all to do except wait,' he said after a pause, 'that's still no reason to talk about the War. I seem to be the only man—at any rate in Hamburg—who doesn't discuss the war endlessly. I find it a great bore. All over Germany, after ten in the evening nobody ever talks of anything else. Whether it could have been prevented, who was to blame. Those who are fools put all the blame on Hitler himself—as if any one man could bring about such a catastrophe . . . but it lets everybody else out to a great extent. The less stupid blame Germany, the Russians, Roosevelt, in that order. Some blame Churchill. But the talk always goes round in a meaningless, pointless circle like mice in a cage because nobody understands what can have happened.'

'You must admit, it is quite a puzzle. I'm sure I don't have even a glimmer of an idea,' Julia said, 'But Georgy has. He'll explain that it is a matter, fundamentally, of the perpendicular structure of power over too small a horizontal base.'

They all laughed at this.

'You only won't understand it,' said Georgy indulgently, 'because you refuse to think in political theories.'

' 'Tisn't that I refuse. I just can't. My brain is a different shape, somehow. But, tell me,' she turned to Luders, 'do people in Germany really blame Churchill and Roosevelt for the War? That's rather nonsense, unless my memory is going. Churchill wasn't in office when England declared war, and the Americans only entered the War when they were attacked.'

'Oh, it's quite irrational,' agreed Luders. 'But people are irrational about the war.'

'One can hardly be anything else about a phenomenon so wildly unreasonable,' said Kerenyi. 'But to blame the British is pretty stupid. They were generous with their warnings before they acted, Churchill out of office as well as Chamberlain in.'

'Don't misunderstand me,' objected Luders, 'I respect the British, especially since they've been in control of Hamburg. And I'm sorry for them, too.'

'It must be hard for them to admit what a disaster the War was for Britain,' said Georgy. 'To know that the only victors were the Russians and Americans and to feel dependent on American goodwill, as they must do. Such a reversal from their war-mood. Traumatic awakening, which they can't allow to become conscious.'

'I recall that feeling,' said Julia with an effect of suddenness, 'after the first War. Naked, you know? Not only money went, everything just disintegrated. Titles to land were invalid, contracts, leases, even identity papers. My mother had to get *visas* to visit her family in Transylvania. And the Czechs cut the railway for some time, at Pressburg. We had to walk across with our bags to a sort of makeshift station on the other side. Even at that age it made a strong impression on me, the craziness of it. And, of course, the humiliation of being treated suddenly as foreigners and having to carry our own things. We didn't have much, fortunately. How anyone can ever have thought *that* would work for long!'

'I doubt if anyone except the Czech government did think so,' Georgy answered. 'Nowhere I went during those years was there any expectation of permanence. Certainly not in Hungary. Everybody knew it was an interim. But very few thought how the gap would eventually be filled.'

'Did you?' Luders wanted to know.

'No. I thought of German recovery, naturally. But like everyone else, I looked upon Soviet Russia as permanently impotent. Especially later, in the thirties.'

'They would have been but for American help,' Luders tone had an unusual note of scorn and bitterness, in place of his normal objective calm.

'You see, we are talking about the War, after all,' remarked Julia.

'I don't remember the end of that War,' Luders looked at her enquiringly. 'And our debacle in 1945 was a bit too much of a good thing for anyone to be able to take an interest in what was going on.'

Julia went to the window.

'It's a lovely day. And we're quite wasting it, because it's clear neither Georgy nor I are going to do any work. Why don't we drive out somewhere and drink a glass of wine? Then we can eat early this evening? I don't feel a bit like eating lunch, do you?'

'A good idea—eh, Berthold? And speaking of the Czech frontier, let's go out to Rommersburg. It's a nice old fort and the wine is good there. Nobody ever goes but the village people.'

As if released from some restraint they at once began to prepare to make an outing, Julia going to get a handbag and speak to the housekeeper and Luders and Kerenyi taking turns at the telephone to apprise hotel and office of their intention.

'I suppose I ought to call Hansi,' said Julia when they were ready. 'I forgot he might want to talk to me some time today.'

'Oh, leave him to stew, Julie,' objected her husband. 'He'll only want to come with us and talk eternally about the scandal we're going to have over Tenius and Hella. I've heard enough of Hella for one day and I'm sure you have.'

Julia did not answer this, except by looking from Georgy to the telephone for a moment, and then she led the way out of the room.

They drove over the Danube into the low, rolling countryside. They were rather silent on the drive as they sat together in the back seat of the large and new car behind the unmoving back of a professional driver, for Julia was concerned with the new factors appearing in the constantly moving, changing complexity of her career, while both the man in differing ways and by differing modes of thought, considered his own business affairs.

Not until they were strolling up the winding cart-path to the modest eminence of a knoll clothed in vineyards where stood a fortified rural house, did Luders revert to the subject of the frontiers. Like many Germans of his age and vigorous type, his mind moved in the empirical practicalities of action, for Nazi schools and War had deprived him of the respectfully accepted mental furniture of history and tradition. He supposed he must once have known of these Danube border lands as a major factor of political balance and action, but if he did, it was long forgotten and he considered, as it were for the first time, their significance. To him all the small countries over the frontiers were a group of settled states cut off from the rest of Europe and only superficially differing, their reality being the dominance of a great power. He had thought neither of the recent nature of this settlement, nor of its temporariness which was now implied by history. In answer to his question about what he could see was a minor fortress, a modest castle, he was almost startled, as if the news were really new, to hear of an ancient series of lookouts in depth towards the East, that reached with a now lost aspect of security to the far side of Czernowitz in the Bukovina.

This small fort, turned in upon its courtyard, had stood fast against generations of assaults of the tribesmen already populating Europe, who then turned to defend their gains against the renewed onslaughts of their kinsmen. Later, the same border defence held elastically, failing here and there, often overrun, or evacuated before its defenders could be slaughtered and ravished, and the homes the fort protected burned, by the Ottoman Turks for three hundred years. The count of years fascinated Luders with a rare insight. For a thousand years this fertile riparian ground was part of an open market, its boundaries constantly changing but never closed, a cultural and trading system; inevitably Luders thought of that aspect. Only for the last generation was the border at first partially closed and now barricaded and impassable. This information, or revival of school lectures, was given with an almost shocking unconcern which Luders did not perceive as an assumption of the mutability of what seemed today and to him a permanent disposition. He was confused by the distances of time and the changes of time, as by the casualness with which they were discussed—that is, as being of present validity—and the implication that the present forward wave from the East could ebb in a generation or could last for a further thousand years. This thought Luders rejected in his mind; only five years ago he lived in another era that was to last a thousand years and he was not disposed to accept such grandiose forecasts. The point was, the frontiers were not unchangingly fixed; if the Danube today was a Russian river, for nearly all recorded history it had very certainly not been, and there was no evidence except the simple assertion of the present conquerors, that it would long remain so. But with what extreme folly and arrogance had these varied groups of related tribes dismantled their common defence only a generation ago. How can any of them have believed, Luders thought pragmatically as they passed under the archway into the court, that an unmanned border and a scattering of separate economic units could be a substitute for a common defence system and a common market?

But he said nothing of this, a little ashamed of his ignorance and a little impressed, too, by a view of his companions which had not before occurred to him, as the heirs of an old and honourable polity. But as it proved, Luders did not need to ask for information; Georgy was in didactic mood.

'The Nazis—the Germans—were awful fools in the thirties,' he said as he stretched his legs luxuriously under the rough table. 'They could have dominated this area right down to the Danube delta in five years without a harsh word and with the co-operation of the Czechs. The people to the north here would have slid back without noticing it into their former attitudes, a sort of grumbling acquiescence in their administrative function, half German, half Slav. The two so-called races are inextricably mixed. There isn't any ethnic border in these parts, you know, it's all artificial. Bohemians and Moravians probably had more representatives in the middle ranks of the old civil service and Army than any other national group, except perhaps the Magyars in certain jobs.'

'Surely that's just the point, they reached the middle ranks but not the upper ones?'

'Yes, that was their point. But in fact, Czechs reached the middle ranks—and by the way that's not true either. A number of cabinet ministers were always Czechs, or part-Czechs, and the wife of the heir to the throne who was murdered in 1914 was Czech. But in general, Czechs reached medium jobs and not top ones just because there were so many of them and in the nature of things, most were just middling people.'

'D'you suppose older people in Prague think of all that now, and wonder. . . . People old enough to know how things actually were and not how they were supposed to have been?' Julia stared dreamily up at the solid blue of the sky through the palpitating sensation of the sun. 'The sky seems so wide, here.'

'They must do,' agreed Luders, pulling a sour face, and followed her eyes upwards, almost wincing in the beating light. He hastily returned his gaze to his glass which jumped and swam for a moment with an outline of white clouds piling towards the north, imaged on his retina. He drank his wine with an enjoyment sharpened by the contrast. 'By God, they're learning what oppression is, now. Can hardly believe that we're sitting in a Russian-occupied area right here.'

'One doesn't see much of it, nowadays. They keep pretty much to their garrisons lately. But, of course, not in the countries where they have real power, sole power.'

'Vienna must have been strange in the twenties. Prague and Budapest might enjoy the feeling of building up something of their own, but Vienna . . .?'

'We were stunned for years. The loss was so total and so unjust, so pointless. People lost their bearings in the reversal of the historical lie, that we were suddenly criminals and the disaster was our sole fault. Like being somersaulted into a mirror, where you know your right hand is still on the right, but it looks like the left and everybody else appears to believe it is the left. More than the loss was the helpless rage at injustice—that really formed me. And millions like me.'

'Yet nationalism is a real force. You couldn't have changed that.'

'It went further than nationalism, it was decadence. None of these small units can exist alone and people who believed they could were a bit mad. Political flat-earthers.' Kerenyi slowly turned his glass to watch the specks of sunlight running through the wine, 'It was a sort of barbarism of the mind, a reversion to a state of innocence where men who helped run a vast, multilingual administrative machinery only a year or so before, suddenly believed that the giant of ruthless power would drop dead because they waved a wand called democracy. And it was only a wand, not one of the succession states had more of it in reality—whatever it may be, if it exists—than would go on the tip of a wand. Oh, parliaments they had them, and elections. They still have. But they all governed through their language policies in fact, and were so busy inventing their own pasts they lost the power to be realists in indulging their own myths. They made alliances with States divided from them by half Europe, while next-door neighbours all quarrelled and took no cognisance of each other for defence—indeed, you know, much of their alliance policy was directed against each other because of their minorities. They all had minorities of each other, poor relations asking for help. None of these childlike dreamers who thought themselves such men of affairs worried about the great angry mass of Germany. Still less of the fearful chaos to the East, not until it had consolidated itself behind their backs. They were all, all, an invitation to violence. And that includes us.'

'But the violence has worn itself out now, don't you believe that? In sheer exhaustion?'

'I doubt it,' said Kerenyi, 'I doubt it. Because we sit here, in the middle of Europe, we think of the War as central European. But the west of the continent was every bit as unrealistic. Think of the League of Nations! And as for exhaustion—the weakness and weariness in western Europe led to more violence, not less. Just as in eastern Europe. I rather think perhaps national irritability is like bad temper in individuals, the result of a lack of vital energy, not a surplus of it. And the psychological pressures on ordinary people in all the mass societies, are greater since the War than before it. I for one don't believe that their frustrations can be made impotent by poverty as in Poland or Russia; nor do I think that prosperity would relieve them.'

'You wouldn't get a hearing for that view in Hamburg,' said Luders cheerfully. 'Since the money reform there's been a terrific upswing of energy: rebuilding, making things, eating for the sake of eating—every sign of real vitality.'

'But of course. It's natural when people lack everything, that they go to work replacing necessities. But I wouldn't expect the concern with possessions to last. It won't be enough for long. Twenty years or so, perhaps.'

'In twenty years a new generation will find new things to do,' Luders insisted. 'The world is full of opportunities. Look at India, Africa. Plenty of scope there for action without violence, enough to use up everybody's energies.'

'Perhaps,' said Julia, but she did not sound as if she believed it.

'I think you're over-pessimistic, both of you. You still feel the Allied Occupation here, restrictions, frustrations. And Tenius reappearing is like a bad omen. But he's only a minor irritation really. We mustn't let Tenius affect our lives.'

'Speaking of Tenius,' said Julia with a briskness that showed she spoke of a practical matter of concern to her own life. 'We ought to persuade Hella to stay away from Vienna after her summer tour. If she's here there will be a frightful scandal over her marriage with Tenius and that will be bad for the theatre. You ought to talk to her, Georgy—or perhaps Hansi would be better?'

'I dare say she's thought of it for herself,' he said and poured more wine. 'Pleasant here, isn't it? Just a little breeze to cool the heat.'

'I feel like something to eat. I'll go and see what they've got.'

'D'you have to go yourself?' asked Luders, surprised.

'It's not a restaurant, you see,' she said as she went towards the kitchen door from which an odour of smoked pork was appetisingly emerging.

'Yet there is a strong feeling of stability here, in spite of everything you say,' Luders said contentedly stretching his legs under the rough table. 'I notice it, coming from Germany.'

'We're a slow lot to change,' answered Georgy. 'Profoundly conservative. I wonder what we shall get to eat. I'm starving now, aren't you?'

'Smells like boiled bacon.'

They both jumped up to help Julia with a big tray, piled with various eatables, including the boiled bacon in thick slices with raw horseradish.

'Some local musicians are coming,' she announced with satisfaction as the plates rattled about the table and the vineyard owner's wife appeared with more wine. 'They are quite good. No kitsch.'

'A queer feeling this music gives me,' Luders said later. 'I keep thinking I'm going to recognise something I know, but I don't quite.'

'You've heard the old tunes a hundred times in concert halls, that's why,' said Julia, lazily surprised that Luders did not know something that to herself, unmusical though she was, seemed like a part of nature, as taken for granted as the present sunlight or the snows of January and no more requiring assertion as an oral component of Danube latency than the whine and clatter of the familiar sudden storms.

'Julie is speaking in shorthand,' explained Georgy with his suggestion of pedantry. 'Mozart, Schubert, Beethoven heard the melodies that fed these more recent themes and adapted them to their purposes of music in infinitely ennobled forms. We listen now to common descendants of an ancient line of harmony, as one might perhaps express it, a continuous euphony.'

'One might so express it,' said Julia laughing at him, 'but I don't think one should.'

'Some of the refrains are delightful,' Luders listened to a repeated phrase with his head tilted. 'It's really very nice here. Very pleasant.'

'Clever of me to think of it, wasn't it?' Julia was complacent.

'No more clever than I should expect of you,' said Luders gallantly, and his shot at an old-fashioned courtesy sounded quite wrong to his inward ear. He had better not try to be anything but his normal self with this so critical audience, he decided. 'Talk to us about the twenties,' he suggested, to change the subject.

'The twenties? They only became *that* afterwards. . . .'

'But the Inflation? The sudden poverty of people who'd always been prosperous?'

'I only saw that period from the supply end, as it were. In the holidays old friends used to come to my stepfather's place in the country with rucksacks and take back food to Vienna. Inflation I heard of from my older aunt.' She turned to Kerenyi with that subtle change of expression that was so revealing for anyone with eyes to see but of which she seemed quite unconscious herself. 'I've told you about the aunts? Naturally the younger two were married by then. Both to former Army officers and both miserably poor. But the older aunt was still living in her house, poor as a church mouse with one old servant as narrow and cramped as herself.

'There were spaces among the furniture. She talked about them all the time and about the pieces of silver and her own jewellery— all inherited, for I don't imagine she ever bought anything of that kind. Nobody ever thought of moving the furniture about to fill the spaces, she would have been indignant, the spaces were the evidence of the crime. She always referred to herself as being robbed. In a way, she was. Some of the things were good pieces, I've no doubt, and she wouldn't know their real value, having just inherited them as the furniture of her parents' home and their parents' home. Robbed, she was, poor old thing and she never stopped telling of the robbers. Someone told her she must ask for foreign currency— the Krone was worthless; and then the buyers would beat down the price to a fraction of what they originally offered and *that* was only a fraction of the real value of whatever it was they fancied. Sometimes the buyers came to the house, sometimes she went to their hotels. Foreigners, they were. Here was the idea of foreignness again, but this time definitely evil, condemned. My aunt used animal terms about them. They were wolves battening on the defeated, sharks snapping the bread out of her mouth, hyaenas drinking the blood of the old Austria dying from a great haemorrhage. It can't have been a very good place for a child. I used to have nightmares. She was a bit mad by then; or perhaps starving. Certainly there was never much to eat, even with the food sent from home. She and the old servant were afraid to eat anything that would keep, for fear things would get even worse. So everything was always rancid, or tainted. The servant went out to work for a family that bought a house nearby and she brought back tales of how rich they were. They came after the War, from Galicia, and *that word* began to be used, and confused with foreigners who had dollars. I thought of dollars as large chunks of gold. I was not allowed to speak to them, the new people. They had a factory and my aunt used to say they'd bought it on a marginal speculation and it cost them nothing. I recall the phrases she used because she repeated them so often. I don't think she knew what they meant any more than I did. But *that word* which was said as if it were a bad word one shouldn't use, got confused with wolves and hyaenas. Of course it had nothing to do with real people. It was all fantasy, pictures out of a jungle book, to me.'

Julia stopped and stared with her eyes narrowed at Kerenyi as if he could clarify the memories of imaginary predators who inhabited a jungle into which the half-crazed old maid had strayed. Predators there certainly were at that time, profiteers and speculators who made fortunes by understanding the nature of money which was something, again, that had not really existed in the former world for the old woman.

'Afterwards,' Julia said vaguely, a little lost in the confusions of what had then been real, was real but given fabulous aspects, and what was only fantasy recalled. 'Afterwards, long after, when we first got the Nazi newspapers in Vienna, I felt that queer sensation that I'd been through all that before. The hideous distortions were like reflections in moving water of my aunt's monologues.

Only later, in the public papers that everyone saw, so they were not quite fantasy . . . I can't explain.

'By the time I went to the Academy the old aunt was dead and I lived with my younger aunt, Cousin Luise, because she had no children. They shared the house with the other cousins. They all went away from Vienna later, Cousin Luise and her husband to Meran and Cousin Helga and the two boys to Munich; for jobs, you know? But all that didn't matter much because there was the Academy then. Cousin Helga's husband joined the Party so I never heard from them after I married.'

'Don't stop,' urged Georgy as she fell silent. 'Tell us about the Academy.'

'The Academy?' she said. 'But you know all that. It was hard work. But, of course, liberty after the Convent. I'm trying to remember when it was decided that I should go to the Academy and be an actress, but it seems to have been taken for granted. My mother and stepfather discussed it, but not in the sense of taking a decision—I always knew what I wanted to do and it was never opposed, not even mentioned as something my father would never have countenanced.

'So perhaps the idea of personal liberty got mixed up then, for good and all with the other idea that we were privileged people. But only privileged because we devoted ourselves to a purpose—a purpose—a very high duty to the public, to everybody in general. It sounds pompous now, but it was many years before I even thought of questioning it—either the special position we were given or its reasons. Of course, we were trained by theatre people who still belonged to the old world, survivors of the flood. That was something real we held on to and we needed something, there were hardly any personal rules left.

'Naturally, all this is hindsight. I wasn't aware of absorbing the tradition of the theatre as something high and serious which we were to continue as a barricade against barbarism. That I had to read about much later to adopt it. But it was very real, very earnest, to us. . . .'

'It may have been more real than the Church at that time,' said Kerenyi. 'Since churchmen intervened in politics actively then, and that brought them into the suspect areas of what was changing, the dissolution of immutable standards.'

'The theatre—music too, I suppose—was what did not change.

The painters and sculptors I knew were all experimenting, all cut adrift from the past and swirling in the flood. The framework remained, for us, simply in the words of the plays, you see. And our own lives, personally, were adrift, too. We were a group and went about together, discussing endlessly. The cinema was the great thing then—we all had a movie period and were going to use films as an art. We meant to regenerate—change, that is—the theatre too, but I can see now there wasn't enough new work for any change to be possible. *Then*, we railed at the Direction of the Academy and the Burg for not introducing new ideas and plays. We couldn't know at the time that the cinema was taking all the energies and talents that might have made the changes we thought were being held up by the old. And, I must say, making no real use of them. Gradually we began to feel a scorn for the screen and to look down on anyone who had much to do with films. But that came a bit later. Yes, we discussed the cinema, and there was love too. We didn't say sex then. We were going to free women from bondage, the State was to care for children, we were affected by Bolshevik ideas—or so we thought —Lenin was a great man and Karl Kraus almost as great. We used to go to listen to him reading his work, and even tried to mutiny our elders into staging *Last Days of Mankind* once. Or parts of it. I can't believe we ever thought it could all be produced, not even at seventeen. . . .'

Julia sat quiet, looking back at the tall, awkward, unhandy creature from which she had grown. The warmth drowsed about them, almost dreamlike in full afternoon, and the musicians sounded distantly, echoing slightly against the solid walls, from a second courtyard.

'Most of us made love a lot. With each other, changing about. But that was something I didn't join in with much at that time. The first attempt was a messy failure and put me off for several years. I began to work hard, instead. I'd finished the Academy before I started another affair, and I suppose because of the long gap, I took it a bit too seriously.

'After a few weeks, I thought I was caught. Then two things happened at once and this bit isn't hindsight—I knew this at the time. I was terrified of course, but I realised that I was frightened of losing my career by having a baby. At first the thought of having a baby didn't frighten me in itself. I suppose I assumed this man would marry me. But I didn't ever even tell him. Because he just faded out.

I didn't hear from him, and he didn't join our group for a week or so. Then I saw him again, but always with other girls. Very noticeably with other girls, which wasn't normal with us because we were a mixed group and not divided into couples. We thought it vulgar to break up the group like that and display our preferences because we believed in freedom; but I knew quite clearly what this meant. And just as I was getting frantic and weighing the idea of telling my mother, the whole thing dissolved into a false alarm. That was a turning point for me. After that, I took care not to risk my work again.'

She turned to Luders.

'Later I had quite a lot of affairs, some I've forgotten among them. But the first two were the important ones. And you know, the odd thing is, as I look back I can see that from the moment I refused to be used, men never faded out any more and I could always do what I liked with them.'

'A dangerous thing for women to learn,' Luders pulled his mouth down.

'Some women have always learned it,' said Kerenyi, 'and the rest never can, so you're quite safe, Berthold.'

'It isn't a matter of how one side behaves. Women behave just as badly to men, but the consequences for a man losing a girl are hurt pride and sometimes grief although that's often much exaggerated. For a girl the consequences often last for life. It's better to know what you're doing and not risk so much. Even if the boy behaves well—and I suppose the majority do—two people are stuck for life with a liaison they thought of as a momentary affair. Afterwards they are bound to build it up into the great love and all that stuff, and that's what makes most marriages so desperately insincere.'

'You're pretty tough on the foundations of Christian society,' said Luders. 'Don't you believe marriages are ever happy?'

'Real marriages, made when young, with children and homes? Very rarely. Only the complete dependence of one side on the other makes it workable. Or, in partly arranged matches, the recognition of mutual benefits. And, then, a certain simplicity of nature is needed, in both people.'

'Aha. Robert and Lali?'

'I hope so,' she answered, for a moment quite serious. 'Goodness knows, I took enough trouble over that match!'

'But we mustn't talk about people Berthold doesn't know. I can't even see the twenties myself, as a time. You were still a child and it was an era for you, in itself. For men who came back from the fighting, still boys but very old boys, it was just one hopeless mess after another. My own inheritance ran out in the Inflation and I had to work the last year of University, already a middle-aged man to the new students.'

'That's where you got your weighty, editorial air I shouldn't wonder,' Julia teased him.

'I doubt that. I was like a hungry cat most of the time. If it hadn't been for loans and free meals from a Jewish friend, whose family had taken better care of their money than my people, I would never have got through my doctorate.' Kerenyi glanced across at Julia. 'That, of course, was Franz.

'As Julie put it,' he went on slowly, 'you began to hear *that word* a lot about that time. I never remember hearing it among people of our kind in my boyhood. But a good deal at the University. And there's no point now in being dishonest about it. A good many of the speculators were really—strangers. Franz himself was always cursing the profiteers for poisoning the social and political atmosphere. The worse were the Russians who fled from the Bolsheviks because they had no feeling of responsibility to anyone or anything. Some of them were real vultures, taking the last pickings of the wealth of the old Empire.'

'The Succession States didn't do too badly at taking pickings, and they weren't Jewish,' said Luders slyly.

'No, they behaved abominably, grabbing the huge investments for nothing everywhere. Not a soul got any compensation for their capital sunk in railways in Bohemia or Rumania, or public building, or the harbour works at Triest, or the tram systems in Laibach or Agram. They were just left penniless. And just as the small rentiers in France never forgot losing their investments in Czarist Russian loans, so these people here never forgot the greed and meanness of the politicians who in the end ruined all of us for good with their narrow selfishness.'

'Yet the people voted for them,' argued Luders, but thoughtfully. 'If one is to think anything of this democracy lark, they have to be blamed for their own ruin.'

'In the first place, nobody voted on any of the Succession States or its government until the fatal aloneness of each was an accomplished fact. In the second, how can you expect ordinary people to understand that they bankrupt themselves as well as their enemies by getting valuables for nothing? Put baldly, it sounds like a sophistry.'

Julia rose quietly and wandered away to inspect a hang of roses growing over a low part of the courtyard wall. They watched her idly as she stopped to exchange a greeting with a group of people near the climbing roses, the men among whom had risen to bow to her. She made some comment to a small boy with them, and there was a general laugh. Then she glanced down at the evening paper, brought with them and lying on the table, read something, spoke again to the child and walked on.

'Do you know them?' asked Luders.

'I don't think so,' answered Kerenyi, glancing over his shoulder. 'People recognise her all the time, you know.'

'Of course, they must. I hadn't thought of it.' Luders was examining a corner of the stone wall which was obscured from his view while Julia sat there. The square stones were balanced together more by their own weight than by the long since crumbled cement that at some time had mended a loose patch. Little plants and mosses grew in the interstices of stone and it had grown together like stratified rocks rather than a foundation of human hands.

'Funny about history,' he said quietly. 'I don't think I ever felt the past before.'

Kerenyi hardly heard him. He was turned in his seat, watching the small boy who leaned on the shoulder of one of the men, evidently his father, and could be seen to be wheedling something from him, ducking his shock head and picking at the man's shirt-sleeve while he traced a pattern in the dust of the courtyard with his booted toe. The man shook his head but reached the child a scrap of paper from a pocket and gave him encouragement in unheard words, jerking his chin to emphasise what he said. Presently the boy seemed to take courage, clutched the paper and ran off towards Julia, but within a few paces of her he lost heart again and stood uncertainly, tracing again his pattern and shyly looking at the unconscious woman from under his brows, bleached almost white with sun. Not until she turned to come back and saw him, holding out her hand, did he make up his mind to ask for what he wanted. Or perhaps he did not need to ask. She rested the paper on a jutting stone and wrote her name with his father's pen, and it could be seen that she asked his name and had to ask twice, he mumbled so low in his shyness.

'It's been there for—how long?' Luders mused, still staring at the stone in the wall. He moved his head to look at Kerenyi and went on in a quite different voice. 'D'you think Europe can be rescued?'

Kerenyi came back to their conversation with a frown, considered the question slowly, narrowing his secretive eyes as he stared at Luders. His look went from his friend to his wife nearing them, and back again.

'No,' he said definitely. 'I don't.' They both rose slightly on their bench as she seated herself with a pleased little sigh.

'You're right, Berthold,' she said smiling at him. 'It is nice here. You can see a little river from over the wall there.'

'Of course, one doesn't say so publicly,' added Kerenyi. And to his wife, 'I see you've found a new admirer?'

'His name is Klaus,' she said as she picked up her glass. 'Ah. I almost forgot. The extradition of General Tenius has been requested from Germany. It's in the evening paper.'

'That won't please Malczewska. She will probably accuse us of having fixed it.'

'She does rather overestimate our influence, I've noticed that.'

'Speaking of influence—I feel I ought to get another opinion for her about her arm.' Luders hesitated and continued carefully. 'I know the doctors here are excellent. Still, with a serious illness, two heads are always better than one.'

'I doubt if she will accept anything from you.' Kerenyi shook his head.

'No reason why she should know,' pointed out Luders with an increase of cheerfulness at the thought of something he could fix. But the pleasant ease of their outing was disturbed and presently, without discussion, they began to collect themselves to leave.

XII

They found themselves at once on their reappearance, within the overwrought swirl of a major, an inevitable, scandal. The limits of what the professional conspiracy of discretion could arrange to spare Hella Schneider, and of what she herself could achieve by her talent for putting her own case in a state of unassailable, unquestionable, rightness were now well overstepped. She was beseiged in her house in Hietzing by reporters of the Viennese and foreign Press. Photographers, naturally unwilling to be fobbed off with official pictures handed out reluctantly by the theatre authorities, were already climbing fences and bribing neighbours to wait in their windows for a sight of the unwilling wife of a notorious war-criminal and the telephone rang incessantly in every room where a contact could possibly be supposed to know something about Hella, her movements or her husband.

It was impossible for Julia to continue her refusal to go to the telephone herself when her old friend Colton Barber rang up from Paris, and equally impossible to answer his probing questions dishonestly. As long as these questions concerned recent incidents her account to the journalist could be convincingly positive for all she need repeat was her knowledge that Hella Schneider had tried for years to rid herself of her encumbrance. But when she found herself pushed towards implying that Hella could never have known either the personal character or the professional duties of General Tenius, she convinced neither Barber nor herself and was forced in the end to tell him that he must ask Hella. Only Hella could tell him what her state of mind was during the War. A long persuasion followed while Kerenyi watched Julia's face as she listened and made vague curved shapes with her finger on the table before her.

'No, I can't say any more,' she said at last. 'I won't say things I don't know and on the other hand, I can't discuss a colleague I've worked with for many years. All I know is that Hella tried more than once to have Tenius officially pronounced dead and when she failed, had divorce papers drawn up for his possible repatriation. That seems to suggest that she did not know what sort of a man he was when she married him, don't you agree?'

That Barber did not agree was clear from Julia's expression of rueful amusement as she heard him out in what was evidently a highly sarcastic and challenging rejoinder.

'Well, obviously it could equally mean what you say. I can only guess and you're guessing the opposite. But I don't know. We are not personally intimate, Hella and myself, and I don't know her private feelings.'

After another long interim she said, rather wearily, 'You had better come and talk to Hella yourself if you think this "story" is really important. She can't refuse to see you, after all, because she knows you quite well. . . . Of course we'll talk to you privately if you come. But not for publication, that's understood?'

'That would be a major mistake, darling,' said Georgy as she put down the white receiver. 'If you talk to Barber off the record, he can't avoid passing the information you or I give him, on to colleagues, and they are not bound by any personal loyalty to you. They can print everything.'

'I know that, Georgy. But what can I do? Nobody in their senses is going to believe we know nothing. And we've known Barber nearly twenty years, we can't refuse to see him. And I don't see why we should, all things considered.'

'Hansi and the others will never forgive you if you admit anything.'

'Then Hansi and the others will have to decide what is to be said. I am not going to lie to Barber, of all people. And, really, the whole storm in a teacup will be dead tomorrow. I can't understand why the papers are so excited.'

'It's largely a question of how much other news there is at any given moment. If there were a mine disaster tonight somewhere, Hella's affairs would be forgotten. But we're in the dog-days and the last sex-story was the abdication of King Leopold in July. Beautiful actress married to mass murderer comes just at the right moment!'

'*Damn* Hella and her beastly films. . . . Why couldn't she grow out of them when every other serious actor did, in the thirties?' Julia was aware of the inconsistency of this view, for she herself had received the full blast of world publicity only a year or so before for the film of *Anna Karenina*. 'She's made several violently anti-Nazi films in Germany in the last couple of years. That hypocrisy will all be dragged up. *Why* didn't we think of all this before?'

'Self-protection, I should think,' said Georgy gloomily. 'And anyway, I did think of it. I just hoped it wouldn't happen. But that notion was sheer self-deception. War crimes of this gruesome nature are always news, the more so since Tenius came here to organize the later deportations.'

'I remember he was here when the big round-up was such a muddle. Now it strikes me as queer. He wasn't really in that department, was he?'

'The unspeakable brute was sent here because he'd already done something of the sort *efficiently* in Kielce. His experience was needed here where the RSHA feared unrest among the general population on account of our being so mixed here, so impure.'

'Oh—that was his earlier career? But surely his later command in Breslau will supply most of the evidence against him? He was there for a long time.'

'Not necessarily. They'll pick on whatever period the German courts have most evidence for. Breslau was so destroyed, the Poles can't have much documentation about it. They will probably choose his quite temporary detachment to Vienna because they can prove it—you see?'

'I don't see, no. The German Courts aren't so very eager to try such cases. Why don't they pick on places where they can't prove things?'

'You're not being sensible,' he said irritably. 'The longer and more confused a case, the greater the publicity. Since they must try Tenius and must condemn him—because the whole world knows he's guilty—they'll use something safe and sure.'

'Don't go,' she said hastily as the telephone began buzzing again. But it went on and on and in the end, Kerenyi picked it up.

'It's Hansi,' he handed the menacing little thing to her.

'I'm beginning to hate the telephone,' she said into it. 'There's no privacy with it. . . . We weren't trying to avoid you this afternoon, we just wanted a breath of air. . . . Yes, half a dozen, including one from Barber in Paris. . . . I said as little as I could, more or less the truth. . . . But be careful, Hansi. If anyone tells real lies it will be called a conspiracy. . . . Far too many people know the facts, you'd never get away with it. . . . Leave it to Hella to tell her own lies, or imply them. I'm sure you're wrong. If she ducks out now everyone will know you helped her, and secrecy would concede Hella's involvement *and the theatre's*. . . . But anyone can discover in half an hour that she was a Party member . . .! What? You'd forgotten that? Hansi, you're slipping. You're losing your head. For Heaven's sake think it over before you make a serious mistake. . . . You'd better talk to Georgy, perhaps he can convince you. You can't say he doesn't know what he's talking about. Here Georgy, you talk to Hansi. . . .'

She gave the telephone to her husband and walked away, trying to ignore the side she could hear of an irascible wrangle which descended rapidly into a real quarrel and ended by Georg almost throwing the receiver back into its rest and turning to her with a face of such saturnine anger as she hardly remembered him ever showing over a professional matter. His detachment and irony were quite gone and it was clear that on both sides subjective passions had gained the upper hand in a deep and painful division.

'The insolence,' he grated, his voice trembling with rage. 'To suggest that I ought to persuade—that I myself should publish an apologia. To talk of patriotism—patriotism, in such a context!'

'Hansi's a monomaniac,' she urged understanding. 'Lost his sense of reality. Do you think we should go over and try to persuade him to do nothing until tomorrow?'

'You'll do nothing of the sort,' he said furiously. 'If Hansi is bent on destroying himself, let him. But you keep out of it. Your name can't possibly be connected with anything so disreputable. Don't you understand what you'd be letting yourself in for? If he does as he threatens and whisks Hella away in secret, refuses any comment from the theatre, he'll turn a personal scandal into a national, political affair of the first order. Hella's been skating on thin ice since the end of the War very successfully. She must get herself out of the mess and she's quite capable of doing so, but the theatre must remain neutral—take the line that it's her private life and nothing to do with the Burg. Any other attitude would be disastrous. Not to say monstrous. By God, Ostrovsky was neutral enough when your reputation was in question and I haven't forgotten it, if you have. Now that he's dealing with a genuine Nazi, he panics.'

'With reason,' she pointed out. 'With me he knew that the truth could only be in my favour and that of the Burg. He could afford to be neutral and wait. Now he can't.'

'On the contrary, he *must* now be neutral. His only possible course is to leave the whole disgusting business to Hella, whose responsibility it is.'

'I should think Hella would rather enjoy a Press conference,' Julia hazarded. 'She'd give the performance of her life.'

The comment dispersed his anger and when the telephone rang again he answered it in his normal dry and reserved tone.

'Ah, Hella herself,' he said. 'Do you want to talk to Julie? Me? This is a signal honour; what can I do for you?' He listened for some time in patient silence to what was evidently a much more rational discourse than the preceding one. Finally, he replied.

'Certainly I can give you some advice and I'm glad you asked me, because I am sure that Ostrovsky is completely mistaken. My tactic would be to send your lawyer out to the reporters straight away and tell them that you will see them all tomorrow in the Press Club—say, at eleven. Tomorrow you turn up looking your best and simply stick to the story you've been sticking to since 1945. You know it all by heart: you knew nothing and as soon as you did know, you began trying to divorce Tenius. You were a nominal Party member only, for professional reasons—don't try to deny that because they can prove it. So long as you stick to your story and don't let them rattle you, you're safe and that will probably be the end of the matter.'

He listened again and then said, 'No, I won't persuade Julie to come too, but what the others do is their own business. Certainly I will come, I shall be interested to see how you manage. No, I can't agree to back you up, you know that. But I shan't need to ask questions, myself, since I know the whole story backwards. If you do what Ostrovsky suggests, you're a lost cause. You are much too clever not to see that. All right. Can I count on that? Eleven at the Press Club. Listen, don't be talked into saying anything tonight. Get a good night's sleep. You must avoid at all cost behaving with the sort of nervousness you showed this morning.'

When he put back the telephone, this time gently, he shook his head and smiled wryly.

'One thing you can't deny about Hella is her courage,' he said. 'For the sake of the theatre, I hope she gets away with it.'

'So do I,' said Julia with feeling. They contemplated, not without a self-denigrating humour, their own mixed loyalties.

'I feel better now,' he said. 'Ostrovsky really had me rattled.'

'It was probably the scene this morning that taught Hella a lesson,' Julia suggested presently. 'She must have realised, when she thought it over, that there are things she just can't scuff over and blur the edges of.'

'If you're right, poor Malczewska achieved exactly the opposite of what she intended.'

'Both Malczewska and Hansi, you see, acted in a crisis out of blind passion. It may be more sympathetic than cold calculation, but it really isn't the answer.'

Frau Lisl came quietly in to lay the table and they saw, with surprise that the sun was gone and the day almost over. It was dinner time.

'I doubt if you really find people losing their heads so very charming. I'm sure I don't. One is bound to forgive Malczewska her desire to revenge herself on everybody she knows, but she can't expect people to bring down her rage on their heads voluntarily—people are bound to avoid her if they can and I admit I do.'

'And as for Hansi, you know,' she agreed tacitly, 'in spite of his great talents in his own profession, they seem to exist independently of any ordinary, commonplace judgment. He has no judgment at all. He manages to ignore the outside world most of the time, so when it can't be ignored, he misjudges situations and people.' Julia lifted her chin with a turn of the throat that Georgy watched for and found always seductive. 'Odd. The telephone has stopped ringing all the time. I suppose they are all going to dinner, like ourselves?'

Kerenyi smiled at her notion that reporters would abandon a good story to eat, leaving their quarry free to make off. He saw that the announcement of Hella's intention to face the Press the following day must have achieved an immediate truce and was pleased without being flattered, that Hella had accepted his good advice at once. His estimate of her shrewd self-interest was not at fault, it appeared. Even as this thought went through his mind and as he took Julia's elbow to guide her to table, he recognised the real source of his pleasure. He was relieved and delighted that they were alone and private. Normally he must have anticipated tomorrow's meeting with a somewhat malicious amusement. At this moment, however, such minor pleasures as the follies and dishonesties of outsiders were only an interruption of a preoccupation much more sharply interesting and enjoyable. He meant to know more of what Julia talked about during the afternoon, much more.

She was unexpectedly devious, teasing and amusing him with jokes and questions about his own youthful erotic adventures, but always somehow turning his own questions away so that the subject was constantly changed from herself to him. Did she know that this tactic must increase his own curiosity and harden his determination, or was her bland refusal to understand his wishes and comply with them an instinctive form of protective manoeuvre designed to retain a certain mysteriousness for her girlhood, since it could no longer be manitained in the present . . .? He found he did not know the answer to this question, but the doubt as to her intention was sharply challenging. It brought a subtle form of violence into his probing which presented itself in his mind—he did not, of course, say it—as a picture of his pushing her into a corner. And gradually, he did so, cutting off the retreat to one verbal sidetrack after another until she was given no alternative but to answer a question suddenly put.

'Why do you evade me? I want to know seriously, not for fun. I can't follow how a woman's mind works and it interests me to understand how you determined on success, professionally. You said yourself there was a turning point, but it isn't convincing, the way you put it this afternoon. It can't be true in the literal sense that you put all your energies into work after two disappointments.'

'But why not true? That's how I remember it.'

'Your vigour is too great. I've known both women and men with far less vitality than you who pursued ambition and sexuality with success at the same time.'

'I think it could be . . . I don't take instruction easily. I have to try things out for myself. Once I tried to understand *why* the Academy teachers told us and demonstrated to us that we should move like this, hold ourselves in such a stance, I was caught by a much more complicated interest in what we were trying to do than I felt before. I began to want to know, not only how to breathe properly, for instance, how to pitch my voice and enunciate the words, but why, by what means, the methods worked. I remember reading about the functioning of the lungs in a big Anatomy. The growing feeling of understanding what we were doing, naturally, made me more and more effective and the experience of success in so small a fashion made me want more of it.'

Julia stopped and stared with a wide, blank gaze at the far end of the long room, trying to recall the state of unknowingness, to undo the years of accumulated experience of her trade.

At the beginning of the second term at the Academy she was still almost entirely ignorant. She knew that her showing at the end of the previous term was not good. Not as bad as that of Fridolin, but bad. As for Fridolin, he was already an obvious candidate for failure. A pity; he was very handsome and would make a fine-looking actor, but he had no gift for the theatre and no determination in his character to acquire skill by hard work. But it was exciting to see him again, Julia could feel this excitement in him too; she did not laugh at him now as the others did, nor join in when they teased him about his name which they all agreed was absurdly old-fashioned and approved his loud announcement that he would change it, no matter what his mother said. His hand trembled when he held hers under the café table so that the others should not see, and they both became warmer than the sunny weather of early spring warranted. With the sensation of holding Fridolin's hand while his palm went quite damp and sticky, Julia was suddenly aware that if he suggested tomorrow that they should not go to the cinema with the rest, she was determined to agree. She was rather frightened when she recognised what she meant to do, the nervousness was almost as great as the pleasure but only added to her determination; she would go with him to his rented room.

Every Tuesday the landlady played bridge all afternoon. They entered the house separately and Julia did not at all like the furtive way she found herself creeping up the stairs. The front door and Fridolin's were ajar and he stood with his back to her, his jacket off and his tanned neck and dark curling hair a sharp contrast with the white shirt. He bit his lip and whispered 'shh' as the door creaked closing, frowning at her so that she could see he was even more frightened than she was herself. Previously he boasted that he knew everything, now she doubted that as she sat, with shaking knees, on the edge of his hard and narrow bed and waited for him to show her what to do. Why was he fiddling with the brushes and things on his chest of drawers?

When he did move it was with the force, not of uncontrollable youthful desire, but with the fear of making a fool of himself. He banged her chin with his head so that she found a bruise afterwards, a glimpse of his eyes in an inextricable tangle of clothing showed a look of one facing an enemy, and then, suddenly he was still. It was some time before Julia realised that that was all. When she rose to her feet, not shaking now, he rose too without looking at her. In silent haste, although there was no reason to hurry, Julia dressed and turned to the small round mirror to make sure nothing showed in her face, which she felt a distinct reluctance to look at. Her hair was untidy, she picked up Fridolin's comb. There was a loud gasp, almost a sob, behind her and she whipped round, startled, to see him staring in horror at the bed cover.

'Oh God,' he stammered, almost weeping with anxiety, 'How are you ever going to get rid of those spots?'

Not understanding, Julia moved slowly towards the rumpled bed. There was no doubt, that was blood.

'Do something,' cried Fridolin. She lifted her eyes from the bed and the three round spots, clearly outlined on the faded pattern of the bedspread, were still printed for a second on her eyes. A thought entered her mind, already formulated. *I* should do something? Why me? She was too much the child of unquestioned discipline, parental and conventual, to know that what she felt was anger, but she rejected the relegation to servitude without even considering it as possible. Since she had helped her mother, who also must take care of unfamiliar household tasks and so was an equal partner with her, at any rate in that sense, Julia had never been requested, let alone ordered, to carry out a menial task. The discipline, from her now remembered father through to the last homily from the aged Mother Superior and on to the instructors at the Academy, was not directed to making her into an underling. She was no washerwoman, and she distinctly framed this thought, too. It brought with it another idea, of a most urgent and personal nature and on this thought she acted; she must get back at once to her own privacy in the half-used house of her cousins, where they all occupied rooms almost as if in a boarding-house, leaving the salons and dining room shuttered and dusty. Julia turned without a word and left Fridolin alone. She walked down the staircase without attempting secrecy. She walked out into the shockingly public street.

The sensation of being exposed to the eyes of strangers made her stiffen; she lifted her head with a movement of pride that was to become celebrated and, ignoring the hard flush she could feel in her face, she stepped deliberately into the middle of the wide pavement and walked without haste towards the Ring and the tram stop. There was no tram there and the absence of waiting passengers told her that one had just gone. So she walked all the way to the IIIrd District, through the parks, across the streets, looking neither to right nor left. It was herself who must be preserved from the knowledge of humiliation, not any conceivable observer of her passage.

No thought of sympathy for the equally humiliated Fridolin touched her. She pushed him out of her mind and never thought of him, indeed she never spoke to him again and the unfortunate boy dropped first out of their circle of friends and then out of the Academy. Nobody noticed that they did not speak to each other, for their group was in a constant shimmer of talk and movement. Fridolin just disappeared; if the episode left any consequence it was that Julia thought a good deal in the following weeks about her dead father. Not about what he would have said to the actual incident; she could not even imagine that. But what he would have thought of her putting herself into a position where she could be privately and possibly even publicly, exposed to a loss of repute, of standing; of his own loss of prestige through her action. She could well reconstruct his views on that subject, for she had often heard them in her childhood when some indiscretion by an acquaintance or colleague was made the opportunity for a lecture on responsibility, on the duty to preserve not only one's personal and family position, but to consider the effect of a folly on the Emperor himself, whose servant one was.

In the actual circumstances of the 1920s in Vienna, these considerations were absurd. And looking back thirty years, they seemed less than absurd; they had ceased to be possible as a factor of behaviour. But at sixteen what one learned in childhood is not modified by objective experience in the real world in which one lives. Julia's perceptions and beliefs were her father's and any knowledge she then accepted of his inadequacies was purely private and belonged to the personality and situation of her mother; it was not valid for Julia. The duty to which privilege was attached as reward was the fundament of life.

The fundament was duly transferred to the career Julia had been able to choose only because her father was no longer there;

and if this was an irony of Florian Homburg's personal tragedy, it was revenged in his daughter's life. She became unable to abandon a task once undertaken; the unloved but deeply respected figure of her childhood was institutionalised into her profession. She must and did prove that she was not the scared half-child entangled in a sordid failure that she appeared on that spring afternoon. Although her character was made resilient and sanguine by her mother's vitality and health, she was her father's daughter.

Talking of this now, in a diffused conversation, hesitating for words and trying to recall what she had never truly been aware of at the time, without making the account unintelligible, Julia brought it out as a much more coherent mental process than it had ever been. Only the hesitancies of her voice, the corrections in the words she used, exposed the vagueness of the deep effects of the episode. It might, she said, have been any other kind of personal failure; it only chanced to be a boy. No, that was not true; it could only have been some contact with a primitive act, nothing less than elemental could have achieved such a permanent result. And it was bound to be something *she* did of her own will, nothing done to her could ever have forced her to view herself from the outside at that age. She remembered her determination to go to Fridolin's room; she did it. The child Julia seduced the boy, he did not persuade her. It was her own responsibility and here she could now see a heritage from her mother's character. Wilful, practical, clear-edged to hardness, she could imagine her mother as a girl doing just the same thing and treating it afterwards with the same common sense.

The account of the afternoon, in the presence of a stranger, Berthold Luders, was considerably different from what she now told him, observed Kerenyi. Julia supposed she may have been protecting herself when she attributed to her second adventure the affects that really belonged to Fridolin. Not out of prudery, since the second brief love affair was as illicit—or not—as the first. But just because of the profoundness of the change it made in her, herself, which was not for the eyes of a stranger. The shock belonged to the first failure; the second was only important because of a few days' perfectly rational fear of pregnancy and because the repetition confirmed what was already decided: namely, that in future Julia would do the choosing and would choose only persons and situations that she could control. The central fact of her character was already formed. Besides, the actual encounter with the second man, whom she still did not name, was by no means the total failure of Fridolin's inexpert attempt. The second lover was far more competent; but he took no more account of his partner as a human being than Fridolin had done, and with less excuse. That fact with the fear of losing her future career through one action, whose consequences she could not foresee or control, was a confirmation of her resolve, not the source of it. Julia still felt what she had been, by then, quite conscious of: she was not going to be used.

She did not want to use others either; that was a difference with girls she came to know well, among them Hella Schneider who, without any known training always used men, and successfully. She had rejected the whole concept of human beings operating on each other as factors in their own situations, as objects. And this must be, Kerenyi saw, a part of her character and not learned; she did not think of it as something high and proud in herself, nor its opposite in Hella as ignoble. Her view of her own character was quite simple and practical and the path she took then she viewed as simply choosing her profession instead of personal indulgence.

Kerenyi saw at last why his determination to subdue Julia was of such fundamental importance to him, and what a responsibility he took upon himself in doing it. His own hubris startled and almost scared him; this was, after all, an unique creature and not only because she was famous in her own world. But his purpose was not changed; he was sure he could not destroy her, but he could release the last barrier to greatness in her and this made him respect Julia as he had never thought to respect any human being.

XIII

'How did your meeting go?' was Kerenyi's first question on coming into the long room.

'Very peacefully,' answered Julia. 'Hansi was obviously exhausted and so worried about Hella that I got my main point accepted with hardly any argument. Thorn plays Antony and we agree that he is to be battle-scarred and wild.' She came close to Georgy with no outward sign of feeling and touched his hand slightly. 'He must look as much like you as possible,' she said softly and turned to greet the guest who now entered, followed by Willy Mundel.

'Is it all right if I come too?' asked Mundel, coming over to kiss her cheek. 'How different this place looks! He's really very good, that chap of yours. A great success. Can't even remember where my room was when I lived here.'

'Shouldn't think you'd want to,' said Julia, kissing him in reply. 'You've evidently met, you two. Now take yourself a drink, Willy, and start telling me every word, every movement of every eyebrow. Between the three of you I expect to get a complete picture.'

'It was better than a play,' said Berthold, holding a glass of some bitter aperitif with soda and clinking the ice cubes round and round in it. 'But I shall leave it to the others to tell you because I didn't know most of the actors.'

'It was rather like a play in more ways than one,' Georgy laughed his bark of enjoyment at anything ridiculous. 'You know that long room in the Press Club, Julie. She came in at ten past, wearing red. A touch of genius, that. If she'd tried to look pale and sad, they'd have torn strips off her. And she came through the main door from the coffee bar, walked through the crowd greeting people instead of slipping in by the end door to the table with the mike.'

'How did she look?'

'Splendid. You couldn't see a sign of strain unless you were determined to find it. Perfectly turned out, perfectly made up. Completely mistress of the situation.'

'The only way you could tell there was anything to worry about, was that she smoked, which she never does in public.' Willy wagged his big head from side to side until his long grey hair flew about. 'I admired her. Can't approve, but one must admire her nerve.'

'The first thing was, the pompous chairman introduced her, a lucky stroke of perfect stupidity. There was quite a loud laugh and the fool looked offended but we were delighted. It was an excellent beginning.'

'So Hella looked round at the chair standing ready by the table with the microphone and laid her handbag down. She said quite calmly, "I just have something to say to you and then I'll sit down and you can ask me questions. I married at a time of crisis in the whole world when nobody was able to think very clearly. There were many unwise marriages made at that time and mine was one of them. It wouldn't be true if I said that I suspected nothing before the end of the War. I did begin to have terrible doubts and I did become very unhappy and uneasy. But that was a time of great secrecy, and I was not only unwilling to admit the truth of my suspicions, I was also afraid. We were all afraid then, all in a state of desperate worry. It is easy to forget that now. But I'm not trying to defend anything. I only claim for myself that as soon as I actually knew what had been going on, just before the end of the War, I began proceedings for divorce. It certainly wasn't my fault, nor the fault of my lawyers—I nearly nagged them into a sanatorium—that a divorce proved impossible until now. That's all." '

Georgy read this statement from his shorthand notebook in a flat monotone and then, as if copying Hella, sat down. 'Of course,' he said, 'Hella didn't need the microphone and never even looked at it, let alone fiddling about with it as people nearly always do.'

'In fact, she spoke away from it,' said Berthold Luders. 'She never raised her voice but everything was quite audible.'

'There was quite a long pause before the questions started, while the flashes went off all over the place and Hella never moved to look at the cameras, but leaned over and said something to Anita.'

'Anita went, did she?' commented Julia. 'Did you hear what Hella said?'

'I did,' claimed Willy. 'She muttered she could use a drink and I absolutely agreed. I wanted one myself.'

'Like all good statements, Hella's pre-empted many of the questions,' Georgy flipped over a page of his notebook. 'But there were still some pretty hostile ones from the foreign Press. Especially the wire service men. They're always the most awkward. The *Trybuna Ludu* man asked some scorchers, too. Wanted to know how often she visited Tenius in Breslau and Warsaw. She said only once, at the time of the wedding, when a Burgtheater company was in Warsaw and Cracow. She insisted she'd never been in Breslau. She knew that nobody could prove that, one way or the other. And her lawyer finally shut the reporter up by pointing out that nobody could go to Breslau after the beginning of 1942 without military permits, so that the point was capable of proof. Which everyone knows it no longer is.'

'The most brutal question was put by your friend Barber,' said Mundel. 'He came in very late—obviously just got off the train. He wanted to know if it were true that Hella put in for a widow's pension with her applications for the official establishment of Tenius' death. There was a bit of a sensation then and it was the only time Hella looked scared, though I don't think anybody would have known it who didn't know her well. She managed to deny it fairly calmly, though her voice trembled a bit. Barber insisted that he knew she had requested a pension, she denied it again. Then some kind soul suggested from the floor that the pension application was automatic in such cases and did not depend on the petitioner for a death certificate—he knew from his sister's case after her husband was missing from his Luftwaffe squadron.'

'Rather naturally, since the pension is nearly always the reason for requesting a death certificate.'

'The lawyer then said that he was only too well aware that Frau Schneider never read legal documents; he often had cause to warn her of how unwise it was.'

'It doesn't seem possible that Hella could have done such a stupid thing,' said Julia. 'I can't quite believe that, even from Barber although he's usually pretty reliable.'

'Barber does his homework, Julie,' said Kerenyi. 'If he says she asked for a pension, I'm willing to believe it.'

'Or at any rate,' said Mundel, smiling broadly at the thought, 'her usual parsimony prevented her deleting the paragraph from the forms. I can absolutely see her weighing it up in her mind—can't you?'

'I suppose I can,' admitted Julia, both amused and disgusted. 'But it isn't like Hella's good sense.'

'Money was always the only consideration that could make Hella behave stupidly,' argued Kerenyi. 'She came in for a good deal of ribbing over her recent films, by the way Julie, just as you said she would.'

'And began to show signs of being annoyed by it. But Anita helped her out by saying quite loudly that there was nothing strange about people being sound anti-Nazis as soon as it was safe to be so.'

'And all the Viennese journalists laughed at that, because everybody knows it's true of Anita's own father after he made a fortune during the War.'

'Was there nobody officially present from the theatre?' asked Julia who was clearly in two minds over the cynicism of the whole scene.

Mundel replied. 'That was the cleverest thing Hella did. She categorically forbad Hansi or anybody else to appear. Not because she cares about the theatre's reputation. Not for a moment. But instinct told her to keep the matter personal.'

'And, of course, her name and her looks ensured that everybody except the east European journalists would be more or less inclined to be on her side—personally.'

Julia shot Georgy a sharp glance at this but replied in the same flippant tone.

'Naturally a masculine group would be unlikely to admit that a woman can be moved by other than emotional motives in marrying. That would put in question the whole male position of domination. And once Hella established that point—implicitly—her position was really unassailable. Which, in fact, proves her own superiority. . . .'

'A positively Shavian point,' said Georgy dryly.

'Julie's quite right,' said Mundel with enjoyment. 'Hella's opening statement established her simply as a woman who had made a mistake out of a temporary infatuation—without ever saying it.'

'So you think Frau Schneider will get a sympathetic Press?' Luders wanted to know, and agreed with a nod that he would like another drink.

'So much so,' said Kerenyi as he moved towards the tray of

drinks, 'that I feel we should really be drinking champagne. As I'm quite sure Hella is, at this moment.'

'Well, "black velvet" anyway,' said Luders laughing openly and using the English words. 'For a rather black joke.'

'There's one good thing about it—apart from the theatre—if she gets away with it,' Julia gave Kerenyi her empty glass to refill. 'The joke is on Tenius.'

'Apparently he was better this morning and has been formally arrested in his hospital bed.' Georgy took her glass. 'The AP man said they had a statement from the Police President and another from the Public Prosecutor to the effect that nothing stood in the way of an extradition order as soon as the patient was fit to be moved.'

'Then he must have been served with the divorce papers, as well?' asked Julia.

'Not by eleven this morning, or Hella's lawyer would have announced it. But probably by now.'

'If one weren't standing in *this house*,' said Mundel, 'one could almost be sorry for Tenius.' This remark with its return to a more seemly view of the events of the morning made the party silent for a moment and when they began to talk again they did not return to their former parade of amusement.

Julia moved over to Luders and asked him about the time of his flight to Hamburg, in case they should need to hurry with their meal. It proved to be at five, so they could comfortably take their ease.

'There's something I would like to say to you, if I may,' Luders went on. 'Though it's tactless and will remind you of things you would much rather not think about. But it's very much on my mind. . . .'

'Go on,' she said, giving him a quiet look as if she knew what it was he meant to say. Perhaps she thought he was going to ask her some question about her first husband, but Luders had the North-German habit of bluntness too well under control to do anything so crude.

'Years ago, when I first met you, I made some impudent and cruel remarks to you. It was in Warsaw and you were just about to go into the theatre. I hope, though I have no right to, that you've forgotten what I said. Whether you have or not, I should like you to know that I was sorry for it long before I knew what an injustice

I did you.' He glanced at her face and saw that she was deeply moved at the memory he revived and for a moment so much moved that she could not help showing it. All her anger, all the impotence of her position at that time came back and he could see it in her expression in the instant before she commanded herself.

'Forgive me,' he said hastily. 'I have no right to satisfy my own conscience at the expense of your feelings.'

'I'm glad you said it,' she replied quietly but with a slight tremor in her voice. 'The memory prevented me liking you and I'm glad, really glad, that you spoke.'

As they walked over to the table and began to seat themselves, she wondered at herself for the first time, that she had never told Georgy of that incident when Berthold Luders in the singlemindedness of twenty, practically accused her of abandoning the Jewish members of her family to their fate. For a moment she could almost see the open, disrespectful yet truculent face of the corporal-driver as she and Hansi Ostrovsky went up the steps to the *Teatr Polska* in Warsaw and he muttered for them to hear 'it always is different'. Those words, now meaningless, seemed to contain all the shame and bad conscience of any German stationed in that city who was not lost to human dignity. Julia knew that many men were made into brutes not only by the constant temptation of corruption in a place where everybody but themselves was starving, but by the very conscience that told them secretly of the horror of what was being done there and which they could only express openly at the cost of their own safety, sometimes of their lives. How right Georgy is, she thought, calmly eating a piquant ox-cheek salad served as the first course. How right he is to spend his life and energy attacking the power of the monstrous apparatus of the State, even here where it isn't power at all. The phrase she used in her mind was Kerenyi's; her own concepts would never naturally have arisen in such terms. His influence is changing me, she must remember to tell him that; and she turned to Mundel to answer some remark about the food.

'Impossible to refuse her,' said Georgy. 'But I can't say I'm looking forward to another discussion with her so soon. You'll be well away, lucky fellow.'

Julia had evidently missed some piece of news and she could guess at what it was but before she could ask, Frau Lisl opened the door and made the windows slam in a sudden burst of wind.

'We'd better close the windows,' she said to the housekeeper and excusing herself, hastily rose from the table to help. 'It's gone quite black to the north. We're going to have a real storm at last.' The truth of this was soon evident in the rattling of the fastened windows and the howl of wind through the gaps where they were propped open to allow some air into the still over-warm room although the temperature was rapidly sinking outside. After a few minutes they needed the lights on and a little later still all the windows had to be securely fastened.

'A good thing I didn't persuade you to lunch with me in the open,' said Luders, looking with astonishment at the rain now lashing against the glass. 'It's a real tempest! I was thinking of eating in the Prater.'

'We'd have been brained by flying branches.' Mundel comfortably emptied his wine glass. 'Those trees are in a shocking state, some of them. Julie, speaking of trees. Did I tell you I've got the permit to rebuild my house at last?'

'No, really? I still think you're mad to rebuild in the Russian Zone.'

'I don't want any other house,' he said with equable stubbornness.

'Is it badly damaged?' Berthold asked to show polite interest.

'Burned to the ground, except for the stone part of the walls and the main chimney.'

The faces of his companions warned Luders not to pursue the subject and he put no more questions. He hardly needed to ask, for he could fill in for himself all but the details of a loss repeated by the thousand six years before. It was too familiar in his own shattered city to need description and if there were any need, he had seen a number of destroyed and abandoned farms and houses on the short journey of the day before. It was very rare for anyone to put an investment into that part of the country which nobody could believe would ever be returned to the free use of its owners, in spite of the theoretical survival of the old property laws.

Kerenyi made some reference to the danger of a renewed attempt at a Communist *coup d'état* on the pattern of the one that failed over a year before, but Mundel dismissed the possibility as having been too great a loss of prestige to its Russian instigators for them to risk trying again.

'It didn't strike me before, but it really is extraordinary that the Austrians have kept their tiny country intact. I mean, when one looks at Germany. . . .'

Kerenyi smiled at Luders. *'Felix Austria,'* he said. 'We're too unimportant for great powers to struggle over us. But we're not out of trouble yet, by a long way.'

'Still,' said Berthold, 'I can't help thinking of what is happening over that border where we sat quite happily drinking and eating yesterday, and felt ourselves as free as air.'

'It seems to have made a great impression on you,' said Julia.

'It did. I never before thought of Europe.'

'You'd better think now, my lad,' Kerenyi said. 'You'll never get off today in this storm. We'd better telephone the airport.'

'I will go over long before the 'plane is due,' Julia comforted him, and they gave their attention to the excellent food again.

But Kerenyi was right and the aeroplane which was to take Luders back to Hamburg on its return flight was unable to land.

XIV

There was a sealed packet lying on the dressing table and for a moment Julia wondered what it could be. But the insignia of her bank on the outside wrapping recalled to her the old jewellery sent for on an impulse, to be inspected. A reminder from the insurance company that rising values made an increase of insurance necessary was the prosaic cause of her sending for these trinkets of heavy gold and large, squarish stones of a past time, dimmed with grime as she now saw, and blinking softly like any other once lively things confined for many years to a vault. For years that part of this almost forgotten treasure trove once her mother's, had lain in paper and tissue, jeweller's cotton and thread, wrapping that contained somehow a breath of the period before the War when they were first sent to the bank. There they lay, consigned later to rural storage and then brought back two years before and Julia had never looked at them, hardly remembered their existence out of a disinclination to consider the implication of their ownerless state; for she certainly did not think of them as genuinely hers. After her re-marriage her mother never wore them; life as a country gentlewoman impoverished by war and in a world shrunk from Imperial grandeur to suddenly inconsiderable proportions offered no use for a 'collier', a tiara folded into a puzzling framework, the springs of which no longer snapped open at Julia's fumbling touch, bracelets that would have interfered with hands otherwise employed than with fans, or even with rolling bandages. One or two of the rings Julia did recognise, but vaguely as if she might have dreamed of their being worn on the tiny hands, as much more physically capable than her own as they were smaller. There was one oval emerald in a setting so antique that she knew it must be at least the fourth generation of inheritance that brought it to herself and which she contemplated with her usual sensible concern as being a possible gift to her adopted family now happily filling her mother's house. One or two of the things she was sure she had never seen, notably a pair of elaborate earrings, and these must have come from her stepfather.

There was another packet, smaller, more expertly packed. Much heavier too, she noted, turning it over. There were bank stamps on that and sealing wax that cracked at its bubbled rims. Inside that more packing, with different stamps. Cologne, she thought, Cologne . . . ? That can't be mine, it's a mistake. She did not open the inside packet but picked up instead the letter of consignment from the bank and read that this was the packet deposited years before in thrifty modesty by a stolid bourgeoise for whom jewels were possessions rather than ornaments and which, by its being numbered and not identified by name, had survived the War and all that the War meant for its former owner. The judgment of the Court of Restitution by which she, Julia Homburg-Kerenyi, was awarded this survival was quoted in this letter as a long file-number and phrases referring to the house in the Rhineland—that was why 'Cologne' meant nothing to her at first sight—reminded her with a qualm of superstitious unease of whence these unseen trinkets came.

It came to her now as a settled matter that of course these still unknown and, by her, unvalued objects must be used for some helpful cause and that this idea was the answer too to the ownership of the Rhine-bank house she would never visit and which was still disgracefully occupied by those who entered it the day after the disappearance of its rightful owner. Since these occupants had themselves done nothing to bring them into conflict with the changed justice of the postwar world, their presence in the property now restored to the heiress, the only surviving relative of its dead owner, had so far been left to the slow processes of the civil courts. Up to now without effect. But if this house with its contents and these packaged jewels were to be offered for sale so that the proceeds could be used for the good of orphaned victims of the holocaust, and if these funds should be put into the hands of an official representative of such victims by herself, Julia, then not only would the unwelcome and to her reproachful, occupation of the house but her own unwilling ownership of it, would be ended. It was only a matter of a few months since she became the owner of these properties but she felt a great surprise at herself that this obvious solution only now occurred to her. There was so much relief in the idea that Julia rose hastily, without opening the still sealed packet, and went to her small writing table in the main living room to write a note to those who could at once translate it into action.

Not until she returned to her bedroom and saw the crumpled paper and the heavy packet lying beside the strewn heirlooms from her mother did Julia consider that, to avoid a possibly embarrassing disappointment to those who should benefit by her divesting herself of them, she had better make sure that the contents of the packet were not, comparatively speaking, worthless scraps of merely sentimental value. Still with a sensation of trepidation and unwillingness, but concerned with her always strong practical sense, by the rationality of what she meant to do, Julia broke the seals of the inside packet and tore away the brittle paper. Inside was a cardboard box covered with imitation leather which already, such a short time later, had an air so old-fashioned that it was almost an antique itself. Carefully wrapped again in coloured tissue paper with designs on it that proclaimed it to be left over from Christmas festivities, were a number of heavy golden chains, bracelets of 19th-century massiveness, two brooches with miniature portraits in the centre and set about with brilliants, and another brooch with what a salesman would have called important rubies. Several rings, one worn thin inside, with solitaire diamonds. A single string of large pearls with a sapphire fastener, the pearls now dim with their long expulsion from the light of day on a thread of silk so fragile that it threatened instant dissolution although it had obviously hardly ever been worn. None of these gifts of long-forgotten occasions was in its casket; Julia supposed they had been so packed as to take up as little space as possible. There was as well a tiny evening watch of platinum with square-cut diamonds that could only have been designed after the influence of the Bauhaus was supreme for those who wished to be modern, and must have been made about the end of the twenties. For some reason this watch was more frighteningly pathetic, more evocative, than the other things. It was probably, Julia thought, the last considerable presentation made to the woman who might have taken it out once or twice a year when going to a particularly notable evening at the Opera.

Under the other, feminine, trinkets lay two dark leather square containers with a more masculine and imposing look, an aspect somehow familiar. They were upside down and on turning them Julia saw without surprise the arms of the Imperial House of Hohenzollern. Medal cases look much alike no matter to which royal court or republican chief representative they owe their origin. One of them was the Iron Cross, second class. The other a later

Iron Cross but still of the First World War, with oak-leaves and swords, a higher form of the decoration.

I wonder where, Julia thought, I wonder where he—whoever he was—won *that*. She knew that the hero gained this distinction almost certainly at the cost of his life unless his rank was above that of Colonel. Stiff papers folded to fit the bottom of the little box were clearly the citations. Julia took these papers out and laid them aside on her dressing table but she did not read them. Such a perfectly understandable action of curiosity would have appeared as a vulgarism, as if she were checking on the credibility of the awards. She laid the two square leather caskets on the papers and packed the jewels back into the imitation leather carton. She knew already that the two medals would be framed with their citations and hung in the dining room under the near-primitive painting of her grandfather-in-law whose death took place far enough ago in time to have been, for one of his kindred, a natural event. There was no sentiment in this determination; it was half an act of piety, almost of superstition, and half an intransigent intention of 'rubbing in' something, something almost like a joke aimed at those who had preferred to forget a wide social fact.

Not only the awards themselves but everything to do with the complicated means by which they had landed at last in her hands was too far away by now for Julia to be inwardly shaken by it. The world had passed on, things were too much changed in the very recent past for such mementoes to inspire either direct anger or a less permissible resentment against having to be reminded of what they meant. She could accept them now with only the residue of enough of feeling to make her sure that they ought to be on record, where they could be seen to exist.

But far stronger than this last sensation was the relief that she would be freed from possessions that only became hers in the legal sense because she and her lawyer, both of whose parents had been imprisoned by the Gestapo long enough for a lasting bitterness to be left in him, were determined that they should not at any rate remain in the hands of their unlawful enjoyers in default of an action only Julia could take.

A satisfying decision having been acted upon which effectively changed Julia's uneasy conscience over possessions that could only be properly thought of as blood money, into liberation, she was now able to examine without guilt the more justifiable heritage from her mother. These are pretty things, she thought, as she took them again one by one in considering hands. I shall certainly have them cleaned and the diadem redesigned so that Lali and I can wear them: the stability of the world was already so much restored that it even seemed not impossible that she might wear a diamond head-piece when not standing on the stage of a theatre. Julia knew quite well that this stability was illusory in outward reality; it was her private world which had achieved a new solidity. She did not stop to analyse this feeling; introspective mental processes remained for her solely reactions to some challenge from Kerenyi. But she was aware of it as an undercurrent of plenitude while her active mind reminded her that her purpose in retiring to this room was to study further the commentaries, histories and annotatory material needed for an understanding of a new and seriously important pro-fessional project. She laid the long-hidden trinkets, the two medals and the 'leatherette' carton neatly away in a drawer and addressed herself to her work.

Julia could hear the rather deep, dragging voice she recognised as Malczewska's before she opened the door of the long room, and knew at once that this early arrival meant that the Polish drama-turgist would be with them the entire evening. She was answered by Berthold Luders and Julia took in his remark as she entered but be-fore her presence was noticed, stepping as she did on the thick car-peting.

'It might be as well,' Berthold was saying in his cheerfully deri-sive tone, 'if you didn't refer to your application for Austrian citizen-ship in those terms before your hosts.'

'Georgy isn't back yet?' asked Julia smiling at them as she came forward. 'What terms, Berthold? If you mean in the terms of an unpleasant necessity on Frau Malczewska's part, I think we should both take that for granted. Of course,' she went on with a slight dryness in her calm voice, 'whether it is a good thing for us to ac-cept new citizens—in our difficult position—who don't even feel bound to disguise their lack of any loyalty to the society that offers them a refuge—that's another matter.'

'Positive feelings of loyalty are probably quite effectively re-placed by the fear of the alternative, don't you think?' Luders pre-tended that it was a theoretical discussion.

'Communism in general, you mean? Or the certainty of long prison sentences?'

'Both, I suppose.'

'Self-interest is always the best guarantee of good behaviour,' said Malczewska bitterly. 'And nobody can dictate what people think to themselves.'

'I don't think anybody wants to do that. Not here at any rate. But we can't be expected to feel as you do. You see, just as you are entitled—here—to think as you like, so are we entitled to object to your hostility.'

Luders laughed. 'Since that's the foundation of your preference for Austria over Poland, you can hardly argue with that, eh?'

'I don't argue with it. But why should I disguise my preference for my own home and people?'

'That's quite different from what you obviously said before,' said Julia shrewdly. 'And, if you can't go home, neither do you have to stay in a place you so dislike. You could go to America, for instance.'

'They don't accept immigrants with physical disabilities,' said Malczewska with a kind of uncomfortable sullenness.

'Ah. Then Austria has some advantages?'

'It seems to be a kind of unwritten policy, to make it easy for people who could formerly have claimed Austrian citizenship, if they want to become Austrians now.' Luders carefully kept up the impersonal pretence.

'Probably. I don't really know, but it may well be. But in Frau Malczewska's case the matter goes a good deal further than that. She comes from Vilna, I believe. At the time you mean Vilna was Russian. It was never Austrian.'

'I would never have suspected you of so much geographical knowledge, my love,' said Kerenyi coming in. 'And historical geography, at that.'

'I'm cheating,' said his wife laughing up at him as he bent down to salute her offered cheek. 'I asked Robert about it when he and Lali were arranging the job with Hella for Frau Malczewska.'

'Why? Did my nationality come into the question?' asked Malczewska, obviously surprised at this.

'Not then, I think. When you first worked for the British at their library.'

'Strange. Nobody ever said a word to me about it.'

'I don't suppose they would,' explained Georgy. 'They'd hardly expect you to be pro-Russian even if you were born a Russian subject.'

'Just because I was,' she corrected.

They busied themselves for a little while with a tray of small tidbits without saying any more.

'I'm grateful to Inglis and Lali,' said Malczewska at last abruptly. 'They did their best and it's not their fault the job went wrong.'

'Well I'm glad that's agreed at least,' Julia was mild.

'I mean,' Malczewska went on grudgingly, 'I'm grateful to them personally. As for the *British*, they owed me anything they could do for me. I don't have to be grateful to them.'

'The British?' Julia was astonished. 'What on earth . . . ?'

'I'm talking about the War,' cried Malczewska with savage impatience. 'If the English hadn't interfered, the War would never have spread to western Europe. Hitler always meant to go east, he would have attacked the Ukraine the following spring if France and England had remained neutral. Then we might have been at least partly saved because we should have been necessary to Germany.'

'What nonsense!' said Kerenyi brusquely, 'you've ignored the Nazi-Soviet pact. Once Poland was overrun neither Stalin nor Hitler needed to take the Poles into account.'

'I'm very far from ignoring the pact. War between the partitioners is the inevitable consequence of dividing Poland. That's history.'

'Ah. Poland as the navel of the world,' murmured Luders.

'The old partition of Poland lasted a couple of hundred years, not five minutes,' Kerenyi objected quietly. 'Neither Russia nor Germany accepted the settlement of 1919, and the independence of Poland was bound to be short. It may be true that Hitler would have continued his drive to the east during the next campaign season—if he'd been able to ignore western Europe—but that would hardly have helped Poland.'

'You're wrong. Neutral western countries would have kept diplomats and journalists in Poland. Then the SS would have been under control, just as it was in Germany itself until after the United States entered the war. And the fighting would have been further east.'

'It's perfectly understandable that you Poles must construct legends about the War to comfort yourselves and blame others for what happened to you. But if Poland was to follow any reasonable foreign policy, it had to be based on the friendship of one of your neighbours, and it had to begin in the early twenties, long before a Hitler could make such a policy impossible. Granted Poland's fear of Russia, the friendship was bound to be with Germany. There was never any sign of such an intention. It never existed.'

'But that's just it!' Malczewska sounded almost desperate. 'You're determined not to understand me! Typical of you radical journalists, fearless attackers of clichés! You're full of clichés of your own. You accept the Allied version of how the War started just because they won—and gave you your licence to publish your magazine. You never seek further. But in fact. . . .'

'Now wait a moment,' interrupted Kerenyi with some warmth. 'I may be a licensed oppositionist, as you right-wing extremists call it. But I must remind you that I was in opposition both before 1938 and after, which was at first damned unpopular and later deadly dangerous. God knows, I don't want to set up as a hero. But you can't simply turn the patience of the western Allies nowadays towards dissenters, into a charge of cowardice on my part.'

'I didn't mean it like that,' Malczewska disowned, although she was aware and so were her hearers, that the gibe was intended to mean just what Kerenyi accused her of. 'I mean just what you say yourself. The Polish Colonels were so stupid they never saw the danger of quarrelling with both their neighbours, let alone the Czechs! They could see only their own 15th-century bravura, and went on seeing nothing else, even after the Molotov-Ribbentrop pact made invasion a matter of days. And then the British jumped in with their histrionic gesture! Just when it could do most harm—just when they should have counselled caution—just when the Polish government should have backed down and waited for the thieves to fall out as Hitler always intended!'

'Whatever Hitler intended, it wasn't visible then and it's a theory now, no more. And as for waiting, the French and British did wait. Until most of Europe was overrun. War between Russia and Germany was by no means certain in 1939. If Stalin didn't expect it, why should Daladier or Chamberlain have been less blind?'

'But they ran straight into the War they all feared!' Malczewska almost begged in her frustration.

'Matter of fact, there's something in that,' muttered Luders. 'They ought to have seen that Hitler moving east was advantageous to themselves. There was at least a good chance that Germany would become embroiled with Russia.'

During this conversation Frau Lisl was coming in and out with large platters of cold meats, cheeses and fruits which she spaced out on the table so that the guests could take what they wished as they felt like eating.

'This hindsight is all so theoretical,' sighed Julia. 'A glass of wine holds more immediate interest—for me, at least.' And she reached for one of the slender green bottles.

'There's just no talking to you,' said Malczewska helplessly. 'You're all, at bottom, abominably frivolous.'

'I suppose I am, though Georgy is sometimes anything but—quite uncomfortably pompous, he can be.' Julia agreed, her attention on the food. 'Have some *Geselchtes*? It smells heavenly. Horseradish? Black bread or white? I'm ravenous, aren't you?'

'I am a bit hungry,' admitted Malczewska ungraciously.

'One thing about 1939 that still puzzles me,' said Kerenyi, reverting to the conversation where the appearance of supper had left it, 'is the failure of conventional diplomacy. One can hardly believe now that the French knew what they were getting into when they declared war. And the British? How can they even have considered going into armed combat with an ally in the state France was in?'

'Bad Intelligence,' said Luders with his mouth full.

'They thought of themselves as the predestined victors—the mood of 1918,' suggested Malczewska. 'If they showed they meant business, Hitler would not attack Poland.'

'Impossible. After Prague?'

'They *must* have believed that the mere threat of help to Poland would give Germany pause,' she insisted. 'They can't have envisaged actually starting a campaign. It would have been obvious at once that they couldn't even reach Poland without going through Germany.'

'Good heavens, is that true?' Julia, who knew nothing of geography, stared at Kerenyi.

'It is an extraordinary thing, that,' he agreed. 'If only a little more were known, one might write something about that. It's always puzzled me.'

178

'If you mention anything so tactless, you'll lose your editorial licence,' gibed Malczewska.

'Can I have some of that paprika chicken?' asked Kerenyi, determined not to quarrel again with their cantankerous guest.

'My dear chap, do let me help you,' Luders offered from his point of vantage near this dish.

'Do you suppose that some other watersheds of history were decided on commonplace mistakes like neglecting to look at the map?' asked Julia.

'Beware of too much pragmatism,' warned Kerenyi laughing. 'Are you by any chance wondering about Cleopatra misjudging Roman strength?'

'Ah, Cleopatra! I hear you're going to get everything you want for the *A & C* production.' Malczewska seized on the subject, using the abbreviation already in use by the company for the Shakespeare play.

'It looks like it, at the moment,' agreed Julia cautiously.

'I think not only just for the moment. At least as far as Frau Schneider's influence goes. She and her allies won't be very vocal for a time. However well her scandal was arranged with the Press, the public will be pretty reserved.' A look shot at Kerenyi showed that Malczewska already knew that the Press conference took place at his suggestion.

'What a place for gossip this is,' Luders took note. 'I see one has to be discreet in business here.'

'That's not gossip,' she said, 'that's news.'

'Did you think of that, Julie?' asked her husband. 'But of course, that's what you were so thoughtful about on the way back from Rommersburg.'

'It did occur to me, I admit,' answered Julia. 'But I didn't want to say much until a meeting or two either confirmed my idea, or not.'

'As a matter of fact, since Frau Schneider has fired me, I can tell you that she herself was calculating on a certain amount of—difficulty. From the moment she knew Tenius was back, as I realise now, she took up two proposals for next summer's festival season and is full of various other negotiations. Just in case she can't play much in Vienna next year.'

'It's still better for me not to talk much about it,' said Julia and since she clearly did not mean to be drawn into a discussion, both

Malczewska and Kerenyi, for their different reasons, dropped the subject.

'I'm still not sure about you as Cleopatra,' Malczewska slightly changed her direction. 'You're too—too imposing. Too much presence.'

'Yes, but I don't see her as the plaything of fate, at all,' objected Julia. 'And I hope nobody else in the German-speaking theatre will by this time next year.'

'How d'you mean? Don't you intend to play it as an erotic drama?'

'That too. But not only that. . . .' Julia pulled the text towards her from a side table and began to illustrate her view of the play by quotations and juxtapositions, and in a few minutes the two women were deep in an analysis of it. Julia was surprised to find that her companion's knowledge both of the text and its historical roots was hardly less than her own. She herself was profoundly preoccupied by it, and after several readings had the main part in her head by a process of her own in which she did not need to commit the lines to memory by rote. Finding they understood each other, they began eagerly to strip the work down to its fundamentals of theme and action, stress and balance and interaction. To a layman they were unintelligible, and it seemed to Luders that they were squabbling, so impassioned did their discussion become, but to Julia it offered a fund of perfectionist and astringently precise stimulus to her own understanding. For the first time in their unhappy acquaintance she discovered the value of the abrasive, combative and uncompromising quality of Malczewska's mind. She was a committed creature of the theatre, to whom nothing needed to be explained and who cared only for the play. Conventions and traditions meant nothing to Malczewska and she took the well-known barriers of public, critics and theatrical technicians into account only to reject their influences.

'There's one big technical problem for you,' she said, flipping over the pages of the script as she counted some complexity with a scowl of concentration. 'All this *movimento*. All this inning and outing. The costumes are going to hamper your concept if you don't get the private sort of clothes much shorter and simpler than the state robes. D'you see how I mean—you'll simply never get about in all that congealed Nefertiti stuff? And a distinct difference would account for Cleo being able to go drinking with Antony in her own city without being recognised, roistering in taverns, you'd expect her to be mobbed if she were seen. They need to be quite divorced from formal clothing in design.'

'But that's clear,' Kerenyi overheard this and unwisely intervened. 'The under garments of the great must have been the loose tunics and loin-binding worn by the ordinary people, so that all Cleopatra would have to do to be private is to leave off her magnificent gowns.'

'You don't understand a thing about it,' cried Malczewska irritably. 'That's just what I don't mean, that vague stab at naturalism. We've had that stupid stuff for generations. I mean she should wear altogether changed clothes, as if she were dressing up as a private person.' She rounded on Julia as if it were she who had annoyed her. 'It's your notion that she was first and foremost a statesman and monarch—yes? Well then, she has to be quite changed when she's being Antony's trollop! Surely that's obvious?'

'You never produced *A & C* did you?' asked Julia somewhat later. 'I mean, you know it so well. . . .'

'I wish I could,' answered Malczewska, in a tone of almost hungry longing. 'I'd like to produce everything Shakespeare wrote.' She laughed suddenly. 'It's odd to think of it, when I started work with my father at fifteen, you were still a pampered child of the civil service patriciate in Vienna. My father was manager and actor too, at the theatre in Vilna then. So I got a liberal education, as you might say. You have to be an all-rounder on that sort of small-town stage and I turned my hand to everything. In the first year or so, I even acted, but I had no talent. Too unable to simulate, too wooden and awkward. But I must have showed a gift for directing quite early; my father used me a lot when he was feeling lazy— that's a euphemism for drinking bouts. I could impose my view of a play on other people, make them see what I saw, somehow. And in spite of the censorship we succeeded in staging several things that were covertly anti-Russian. Sometimes my father went too far and we got into trouble. *Julius Caesar*, for instance—a bit too anti-tyrannical! Another time, it must have been towards the end of that War, because there was rioting, I remember. We produced an adaptation of Tolstoy's *Hadji Murad* done by a young Polish writer, and they both landed in gaol—I was let off lightly, being a girl of eighteen or thereabouts. Then there was the Revolution and that was marvellous. We could do as we liked.'

'And when the young writer came out of prison, you married him?'

'How did you know that?' Malczewska's voice changed to quick suspicion.

'Everybody's voice changes when they speak of somebody they care about.'

'Yes, I cared about him. He was handsome. I never fell out of love with him again, though we were never happy. There were always other girls, and I made a fuss. If I'd known how little time we had for private worlds, I would have been different. But I wouldn't have been, of course.'

'One never is, I suppose.'

'The last time I saw him, the day the reserves were called up in August, it was our wedding day. Silly, isn't it? And I wasted time worrying because his tunic was too tight. . . . The boy was eleven then, they had the same name. He was captured in the first days with his whole company. After that everything became all savage and bloody, life was like wild beasts gone mad in a menagerie fire. I saw one once, in a circus. They say animals don't behave like that in the jungle, only when they are denatured by man. There wasn't much disorder to be seen by the time you visited Warsaw in 1942, it was almost organised, the killing. Like in Napoleon's time, order reigned in Warsaw. The only other man I ever went to bed with was that poor little SS Lieutenant, Schultze. . . . Yes, we only had eighteen years together. It's not long for a lifetime, is it?'

'You must have hated Schultze, poor boy.'

'I did. I did.' She stared in front of her, the ruined features set in familiar hatred. 'Poor boy, and he knew. I think he took it as punishment. He certainly knew why I did it, and what I was doing, because he used to offer me tips without me having to wheedle them out of him. I could never have gone on with it, just for the Underground. But I felt I was protecting the boy by knowing what their orders were in the district.'

'It's a mercy one can't know what is going to happen. If I'd known. . . .'

They were silent for a space, filled with the bitterest memories, until Julia shook her head quickly with a movement like a shudder, to free herself from such thoughts. She did not tend by character as Malczewska did, to dwell on the irrecoverable past but that, she now told herself, was no virtue of hers. She was able to continue her profession, and prosperity was assured to her. She had by no means lost everything, friends, language, country. She did not, at that moment, extend this thought of comfort to her private life, yet the sensation of that afternoon returned, a largeness, a full spaciousness of being, which was new and which she was not used to. To draw them away from hateful memories, she changed the subject.

'You must have been producing your *Hamlet*—I remember you telling me about it—when I was still at the Academy?'

'No, no. That was in '33 and you were well established by then as a future "great". I saw you about that time as Helena, when we made a long visit to Vienna. How we envied you the Burg!'

'I had a lot of luck in those years. There just didn't seem to be much competition among the younger actresses, and roles fell into my lap.'

'There's no such thing as luck,' said Malczewska. 'Not in work.'

'Not directly, perhaps. But I had luck in an important indirect way. I was settled and happy after I married. If I'd gone on diffusing my energies in scattered love affairs, I shouldn't have been so single-minded. That was in '31, when we married. It was Georgy who introduced us, you know. . . .'

'Did you have so many love affairs, then?'

'Many? I don't know what many is, but I had several. Not all of them actual affairs, you know, but all accompanied by that frantic excitement and the upset of judgement and the loss of self-confidence. Looking back now, I don't think it suited my temperament. It does suit some people, but I was so strictly brought up to feel *responsible*—I suppose that is a part of me that comes from my father, like your talents from your father—that I always felt much was expected of me. Even before I was pampered at school, being the youngest and the prettiest too. I had great notions of myself as a girl. It all sounds rather humourless now, but you know how it is. In those days one was supposed to take things seriously and I just never got out of the habit. Not until this War. That broke it all down, with every other standard. Even the way we talk. My father would turn in his grave if he could hear me sometimes. But when things are dominated by people like Tenius, really everything is either destroyed or else it loses its reality. I mean, I can't say it properly, but it's impossible to believe that even the most beautiful words matter when—when. . . . I don't know, just everything is horrible.'

'But later—for me, anyway—you cling, you absolutely grab, at what is always valid. You have to, or you'd go mad.'

'That's true, that happened to me, and then the belief came back gradually that what we are doing is important, that it does matter not only to do it but to do it well, as well as one can.'

'You see,' said Malczewska slowly, almost shyly, 'Tenius is a catalyst, forcing us all to identify ourselves again, state our positions, as you might say. I've thought of nothing else for days, going through a whole series of violent changes of opinion about him.'

'Changes of opinion about Tenius?' Kerenyi asked with surprise, as he caught the name.

'Yes, about him. At first I assumed he must be dragged back to Breslau where at least we could be sure he'd be tortured before he was hanged. But then—I don't know why—it seemed less and less important what happened to him. As if he were dead already, almost, and the only thing that mattered about him was what he could make *me* do. As if he no longer exists but what he represents is still there in some mysterious form, an influence. And what matters is how far that wicked influence can still make us behave in his kind of way; us, who still live.'

'Hmm,' Luders sounded dissatisfied at this vagueness. 'But will he be dragged back to Breslau? I'd rather have a hint at what the Polish exiles mean to do than some miasma of influence.'

As they could all see from her expression Malczewska was about to answer him sharply. But she changed her mind, hesitated, and narrowed her eyes to consider what she said.

'As a matter of fact, I don't know,' she said at last in a self-consciously off-hand fashion. 'Our people are pretty annoyed with me for breaking with his wife just when they wanted all the information as they could get. They haven't told me anything for the last day or so.' She shrugged her shoulders, crookedly pulling against the useless arm. 'There's talk of putting me before a secret tribunal —a sort of *Feme* court—for disobeying orders. . . .'

It was not because the other three knew Malczewska would not tell them about the conspiratorial methods of her countrymen that none of them asked more questions about this piece of news. They reverted to more general comments because her manner of answering Luders betrayed a disingenuity which she either was unable, or did not entirely wish, to hide.

The very circumstance that Malczewska was there, at her own suggestion that evening, suddenly became a new factor in the situation. It was possible that she was present at the orders of the exiles; even possible that the awkwardly managed scene with Hella Schneider had been deliberate because they—Kerenyi and Luders—were more important potential sources of news about Tenius than a wife so determined to have no direct contact with the sick and abandoned scapegoat. The intense interest in Julia's professional concerns, though certainly real enough in itself, could have as well another purpose underlying but not conflicting with its half-suggested one of working her way into a new job. That ambition on Malczewska's part was fairly clear and understandable, but it may not have been her only intention in engaging Julia's interest. Julia herself did not work out in her mind these implications, but simply behaved with discretion about a possibility which would need further consideration and some discussion with her colleagues before it could advance towards realisation. If she took the statement about the exiles' anger with Malczewska at all seriously it was solely as another evidence of that romantic attitude in the Poles which the Polish woman herself described as of the 15th century rather than of their own time.

'Don't see how Tenius could be dragged very far without the people doing the dragging getting themselves as well as Tenius into the hands of the Polish secret police.' Kerenyi was in the act of lighting a cigar as Luders spoke.

'He wouldn't have to be taken far,' replied Malczewska. 'Only behind the locked doors of a dozen houses in Vienna. I know of at least two in the IVth District. From then on he would never be seen again, only heard of as having been tried and executed.'

'What? Even now—still?' Luders' voice betrayed the levity of unbelief.

'It's probably true, I dare say,' said Kerenyi. 'And no doubt some of the exiles are in contact with the Polish or the Russian police, if not in their pay.'

Malczewska did not flare up at this imputation and her self-control confirmed the two men in their supposition. For Kerenyi's provocative remark was intentional, and if Malczewska were really acting without a second and covert purpose she could be expected

185

to deny the charge of co-operation with the hated Communist police with all her usual asperity. But she did not do that; indeed she made no reply at all.

Only as she and Luders were leaving did Malczewska return to the subject of Tenius. As the two women shook hands at parting, Malczewska looked from Julia to Kerenyi and Luders and her dark face showed once again the hoarded anger that was its settled expression.

'Fate's played us a dirty trick over Tenius,' she admitted, her harsh voice almost a murmur. 'Ill, hunted, it takes all the salt out of revenge. Sometimes I have the terrible suspicion that the whole tragedy, from first to last, has no meaning.'

XV

In spite of the two separate conversations during the evening, Kerenyi did hear his wife's remark about his having introduced her to her first husband. When they were alone, later, he asked her about that, about the occasion which he no longer recalled and about the circumstances of it; but she did not carry the event in her mind as one clearly frontiered incident any more than he did. The moment of introduction was merged into a diffused memory of its consequences and just as Julia retained no memory of meeting Kerenyi for the first time, or rather, no sense of once not having known him, so the first meeting with Franz Wedeker had spun itself into the web of what was gone, the resurrected past of before the War and the still vivid past of the War itself and its ending. They were clear that it must have been late in 1929 or early in 1930 and Julia was sure that it happened during cold weather for she carried a picture of snow both spiralling in a fierce wind at night and of snow lying in drifts with the sunlight on it, among tall beech trees.

They must, she thought, have gone walking in the Vienna Woods, perhaps the first time she and Franz did something alone together. It was strange that an occasion so momentous should have blended into generalised recall and they decided that it must have taken place at one of many gatherings where a number of strangers came together, perhaps a gathering that repeated itself several times within a few days—the New Year? Carnival?—so that one moment had spread itself over a period and the future lovers were hardly aware of when they became conscious of each other, of standing out from the surrounding movement of companions. That this happened quickly was definite, for Julia could see as if in a mirror a moment so soon after the first awareness that it caused her a trepidation she could still feel. A sensation was held for ever of being slightly shocked at herself for yielding so quickly to what then seemed a momentary desire.

Franz embodied a particular elegance of outward form paired with a matching fastidiousness of mood and of movement, a very refined tactile delicacy which reflected his—later discovered—spiritual sensibility in a combination unusual for a man, or at any rate unknown until then to Julia.

She was, she knew, of much harder material than Franz had been, made of a clearly outlined, tensile moral fabric like a metal. She knew now that this hard, vibrantly sprung inner quality was exactly suited to challenge a much gentler nature, although one accustomed to a seductive success with women which gave his approach a certainty and confidence one might not have expected in so apparently diffident a person. Thus his progression from attraction to action was swift and had a charm of unexpectedness as well as its more expectable, ardently desired sensuality. Coming as it did, as one of a series of only partly realised amorous experiments, which could equally easily have become habitual or have been dropped altogether as not worth the trouble, the first encounter had a quality of triumph. It seemed easy; it not only just happened, but happened with a completeness and pleasurableness that invited repetition at once. Within a few days the repetition was an obsessive passion that effectively shut out the rest of the world and made any further experiment for either of them as impossible as it was unnecessary. Franz and Julia had found what is probably much more rare than the constant harping upon it, which already then dominated all the minor arts and imitation arts, gives many people to suppose; they found satisfaction in the flesh without effort or pretence, pleasure without trying. As the knowledge that this pleasure could always be repeated, extended, and was not going to lessen dawned upon them, the obsession released itself and their relation took itself for granted long before it occurred to them to marry. What was taken for granted was an intimate erotic and emotional concern with each other, and not each with himself and his own body; it was the other who mattered. Because everything they did and felt came so easily and naturally, not only their mutual relation but their own characters began to return to a state of innocence, all their varied previous experience became meaningless and they lived together in a childlike erotic exclusiveness which was hardly touched by the transition to marriage.

Because of the difference of religion this transition was an unceremonial formality and probably neither of them ever realised it as the fundamental change of impressive import that the wedding is to most lovers. In fact until, years later, outside forces thrust a tremendous responsibility upon Julia, and an equally shattering loss of responsibility on Franz, they were not really married in any psychological sense. Julia moved into a domestic arrangement already in existence for several years since the deaths of Franz's parents within a few months of each other; her profession reduced her small housewifely concern to little more than a relief that nothing new was expected of her. It was some years before the remark of a casual acquaintance drew either Franz' or Julia's notice to their childlessness and this state seemed as natural as the rest of their relationship.

It was in Julia's work that the fruit of their marriage issued in the outer world, not in children. Educated by her husband's sensitive artistic insight, and released from the search and the dissatisfaction of incomplete love affairs, she became an almost infinitely better actress and what she said to Malczewska so many years later was no more than the truth—Franz liberated her power.

On the professional life of Franz the effect of their communion was less immediately positive. The simplicity and realness of their private life was the first influence that made him, although unconsciously, critical of the strains, compromises and insincerities of political activity. Even if the proscription of opposition parties had not soon almost entirely retired him and his fellow-Socialists from public life, Franz would probably have turned more and more towards theory and less towards action. The notion that a political opinion obliges its holder to engage actively in public life was in the thirties even more widespread than later. This was especially so in central Europe where a universal factional concern with political affairs shadowed in advance a similar development of equal negativeness in western Europe and one immensely more unfortunate in the eastern part of the Continent. Franz Wedeker was one of the first political thinkers to realise that the obsessive minute concern of the general public with the administration of affairs is not a sign of a healthy body politic but rather of the decay of serious political life, leading to the diffusion of ordinary people's genuine and proper concern for their own interests and to the universal lying of constant propaganda.

These memories, disentangled in the course of a long and rambling conversation, led back imperceptibly towards the present until Kerenyi said with an air of ruefully comical surprise that he supposed their present venture into matrimony was, in reality, the first marriage of either of them instead of the second.

'My first was a wartime love affair. I was still in my *teens*, come to think of it. It hardly survived the separation, when I went to Krainburg and first met Franz early in '18. And you, by your own account, scarcely took note of the change—if it was a change. One did, looking back, always have the feeling with you and Franz that there was none of the thicket of complications between you that make up marriage. Other people too have said that, from time to time in the past, about you.'

'You do remember your own first meeting with Franz, then?'

'Oh sure. We were both volunteer officer-cadets and we'd both cut off the University to volunteer, so friendship was almost inevitable when we were thrown together. And we were posted to the same unit, as well. I arrived in the evening and the mixed lot at base, waiting for postings, were pretty cool to me because I'd been sent by some chance to a completely German and Croatian Mess. The Hungarians were very unpopular by that time and they probably expected to get the usual ranting chauvinism from me. So I kept as quiet as possible. And Franz was keeping quiet too, for other reasons.'

'You mean, because he was Jewish?'

'Oh no. That was only a drawback if you insisted on emphasising it and Franz was always bored by the nationalist questions. Even as a boy he was too bright to be fooled by that illusion, though of course he didn't say so openly in the Mess or he'd have been in trouble with the various cliques. No, he just hated military life, which I rather fitted into.

'D'you know, I even remember our first conversation? We'd been collecting some piece of equipment and walked back to our billet together. He was being funny about his name—too ordinary, you know. All his family wanted him to have some much grander name, but his mother had a crush on the Emperor and insisted on Franz when he was born. Wedeker, he said, that was all right, they'd already fixed the surname. And then his mother goes and spoils everything by naming him Franz. . . . It was typical of Franz that he made fun of his family's ambitions in just the same way he treated every other snobbery, and did it so naturally that I don't think I ever heard his background mentioned by anyone but himself. I suppose it may really have been a kind of defensiveness, but if it was, it wasn't noticed. And boys of that age can be fairly brutal to each other—no, I think it was natural. In fact, at first it was he who took me under his wing. It was bad then to be a Magyar except in an Hungarian regiment. It was all right after we were posted up the line. After that things got so rough there was no time for anything but hanging on to life and limb.'

'Odd, I've always heard there was a lot of anti-Jewish feeling in the Army.'

'Well, most of the Jewish officers were lawyers or doctors so they tended to be in non-combatant branches of the Army and that separated them from the rest. But Franz was just a stray cadet as I was, and posted to a unit where he was saddled with duties really belonging to much older officers. The men liked him because he cared about them as much as he could in those conditions. We were sent to a sector high up among the crags, and wounds were terrible. There was splintering rock as well as shells and shrapnel, and it took a long journey down the mountains even to a dressing station. You can imagine we lived like chamois at the best of times, and mostly it was not the best of times.

'The men knew what an officer was worth who worried about their rations. Everyone knew how badly off the Italians were, they had hardly any officers up at the front and the men suffered shamefully from bad food and neglect. That is, our men knew until about August. Then they began to get shifty, about the time we were moved down to the Isonzo flats and the mass straggling started.'

'You were still together, then?'

'For a few more weeks—I can't remember exactly, but I was sent to the reserve and we were separated. Not that there was any reserve, by then.'

'Why? Were you wounded?'

'No. I'm afraid because I was Hungarian. We were known to be defeatist and there was a lot of separatist talk that affected the other nationalities in mixed units; a lot of regiments were very mixed by then. I was pretty ashamed at being taken out of the line in that obvious way. I think that may be why I came here to Vienna, after, instead of going back to Budapest.'

'Poor Georgy.'

'I can never explain how it felt, not even now.' He got up and moved restlessly to and fro, angered by an old injustice. 'We weren't defeated, and certainly not by the poor bastards of Italians. The War was not over, it was something quite different. The whole administration dissolved and left us helpless. We didn't know where we belonged, or whom to turn to. One day I was ostracised as a Magyar, which was unjust; the next as an officer when Soldiers' Councils appeared from nowhere. That was even more unjust. The Emperor's manifesto, and then the offer of an armistice, we just heard of them from afar. Nobody knew what was happening, the men began to give up their weapons, and the Italians came in and claimed hundreds at a time as prisoners. That was too much. I just cleared off; I wasn't going to be captured by a mob like the Italians. The regimental depot was at Klagenfurt by then, and I shall never forget the empty barracks when I tried to report. . . . Then there was the proclamation freeing us from the oath to the Emperor. I was only eighteen and at that age such things have an immense power over the mind. I was frightened by the thought of the broken oath, but even more frightened by being left alone when it was lifted. Afterwards we were all ostracised again, as criminals responsible for the whole War, as if we'd done it all ourselves. All I needed to do to escape that odium, was to declare myself a Magyar and then I'd be a citizen of a Succession Democracy under the patronage of the former enemy. I just couldn't do that. There was a lot wrong with the old Monarchy, but it wasn't criminal, it wasn't militarist, and it wasn't solely to blame for the War.'

'I've never thought of that, about being scared of being left alone when the Army dissolved. . . .'

'It's not a thing women would think of. But millions felt it, then. In Germany much more than here. That is where the Second World War began. The Inflation, and then the Depression later, only increased the trauma, they didn't deal the wound. Foreigners said later that the Germans—that included us—were a nation of sheep. But we'd always been able to trust our government, up to then. The trouble came from a virtue of the old order, not from a fault. It was the injustice, the ostracism. The whole of central Europe was a witches' cauldron of fear and anger for years, brewing away shut off from the outside world. And just as the fear began to heal, the anger to fade, the Depression threw everything back into hunger and misery again.'

'Perhaps in a way, Malczewska is right? Nobody abroad ever wastes a second of remorse for the Depression, and that, at least, can't have been our fault.'

'It goes deeper than that. Malczewska does have some reason in what she says, though not at *that time*. All the great powers wanted the first War. And a lot of people wanted the second, too. Not only in Germany.'

'But, Georgy—Hitler!'

'Of course, Hitler! A raving maniac. The remarkable thing is not that a Hitler appeared out of the mess, but that he didn't appear years before. But the time was ready for brutes. About the same time in Russia, Stalin was seizing power by the same mass-methods —only even worse.'

'Ah, politics,' she said. 'I'd rather hear about your love affairs.'

'And I'd rather hear about yours.'

'They ought to make you angry. You're unnatural.'

'They do, a bit. Just enough to be exciting.'

'Just the same, I notice that you don't tell me much about your wild past.'

'Trouble is, there were so many of them. I've forgotten half.'

'Georgy! Don't brag about your conquests. It's terribly vulgar.'

'Brag?' he said. 'I'm ashamed of it. I was always extremely choosy, as you will be the last person on earth to deny, so they were all delicious creatures and it's a sin to have forgotten them.'

Julia was just about to say more when he went on, abruptly and in a different tone.

'Did you ever have a lover during your marriage?'

'Not while Franz and I were lovers, no. Some time after it ended, there was Nando.'

'Yes, Nando was your safety-valve, that was always clear. I often wondered if anybody else noticed that aspect of your affair with him—it could have given you away.'

'I think Nando himself did, gradually. I think that's how he knew—as far as he ever knew.'

'You never said anything, of course?'

'Never. But equally of course, he knew something. After about the end of '41.' She ventured no nearer to that crisis in their lives which brought her to the verge of a nervous breakdown and cost Kerenyi his child's life and its mother's.

'I wouldn't like it if you'd been unfaithful to Franz,' he said.

'I was never even tempted, not once. But when it ended, it was so final, so irrecoverable that there was nothing there to hold on to. Simply nothing.'

'I think that was inevitable. In all the accounts I've heard of one partner hiding the other—and I've heard a number—there wasn't one where the personal bond didn't crumble away under the strain.'

Julia was silent for a space, and then she said, miserably, 'D'you suppose we shall always talk about it? Now that we've started?'

He looked at her with his steady, searching look which stirred her painfully, made her feel uncovered.

'I don't think so,' he said at last. 'It's just—we have to know.'

'I don't feel that about your past.'

'No, you didn't love any of my women. But I loved Franz.'

'The destruction,' she said, and putting up a hand, found there were tears on her face.

Yet for the first time she felt, with a sense of shock, that she would not now have it otherwise. Being unable to deceive herself, she admitted this sensation in spite of the shame attached to it. His eyes still penetrated her whole being; she was for the first time in her adult life altogether defenceless, at the mercy of another human being who could see, she knew it, into her innermost thoughts and beyond thought, beyond feeling into a realm of being in which, had there been words, the word emotion would have been meaningless. But there were no words, nor any other contact. There was an instant during which she might still have resisted the silent force of his will and in that instant she knew the fear of losing herself that she experienced once long ago in an outward crisis of fear and desperation; against this inward crisis her resilient hardness was no defence, for her own will was dissolving until nothing was left but his implacable intention. In the moment he saw that she would not now have it otherwise, that she abandoned the past and was conscious of abandoning it, he knew his moment was come and he could now subject her and rob her of her pride so that she could never again raise it like a banner against him.

This was the moment of battle threatened since the night of their return, but now the outcome was not in doubt. She took a step backward, just touching the Chinese cabinet so that her back was now literally against the wall. But he still did not move, only smiled at her.

'What is it?' he asked quietly, predatory and mocking. 'Are you afraid of me suddenly?'

'I think I am, a bit,' she said breathlessly.

'But why? You know I would never do anything you didn't wish me to do.'

'That's just what I'm afraid of.'

XVI

It was beginning, thought Hansi Ostrovsky, to look as if Hella were right and he glanced across at Julia for the tenth time during the discussion. He was aware of looking too often and in a particular way, but the exhausted vagueness, the dreaminess of her demeanour were so irritating to him that he could not resist the impulse to examine her face, to find in it an evidence, a lever for a reproach. Hella had repeated the remark made at the Heurigen more than once and the idea that she expressed in a slightly libidinous, smiling insinuation as 'devouring each other' was firmly now in Hansi's mind. He disliked it, and denied it with the welcome support of Monika, who thought it funny because to the adolescent the whole field of sensuality belonged to her own extreme youth and was still narcissism; she could not attach it to anything outside her own sensation or what could be visibly transferred from an innocent state of self discovery. He knew that the mirror image of her own delicate lasciviousness was what Monika found in his embraces and imagined in those of others, others turned always towards her own person. He adored this self-absorption in Kiki and would have been relieved to accept it as valid for this other relation whose atmosphere would otherwise constitute a threat, the menace of a passion that was more than a pleasant way of passing the time between more serious preoccupations. The possibility of such a comprehensive feeling attacked his own careful relegation of intimacy to a small fenced-in area of life, which is all he believed it could ever be because he had always made sure that that was all it was for him.

This system of self-protection was now assailed and in a way that undermined more than his love affair with Kiki, for here were no protestations, and no repetition of anything known or observed before in Julia's private life. She was simply turned wholly towards something else, not there; and this absence was new in her. Just after the War, he thought bitterly, she was 'there'; very much so, the powerful consciousness consumed with resentment, scorn, rejection and self-questioning—but there. Rage, hatred even, but presence.

How had Hella known that this would happen? The first slight references came before the sudden and private wedding, weeks before the end of last season, before Julia requested two alterations in the last month's programme: which ought to have warned him. They were obviously plotting then to go away for the whole summer, serve them right that all the conversations which gently converged in plans for this coming season were made without Julia, and ignored her own express wishes. That he himself had forgotten completely about the proposal of the Greek trilogy was not surprising for there had been nobody to remind him, to press the idea. Instead, the two Shakespeare plays; and now, now that *Cleopatra* was left alone to bear the weight of its own risks without the certain success of *Macbeth* to support it, by the incredible ill-luck of Tenius turning up again, Julia was behaving like this. It had seemed such a symmetrical arrangement, and now half the season was spoiled. Should he perhaps have refused to give in to the demand to drop Hella's long-awaited chance to play Lady Macbeth? No, that would have been asking for trouble with the public, always ready to find its own smiling cynicism in its self-elected mentors—just that play, in the circumstances . . . ! Hella herself had not even argued.

'We shall have to go over all this ground again,' Hansi said, looking with exasperated resignation at his watch. He did not explain what he meant because of a feeling that in Julia's mood it might be unwise to push her. This warning was a memory from the War when sometimes the strains of some extraneous preoccupation would disperse Julia's concentration. But that was a grasp from outside pulling at her, a pull from something Hansi recognised, but was then dimly aware of not wanting to consider. Now he was bewildered as well as irritated by a sensation of her inner will failing; formerly she clung to work as a refuge and concentration might sometimes be forced, but always forced by herself, as a relief from that other concern.

Ostrovsky was not the only one present who noticed that Julia was not herself. Jochen Thorn was aware, although he did not show his awareness as Hansi did, that she kept catching at his thoughts, listening to his contributory ideas laggingly as if they were beyond her comprehension rather than familiar before he got his words out, as they should have been.

A little later Monika came in, only slightly unpunctual, to collect her lover for the midday meal.

'Shall I wait?' she asked, before greeting the people at the table and then, her eyes fixing on Julia, she stared.

'You don't look at all well,' she said. 'Are you all right?'

'A bit tired,' said Julia, smiling mechanically. 'This Hamburg friend of Georgy's likes night-life.' Monika was satisfied but Thorn stole a look at Julia's shadowed eyes and the lie was patently obvious to him; he was notorious himself for his love affairs and knew perfectly well that this visible hangover was not the result of dancing until dawn.

'Where did you go?' Monika wanted to know and Thorn at once covered the hesitation of Julia's answer with a loud question to Hansi; for the possible choice was small and there was a danger that Julia would pick on a place at which one or other of those present had really been the previous evening. Julia did not look at them as Hansi pulled round a chair for Monika and in the movement both her question and its lack of an answer were lost. The knowledge that she was betraying herself made Julia try to pull herself together, but the very cause of her exhaustion made it difficult for her to take her own dignity seriously for more than a few moments, and the implication that she had been at a night-club gave her a spurious cover which allowed her to yawn openly.

'You don't seem to be taking much interest, Julie, I must say,' Hansi was suddenly openly fretful. 'I'm beginning to feel frightfully worried about the whole production. . . .'

'Beginning?' said Julia, yawning again. 'You haven't liked it from the first. If you hadn't been dissuaded from the Greek plays, you'd never have let yourself in for anything so dangerous—but you felt you had to offer me a consolation. . . .'

'How—dissuaded?' Hansi began, and then was struck by the openness of Julia's attack, that she did not bother to hide what she meant, as if she could not bestir herself to be diplomatic. This was so far from her usual practice that he was again disconcerted and was tempted to reply that a major production could hardly be called a consolation prize, but was rather an advance on anything Julia herself had laid claim to. An obscure sensation of dishonesty in himself stopped him.

Kerenyi, he thought with a jealousy that existed only for the theatre, I never liked him really. Always knew there would be trouble with her if she married him. Disruptive brute.

'Oh, it's the challenge to the prejudices of the public Hansi fears,' offered Thorn, as an olive branch. 'We shall all go through several attacks of nerves before this thing is launched—you'll see.'

'It will be worth it, though,' said Anita, and pushed up the spectacles she lately wore for reading. 'Lunch time. The German art historians again tonight. See you at Sacher—yes?'

As they dispersed, Julia and Thorn were left together at the table gathering up papers.

'As your future dominating lover,' he said, pulling his aquiline features into a theatrical scowl, 'I advise you to get some sleep this afternoon. You look like hell. Beautiful hell, naturally, but hell.'

'Thanks,' she said, 'I will.'

Quite a chap, he thought looking after her as she went; quite a chap. I was wrong in the War when I thought they were lovers then. It could never be like this now if it weren't a new passion.

She was so intensely impatient to be at home that it did not occur to her that the domestic luncheon was establishing itself, exactly as she had denied it would. But as the cross-draught of full summer greeted her at the open door she became aware too of a great difficulty in facing him. Her heart, that excellently attuned organ the presence of which she rarely had occasion to notice, lurched within her and began to beat heavily. She would have turned away but that she could see him awaiting her through another open door. Equally impossible to show the cowardice she felt; the indecision drew her into the long room, all light and colour.

The tall, slightly crooked figure turned, the hawk nose and deep-set eyes, so familiar and so strange, faced her and for a second she saw reflected her own panic in a quite different form, as he took in her exhausted face.

He moved towards her and she towards him until he could take her hands and kiss one after the other. He did not ask how she felt because he could see that whatever kind of a morning she had passed, she was now easy in the display of his concern; the unsureness went and she leaned her weary head for a moment against his scarred neck.

'What! Champagne?' she asked, over his shoulder, softly.

'But of course. Luders sent it. Trust a German to do the right thing in the wrong way. Or at the wrong moment.' .

'But, it's very much the right moment. Champagne—and French at that—makes just possible the return to kitsch.'

'I think he can't have intended it quite like that?'

'No. I suppose an apology for his—even for Tenius'—presence . . . But that is surely the essence of tact, to answer a state of affairs with the right answer without knowing the circumstances?'

'Hm. I don't think I care for you finding Berthold a genius of tact.'

'Why not? Tact being the correct attribute for an outsider. . . .'

'Ah. That's better.'

All this time he was kissing whatever part of her neck, hair, forehead, he could reach from his superior height without changing her chosen position. And presently she raised her head and looked directly at him, whereupon he kissed her hands again in thanks and released her, to open the champagne.

'It's queer Barber didn't come round while he was here for Hella's press conference,' said Julia idly, as they stood side by side at the open window.

'I think he's still here, but presumably working hard. He'll show up when he has time. I can't imagine him being in Vienna without seeing his one-time enemy.'

'Is this Hella scandal such a big story for his paper, then?'

'I wouldn't have thought so. But he's probably doing his homework as he says, while he's here, on the Vienna end of the future trial. Going through whatever official documents there are and so on.'

'Allied or Viennese documents?'

'Both, I dare say. All archives are open to his newspaper, you know. Well, all avowable ones.'

'When I have time to think of it, I'm still worried about Tenius being tried. The defence would be only too glad to drag you in, if it could. Imply that everybody was involved and only a few are being made scapegoats.'

'If the defence gets Malpas, he'll drag in God and all angels. And I expect they will get him. He's done most of the big SS trials since Nuremberg. But I'm sure now Berthold is right. There's nothing to do but face it out and tell the truth.'

'Do you really think you may be called as a witness?'

'Only if the defence can find contributory evidence as to Tenius having condemned the gas chambers fearlessly to his Party chiefs, I should think.'

'Contributory evidence?'

'Besides his own report. That alone would be too easily torn apart as a tactical manoeuvre—as Berthold said, it's as much evidence of Tenius' knowledge of his own guilt as anything else, by itself.'

'Berthold got off this morning?'

'Yes, at last. He will telephone when he's coming back.'

All the time they spoke, other things which would not be spoken of, were returning in disjointed glimpses, images distorted by overwrought senses and by lack of sleep into the visionary flickers of delirium, the dreams of fever. In the open windows across the street a dark, loose curtain billowed in the breeze and streamed out, changing its colour to red in the sunlight and then collapsing back over the window's edge as the wind dropped its force. Kerenyi saw her head thrown back in a moment of unbearable tension and felt her hair in his grip and then instantly the dark hair was flung out over pale linen as he awoke for a moment in the heat-misty dawn. He thought, Berthold must just have been leaving his hotel then for the drive out to the airport, and it seemed incredible that anybody should do anything so senseless.

The housekeeper approached without sound and handed Julia a note on an oval tray. This was unreal and the slight musical chink of a gold bracelet he had given her was unreal and so was the stir of white silk on the edge of his vision as she turned, saying something unheard to Frau Lisl. He was so intently aware, enmeshed in her being that these sounds and movements reached him as if after an interval, and through a mist which was actuality and which obscured reality. Julia said something and he knew without hearing it that she said 'it's from Robert' and offered him the note, already open—so she had taken it from its envelope? Automatically he put out his hand and felt a tiny jump in her own as he took the paper. She was looking at his hand, not at the note, and knowing that she too relived some moment, he raised his eyes to hers and with a shock felt as if with her eyes he saw his hand approach her, the still new gold band on the ring finger gleaming in a deflected faint light.

He was obliged to shake his head to clear it and he took a drink from the funnel-shaped glass before setting it down to read the short message that shivered a little in his grasp and told him that Robert would like to dine tonight, but if for some reason. . . .

They returned to here and now and, amazingly, the sun glowed; there was no deflected shaft of distant light in darkness; it was broad noon.

'If Robert's come up to town again, that must mean . . . Tenius.'

Kerenyi did not reply, but was transferred back to rationality with the thought that if Julia were right it was going to be difficult for Robert, whose duties enforced extreme discretion upon him.

'I feel as shaky as if I were ill,' said Julia. He saw that she referred to having dropped the envelope, with a brilliant red express stamp across its corner, and he bent down rather awkwardly to pick it up.

With unusual exactness Julia made a final inspection of her face before leaving the glass. It'll have to do, she decided of that familiar attribute, though my eyes still look a bit queer; thank heaven at any rate for an excuse not to go out tonight with those boring art people. She heard the doorbell in the distance and knowing Robert's punctuality, did not need to look at the clock to see that it was just gone eight o'clock.

As she came through the door by the wall of books a man of about thirty entered by the other door. He was in uniform, trim and smart; a square face, reserved and even careful in expression but with expressive brown eyes that searched the long room with a slightly nervous eagerness while he pulled at his tunic with the habitual gesture of one used to Army discipline, although it was already quite straight.

'Julie—darling—it's been an age,' he came quickly forward, speaking with the light, constrained modulation of English training. He spoke in English and Julia answered in that language as she held his shoulders, only a little taller than her own, and kissed his cheek.

'How nice you always smell,' she said appreciatively. 'Dear Robert, how are you all?'

'Portugal water,' he was pleased at her compliment. 'We're bursting with bucolic health, though Sebastian's a bit cross about the new baby. Lali sends her most special love.'

There were details here to be gone into for both of them after a separation of months, and examinations and appraisals to be made of the redesigning in the apartment. Between his being very brown and the astonishingly effective newness of the room they were in, which quite changed those pieces of furniture he recalled from its old shape and appearance; and between the new baby girl and its mother and the account of Greek islands which Robert had never yet seen, they very pleasantly brought themselves up to date for some time, talking both together. They dropped quickly into German, which Robert spoke almost perfectly, with the neutral tone and accent of a foreigner who avoids regional differences, although he frequently used Austrian expressions that might have puzzled a North German like Luders, if he had been present. At one point he broke off his narrative at some expression Julia used and stared at her with a freshened delight that contained something naïf and still boyish.

'Your voice!' he said, 'one always forgets how marvellous it is when you're not there . . .' and without pause they tumbled again into their double narrative and questioning.

The time was not long enough for any question to have arisen as to where Georgy might be—he was discussing a disputed evaluation of the just ended Salzburg Festival with the music critic of his journal—when that other member of the new household entered. So far the newness of the household had been confined to the rebuilding of it, to its framework; but some nuance of expression in the greetings of the two men introduced an implied question as to deeper innovations than removed walls or white paintwork. Not that anything was said by any of the three, but with the recapitulations of news it was apparent that the change was not completely taken for granted yet, that a possibility remained in the minds of close friends—though certainly not posed in words—that the new arrangement could not be quite assumed a settled affair. Somewhere there was a faint surprise that things had gone this far, an adjustment was required to envisage Georgy as entirely belonging here.

Kerenyi himself gave so little consideration to any domestic environment and so little felt any such thing as belonging to himself or as him belonging to it, that he had not, so far, been surprised to find himself living in the house. The adjustment of his mind to marrying the widow of his friend had, after all, been made at sufficient leisure during the four years of her own slow recognition of its inevitability. She had struggled with this idea for long enough and at last accepted it with many reservations, so that its appearance as a permanency was bound to be tentative in the minds of onlookers, even onlookers as loyally committed as Robert Inglis was.

The irreversability of what Julia had been persuaded into doing—that is, of publicly declaring her private involvement—and declaring it, though quite alone but for priest and witnesses, in a place sacred to their whole history as well as to Him who was called upon to witness the action, was only a few hours old in her mind. There was, certainly, from the afternoon of the ceremony no way back from the public fact of marriage since it was proclaimed in the Chapel of the ancient Imperial Palace and by a priest of their religion which admitted of no second thought in the matter. But in Julia's mind there had remained a split. The declaration which committed her to overt success no matter how shaky that success might appear to herself, committed her as well to the retreat into complete hypocrisy in the case of failure. But it was only in the last twenty-four hours that Julia faced an even more intractable commitment; the admission to herself that her entire being was tied to the achievement of a perilous balance—it could only be perilous for two such natures and two such highly formed personalities—in this intensely intimate relation. Hypocrisy might still save face in public, but nothing could save her from the inward crumbling of confidence if they now failed to establish a harmony; she was now totally involved with a creature as hard as herself and cleverer, who was capable of imposing his will on her to any extent he desired. No amount of respect and consideration shown by Kerenyi to her now in accordance both with his own decency and with the old customs of their society could alter this secret knowledge.

Instinctively recognising that the overflow of these emotions must be too strong to be disguised, especially from someone who knew her well and as a private person rather than as her public self, Julia had already suggested that they should spend the evening somewhere else than at home. The immediacy with which Robert welcomed this idea with a slightly too great eagerness told her how wise this evasion was on her part. It was necessary for them to be not only away from here, but in the open air, so strong was the emanation of feeling which they all spoke of as the intensity of accumulated heat at the end of a hot summer, so that the city buildings gave off almost as much warmth in the evening as they had absorbed from the sun in the day.

'It won't be much cooler on the river,' Kerenyi warned them as they emerged into the exhausted airlessness of the street.

'But at least a little fresher,' hoped Robert, opening the car door for Julia to sit beside the driver's seat.

It was a good deal fresher on the river bank, there was even a slight breeze and after a pause for recovery they began to feel that they could eat something of what was offered them deferentially by a pallid elderly waiter who was glad to see people who were not only not tourists, but arrived in such a magnificent motor as was now dwarfing the other cars in the courtyard. Kerenyi had engaged a table by the railing, where they sat at the edge of a wooden terrace over the water, swirling and gurgling darkly as it pulled against the obstacles to its flow formed by the supports of the restaurant platform. It was almost dark. An impenetrably moonless night that subdued the lights about them as thick curtains subdue sound, descended over the wide swirl of the Danube, on the great flow of which could be heard the thudding and deep purring of barges and ships as they passed almost invisibly out in the stream. Huge trees rustled softly overhead, absorbing the chatter and chinking of the eaters and the rapid but weary tread of waiters.

Julia sat, as always in a public place, with her back to the rest of the company, so that she could stare out at the reviving black glitter of the swift waters. On either side of her, her two companions sat by the railing, each with one elbow raised to rest on it, half turned in their chairs towards her. Since the other tables by the railing were all occupied by foreigners they were as private as if in their own homes. And they began to discuss both the entirely renovated apartment of the Kerenyis and the imminent return of Robert's family to his requisitioned house in the city from their summer in Styria. Alterations were needed there because of the arrival of a third child in the family and these claimed their detailed attention for some time. It might have seemed that these alterations were what brought Robert twice to the city during his leave, and as yet nothing was said to contradict that supposition.

Two hours passed quietly before Kerenyi asked Robert if he knew of the return of Tenius and his sudden illness.

'I read of it,' replied Inglis. 'And remembered his name, of course.' There was a silence between them. 'I very much hope I shall not need to know any more.'

'So do I,' agreed Kerenyi. 'For you and for myself.'

'I think it very unlikely, don't you, that you could be involved?'

'An outside chance, but it could happen. It depends on the defence.'

'I don't really see how you could help the defence. The use of that approach would be almost as damning to Tenius as to have no defence at all.'

'You've obviously thought it all over, Robert,' said Julia.

'Yes.' A hesitation as to how to frame his words, and then cautiously, 'I've already reminded the British war-crimes people of that old enquiry that came through to me, so that I have proclaimed an interest in the case without going into details. I know the man in charge and he will certainly let me know at once if either the prosecution or the defence ask for any further information in Vienna. I discovered, by the way, that the old enquiry of 1946 was caused by Frau Schneider trying to trace him. Did you know that?'

'No, but now you say it, it's obvious.'

'What a memory you must have, Robert, to recall such a slight detail from five years ago.'

'The name is unusual. I never heard it except that time.' Robert waited again before he continued, 'It is, as you know, nothing to do with me—not for years now. But I did rather wonder at Tenius being able to come here. I would have expected the Polish authorities to try him.'

'Oh, it's Russian policy to release such prisoners with the maximum emphasis on war crimes. The publicity is much greater and more effective if he's tried in a western court. Malczewska was pointing that out to us.'

'You know, I didn't think much of it at the time Lali suggested it, but in the last days it has seemed odd to me that Malczewska accepted that job from Hella Schneider. It only seems strange in the light of his reappearance, I suppose, but however much Malczewska wanted to get a job more suited to her than the library it strikes me as unlike her to take anything from Hella, who was a Party member, quite apart from her connection with Tenius—and he killed an awful lot of Poles, after all.'

'The same thought struck us two days ago,' said Julia quietly.

'In fact, Malczewska practically forced the idea on us,' added Kerenyi.

'She did? She's playing a very double game somewhere.'

'She almost told us that, too. But the exile Poles are displeased with her, according to her own account.'

'But why—I thought she was so thick with them?'

'She turned in the job with Hella—said she couldn't stand it any more—with some pretty insulting details.'

'I didn't know that.'

'It's only a day or so ago.'

'If the exiles are angry, she must have had some role to play?'

'One may have been proposed to her when Tenius showed up, I think.'

'And she turned it down?'

'That's the implication.'

'I can only think of one thing the exile Poles would want with Tenius. Have you reported this to the police, Georgy?'

'No. I don't look upon it as my business. So far we are only making guesses. I have no wish to get Malczewska into trouble in Vienna, just as she is taking out citizenship papers.'

'There's a point of view that would say that is just the moment at which Malczewska becomes our business,' said Julia.

'Very true, and I thought of that, too. But if anything happens, Malczewska is bound to be involved, so that there's no need for me to intervene since it would come out anyway.'

'Ah. Of course.' Robert was measured. 'And as for the police, they are watching Tenius constantly, for their own reasons.' He waited once again and when he continued his thoughts, the preciseness and conventionality of his conception of what was correct was very noticeable in his slightly stiffened tone. Or perhaps that impression came from his deciding now to speak in his own language so that the likelihood of waiters or other guests understanding of what he spoke was lessened.

'It has occurred to me that your possible involvement may come from a quite different cause than that old story of the report by Tenius. That is, because of the great difficulty—that has already been mentioned by my man in war crimes—of getting evidence of any kind as to Tenius in Breslau. If the prosecution decides that a much smaller crime . . . I mean, naturally, in the legal sense, since numbers can't have any real place in crimes of his kind . . . is easier of proof, then the SS *razzia* of October 1941 in Vienna would offer what one might call a firm handhold. You see my drift?'

'You mean, there would be a public call for witnesses and other evidence?'

'Yes.'

'A call we couldn't refuse to answer,' said Julia quietly.

'It's even possible that the trial would then take place in Vienna,' said Robert, equally quietly.

Neither of his hearers made the slightest sign that what Robert was telling them was not simply a possibility, but a definite proposal of which he already had some official knowledge.

'But a demand for extradition has already been agreed to?'

'That could be withdrawn if the Allied Control Council asked for it to be. I happen to know, for instance, that a senior officer of the American staff was born in Poland.'

'But the Soviet members of the Control Commision must be against a trial here? They would obviously prefer a trial in Germany and on the basis of the years in Breslau.'

'Yes. But that fact alone makes it certain that the other three members will press for a trial here.'

Kerenyi said, 'I must find out tomorrow what the issues before the Control Commission are at the moment. If the Soviet members have some project of importance to themselves to put through, they will give in over Tenius to get co-operation in their own plan.'

This was the point to which the whole oblique conversation had all the time been leading and now that it was stated the talk changed to other matters. They talked about the coming programmes for the Opera and theatre season and a series of concerts to be conducted by Furtwängler with the Vienna Philharmonic at the end of the year. Presently Kerenyi put his hand over Julia's, lying on the table; she turned her own hand upwards and they sat there linked while they talked.

XVII

Not everyone who discussed the case of ex-General Tenius that evening did so with such urbanity, nor in such pleasant surroundings. There are small places of entertainment in the district of Vienna that lies just across the Danube Canal from the inner city, and which the Viennese call the Leopoldstadt, which neither the three diners on the river nor the kind of tourists who surrounded them there were ever likely to visit. The whole of that district remained many years behind the rest of the city in hygiene, policing and transport services and failed entirely to resemble other working-class districts where large tenements shouldered each other, with dilapidated houses from the 17th and 18th centuries next to blocks that were modern in the twenties of this century and brand new ones still in the building process. These working-class areas are distinguished by wide main streets, by the frequency of offices of the various public welfare services, by an almost painful orderliness and cleanliness of the open parts of the houses. Though the people who live in the tenements may be crowded, pallid and pinched and the older tenants show many deformities and a smaller stature than the young, and although tuberculosis is still a problem in these 'one room and kitchen' homes, there is a pervading atmosphere of a law-abiding community that feels strongly its social cohesion, its established right to be there. Work is the key to living and jobs are held for a lifetime as a rule rather than the exception. People do not move house much in those labouring districts, and the eye of the neighbours is a sterner censor of behaviour than the priest because the neighbours are always there and everybody's life is public business. And where homes are inherited for generations from parents to children, or rented from the city authorities according to a socialist-party card there is little chance of keeping secrets. These districts lie further from the centre of Vienna than the Leopoldstadt, but they are much more Viennese, for the population is stable and whatever its political affiliations, is profoundly conscious of belonging together and belonging to the city. So much so that it might better be put that the working classes of Vienna think of their city as belonging to them.

Nothing of this description fits the IInd District. Except for the road leading through it to the Prater, no street seems wide even where it is, so crowded and confused, so bent, are the thoroughfares here. Even the respectable shops, coffee-houses and hotels carry a slight tinge of dubiety from their neighbours. The whole area is sleazy with a more than physical shabbiness; there are places here where it is unwise to ask too many questions and where the women coming out about midday in wrappers to buy bits of food are subtly different from the working class women they superficially resemble. They carry an air with them of only just having got out of bed in a town of notoriously early risers; and something bold and coarse in their homely faces and the way they move their either noticeably fat or very meagre bodies implies a familiarity with men that has little to do with family life. In the evenings they cross the canal to the chief streets of the city and in spite of their lack of looks and failure to attempt any spurious glamour, they do not lack for customers there. Of the floating population of Leopoldstadt, they are borderline cases.

The area was decimated during the War by Tenius and his like, but the cramped quarters of respectable Jewry now contain tenants many of whom are well on the other side of any border drawn by society, even illicitly in the sense that limits exist for the night women. There are houses where the inhabitants lack any genuine 'papers' as they lack any avowable job. Among the minor and major criminals are others whom even the criminals avoid, between whom and the burglars and fences, the ponces and pickpockets, an undeclared war is endemic so that none of the one class can depend on safety with the police from the other. Most of them came there after the War, few were born in Vienna, still fewer have ever candidly been through any of the various bureaucratic forms. Where they have some settled identity it is one accorded them during the chaos of the end of the War and may as well have belonged to another wayfarer as to the one now holding it. Such identities, where not simply bought or stolen, were almost all passes issued to stateless persons; a number of deserters from the Red Army, still more stragglers from the great migration of peoples that took place between 1939 and 1949. These often claimed brotherhood in the melancholy caste of concentration camp inmates, a sure means of claiming sympathy or accounting for a rancid hatred of the society they lived among but not in; some even had documents or tattooed numbers to prove this, of some it may have been true. Many of the younger ones were abandoned or lost children from eastern Europe who had wandered this far before the re-establishment of administration prevented their further journeying.

These young people now in their late teens and early twenties were the fiercest and most ruthless of a mainly cowardly group, for since they really had no identity and in many cases did not themselves know who they formerly were or even where they came from, they had nothing to fear; and being unemployable, nothing to hope for. Most of them lived by hanging about one or other emigré group when they were not engaged in thieving; alternatively all the girls and most of the boys practised prostitution and this means of money was steadily growing in worth as more and more tourists visited the city and found the old-fashioned Viennese whores too simple for their tastes. Tourists paid well for the mixture of intricate vices and pathetic tales of Auschwitz or Buchenwald—it was always one of the larger camps. The superficial pity added to the enjoyment of the vice, and travellers would often tell their friends of these encounters, leaving out the major facts.

A 'night-club' was advertised in a side street of this area, simply by the universally understood English words. A dim pink light led down cellar steps bedizened with painted decorations that would have been vulgarly contemporary in 1935. Coats were given up at the bottom of the stone steps to a hugely fat woman with a look of leering toughness, who sat there summer and winter inspecting all who went in and out. A creaking swing door led into a dank room with café tables from which two steps led down to the smokefilled racket of a small dancing square surrounded by more tables bathed in red lights. The scabrous appearance of the band and the waiters was borne out by horrible noise from the one and doctored drinks from the outer. The place smelt of damp, dirt, spilt spirits and stale tobacco with threads of various cheap scents and an undertone of the carbolic occasionally slapped over the indescribable floor which was fortunately invisible. Its one advantage at the end of August was that it was never even slightly warm. A number of the small tables with their red covers of artificial silk were occupied by the more foolhardy and less discriminating kind of holiday-maker, under the impression that they were seeing life. The touts who had slipped ill-printed invitations into the pockets of the tourists earlier in the day were now drinking at the bar; not one of the dance hostesses would have been safe even to dance with, and only a man blind drunk or consumed by a death-wish could have considered any of the other proposals made by them.

The tourists, however, were mainly innocent provincials and foreigners, so that to feel themselves as onlookers in a den of vice was all they wished for; they would have been rightly frightened although for the wrong reasons, to take part in what they took to be an orgiastic scene in which they would display their unworldliness.

In the far corner from the bar and the other side of the small bandstand was a larger table, obviously the one reserved for regular customers or the owner's cronies. Only a policeman would have taken note that behind it was a door let into the wall and obscured by the 'jazzy' decorations. At this table sat two middle-aged men of a type that Robert Inglis might have recognised from a few years before this, when his job was to 'screen' displaced persons. Not that they were noticeable; neither was. They both had smooth, rather fat faces, broad and low-set bodies and clothes exaggeratedly tailored from expensive cloth. Both, of course, drank whisky which came out of quite different bottles from those products of 'Scotland' which were served at the customers. They drank real scotch whisky, 'pure' as they said; one of the democratic realities of the postwar world, from ambassadors, to artists and 'intellectuals' and from them to gangsters and successful blackmailers, everyone who could afford it drank the guarantee of excellence as the advertisers were quite truly beginning to call it. From time to time these two men were joined by one or other of three very young men whose manners—if they could be called that—betrayed great respect for their hosts and a nervousness of any misdemeanour which could not have been surpassed by the backdrop of customers. Evidently there were places of greater sordidness than this 'night-club' about here, and the young men betrayed a consciousness of being in a place they must live up to.

Yet there seemed to be some difficulty of understanding. One after the other the young men demurred at some point or another, asked for a day to think it over or discuss it with a friend. It must have been some very unusual task that was being proposed to them, for their slack mouths, sad eyes, twitching hands and tawdry smartness of apparel which in each case badly needed renewal, all proved how little they were likely to draw any lines.

It wasn't so much, they more or less expressed themselves, that they minded a kidnapping. But a hospital, full of awesome nurses and watched by the police who, they made clear, did not count as adversaries but still . . . At night, wheedled those offering the commission, nurses are few and far between, and though orthodox exits are closed the old buildings offer a variety of other loopholes. And the money—with politely noncommittal glances—was good, was it not? Well, yes, the money but they had heard . . . none of them said exactly what he had heard.

In a close-knit underworld discretion is necessary; none of those summoned as candidates for this commission could be shouted at or blackmailed, for all those who could be blackmailed could also, in the end, be traced back to those who could blackmail them, such being the nature of their co-operation in more everyday affairs.

By three o'clock in the morning an air of weariness, even of failure, settled about the table at which the two middle-aged men still stoically sat with their glasses of whisky and the unused syphon of soda water. The inhabitants of the city with all their melodramatic or dull, lawful or illicit, night lives were nearly all fast asleep. Most of the first shift of tourists were gone to nurse already threatening hangovers, and had been replaced by those who came on in the flush of alcoholic courage from more reputable establishments to 'see life'. The fearful band made even more frenetic noise but with longer pauses between the bursts as their drug-staggered hands and lungs slackened in energy. A man entered and looked about him who was as far removed from the three young men who one by one had gone away, as a great crag of the Alps is removed from a hillock of the Surrey Downs. A mask of a face that might have been carved by a hatchet from some intractable wood, a lurching gait caused, not by the wounds of violence for that was almost normal about here, but by some disturbance of bodily balance which had its root in a mental upheaval or a gradual mental collapse. A stammer of speech, issuing from the closed side of his set mouth —this, at any rate, the two men recognised as the result of years of prison.

Those near the larger table looked round, and they looked round whether they saw the strange man enter or not. He spread a stain of some moral indifference quite beyond ordinary experience about him and even the two middle-aged men became uneasy as they took him in while he came up to their table, bowed politely with one gangling hand on the back of a chair and then drew the chair out and sat at the table. Still, bound as we all are by the conventions of our own group, one of the two men raised a hand that brought a waiter flatly running with a glass and whisky. The newcomer waited for this ritual to be completed, with one elbow resting on the table and his forehead upon the hand, in a leaning forward position, while he looked about him with pale, blank eyes at the other tables, the band and the waiters.

He did not drink the whisky but poured soda water into the separate glass provided, and drank that. An odd jerk of his head conveyed that he had been too long away from alcohol to risk it and the two middle-aged men understood that. He was evidently thinking what he should say through some fog of stupidity, or a distance of not talking much.

'Released three weeks ago. See?' he said at last. 'I've been inside since '46. Death row, they call it, see? Lawyer—clever bastard —found I was born in Bruck an der Leitha, not here at all. Me old woman must have taken a holiday, I reckon. So they had to let me out. Not in the jurisdiction, they said. All a great big mistake. I'd told them all the time I was born in Waehring, believed it, too. You got to hand it to them Yankee lawyers. Objective justice, that's what this fellow called it. See? Anything wrong with the papers and you're sprung, just like that.'

Neither of the two middle-aged men said anything in reply to this disjointed credential.

'I hear you're looking for help. A certain party, who's in hospital. I can help you, because I've got to go into hospital myself. I can go in tomorrow. Boils, I've got. Otherwise nothing wrong with me. See? Once in, the rest's easy. Just got to find out when the police is changed, of an evening, or nights. They usually always stop to have a chat, changing shifts—sometimes five minutes or more. I'm used to all that.'

'Where was it you left, three weeks ago?' asked one of his hearers. 'Excuse me asking.'

'Landsberg,' answered the stranger, and at the mention of the

American war-crimes prison in Bavaria, both listeners pulled down their mouths and shrugged their shoulders as if confirmed in some guess.

'No good. The police will be watching you.'

'Of course. But I'll be in hospital, see?'

The simplicity of this idea engaged their professional approval, although they tried not to show this.

'And I'll still be in hospital, when he's gone. They're bound to suspect something, but what can they prove? There I am in bed, with a hospitalisation card from the US Prisons Administration, Berchtesgaden, to continue treatment interrupted by my release.'

'But you would be in a different department. Even a different building.'

'No. He's been moved to the special ward used for prisoners who need urgent treatment. I shall be there too, being as I've got my card. See? It's just one ward, surgical and medical all together, with four beds. He's alone there now.'

'You seem to know a lot about this,' said one man, hiding the fact that the removal of Tenius to a special room had been unknown to him until this moment. 'But this special ward will be guarded. His room was watched before, constantly.'

'It's not guarded as I'm used to being guarded in the death cell. The hospital is old, the windows upstairs aren't all barred, and a backstairs from one side corridor has an ordinary door to it. Locked, of course, but you could open it with a nail file.'

'But how do you know all these details?' one of the men asked, and now he showed his interest by his surprise.

'I was there, today. Getting the hospitalisation papers. See? I only have to go into that ward because my treatment goes to the prison-service account. I'm a free man, for the moment. They won't get me again for months. So I have time.'

'Time? For what?'

'Time to be got away. It's all arranged. My friends it was, who got the birth certificate about Bruck an der Leitha to the lawyers. They have the transport all ready for me. You see—that's why I can help. This other fellow can have my place. He's urgent but I can wait a month or so.'

'Your friends . . . they would be . . .?' His elbow jerked by his companion, the man who spoke did not name those to whom he referred aloud, but ended with an enquiring glance from narrowed eyes.

The stranger, who was about to answer, saw something in this unfinished question that made him hesitate. He considered slowly the implication of the question having to be asked at all. For the first time it trickled into his hesitant consciousness that these two men to whom he had been sent might not wish to remove Tenius from the same motive as his, or rather, as that of his friends. And now that the discrepancy was present in his mind, he became dimly aware of a memory in the demeanour of the two men before him. Something stirred from the past, some recognition of men like these with whom he had dealt before in very different circumstances. As those of slow and blurred wits do, he felt around this recognition cautiously in his impaired mind without being able to formulate it to himself. His long silence, although it might have been explained by the way his gaze wandered over the gradually emptying dance room, gave a warning to his companions.

'But why are you willing to give up your place, as you call it?' asked one of them, filling the threatening length of the gap in conversation.

The stranger looked at him directly, moving his head with a curiously deliberate heaviness.

'Our lot sticks together. See?' The words came out with a pride in solidarity that overcame gathering suspicion. 'You have to when the whole world is against you. This man in hospital—he'd do the same for me.'

Someone at the bar meanwhile spoke in an undertone to the bar-man and this employee now came over to the large table without being summoned. He acted as if one of his bosses wanted a fresh drink, but as he bent over to wipe ash from the tablecloth with a dirty napkin, he muttered something under his breath and glanced briefly to the side where his informant still waited by the bar. As soon as the two men looked across and identified this latter, he quietly left the room as if his purpose were accomplished. Immediately, the bar-man too went away, to fetch another ashtray.

'There was only one release from Landsberg reported in months,' one of the two men now said. 'You must be Benda? The Ulrich Benda who was in command of the SS Hiring Office in Lodz?' This was the official title of the forced-labour contractors' department of the SS, and Benda was indeed in charge of it and wielded the power of life and death by means of it, for several years. During this period it was not unusual for the population of the town to fall by thousands in a month.

The stranger, like many more intelligent people, hardly noticed the intervention of the bar-man, a figure to be expected in such a place and who had already approached their table several times before, during the conversation. He was startled, as far as a quick reaction was possible to him.

'How d'you know that?' he demanded, his suspicions now well forward in his mind.

'I read it in the papers,' said the same man, and there was a suggestion of a sneer in his voice which he was powerless to force into neutrality.

'I guess my friends were misinformed . . .' began Benda heavily, and began to lift himself laboriously out of his chair.

'No, wait a minute,' intervened the other well-dressed man. 'My chum here gets a bit too witty, sometimes. Don't get him wrong. We are just removals men. We move bodies. That's what we get paid for, and we work for anybody who pays well.'

'I was told you were already half-way in action in this case,' Benda worked it out in his badly co-ordinated fashion. 'And we would co-operate with you.'

'So we are. And that argues that we already had a buyer for this body. Doesn't it?' The man leaned forward, fixing Benda with sharp eyes to hold attention on what he said, and to stop Benda thinking further. 'We haven't even spoken of money yet.'

'No, I didn't know you already had an offer. I was told you'd helped my friends before with snatching jobs. That's all I was told, See? I came here so you wouldn't have to get in touch with them— with my friends. The case being urgent.'

'And a very good idea, too,' the man assured him. 'It saves at least a day.'

But something in the atmosphere was now so heavy with memory for Benda that he was at last sure of something very wrong. He could not know that the two kidnappers had already failed with several candidates for the internal side of their task; that of opening doors in the hospital, helping the sick man to put on outer clothing, and perhaps supporting him to the side entrance where a car would be waiting. Therefore their disguised eagerness to enlist his own services appeared as added evidence of the urgency of their desire to lay hands on Tenius for quite different purposes from those of Benda's friends.

'We'll split our fee with you,' offered the man who had not spoken for some time. And this reasonable offer was fatal to their purpose, as the second man demonstrated by turning on his friend with suppressed violence and telling him to shut his mouth. But Benda had heard and understood that he was to be used. Long habit of caution schooled him not to betray himself, but he got awkwardly to his feet at this second attempt. Clumsily, he stepped to one side of his chair as if drilled to the movement, put a coarse hand on the chairback and pushed it back under the table top. Then he bowed stiffly.

'I'll let you know,' he temporised. 'You'll be here tomorrow, I guess?'

He meant, since it was now four o'clock in the morning, that same night. There were still a dozen drunken people present in the bar apart from those whose employment or constant attendance there would prevent them either intervening or talking. There was nothing to be done as Benda plodded unevenly out of the place, except vent disappointment on the unwise partner who had shown their hand. They could not even earn some part of their fee by warning those who employed them that the SS fraternity would remove Tenius from his hospital bed in a day or so; that would ensure them never again earning a penny from this wealthy organisation. All they could do was to claim the extreme difficulty of the task proposed as an excuse for not yet having succeeded in planning it. Between acrimonious reproaches they discussed the possibility of bribing some member of the hospital staff as an alternative to breaking in from the outside.

Benda made his way slowly up the clammy steps and out into the warm glimmer of dawn. An idle breeze, already heated from accumulated sunshine, frisked waste paper round his feet, the remains of touting leaflets thrown away by tourists as they departed from 'seeing life' in the night-club. There were already single figures moving about. A market truck rumbled over cobbles, its noise almost ceasing as it turned into the asphalted main street. Benda turned the corner after it, and looked about him to pinpoint his position in a district he knew only very slightly and where he had not been for many years. The shop-lined street bent here. Across it, Benda saw a street entry where the pavement was at first wide and then narrowed suddenly where larger houses took up its width. There was a mean wineshop, its shutters closed, a large padlock on its outer door. The signs on each side of the door showed shabby old paintings of grapes and the names of wines with their prices. There was nobody about here. It was now daylight. Somehow it seemed to Benda that a crude wooden chair should stand on the wide pavement near the wineshop, that a crowd had just withdrawn, that he knew this place. The shadowy picture of a hungry, meagre woman pushing forward a glass of raw wine on a dirty tablecloth, and then retreating from the table with a twist of fear about her pinched mouth, rose from a distant past. Benda turned himself about but the memory, if it was a memory, was not to be recovered, though for a moment the impression of remembering was strong enough to disturb him. He walked on towards the city, where he could mount a tram, a shambling, gawky figure with its head bent. As he reached the tram stop, he thought after an interval of thirteen years, I wonder what ever became of Horst. But as the tram ground to a stop and he moved forward into the roadway to board it, the thought was lost and he forgot it without identifying its cause or even recalling clearly who Horst had been. Many, many men known, seen, half-remembered, had disappeared during the six years of Benda's active career while he, in secure corners wielded powers rarely accorded to men of his less than commonplace stamp. What survived of Horst was long since ploughed into the dark earth of vast spreads of maize south of Sebastopol together with the bodies of those he thought his enemies. All that remained of the vast unthinking hordes of human lemmings, driven to and fro over the body of the patient earth, was that the sturdy maize stalks grew higher than before their senseless struggles.

As the tram trundled stolidly towards Benda's lodging, a sparely equipped room in a discreet hostel which called itself a boarding-house but where no unadvised arrivals were given shelter, he thought with apprehension of the continuation in hospital of those blood-tests that made him feel faint and the hypodermic needles from which his hard flesh shrank cravenly.

Later in the day, after sleeping, Benda discussed with the leader of the hostel his experience in the Leopoldstadt night-club and it was agreed that he should enter the hospital the following day. Benda dreaded the treatment and felt a dull reluctance to leave the shelter of the hostel where everyone, tenants and staff, were of his own kind. But it did not occur to him to object or try to put off the unpleasant moment; he was proud to be able to help a senior officer and the knowledge of his own friends' approval and watchfulness for himself as for Tenius, supported him in going back to the outside world in which he was an outlaw. As his adviser told him in a rallying tone, it was not for long.

XVIII

'I'm getting more than tired of Hella's problems,' Julia admitted, as Hansi Ostrovsky accused her of looking out of the window and not listening. 'I've been keeping my eye on Jochen's watch—he's fortunately such an immobile person—and for eleven minutes, this time, we haven't once mentioned the costume designs. We have talked solely about Hella and whether she will try to involve us all in her own temporary eclipse. And what makes it so boring is that we all know the answer.'

'Of course, she will try to involve us all, you mean?'

Julia did not even answer Thorn's remark; she looked at him with a shrugging turn of shoulder and throat which tipped up her chin scornfully, and this imitation of a mannerism of Hella's when displeased was so expressive of their agreed attitude to the subject that both she and Thorn began to laugh appreciatively at her own joke.

'What happened to your watch, Julie?' asked Anita, laughing with them to show Hansi she agreed with them.

'I dropped it into the bath—wasn't it stupid? Now it's at the watchmaker's, who is doubtful about its recovery. His idea is that I should have a new one, needless to say.'

'I don't think much of these designs, anyway,' grumbled Hansi. 'They're entirely derivative—derived, I mean, from all other recent theatrical costumes of antique periods. I don't see a sign of talent in them—they are just vaguely Greek with a French tinge—could almost be an imitation of the *Palais Royal* in Louis XIV's day. Except for the peacock's feathers, and they make them look a bit Napoleonic, there's nothing faintly Egyptian about them.'

Julia was reminded of Malczewska's ideas and said obliquely, 'We ought to get a new designer. This stuff just creaks with weariness. And the headdresses! How d'you suppose old Cleo could go roistering in the taverns with her swashbuckling Antony in these things? Like going to an Heurigen in a tiara!'

'I daren't,' cried Hansi. 'There was another row about using guest technicians only last week. Our staff is so large, and the Union makes life impossible for outsiders with all their damned obstructions.'

'Not even an adviser?' offered Anita.

'That's an idea,' agreed Julia. 'I think I'll get some designs for my dresses done outside. . . .'

'Here he is, now,' said Hansi, meaning the designer, who entered the room at this moment. 'Peter, we feel some modification is needed in. . . .'

At this the artist who was to design the stage sets groaned only half under his breath, and when Hansi looked at him appealingly, lost his temper.

'Modifications can only make them worse,' he said with sudden fury. 'They are all bloody bad and not fit to be on my gorgeous sets. Even little Monika could do better in her first year.'

'How dare you say that!' Peter's outrage made his voice almost a squeal. 'They are beautiful designs. I went right back to—'

'There you are,' shouted the stage designer at Hansi. 'Just what you said. He looked at old designs. One thing's sure, though, you never looked at anything Egyptian, you stupid old queen. You ought to be doing dresses for the circus, not the Burg!'

'I say! Watch it, Florian!' cried Julia, delighted at this outburst. 'I didn't know you were so keen on *A and C*!'

'Of course I'm keen on it! It's a chance at last to create something fresh. Unpopular masterpiece, public prejudice, marvellous poetry, a not too bad cast! Of course I'm keen. We can show what it ought to be. I doubt if it's *ever* been done as it should be. . . . Who wouldn't be mad to do it? And this old fairy here, comes up with dreary old tart's evening gowns like one of those horrible drawing-room dramas in London with people drawling at each other. "My dear, you don't understand." Who was that fellow—Owen Nares!'

'Oh, Lord, Florian, that was before the war, all that,' Hansi was shouting now as well. 'All that stuff is as dead as the dodo in London.'

'Just what I mean! That's what these dresses make me think of.'

'How on earth did we get to London?' asked Anita plaintively. 'I don't see what that's got to do with it.'

'It's got to do with it that Peter was there in the War and he's never got over the idea of being well-bred and restrained. That's what it's got to do with it!' He stopped to catch breath and then burst out again. 'All this stuff! It looks like negligées for girls in brothels pretending to be ladylike! All we need with this junk is Luigini's ballet and we're all set to be the laughing stock of Europe!'

'But Cleo was a *Queen*,' pleaded Peter, becoming involved in spite of the insults, in the battle. The use of the word just used against himself was so comical in its emphasis that they all burst out laughing and he was obliged to laugh too.

Florian clutched at his short black hair, trimmed forward on his forehead in the new French style.

'Cleo was an oriental despot who lived on male juices!' he almost shrieked. 'She was a human tigress just at the point in her life when she discovered there was one man on earth she couldn't use in her bed and ignore elsewhere. D'you want me to put it in four-letter words for you? You're supposed to be designing clothes for a woman who is destroying herself, not for Princess Cissy!' He turned on Julia as if rather to strike her than to gain her support. 'Look at her! Is this a frame you can drape with laces? You want to cover that rearing head with feathers, you batwit? She's savage, virulent, violent. She's tearing Antony in strips with her talons and drinking the blood. She's torturing herself as she tortures him and loving every minute of it. She's the Dark Lady, bearing out to the edge of doom her own destructive nymphomania, and her lover's raging lust. They don't know any longer whether it is power or the unbearable longing for each other that drives them, but it drives them literally to distraction until they pull down the pillars of the world about them. . . .' He paused for breath and rushed on 'You clown! She has to be almost terrifying! She's a slinking, fabulous beast, larger than life . . . haven't you even read the play? Or can't you read?'

He plunged at the table and grabbed up one of the scripts. 'Where is it, that passage? Hell, I can't put my hand on it . . .!'

'You'll tear it. And it isn't a passage. It's the whole play.' Julia pulled the script carefully out of Florian's hasty grip. 'Listen, Peter, I'd like you to talk to Frau Malczewska about my own costumes. I'll pay her a fee as consultant myself, to save trouble. But she has some ideas about the production that I think could help us. Now, wait. You mustn't feel you are being pushed aside; it isn't that. Everybody needs new ideas sometimes, and that includes me. Don't take any notice of Florian's tantrums. You know what he's like when he's keen on something. . . .'

'If your things are going to be changed, I don't see why mine shouldn't be, as well,' Anita claimed.

'Well, if one set of dresses is changed, then they will all have to be at any rate, a good deal modified,' Hansi proceeded cautiously.

'All the lines must be clean and straight, stiff materials, and for Cleo direct from the shoulder down to increase her presence. Look, like this—' Florian began to sketch furiously on the block before him with a pencil. 'And decoration, if there must be frills and furbelows, belongs on the two waiting women, to emphasise their essential triviality compared with the Queen, with Egypt.'

Peter said nothing, sulking with as much dignity as he could pretend to, while the discussion went on, drawing him gradually back into itself by a mixture of bullying and cajolery. As they worked on each other they began to feel a familiar but rare sensation of unity which was the first sign that a project was now in train which could, and it was still only a distant possibility, prove to be one of their great achievements.

Jochen Thorn was little concerned in the argument about costumes, since the accoutrement of Mark Antony is decreed by history, and the Roman uniform was to become by its unchangeability, the fulcrum on which the visible coherence of the production turned. His silence was far from dividing him from the loud discussion in which he hardly joined, indeed it formed the noisy background he needed for his own increasing grip on the relationship of his own unit of the group to its other main unit. He began to experience a visional connection between Julia's real life and the meaning for her of Cleopatra. This grew naturally from his perception of Julia's exhaustion on the last occasion they worked together in this room. But it stretched back in his memory to scenes years before when his intense sensual appreciation of women was for short periods of time concerned with his colleague. He recalled, not as an event but rather as remembered feeling, the latent terror and pain in Julia on the day in the rehearsal room at a time when he scarcely knew her which communicated itself to everyone else there, ostensibly as the aftermath of the capture of Kerenyi's unknown and lost girl. For years now Thorn had attributed that communication of fear to the presence of Julia's husband in their home, which he then first apprehended without knowing it. But now he drew something even more deeply hidden from that memory; an unrealised and unavowable passion of jealousy and resentment in Julia of which the object was not her husband but Kerenyi, her husband's only friend. His recall jumped to another moment, three years later when he, Harich and Ostrovsky left Kerenyi to walk home with Julia in the late evening and he, Thorn, expressed the expectation that the pair were going home for the purposes of love. He could feel that moment now in retrospect, could feel himself looking after the man and the woman walking away in the narrow and aged street only seen as moving shadows. His perception then was not as wrong as its factual incorrectness implied. A passion of desire was present then; his faculty had not deceived him. He had taken for physical actuality what was then buried like a subterranean volcanic fire over which the two of them walked, the one deliberately banning knowledge and the other unable even to admit it to the mind.

No wonder, Thorn thought, the explosion is now so violent. And no wonder this play of all others is destined to commemorate its violence. Only a few days ago they could all feel the absence from them of Julia's energy. Since then, something crucial had changed, and Thorn was fitted from his own experience to identify what it was. Julia was abandoning some barrier and some territory of her being, always before defended, was invaded; the territory of spiritual force until now kept apart from living, which had been devoted to her work alone. She will stand or fall by this production, Thorn formulated his perceptions to himself; either she will succeed in fusing reality with art, Kerenyi's demands on her whole self will transport her from potential to real greatness, or she will never complete her development.

Willy Mundel, coming from some other business, now joined the meeting and seated himself half sideways to the wide table close by Thorn. He was one of those whose doubts as to the public acceptance of Shakespeare's masterpiece made him uncertain of the theatre's choice of a production so costly in time and money. He listened for some time without making any contribution to the discussion, in order to catch up with their progress, and as he gradually joined in, he showed that his doubts were still unallayed.

Presently, in an undertone, Thorn taxed him with his lack of confidence.

'You'll inhibit us all unless we can persuade you,' he said and their remarks went unheard owing to the constant argument and their proximity to each other.

'I can't help feeling that too much depends on you and Julie,' Mundel explained. 'Above all on Julie. And she has a good deal else on her mind and will have for months.'

Thorn gave him a surprised glance at this unnecessary candour, but Mundel went on to show his colleague that his thoughts ran on a different track from Thorn's.

'There's a rumour about this morning that Tenius may be tried in Vienna. Julie and Georgy would be bound to be involved if that came true.'

'Ah. I thought for a moment you meant . . . something else.'

'Something else?' Mundel looked at the unwitting Julia across the width of the scattered table, as she once more intervened to protect the costume designer from Florian. A gesture flashed a gleam from a ring on her hand and a flicker of pale green linen as she turned emphasised the elegance of her tilted head. Mundel knew Thorn too well to underestimate his knowledge of human nature and he now watched Julia with a stringency which neither his carefulness not to be noticed nor his affection for his old friend could soften. His examination was professional and not personal.

'Another kind of involvement that could interfere . . . ?' suggested Thorn in a murmur hardly to be heard.

Mundel did not answer, but after a while he shifted his massive head a little so that he could look into Thorn's face. Not even a lifted eyebrow betrayed that they understood each other. Only a look passed between them, a look which assured Thorn, whose own professional reputation would be at stake in this production, that nothing Mundel could do or might fail to do would be allowed to increase the chances of a failure.

So one more member of the team was committed to unstinted loyalty to the growing project, and it was noticeable that besides Mundel, Hansi Ostrovsky too began to shed his reservations after that morning and less was heard of them. His unbounded ambition for himself and the theatre was fired, first by the enthusiasm of the stage designer and then by the increasingly strong authority and dynamism of unity in the group round the table.

'Depends what you mean by going well,' Julia answered Georg's habitual question later in the day. 'We wasted a good deal of time at first, discussing Hella and her sex-life again. But after that we really got down to business. I think we are properly started now. Most of the cast were there for the first time except the new boy who is to play Octavius Caesar. You haven't met him, I think. He's obviously going to become a big challenge to Wally Harich, so it's a good thing Harich isn't playing Mark Antony. I think Thorn is better, he's much harder and clearer in presentation than Wally. Wally's got a romantic aura, that doesn't suit Antony. Thorn will make him a real soldier of fortune, harsh, ambitious, a tough you can imagine sacking towns and ravishing the maidens.'

'Then it did go very well?'

'Yes, I think so. I think we've got a grip on it now. Difficult to tell at once; the whole morning was one long row, in fact. But the right kind of row, if you know what I mean?'

'I saw your new boy at Salzburg last week. A genuine find, a "golden lad".'

'I'm really beginning to hope that this will be a major event— *A and C.* If we keep up our drive we could set a new standard for this play, a breakthrough. It belongs so much to the classic theatre, and yet is half unknown. So it's absolutely our "thing"—you see? And there is a new feel about in the air that things can be spoken of, demonstrated, that were tabu a short while ago. . . . Difficult to express what I mean. Not only sexuality—I mean the savagery of war, the rawness of empire-building, the cunning of politics—if we can strip it of babyish sentimentality—make it rough and crude. Florian was splendid, he's a great talent. Ought to begin producing, perhaps. . . .'

'How are his set-sketches?'

'There you are! They're almost revolutionary. The palace is just tall blocks with dark drapery coming down stark, very suggestive— anything could happen in such a place, a looming depth and height, a labyrinth. And the Roman scenes are blazing with light and rather naturalistic—brilliant idea, the contrast.'

'What's he done about the sea battle?'

'Wire constructions. He wants them to move rhythmically, to suggest the oared galleys, and billows of drapes with heraldic signs. Some of them move, fall underfoot and are trampled. It will be a beast to stage-manage.'

'A good deal depends on the music. . . .'

'That we haven't heard yet—it isn't written, I think. Florian is going down to Innsbruck tomorrow with his designs and the recording—Oh, I didn't tell you—Thorn and I used that gadget Luders brought me to record two passages for Branden to listen to.'

'Webern's pupil? He got the commission, then?'

'Yes, thank God, Hansi decided not to economise on that.'

There was a long silence. Then Julia spoke again, abruptly.

'Do you believe it really—that a man and woman can destroy each other?'

Kerenyi thought for so long that she supposed he would not or could not, answer her.

'Yes, I do,' he said at last. 'Physical love can be a dominant of the whole human being, in certain circumstances. Like a key that unlocks a whole house. And if two people debauch each other so that they are stripped of every defence *in their own eyes*, and yet are not absolutely loyal to each other . . . If they maintain reservations in the mind, in other actions—as Antony and Cleopatra did —then the inner treachery can corrupt their natures and even the whole basis of character, like insanity. The shamelessness of total abandon—I mean the loss of shame—must become shameful if it isn't in the most real sense, pure and exclusive. If two people give themselves away, literally in the sense of the original words, and the gift is not total and mutual, then they must be—literally again —lost. Isn't that so?'

'I suppose it is. It sounds logical, even simple. But it's quite possible to have long and exciting—satisfactory—love affairs and not give one's whole being away.'

'But once one's whole being is given, then one can never withdraw the giving. Nothing, as one says, can ever be the same again.'

'For both?'

'For both.' And after another silence, 'You must have known this as well as I did, because you were always careful to reserve some part of yourself. You said so to Luders and me, of your early encounters. And it was just as true for Nando—even for Franz. Wasn't it? It was not just rage that made me say it when we quarrelled, was it?'

His voice was quiet, even soft, but she felt the ruthlessness in him. He meant to force an admission from her, and this time not in actions, but in words.

227

'Yes,' she said slowly, knowing that she must say it.

'But it is different now, isn't it?'

'Yes,' she said again, and was grateful that he did not need to force her further. The silence that characterised the depths of their relation to each other, which swelled like an underground flood beneath their talkative surfaces, the varied but explicit and discussed facets of their lives, this silence had now been broken. And it was Julia herself who spoke the question that led to its being, just for a moment, ended. The admission that Georg was bound as well as herself, by the extremity of what passed between them, was already made in silence behind their conversation as they stood drinking Berthold's gift of pre-luncheon champagne. The simple words they now exchanged took on, by their quietness and by the long pauses between them, a great solemnity, a quality of ceremonial. A treaty was here ratified, months after its signature. And it was Julia who, by her question, admitted the need for assurance; her husband only required her, by repeating the single word 'yes', to endorse that confession of dependence just as he confirmed his equal dependence with the word 'both.'

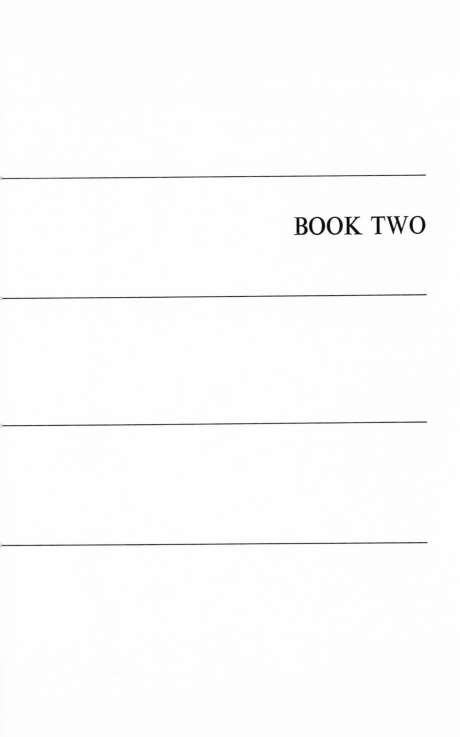

BOOK TWO

XIX

Derided by all arbiters of taste, melodrama continues inconveniently and unfashionably to exist in real life although banned from the arts excepting only in the works of one or two painters, sculptors and poets whose fame is beyond attack, and who are in any case long dead.

It was not chance that the two groups of conspirators determined to remove the former General Tenius from his hospital room on the same night. It was, rather, that the work on this project by two somewhat similar unofficial organisations was bound to take about the same length of time to arrange in the circumstances of secrecy and caution attending it. The Polish exiles who were ready to deliver Tenius to their hated and successful rivals for arbitrary control in their homeland, if only they could effect their vengeance on a common enemy, took rather longer to arrange their kidnapping than the brotherhood of the former SS. This was because they were not only more loosely bound together by less effective loyalties, but were forced to employ outside help as well. But they began their work earlier; their plans were ready to be tested on the same night that the neater, more practised, more compact plan of Benda's friends was also ready to be put into action. Because the two groups, warned by the abortive attempt at co-operation through Benda, were wary of each other, they maintained strict security precautions. Thus neither group knew that the other had set that September Sunday evening.

Those whose turn of duty falls on a Sunday or a holiday are always a little slacker in their attention than on a weekday, and there are fewer people to each shift. In addition, hospital staff are usually tired and relaxed on Sunday evenings after the rush of afternoon visitors. For these sensible reasons both groups fixed on the time of change between the evening nursing staff and the night nurses. The solitary police guard was due to be relieved half an hour after this time, and was already on his way home in his mind. The only part chance played in the whole matter was that it happened to be the birthday of the young policeman's baby son, his first child. So to the lassitude of Sunday evening was added resentment at being on duty on his son's birthday, and the celebratory drinks offered by some of the hospital staff for this occasion. It is clear that the junior policeman was not a clever young man, or he would have arranged to exchange the unwanted, but higher-paid Sunday 'turn' with one of his colleagues.

It was dark and the new moon was obscured by heavy clouds; it was beginning to rain, heavy drops that rattled on the leaves of the trees in the courtyards of the old hospital. The wind rising at the approach of a downpour made a variety of noises down corridors and through open windows; a parsimonious and poverty-ruled city administration provided only weak lights and these were turned off in unused corridors under a strict rule of economy. There was therefore every prospect of confusion with the tired hospital staff interrupted in their last jobs by the need to close windows hastily, with unaccustomed sounds already present, shadows everywhere, and the Sabbath lack of concern at a glimpsed stranger, possibly a late-departing visitor.

The penal ward was situated in one of the oldest blocks of the venerable buildings, on the ground floor where all windows were barred with ornamental ironwork over the whole hospital complex, so that one who did not know the place well would see no difference in that flight of four windows from any others. The passage was connected with the administrative part of the buildings, and on the other side of a locked door were only empty rooms. A side passage led on the left to a flight of bare stone steps worn into hollows by thousands of feet and going down to storerooms in the first basement. On the right a turn led to a cross passage and a few yards along there was an outside door, used by the police guards, which was always locked by a massive old key. A stray bomb fell near this door during the last week of the War, and in repairing it the panels behind its bars had been replaced with glass to let light into a dark corner. A glass-cutter could easily remove a section of this door silently and pass a hand through the bars to open the bolt inside. The lock was to be taken care of by a pass-key. Well-organised criminals can usually get hold of pass keys for hotels, museums and other semi-public places if they are willing to pay for them. Once inside, the kidnapper was to approach the penal ward quietly, wait for evidence of the guard's whereabouts or make certain of his absence, and then, when opportunity offered—there was all night to use if need be—slip into the ward, cover Benda's mouth with a pad soaked in ether and overcome any suspicion in the half-sleeping Tenius by showing a forged SS membership card and using their jargon to urge him to speed. The movements of the guard were already known; the only serious danger was that this man might be indulging in a rest on one of the unused beds in the room, from which any unexpected noise would awaken him. A small car of old design was parked, empty and convenient, a few paces from the outside door and there were already enough cars in the city for this to cause no remark. Its driver waited across the street for the opening of the door; at this signal he was to cross to the car, open the doors, start the engine and drive off when the two passengers were inside. Entry was timed for just before the guard change. In case of any trouble from the guard, the burglar carried a short weighted club hung inside his trouser leg, the side pocket of which was removed for speed of access. However, once the entry was made, interruption was unlikely, for the intruder could simply bide his time.

It was a plan the disadvantages of which were also its good points—it was both slack and flexible. The man who was to carry it out was familiar with the layout of the rooms and corridors, having visited the similar wards immediately over the penal ward on several visiting days, enquiring for a non-existent friend and wandering about in apparently fruitless or aimless fashion. One day he even left the hospital by the door he proposed to use on this night. Anyone looking lost and confused on hospital visiting days in a large city can traipse about for some time without causing more than questions as to which department he wants.

The second organisation was much simpler. Benda had been passed a key cut from a model he himself took in children's coloured clay, by his 'brother' who visited him from the boarding house. To receive this visit he was obliged to leave the penal ward where visitors were, of course, not allowed, and go to a waiting room. The clay impression had been taken while the key lay on the guard's table beside his uniform cap and the policeman was gossiping with a male attendant from 'Men's Surgery', the department adjacent to the penal ward in the direction away from the administration offices. Benda was a walking patient but since he spent most of his time lying on his bed he seemed to the guards to be as stationary as

Tenius, whose much improved condition had been carefully disguised in the last days at Benda's whispered instruction. He was believed by the staff to be suffering from a trauma following release from imprisonment, not uncommon when the prisoner has a heart ailment and has already undergone the shock of re-arrest. Benda carried a stimulant for Tenius in small phials with the precious key in his pocket. He kept his normal clothes on after his 'brother' left and appeared to be laboriously writing letters.

The guard was ready for his relief. He rose, yawned widely, stretching his healthy young face and showing a good set of teeth, glanced about him and strolled out to see if there were anyone about to talk to. The cubby-hole where his chair and table stood near the entrance to the room was dimly lighted and the ward already glimmered in its night-lighting, one small bulb over the bed occupied by Tenius, and one over Benda's empty bed beside which he sat bent over the paper spread on his locker.

Benda slipped with surprising quiet for so unwieldy a man, across the room and took the clothing belonging to Tenius from a white-painted cupboard. The door squeaked but nobody heard it. Under his bed covers, Tenius began awkwardly to dress. Once in his underclothes, he slid his gaunt legs out of the bed and Benda pulled on trousers and, helping Tenius with a hand under his elbow, held his jacket for him. He then gave him the ampoules of stimulant, and the prisoner moved to the angle of cupboard and wall, where the shadows were darkest. Benda murmured in his ear.

'Once in the street, we walk to the right. About twenty metres on there is a turning on the far side of the street. See? We cross the road and a Mercedes is waiting just in that turning. Walk fairly slowly, don't turn your head. I'll give you some drops as soon as we reach the car. Take it easy, no need to worry. Everything is taken care of. Just follow me when I signal you and make no noise.'

Benda then left his charge and went to look for the guard. At one end of the main corridor the empty offices were in total darkness. Farther along the other way the man in uniform kept a look-out for his relief, facing away from the ward and listening to an invisible voice in the surgery ward. He was about thirty steps away from Benda and the wind and rain caused a flurry of sound, so that in order to hear better what was said to him, the policeman moved into the doorway and stood there, hands on his leather belt, relaxed.

This was perfect and Benda made a move with his right arm

behind himself. Tenius could be heard crossing the bare hardwood boards of the floor. Benda pointed to the side passage, making a gesture as he did so as to which direction Tenius was to take. Then he moved two steps out into the middle of the half-dark corridor with its completely dark offices while Tenius crept across behind his back. They were quite safe, for if the police relief appeared a minute or so early, he would be heard approaching and greeting his colleague.

Benda had the key in his hand inside his pocket. He waited a moment, as he had been instructed, then as the policeman spoke to his invisible interlocutor, Benda moved into the side passage, withdrew the key and followed Tenius to the door.

At this moment the cut section of glass was lifted silently out of the door panel from outside. Neither man noticed anything for each was concentrating on keeping quiet and listening to the murmur of the policeman's voice which could still be heard behind them. It was the scraping of the bolt being drawn that alarmed them. It was quite dark, but Benda's eyes were now accustomed to the gloom and he could take in the lighter movement of a hand through the space in the door, as it groped for the bolt, oiled by himself in preparation the day before. This half-seen apparition was so strange that Benda thought he was imagining it and somewhere in the depths of his halting mind he had a sensation as if it were his own hand groping through a hole in a door for a bolt. He could almost feel a splinter scratching the back of his own hand. There was some threat attached to this movement which bewildered Benda and as he realised that a man was entering the door from outside, he also had an urgent, a visceral impulse to unlock the door and fling himself through it. So strong was this impulse, that without working out the course of what was actually happening or even taking it in, Benda repeated a movement he had practised several times in the last few days. He slid the key into the lock, turned it while the bolt slid back as if in his own searching fingers, and pulled the door inwards towards him. With his left hand he pushed Tenius against the far side of the passage. As the door answered his pull, his free hand caught at Tenius and touched his arm; he was still holding the key by which he pulled the door, and his eyes were fixed urgently in the dark on the whitish and mysteriously separate hand. The foreign hand which was his own was wrenched sideways by the opening of the door and the weight of a man behind it stumbled forward off balance. Benda stepped back, the door flew wide, Tenius moved like a shadow pushed by Benda's free hand out into the open and a man's solidity fell with a high-pitched cry against Benda's body almost softly, at the last of its fall.

The tumbling impact of a human mass caught Benda across hip and groin, but as the fall was slow and he himself was swaying back away from the door, it was not violent. From the far distance came the memory of a unique sensual pleasure, more piercing than anything else he ever felt in the many times he sought to recapture it, by his own violence towards others.

'Go. Quick,' groaned Benda, his whole uncouth frame quivering in the joy of saving Tenius; the sensation of reversing violence was infinitely rewarding, an access of pleasure in which the yells of the falling man went unheard by him. Tenius, bewildered by the noise and confusion of movement, rushed out of the door and from habit did precisely what he had been told to do. He stopped his rush and walked to the right twenty paces until he could see a street entry across the road, never turning his head and not hurrying. Then he crossed into the sidestreet, and an old Mercedes, still wearing its *Wehrmacht* paintwork, waited. A door was held open for him, and he scrambled into the back. The driver was in the act of asking Tenius where Benda had got to, when the sound of several shots fell on their ears. They searched each other with scared looks and for an instant the driver panicked and began to open his door, but training made him stop. He slammed his door again, put the big car into gear and the idling engine moved it gently away from the curb, out into the roadway. Accelerating gradually to avoid any notice from a possible onlooker, the driver turned left into the next opening, and in a few moments was mingling in the traffic of evening down the main thoroughfare that ran along the outer wall of the hospital, towards the inner city.

The intruder's impact made Benda stagger backwards, and as if to stop his retreat he felt the sensation of great blows at his back. An infinity of a few seconds threw him upright with repeated shocks, while a torrent of scenes tore through his brain picturing a thousand releasing pleasures achieved through savage cruelty on helpless bodies. In the moment of death he experienced a new, a perfect joy and knew with an explosion of revelation in his mind and body the truth that it is better to give than to receive. Without knowing he was dying, he was enraptured that he was giving Tenius, his comrade, life.

The young policeman, frightened and bewildered, stood swaying a little on his feet from the recoil of his heavy duty weapon, choking on the fumes, hardly knowing where he was or what had happened.

XX

'Delighted to see you, my dear fellow,' said Kerenyi, hardly lifting his head. 'Find a chair. I must just finish these galleys, and I'll be with you.'

Barber did as he was told and picked up something to read; he was incapable of sitting still for a moment without some form of printed matter in his hand, but scanning the political journals, he was quite at home and a companionable silence was filled with the familiar rustle of papers. It was not an unbroken silence, and now and again one of them made a comment on what he was reading, more to himself than to the other.

'I do it in the evening to get some peace,' said Kerenyi at last, shuffling the galley sheets into a neat pack. 'The office is a bedlam in the day time. When did you hear?'

'Just before I came over to you. I telephoned the apartment, but no one was there.'

'Julie's at the theatre. It's the first night of the new season for her.'

'I hear the Cleopatra production is going to be the biggest thing of the winter.'

'You do, do you—where d'you hear that?'

'From that very strange Polish woman who was working for Frau Schneider. I tracked her down to ask some questions about the Tenius affair but all she would talk about was Shakespeare's gypsy having her lust cooled by the third pillar of the world.'

'You're mixing your quotes like the poet his metaphors,' said Kerenyi laughing. 'It sounds pregnantly phallic, but this escape of Tenius is no joke. Apparently a man was shot dead.'

'So I hear.' Barber rose and, dropping his reading matter down beside his chair, he lounged across the short space to the wall and examined a map of Europe that almost filled it. 'A fellow-patient of Tenius. He's dead. A second man got a glancing shot in the hand. That's all the agency here seems to know, so far. Tenius got clean away.'

'You mean the guard got two other fellows while Tenius was making his getaway? That sounds awfully unlikely to me. Tenius is a very sick man.'

'That's what puzzled me. Would a man in the condition Tenius is in be able to stand an exchange of shots and still make a burst of speed and get far enough away, without pausing for breath, to escape? The shots must have been heard, both inside and outside the hospital?'

'Bloody funny story—you sure the agency man got it right?'

'Of course I'm not sure. What d'you think I came to you for?'

Kerenyi reached for the telephone, but he looked up at Barber who was now turned again to face him, and dropped the instrument back into its fork.

'What is it?' he asked, puzzled by Barber's anxious look.

'Something the Pole said worried me. You know her, she said. Is she hysterical?'

'Hysterical? Not quite the word I would use, but certainly in a state of overstrain. I'd say, practically unhinged. Her story is a fairly frightful one.'

'Her story? What story?'

'I mean her life history. She was in the Warsaw Home Army and lost both husband and son. She's crippled, too, as you will have seen. A neglected wound.'

'D'you think she might be suffering from delusions?'

'What did she say?'

'She was scared of me, to start with. Insisted on seeing some proof that I was who I said I was. Fortunately, I had my passport on me, and my collect-cable card from Radio Austria. She didn't know what that was, but the explanation seemed to convince her. Then somebody came to the door of her room and said she was wanted on the telephone. She was obviously scared out of her wits and called back to say she wasn't at home. And as I was leaving, she said something so weird I thought she might be a bit touched.' At a jerk of the head from his friend, Barber went on, slowly. 'She said, sort of under her breath, "They'll get him, and if they know I've been talking to the Press they'll get me, too".'

'You didn't ask her who "they" were?'

'I did. She didn't answer me. She gave me a kind of sleep-walking look as if she'd only half heard me.'

'Probably not aware she'd spoken aloud.'

'When I got back to the Bristol, the local agency man was on the line, with this news about Tenius and the shots. Naturally, that made me take what this Polish woman—how d'you pronounce her name, anyway?—what she said, a bit more seriously.'

'Malczewska,' said Kerenyi, writing it out to show Barber how it was spelled. 'I don't know her first name—nobody does, she's always called by her surname, like you.' Barber picked the scrap of paper up, and then reached into his pocket for his notebook to make a correction.

'Well, that would explain Tenius getting clean away,' said Georgy, considering. 'She must have meant the exile Poles when she said "they" would get him, and Tenius would be "him". There may have been a whole gang of them there. It looks as if it may be not an escape, but a kidnapping.'

He swung round on his circulating desk-chair and swung back again, catching at the edge of the desk to stop himself. 'I wonder if she really is in danger,' he said. 'Did she answer your questions about Tenius, once she knew who you were?'

'I was asking her about Hella Schneider, not directly about Tenius. She answered readily enough, seems to dislike Frau Schneider a good deal and was clearly glad to put in a bad word for her. But when I brought the conversation around to Tenius himself, she said she didn't know him at all, had only heard of him. Then she began talking about Cleopatra. I don't know that her remark just as I was going was anything to do with Tenius, you know. . . .'

'Well, unless she knows several people whom somebody wants to "get", she must have meant him. It's a fair bet she meant Tenius —she's been obsessed about his return. But if she was so scared to go to the telephone, how did you get into her room?'

'The landlady let me in, and I talked through the door at first; Malczewska's door. She recognised an American accent, of course, and that may be what made her open her door. Then I showed her my passport and so on. . . .'

Kerenyi looked at his watch.

'How much time d'you have before you must file? Your deadline must be in the middle of the night, eh?'

'Between midnight and one o'clock is the latest except for a real big story.'

'We've got time, then. I think I ought to make sure about Malczewska before I start telephoning. No good calling her. I'll go over there. You want to come with me, or will you wait here?'

'I'll come with. We'll use your car, shall we?' Kerenyi was already rattling his car-keys. He locked the office door, leaving the lights burning for their return, and they made their way back to where Barber had come from, to the 'wrong' part of the IIIrd District behind the main Customs and Excise Department of the city.

The large, extended blocks and courtyards of this necessary but unpopular authority were silent and lightless, the high gates locked.

'Creepy around here after dark,' commented Barber, as they left the old car under a street lamp. 'Glad I don't live here.'

'Perfectly respectable neighbourhood,' replied Kerenyi stooping a little to find the right bell-push at the house door. 'Cheap, that's the point.'

The plump young woman who finally opened the door to the bell marked '*Hausbesorger*' was not difficult to pacify; both Barber and Kerenyi received the impression that a few minutes' chat with a couple of strange men was even more welcome than the extravagant tip she was given for her trouble. As she pointed out not without a flirtatious smile, at this time of an evening and me all alone here, my husband works nights, you know.

'Janitors have changed a bit since my young days,' remarked Georgy as they paused for breath at the second landing.

'Christ, these stairs,' muttered Barber. 'Second time this evening.' And they resumed their steep climb, grumbling. On the fourth floor the landlady who let rooms to quiet single ladies was less accommodating. They were obliged to assure her of their entirely business interest in her tenant with much talk and a quite large note before she agreed to retire after locking her door to the stairs twice. But not more than half an hour, I have to get my sleep, and please leave the room door open. This is a respectable house.

The tenant liked visitors at half-past eight in the evening as little as her landlady. She could hear that it was indeed Kerenyi from his voice, through the barrier, but still hesitated before opening to them and they heard that key turned twice, although the flat door was secured.

'My dear Malczewska,' protested Kerenyi, 'this house is burglar-proof, and you can't really suspect our morals, either. So be a good girl and offer us a drink. We have only your own best interests in mind, I assure you.'

This deliberate lowering of the atmosphere seemed to reassure Malczewska and she managed to produce a bottle of vodka and a reluctant grin.

'But it's all very well,' she said. 'I really am scared.'

'Ah, Wyborova. Very good,' approved Kerenyi and threw the spirits straight down his throat. 'So far from wanting to belittle your fears, I am sure you should have some protection. As you see, Mr. Barber came straight to me, and we came here before he even reported to his newspaper.' He looked round the room, crammed with dreadful and useless pieces of furniture and saw that there was no radio visible. There were books spread over the tapestry table cover but no newspaper. 'Is this chair safe?'

'Not really, none of them are. But it will take your weight, I think, if you don't move about much.'

She seated herself where she had clearly already been sitting, in an imitation renaissance throne which creaked loudly at her negligible bulk. Warned, Barber tested another of the chairs at the table carefully before trusting himself to it.

'Tenius is said to have escaped,' Kerenyi told her. 'But from what we know so far, which is not much, it may have been kidnapping.'

'Let's hope to God it was,' said Malczewska. 'Then they will be satisfied and leave me in peace.' Then she seemed to take in what Kerenyi said, and glanced quickly from one man to the other. 'When? What has happened. Tell me, quickly!'

'When I got back to my hotel from talking to you, there was a message from the news agency—you know, we have a subscription with them, really mainly for east European stuff but . . .'

'For God's sake,' Malczewska almost shouted, 'what does all that matter! Tell me about Tenius!'

'Oh. Sorry. Stupid of . . . Well, the message said there had been a shooting affray at the hospital where Tenius was confined, and the prisoner escaped. Two men shot, one who died at once. That was the message, but as Kerenyi points out, there were two men present, it seems, the second one slightly wounded, so it looks as if it might be a kidnapping. Or, Georgy, it might have been an attempted murder.'

'I think everybody who wants Tenius, wants him alive.'

'Yes, but maybe we don't know about everybody?'

'The ones I know about most certainly want him alive,' said Malczewska grimly.

'It's true, there must be a lot of people about who nurse powerful grudges against Tenius, and some of them have more simple ideas of justice than even the exile Poles. They'd cut the court scenes out altogether, I dare say, as a waste of time.' Kerenyi did not, of course, mention his own and Julia's wild surmise about the wife of the missing man. And that does now seem absurd, Kerenyi said to himself, as they all three sat considering their news. Once Tenius was under any kind of official surveillance, obviously Hella wouldn't think of approaching him for any purpose. It was only while the presence of Tenius was unknown that she might just possibly have thought. . . .

'Have you thought?' he said aloud. 'It was almost certainly an escape with the aid of the former SS men. They are well organised and they had time to make their arrangements. I think I'll put my money on them. But we'll go back to the office now and talk to the Police department and some of the Vienna newspapers. Provided you don't go out tonight, you seem to be pretty secure up here, Malczewska. You can lock us out and that sexy little girl didn't seem to mind us interrupting her evening, so she will unlock the street door for us again. But if it turns out to be a real escape, then I think you ought to go out only in the company of friends for a few days, until we all know what is happening. I should imagine your exiles have quite enough on their minds at the moment without you, but one never knows.'

'There isn't anybody I could ask to go about with me,' replied Malczewska bitterly. 'I have no friends.'

Small wonder, thought Barber to himself, but he felt sorry for the ugly, badgered creature, as she put up a shaky hand to her head.

'Just at this time, when the crucial stage of getting my citizenship is going on. . . . I suppose I shall be refused, now.'

'I don't see why Tenius should affect your private affairs,' said Kerenyi, trying to encourage her. 'You've had nothing to do with him escaping, or being abducted, have you?'

'Will the Aliens Office believe that? And I left a good job with that bitch Hella Schneider, just so as to have no connection with them! At the risk of making enemies of those thugs. . . .'

Naturally, that was why she was so upset at Tenius showing up, thought Kerenyi. *She cares more than she admitted for her Austrian papers.*

'You see, it has been complicated anyway. I can't prove anything about myself. All I have is the identity card issued when I went to work at the British library. Before that I had a DP card, and I was lucky to get that. The officer was in two minds as to whether or not I was a prisoner of war, or something. Since then I've kept quiet officially about being a registered member of the Polish Home Army. But for the Aliens Office I *had* to tell the truth. You never know, they might find out afterwards. . . . And I haven't any sponsors, not ones that count.'

'Robert Inglis would help you, I should think,' said Barber.

'I don't want to ask him,' she argued sharply, and caught her breath before she added, 'it might do more harm than good to have Allied backing, don't you think?' She appealed to Kerenyi with the awkward sullenness so typical of her embattled pride.

'But if you need sponsors, why on earth didn't you ask us?' cried Kerenyi, annoyed at her stubborn independence. 'Just so that you could go on resenting us, I suppose. Here you have respectable and publicly known people, who could sign whatever it is for you, and you never even mention the matter! How can you expect help, if you don't even tell people what's wrong?'

'It didn't occur to me that you would. . . . Honestly, it just didn't enter my mind that you and Frau Homburg would sponsor me. I'd sort of thought of somebody official.'

'Well, on that level too, Julia and Hella are both officials. They're civil servants in a sense, with life contracts. There could hardly be a safer guarantor.'

'Frau Schneider would never lift a finger for me,' cried Malczewska, staring at him in unbelief. 'You must be crazy!'

'Frau Schneider-Tenius will be only too pleased to offer you help by the time we're finished with her. You can bet your life on that. If she wants the support of the Press and her colleagues in the next few months, she will have no choice.'

'She'll find some way out of all this, I'm sure she will. She's as cunning as a fox, that one.'

'It's a very bad modern habit,' adjudicated Kerenyi, 'to confuse genuine moral disapproval with dislike or it may be, envy, of somebody's sex-life. Lots of women like going to bed with brutes. Hella isn't unique in that taste. She's not a bad lot, Hella, no worse than many I could name. Her only real fault is her love of money; the rest—her too naked selfishness—is the result of bad upbringing. Most people learn to hide their ruthless concern with their own advantage. Hella never did, that's all.'

'Well, I won't quarrel with you just now,' said Malczewska, showing a rare flash of humour. 'If you really mean that you and Frau Homburg will sponsor me?'

'I'll do more than just sponsor you. I'll get in touch with the Aliens Office myself, without waiting for you to suggest it to them. I don't know anybody there, it's true, but I know several chaps in the Police President's department and they will tell me whom I should go to. And speaking of the police, we'd better get about our business if you are to get a story tonight, Barber. Now listen, Malczewska, do you really think these roughnecks might blame you for the escape of Tenius? If that's what it is. For all I know they may have some reason to blame you, I take it you haven't told me everything you know about them. If you really fear them, stay where you are and get that funny little soul downstairs to bring in food for you. Eminently willing, I should say, for a few schillings. Don't go wandering about the city just to prove to yourself you're not frightened.'

'I don't know that I'm so scared of the exiles,' muttered Malczewska. 'It's the Polish Embassy here I'm afraid of. I was obliged to get in touch with the Embassy months ago, because the Ministry of Interior wanted a definite statement that no papers from Warsaw could be found. My birth certificate—all that. The interviews I had there were unpleasant, I can tell you. First they tried to persuade me to go back home. Then they suggested that if they made a search in Warsaw as a favour to me, I ought to show my gratitude in some way they didn't go into. I was forced to have a row with them so that they would reply to the official enquiry from the Aliens Office with a blank refusal to search. They were stupid enough to fall for my trick, but they don't like me, and they said so. They think I'm too friendly with the exiles, and of course, they don't believe that *they* have quarrelled with me too. . . .'

'Have they got anything on you?' asked Barber, and both men showed that this complication was one that was to be taken seriously.

'No. But they know I was working for Frau Schneider and of course, they guessed that the exiles would use that if they could. So you see, they could now go to the Viennese police and inform against me. Or even get hold of me to interrogate me themselves. Those things do still happen.'

'But you refused to help the exiles,' persisted Barber. 'The police will interrogate them about Tenius now, for sure. If you refused to help they will speak of you with hostility, which can only be to your advantage with the police?'

'But I didn't refuse to help, that's just it. I stalled and was vague with them, and then did nothing. They already suspected me even before I threw up the job with Frau Schneider. And they are quite bright enough to know how to put me in the wrong with the police here, in revenge. They must know I wouldn't do anything actually against their plans, but they will pretend to think I am somehow involved. Don't you see?'

'The police would take the view that you ought to have reported any attempt to enlist you in a kidnapping plot,' pointed out Barber. 'You really are in a mess. I see what you mean.'

'Do the exile Poles know about your naturalisation request?' asked Kerenyi shrewdly.

'Good God, no! I've been terribly careful not to say a word to any Polish acquaintance outside the man in the Embassy.'

'Well, then, they probably feel a general malice against you and nothing more. Unless for some reason your name comes up, I don't see why the police should show any interest in you.'

'I'm afraid they will mention me. There's quite enough malice there to make them do that.'

'So you have two separate worries, in fact.' Barber held up his hand and pulled down first one finger and then another, to demonstrate. 'First, the exile Poles may try to involve you just to cause you trouble as a fellow-exile with dubious papers, as they think. Second, the official Poles may try to put pressure on you in the belief that you do know something about Tenius. Is that the situation?'

'That's about it,' she said, pressing her lips together and shaking her head.

'I wouldn't be too sure that the exiles don't have contacts in the Polish Embassy. I think it's a Legation, by the way. All these exile clubs and organisations are riddled with informers, as I suppose you know.'

'Not the Poles I know,' she said.

'When I said just that to you a short time ago, you didn't answer me,' Kerenyi pressed her.

'You know why that was,' she countered with a desperate look of bafflement at their insistence. 'I didn't want to antagonise your wife just when it seemed as if she might help me get a job. You know that perfectly well.'

'Are you sure that is all it was? We all had the impression after that evening, all three of us, that you were hiding something.'

'Well, I was. I was hiding what I've just told you. But that's really all it is. The only thing I've done that's illegal, is what Mr. Barber said—I ought to have reported to the police that there was —there might be—a kidnapping afoot.'

'Well, it seems to have been fairly vague at that time. I don't think it's very serious, do you Barber? I mean, it would be rather unnecessarily officious to go to the police just on such hearsay?'

'I don't think I quite agree. In ordinary circumstances, yes, but she's in constant touch with one branch of the police over her citizenship. You see?'

'Ye-es. But these exiles are always plotting something or other, and it hardly ever comes to anything. Malczewska can quite well maintain that she didn't take it seriously.'

'Hm. It's happened, hasn't it, after all?'

'Oh don't!' begged Malczewska. 'I'm so scared and you're making everything worse. It's like being caught in a net. Whichever way I struggle, I only make it worse for myself. I ought to have cut off all contact with the exiles when I first put in my naturalisation request! *Why* didn't I think of it in time. . . .' She put her good hand over her eyes with a gesture so forlorn that her two visitors feared that her nerves were going to give way altogether.

'Here, have another drink,' said Kerenyi hastily. 'Listen. You're all right tonight. Don't get upset. I tell you what—I'll have a talk with Robert. We're meeting after the theatre for supper. He knows about these things and perhaps he can think of something to get you out of this confused situation. You know you can trust his discretion.'

'I don't want to ask Inglis for help,' she almost groaned. 'I told you that before.'

'You won't have to ask him; I shall.'

'No!' she cried wildly, with so frantic a look that Barber started up in alarm. 'I can't go to . . . you're not to ask Inglis for anything. Not for anything. I . . .'

'Look here,' said Kerenyi slowly. 'There is more to this than you've told us. Why should you have a bad conscience over Inglis? Malczewska, you'd better tell me what is on your mind. If I got Robert and his family involved in this without knowing what I was doing, I'd murder you with my own hands. And I'm only exaggerating just a little. Believe me, any hope of help from Julia would be lost for ever if you allowed that to happen.'

'Conscience?' she wailed. What makes you think . . . .' Her strained voice broke and she began to cry angrily and despairingly, trying to lift her helpless arm to shield her face so that both men were constrained to look away in painful embarrassment.

'Pull yourself together,' said Kerenyi coldly, so that Barber stared at him in astonishment and began to protest but was silenced by a gesture. 'Come on, tell me the truth. It's taken long enough to get around to it, God knows. But now you're going to tell me, and fast. We've still got work to do this evening.'

Barber reached the weeping woman his handkerchief and she struggled for a few minutes with her hoarse sobs until she could command herself enough to speak.

'One of my appointments at the Polish Embassy,' she managed to get out. 'There was a second man there. He didn't recognise me, but I remembered him. He was a Russian and I've seen him before. That's all I'm going to say. You don't know what I'm talking about, but Inglis will know if you tell him we saw this man together at the "*Papagei*", years ago.'

'You mean the Russians are interested in kidnapping Tenius?' asked Barber, forgetting his chivalrous concern in his surprise. 'That's nonsense, that can't be true. The Russians released Tenius from prison camp so that he could be tried!'

'Of course, you fool!' she almost screamed, and then lowered her voice with a terrified glance at the door of her room. 'They're interested in getting as much anti-German publicity as they can out of Tenius. They can make as much out of an escape as out of a trial. They don't care which it is, so long as the propaganda noise is loud. Don't you see, they use you newspaper people without you knowing it? What simpletons you are!'

'Well of course, we know that,' muttered Barber, defensively.

'Perhaps they were following Tenius to get a line on the Odessa people?' hazarded Kerenyi. 'Anything is possible. Or Malczewska may be right about the publicity value of an escape. Or an abduction by the emigré Poles, alternatively.'

'It doesn't matter what it is, so long as the publicity is widespread enough,' insisted Malczewska.

'Are you quite sure this man didn't recognise you?' Kerenyi's voice was still full of suspicion and his concern for Malczewska's safety now had a reluctant tinge.

'Quite sure,' she answered, stifling a renewed burst of sobs so that she could hardly be heard. 'He was just leaving the room as I came in, by another door. I hardly noticed him, but I had trouble closing the door as I went into the room. My arm, you know? So I had to turn round and close it with my left hand, and I saw out into the hall-way. He was walking across and I saw him clearly, but he didn't look round at me.'

'And you're sure of identifying him?'

'D'you think I'm ever likely to forget?' she asked savagely. 'Even if I hadn't seen his face, I'd be sure. He has a particular way of walking.'

Kerenyi rose as if the whole matter was of no further interest, and Barber rose with him, following Kerenyi's lead in a situation he did not fully understand.

'Of course, you understand I must tell Inglis about this at once?' Kerenyi said as she unlocked her door and stood waiting for them to go out into the corridor.

'Oh yes,' she said helplessly, turning her head away. 'In a way I suppose it's best.'

She did not watch them start down the stairs, but closed the flat door at once behind their backs, and they heard the key turning again, and her voice answering some grumbling query from her landlady.

XXI

'Oh, you know what the beginning of the season is like,' said Julia. 'Rather dull audiences, rather slack performances. Unfair, really. You're very quiet, Robert, tonight. Never mind, Lali will be back tomorrow.'

Robert allowed Julia to assume that his preoccupation was due to loneliness.

'They've just finished painting the baby's room in time,' he agreed tacitly with her remark. But for a moment he looked a little apprehensive, reminding Kerenyi of the unsure boy he first knew in 1946. Robert has grown up, he thought, it's astounding how authoritative and competent he now is with anything to do with his job. But still a bit scared of trying to deceive Julie.

'I shall be glad to see the children again,' he said, 'we've missed them haven't we, Julie?'

'I don't know why I never get any sympathy,' complained Barber. 'I'm lonely all the time, but nobody ever comforts me.'

'You're a confirmed bachelor,' explained Julia, 'but Robert is very much the family man. But I was going to single you out for attention, so there, you are quite wrong, you see. Tell us about this escape story, or wasn't it an escape?'

The three men carefully avoided looking at each other at this, but Julia noticed with amusement that they must have hoped the subject would not be touched upon.

'I was afraid you'd be in a rage when you heard about it,' said Robert, recognising her expression.

'I was, but that's hours ago. I heard in the interval,' she replied, 'and on mature reflection I've decided that if the brute gets away it is probably all for the best. Nobody wanted a trial, if we're honest, did they?'

'Mixed feelings, I think, all round,' agreed Barber. 'I played the story down, but the popular press will make a sensation out of it and I'm afraid there will be as much publicity as if there were a trial. You may all still be involved.'

'So it was an escape, then?'

'Did you think it wasn't?' Robert asked her curiously.

'Couldn't tell from the short report in the last edition of my dresser's paper. It was a bit garbled, I thought it was an abduction.'

'So did we to start with. But the police were generous and told us what they knew. Which proves they have no present hope of catching Tenius again. He's got clean away, it seems.'

'I doubt if the police really care much about laying hands on him,' hazarded Barber, 'except that they don't like being made fools of. But the policeman on duty did get two of the abductors, or liberators, and that no doubt soothed wounded pride.'

'There is a lot of feeling against all these war-crimes trials,' said Robert. 'I know a man whose job it is to assess public opinion for the Control Commission. He told me that every trial produces a crop of jokes about "victors' justice". And not only among the suspect types, either. Ordinary people resent the trials and have no feeling that they are either necessary or fair.'

'It's the mistake of putting soldiers on trial,' said Kerenyi. 'If the trials were confined to real criminals, public opinion would be for them, or at least neutral. But they believe the generals are tried out of professional jealousy; and after all, soldiers. . . .'

'It's a nasty precedent,' said Barber. 'In any future war, officers are going to be put on trial for show after being captured, and that can only reduce standards of behaviour still further. Don't you agree, Georgy?'

'Inevitably. I gather prisoners are treated shockingly in Korea.'

'They never signed the agreements about the rules of war,' said Robert uneasily. 'But what bothers me about our war-crimes trials, where they are justified, as in the case of Tenius, is the artificiality and the backward-validity—what's the word—of the laws under which they're tried. It's against all the theory of law to make a law and then try people under it for things done before the law existed.'

'You mean, they should be tried for murder, conspiracy to defraud and the like, according to the penal code of the country?'

'Well, at least ordinary people could then see what the crime was and why the trial is held.'

'D'you think Tenius will get clean away?' asked Barber suddenly. He looked at his watch, still thinking of deadlines, seven hours behind in New York. Robert followed his gesture and glanced at his own wrist quickly.

'Probably coming up to the Wechsel right now,' he said. 'They usually go as second driver on lumber transports or food trucks. Gustav Müller, motor mechanic, of Vienna, Hernals, aged 52. The border controls never even look at trucks that cross the Zone frontier regularly.'

'You mean you actually know what route they take?' asked Barber incredulously.

'Not all of them, by any means. . . .' Inglis hesitated noticeably.

'I'm only asking privately,' added Barber hastily. 'I shan't use anything you say.'

'I'm guessing, in fact. But the dead man is well known to us, and if it's his friends who are involved, we know where he was living and what his resources were.'

'Then couldn't you order—I mean somebody order—an inspection tonight?'

'Of course. But if there's going to be an Allied inspection— there is sometimes—they always seem to know well in advance.'

'The Austrian police?' asked Barber.

'I suppose so. Why wouldn't they drop a warning hint? Not necessarily knowing that the driver or co-driver are not what they seem. Just helping a regular road-user to avoid trouble. The trucking companies and their drivers are all, quite properly and naturally, familiar with the police and the pub-keepers along the main roads.'

'But surely someone would recognise a strange driver, just because they are regular travellers?'

'No, I don't think so. The bigger companies employ—let's say —a dozen drivers, and mechanics and others. Some are tall, some short, some young, some getting on; there's bound to be a type that more or less fits. Identity cards are worn to greasy blobs, the border patrols think they recognise a man they saw last week, one of a recurring stream of faces that they don't look at any more than you look at the postman.'

'But the real drivers must know,' objected Julia.

'No, they don't *know*. A chap comes up to him just before he goes on shift and says is it all right if his brother-in-law stands in for him tonight; he's got to go to the dentist tomorrow. Next week the driver's got a party coming up and will do the same himself to get a free night. The night foreman may know that a stand-in is being used, but unless there are a lot of the thefts he doesn't want to interfere with a conscientious employee. The regular drivers don't take criminals, they'd lose their jobs. They know all the wide boys who could get them into trouble. And if anybody thinks there's something odd about a certain man, well there are a lot of people who aren't too keen on the Allied checkpoints for all sorts of reasons. Maybe a girlfriend down in the country and the wife mustn't know or he's trying for a new job and doesn't want to make a fuss before he's sure of it. It's all on a much less strained level than one thinks from the outside. It isn't at all conspiratorial. Nobody comes up to the boss with his hat pulled down and dark glasses on, muttering out of the corner of his mouth. Truck drivers are quite a fraternity, you know, news passers, message carriers, taking a parcel one night to a chum's old mother, bringing a basket of apples back from a cousin's orchard to divide up between the boys. They don't think anything of it and why should they?'

'What a funny, mysterious little world that one doesn't suspect the existence of,' said Julia.

'It's only mysterious because you've never lived in the working-class world, darling. Now if *you* tried to hitch a ride with a truck driver, you'd frighten the life out of him. He'd know at once there was something wrong. But a shabby, elderly fellow in overalls, released from P.O.W. camp and looking for a job . . .? He's brought along by one of your mates and you were all in the army a year or so ago, weren't you?'

'But aren't all the various Allied security police alerted when somebody like Tenius escapes?'

'Of course they are. But it takes an hour or so at least. First the local police are called, or report it, as in this case, since there was a police watch on Tenius. The immediate police work, including a man shot dead and probably some damage in the hospital, that comes first. Preliminaries dealt with, a senior is informed. He telephones the department that works with the Allies. Then the Allied duty-officers are told. The duty-officers inform their own security police. It all takes an hour or so, and today is Sunday. In at least one of the various offices there'll be only a subordinate on duty who may have trouble finding his superior to report to. By the time they all get cracking, Tenius is way off on his travels.'

'If he doesn't have another heart attack,' said Kerenyi.

'He'll have the drugs prescribed for him in hospital,' pointed out Julia.

'The arrangements for the journey don't even have to be made hastily at the last moment. Since the escape from the hospital was planned well in advance, you can be sure they've fixed up his transport as well.'

'It seems frightful that a special watch wouldn't be on duty, when there has been so much publicity about Tenius,' Barber was hesitant, not wishing to appear critical of Robert.

'There was a special watch,' pointed out Kerenyi. 'Who seems to have acted with great zeal.'

'I mean . . .'

'It's more complicated even than I've made it,' said Robert. 'Allied politics comes into it. It's a Russian plan, releasing Tenius for trial, and no matter how keen the American or British authorities are on catching war criminals, it spoils their ardour a good deal to know that whatever they do will be used for Soviet propaganda. Then, experience with people under the protection of the SS survivors' brotherhood has been so unsuccessful that security officers don't try too hard because they have little hope of a catch. And I know they've been so cut down in numbers in the last year that they just don't have enough staff for anything like the big round-up needed for this sort of thing.' He hesitated and then went on, looking with a rueful smile at Julia. 'But the biggest factor is the civilian population. Just the very casualness easy-going and tolerant, lazy perhaps, that allowed so many people to slip through the hands of the Gestapo in the war here, operates now in favour of escapers like Tenius. I doubt if one in ten thousand people would actually take any trouble to help catch him.'

'Especially when it means being involved with the police,' said Julia, 'so time-wasting, the bureaucratic machine.'

The word bureaucrat reminded her of another concern and she turned to her husband to mention it before she should forget again.

'I have to see Malczewska tomorrow, about these designs. D'you know her telephone number, Georgy?'

He put his hand at once into his inside pocket to produce his address book, but the glance he exchanged with Robert and Barber told her that she was introducing a complication into some situation she was not supposed to know about. Georgy slid the notebook back into his pocket.

'Tell me when you want to see her and I'll collect her and bring her over,' he changed his mind.

'Oh, it's not all that urgent,' she said, pretending innocence, and enjoying their ever so slight embarrassment. Then, quickly, 'She isn't involved, is she?'

'Not with the police,' said Georgy, giving up the idea of a silent deception. 'But there may be . . .'

'There, I knew it, that evening with Berthold. What *has* she done?'

'Apparently nothing, but various people will have to be convinced that she had nothing to do with the escape.'

'But Malczewska is the last person on earth to allow Tenius to get away,' protested Julia. 'That's ridiculous. Who could need convincing of that!'

'The exile Poles were on the scene of the escape; it's a most extraordinary mixup, the whole thing. Malczewska is worried sick about losing her chance to get naturalised.'

'But that doesn't prevent her working—rather the contrary. . . .' Julia glanced from one face to the other and made some instantaneous mental adjustments. 'All right, Georgy, you bring her to our place tomorrow for coffee. I have a meeting in the morning. Can you manage about four-thirty in the afternoon? Or does that clash with something in the office?'

'Four-thirty will be fine,' said Georg.

'A meeting about *Cleopatra*?' asked Barber.

'No, about the history of the theatre. So you know about Cleo?'

'Half Vienna is discussing the new production. Either for or against. My "red" contacts say it is disgracefully expensive and won't be popular.'

'The sea battle will be popular. You'll bring Nando to see that Act, won't you Robert?'

'He'll love that. Death and destruction, alarums and excursions.'

And, at first to fix the change of subject, but soon for its own sake, Robert told them of the glorious summer, when rain fell just enough and during the nights. So hot was it that the children played all day practically naked, filled with sunlight and the fruits they constantly took as natural booty from the trees and plants about them, the older boy roaming about with the children of neighbours until his sturdy little frame was hard as wood and almost as dark. The younger clung to his mother's presence, mysteriously aware of his coming displacement and half sulky, half excited at the idea of what he was aware was happening. He made no clear transfer from births among the farm animals, the rapid heart-beat and muffled kicking he could equally feel when he lay half asleep, curled up with the Alsatian bitch in the shade of the hanging roses by the garden wall, and when he clung, rapturous with jealous love, to his mother. The puppies arrived on the same day as the baby and without much more disruption of his small world. Only the suddenly stern and pale face of his father during that morning taught him that something serious was happening. The arrival of the district midwife and nurse was no novelty for she had been going to and fro for weeks. He might have noticed being left alone, but his brother took him on an excursion to the nearby brook to play at fishing. Not until their return, fetched by the nursemaid, did the memory of his father's look frighten him, although there was no trace of that look any more. When he began to whimper, half really awed into fear and half to claim attention, his father took him up to Lali and read to them both Sebastian's favourite stories. But when the baby in the adjoining room raised its cracked wail, so unlike any other sound, Sebastian showed no curiosity, only looked at father and brother for guidance, his round little face trembling with some primitive grief which struggled with the already recognised need to spare his mother any fuss, as she lay there languidly smiling.

'Will she be flat again, now?' he asked Nando as the latter slowed his pace to a step on each tread of the stairs, going down with him. Then he turned and saw that his brother was silently crying. He did not feel so lonely then, though they cried companionably, sitting at the kitchen table to eat supper with Nanny Margarete who had been there all summer with them.

Sebastian spent much time in the following days with Dora, the Alsatian, and her puppies and was unconcerned with his mother, to punish her for not being allowed to get into the big bed with her. There were a great many things to do, and by the time the new baby could be seen downstairs, he had forgotten being cross with his mother and though she seemed to encompass him as much as ever with that atmosphere he was only aware of when it was lacking, Sebastian began to put on little airs of being too big for that sort of thing.

In all the surrounding country the harvests were in, except for the tall thickets of maize with their hot, dusty smell. The shooting season had begun and everyone about the place was additionally concerned to keep an eye on the two children in case they should wander anywhere near the guns, which caused indignation on Nando's part.

'The tragedy is,' went on Robert in his careful, rather slow voice, 'the people round about are so overworked that they can never enjoy their lives as they might do. There are hardly any labourers, and some of the neighbouring places have no house staff at all. The women have no time to make preserves, or embroider, the men no time to carve and as for music, they hear that only in Church. Nobody sings the old songs any more, not at home, anyway. Those who do these things now, make a profession of them for sale, and there isn't much of that in Styria, where there aren't many foreigners. The local people buy machine-made stuff; cheaper to buy, easier to keep clean. There are families in the district who were wealthy landowners a couple of generations back, and now they are almost poor-whites. They just can't get labour and their own men were decimated by the War.'

'It goes back before that,' said Julia. 'I remember my mother, she worked like a slave. And they leased most of the land, in those days. But, Robert, we seem to be able to get people now?'

'Well, look at the wages you pay,' said Georgy. 'Farmers can't afford your sort of money. The place is run as a luxury for us.'

'It won't be in a few years,' Robert promised. 'I mean to make the stables pay.'

'But you. . . .' Julia stopped and looked at him closely. Robert returned her gaze, with a slight mile of reassurance which yet had something in it of the challenge to defend a decision and a hope of their understanding.

'Perhaps you would prefer me not to take it over,' he said as if making a joke. 'But if you want it to earn money, the horses can do that; no professional breeder will have your interests at heart as Lali and I have, but there's no doubt you could get one.'

'I hadn't thought of it,' she said, a little blankly, and Kerenyi noted with amusement that Robert was taking over more than the stables.

'We have time,' he said easily. 'Robert's commission runs for a year, yet.'

'I think you did think of it,' Robert's voice was very gentle, 'or do I mean, it was in your mind?'

'Here comes Ostrovsky,' interposed Barber, who was facing towards the door of the room they sat in. 'Who's the girl?'

Hansi Ostrovsky and Monika stopped by their table in its high-backed booth with just that air of stopping for a greeting which assumes an invitation, and were duly asked to fill up the two empty places at the table.

'This is a fine state of affairs,' Hansi looked even more worried than usual. 'I've just seen Hella. Three theatres still left on her tour have asked her to "postpone". She's in floods of tears at the moment, I had to leave her to her mother and the doctor to give her a sedative. Of course, she'll have to cancel the whole tour.'

'But can the news of the escape have got about so quickly?'

Hansi looked gloomily and suspiciously at Barber, only glancing away irritably because the waiter hovered with the bill of fare.

'Bring us whatever the others had,' said Monika to the man nervously.

'The telegrams came before the news was out. No, it's worse than that. Poor Hella just isn't wanted.'

'How damned unfair,' Kerenyi scowled, 'but unfortunately, to be expected. A lot of people will have cancelled tickets.'

'And she missed one performance, staying here to deal with the divorce papers. I've no doubt the company got jumpy; that always asks for trouble on a tour.'

'She was quite desperate,' said Monika, 'I was almost frightened.'

'Poor Hella. She missed a performance for Tenius once before. Now it's caught up with her.' Hansi looked sharply at Julia and old, bitter memories rose in the look between them, while the others were silent, not knowing to what she referred.

'That oval dining room in the hotel in Warsaw,' Hansi said suddenly. '*We* were talking about divorce, then.'

'I thought everything was going to be all right, after the Press conference?' Monika ventured.

'A lot of people have thought that, one time or another,' said Barber. 'But sometimes ordinary people make up their own minds. Manipulating the newspapers is not always enough.'

Hansi was talking, not without unease at the presence of a foreign agent of the force of publicity, but assuming correctly that such internal affairs of the Burgtheater were not of interest abroad, of the need for a careful balance in the coming season. Only if

Hella performed just enough to avoid the appearance of having been banished, would it be possible to keep the theatre out of the unavoidable public controversy. The idea was insinuated without being spoken, that Hella would expect to be provided with appearances and that this was essential for the sake of continuity. It was not, as Hansi pointed out with his curiously opaque tactlessness, as if they were still in the immediate postwar period when every whisper of the Allied representatives in Vienna must be obeyed. They must, without making it assertively obvious, maintain the fundamental function of the stage, to provide those who paid for it with both amusement and spiritual nourishment. The underlying dialogue between audience and professionals must continue unbroken, but the way in which Hansi put this made it so much a matter of official policy, almost of governmental weight, that it became clear that the daily work of those who made up Hansi's 'fundamental function' was not fundamental but a part of politics; they were not simply and entirely concerned with the audience, but were being used for something outside their work. It was to return to, or was already considered to be, part of a concept larger, more important, than itself.

'The Directorate, one gathers, agrees with your attitude?' asked Kerenyi. And at a slightly startled but worried look from Ostrovsky, as if this was unchallengeable, he continued in a more forceful tone. 'This means, then, a slow and as far as the public goes, a secret change of theatrical policy. You are, in essence, agreeing with the wartime view of the theatre as a political factor. In the last years it has been agreed, as I understood it, that the whole energy of the theatre administration should be directed to the opposite purpose. That is, gradually to take the theatre out of its non-theatrical framework and re-establish it as a genuine dialogue between public and professionals, between the stage and the world. That is, to my view, the only way we can recover any genuine interest in the theatre, stimulate a real communication so that new ideas can move and new plays be written which would have the same relevance to our world as the classic plays—one thinks of Ibsen or Schiller, perhaps —had to theirs. Your accommodation with what you think to be political necessity will strangle communication and make the theatre into a sterile historical object again.'

'But you are taking my views much too far,' protested Hansi. 'I am speaking of a quite short period, during which we must be careful to avoid political interest in ourselves, just in order to keep our freedom of action in the future.'

'Nobody keeps his freedom of action by giving in to pressure. Here less than anywhere, because here we are under the constant pressure of our own so evenly balanced political Parties. Where every stupid Party boss can prevent the theatre and opera budgets from being passed if some favourite scheme of his is not agreed to. That is a burden you can't get rid of, because your money depends on it. If you agree to its being widened as a matter of agreed principle, then you have reversed the policy—not the practice, unfortunately—which the theatre administration has been committed to since the War.'

'What you mean, Hansi,' said Julia, 'is that the company must protect one of its members in a matter that has nothing to do with the stage. You are deliberately taking the theatre into politics.'

'Would you wish the Allied Control Commission to enforce some kind of inspection of our personnel and programmes?' asked Hansi indignantly. 'I assure you, that could happen.'

'Rubbish,' she said brusquely. 'It's as simple as abc. For her own sake, Hella keeps quiet for a month or so. The Burg has nothing to do with it at all. If she is either suspended or insists—or you insist —on a demonstrative appearance, you invite interference.'

'But Hella is insisting. Her view is that only an announcement that she is to play a major part in a major production this season, can recover her own and the theatre's position.'

'And you have agreed to that view?' Kerenyi's question was really a statement. 'Have you forgotten that Hella was, in fact, a Party member? If you allow this, you'll get on very slippery ground. So far, Hella's position is shaky but recoverable; that of one who admits a mistake. We had this argument over Hella's Press conference, and she herself saw then that any intervention from you— that is from the theatre direction—would be bad for her.'

'Exactly. But she now sees herself as cleared, and expects us to back her up for our own sakes.'

'You will force a public row over Hella's Party membership.'

There was now an increasingly definite climate of animosity in the discussion which made the three supposedly neutral observers of it uneasy and they began to exchange small remarks between themselves, in order to disclaim any interest in what was being said.

'Hella was de-Nazified, like the rest of us. That is all ancient history.' Hansi's tone was so irritable that Kerenyi understood that he still resented the battle between them on the telephone, in which he, Kerenyi, kept Ostrovsky out of Hella Schneider's meeting with the newsmen. He thinks I went behind his back then, thought Georg, and I suppose I did.

'Julie, you will at least think it over? You won't take up an uncompromising position? I know what you're like when you once get your heels stuck in.'

It was a personal appeal which went back almost to their childhood, and an appeal, whether Hansi was conscious of it or not, which went over Kerenyi's head, cut out his later influence implicitly by asserting an older loyalty. Hansi is jealous, thought Kerenyi, and he saw clearly that Ostrovsky would, without saying anything, or knowing of any need to say anything, try to turn Julia away from himself, convince her that a complete communion between them was inimicable and not beneficial to her work. Convince her of just that danger of giving her inner self away, which she had instinctively always felt. The barrier will go up again, he said inside himself, and she won't know how much the two hang together, her achievement in her calling and her relationship with me. He felt an angry fear which was only partly egotism. For the first time he knew that he and Ostrovsky were enemies.

Julia was denying taking up any position. Up to a few minutes ago, she believed that they all agreed in their attitude to Hella and her difficulties, including Hella. Hella was afraid of losing her hold on her career if she withdrew from it for a month or so, and that was understandable. A compromise must be found, one that would satisfy no one, but would bridge the cleft of interests, which at bottom were a common interest. There was no question of a retirement, not even for a time, by Hella. That would be almost as bad as an open breach, or an open defence of Hella's really indefensible situation. It *was* bad luck that she had not managed to divorce Tenius before his return. Human relationships hardly counted in this case, for the relations between Tenius and Hella never had been above the cold level of a marriage of ambition on both sides, in which each was using the other, sensually in private and interestedly in public. The practical point was that here was Hella, in the slang phrase, stuck with it; and the cure for her disorder was time and discretion.

'What part was it Frau Schneider wanted, Hansi?' asked Mon-

ika. 'I mean, after you told her the *Macbeth* production was put off?'
The questions were not intended to produce answers, but to show
Robert and Barber that she, Monika, was intimately involved in
the professional lives about her as much as any of them and much
more than the two outsiders.

But they were extremely unwelcome to Hansi at that moment,
and he felt a spasm of violent annoyance, a desire to give her a
sharp slap that would be more painful than a love-pat, but would
show her—what? He had a sensation of Monika's smooth, almost
childish body naked and to disguise his momentary anger as desire,
he leaned over and kissed her dear little nose, to show her whatever
it was. Monika laughed and rubbed the tip of her pretty nose,
pleased at the look she was getting from Barber and delighted at
having changed the course of the talk. For, in fact, no more was
said just then about Hella Schneider, as if everyone agreed with
Julia's suggested compromise; the Englishman assumed an ex-
pectedly prim expression at the public caress, while the American
began to tease her in a heightened aura of her desirability. Hansi,
however, knew that Julia's sharp wits registered the question and
that she would return to it on a more appropriate occasion.

XXII

The habit of always returning together to their own privacy and to the same surroundings was, as Kerenyi admitted, growing rapidly on him. There was a good deal to be said for a certain atmosphere of domesticity, it provided a base for excursions, not necessarily of physical movement, and he was finding that work was easier in the changed circumstances. Always to return to the same place was not new to Julia and she was still slightly surprised to find in herself an urgent wish to be there again when she was away from home. To return home had for years been a threat of anxiety which no amount of devotion could sweeten. Once there was compulsion in the thought; she *must* get back. She was forced by circumstances which contained a fear so dreadful that she could neither face it openly in her mind, nor ever forget it for a moment. The memory of this was sometimes still present to her. Not frequently now in their own home, for it was so changed in both outer and inward aspects, but in the entrance to the house, the always shadowy and chill hallway, the lift with its jerk and so-familiar groan of effort, the curtained inner window where for years the possibility of danger watched. Passing through the hallway could still reproduce the sensation of caution, reluctance and apprehension.

The new occupants of the porter's lodge were much younger than the former people, with jobs and lives of their own outside the house so that concern with their neighbours and the tenants no longer made up their whole interest. Anyone could now come and go, and the knowledge that nobody was interested was part of the post-war atmosphere, a lightening, an unnoticed sureness that these new people were simply Julia's employees with no other duties in the house but to keep the door and clean the public passages. The change was noticeable on the present occasion because the janitor was wheeling his bicycle through the hall to a back passage as they entered, coming back from an evening shift at the garage where he worked. His cheerful and unconcerned greeting, lacking in the oppressive respect of everything the Pichlers said to her, but lacking too the implication of anything behind the words themselves, almost startled her.

She encompassed this by the comment in the lift, that he was a nice fellow, and this gave rise to Kerenyi's expressing a whole amplitude of comfort and enjoyment which was fresh to him, and as she had gradually noticed, new to herself.

The profound difference between an external worry about Tenius and his escape, with all its tiresome and complex details, and the obsessional anxiety of the War Years—the end of the War was missing from her conscious thought and was never admitted to her mind—struck her almost with a shock, as if it were actually something new which had only just happened with the sight of the man downstairs. She spoke of this to Georg, stumbling slightly in her effort to put into words what she avoided thinking of as a rule. It was, the whole period and its black emotions, he answered, an artificially induced psycho-neurosis from which healthy minds could recover. And, thinking of Malczewska, he went on to surmise the pervasive mass psycho-neurosis still smothering great tracts of Europe in its breathless pall. Kerenyi thought of this pall as a future endemic social danger, the danger of spontaneous explosions of rage. He mentioned Poland in passing, and this brought Malczewska into Julia's thoughts as well.

'What was it about Malczewska you three were trying to hide during supper?' she asked. 'Before Hansi came in?'

It was agreed that Julia did not need to know precisely what Robert's interest in Malczewska was, and Georg now gave her a generalised account of the events of the evening, explaining only that the Polish refugee could give both Robert and the Viennese police information they valued, and thus smooth her own path to naturalisation with the authorities. Robert, he said, had at once suggested that a rapid transfer from homelessness to the possession of Austrian citizenship was not only Malczewska's dearest wish but her only protection against renewed attempts to embroil her in either emigré or Communist affairs.

'If we backed her it would be even quicker,' pointed out Julia.

'Would you do that?' he asked. 'You might perhaps even induce Hella to sign her petition? It's been hanging about for months, apparently, because the poor girl can't even prove she was born, let alone find sponsors.'

'Hella! I wonder if I could—that would be a real triumph of diplomacy.'

'To judge by this evening's conversation,' he suggested slyly, 'you have Hella's pawns in your hands. You might as well use your advantage.'

She laughed softly, enjoying being managed.

'Something else I noticed this evening: you've lost your attraction for Monika almost as quickly as she discovered it.'

'She's at the age of half-fantasy when the real attraction is her own sensation of desire. It disperses itself like a lure towards whatever is new. Or rather, untried, since she seems to prefer men much older than herself.' He considered Julia caressingly. 'I wonder if you were ever like that?'

'Oh yes, I remember it. A drenching of the atmosphere, like flowers in a garden. If it hadn't been cut off sharply, I expect I'd have turned into a voluptuary. As it was, I turned ambitious. Only I think we were more conscious of it, then, because there was still the guilt feeling. That's disappeared now.'

'A great loss, I wouldn't be without it. Not that I believe it has disappeared. Or not for long. Too indispensably part of pleasure.'

'I must see if I can't recover that atmosphere somehow, with Cleo,' she mused aloud, a habit that was growing.

'That shouldn't be too difficult,' he said, 'in the circumstances. Just don't let it get attached to Thorn, will you, though? He's a bit too experienced in those matters to make a good rival.'

'There's always a danger of that,' she considered, teasing him with a serious air.

'What you will have to do,' Georgy went on, now really meaning his words, 'is to try, in the intimate scenes, to switch off your "presence". You know? The trick you have of creating a space around your person?'

'You had better come and stand in the wings from time to time.'

'Darling,' he said touched into an unusual softness. 'That's the nicest compliment you ever paid me.'

'In words, anyway.'

In the stilly night air of the streets, an aeroplane drew across the sky, trailing sound.

'Will Berthold come back, now Tenius has escaped?' Julia asked, and was surprised afterwards, that the sound brought with it the thought of Luders and not that of air-raids, as an aeroplane at night usually did.

'I suppose so. Though I don't know—perhaps not. Unless he's caught.'

In the morning, a soft grey light flowed in at the window, and as Julia turned her head towards the glass, this dimmed and sunless light seemed only slowly to emerge from soundless billows in the deeps of the sea. She drifted up glassy, grey-green rollers and was unnoticeably carried by them on to some far shore on which sand and vaguely outlined rocks, boulders, perhaps even cliffs bounded the uncertain line of change through sea and air and what was not yet land, but a sensation between floating in the sea and resting in only just less billowing and supporting sands. Now she was on the shore and the slow boom of the sea's withdrawal echoed as if still under water, in the recesses of being. She was entirely alone here but not alone, connected with being and meaning. As she turned and began to raise herself on the shore the illusion which was not illusion faded into memory; she raised herself in bed and she was alone and there was no sunshine through the windows from which the curtains were already drawn back. Passing from one state of awareness to another without either effort or break, she drifted to the windows and saw that autumn was there.

Then sounds penetrated, and sliding hands into the sleeves of a dressing gown, yawning and pushing the hair off her forehead, Julia slowly moved into the long room where Kerenyi sat drinking coffee and muttering critical comments to himself over the morning paper.

He looked up with instant awareness of her arrival, although she made no sounds, and his face changed entirely.

'I think I dreamed of Greece,' she yawned again. 'The sun's gone, at last.'

She was puzzled by the feeling that it was not of Greece she had dreamed, and that it was not really a dream, either. She stretched lazily as Georgy poured her some coffee and pushed the cup slightly towards her on the bright pink linen cloth.

'Such a pretty colour,' she said sleepily. 'What do the papers say about Tenius?'

'General self-righteous indignation. Nobody cares, everybody pretends they do.'

'Bit like the way I feel about it. I did care, when I actually saw him I cared a lot, but it doesn't seem to matter much any more.'

'I hope you're not going to be self-righteous, though?' he said, smiling at her languid air.

'Oh no,' she sounded slightly shocked at that notion. 'I'm sorry about the man killed, though. Couldn't the policeman have shot him in the leg?'

'They were all three—four with Tenius, I suppose—moving about. I doubt the guard had a clear target. But you need not be too sorry. He was a really bad lot, an ex-SS thug released on some legal quibble from Landsberg.'

'Give me the paper,' she demanded, cutting the top off an egg. 'You knew all this last night. I want to see.'

He passed her the newspaper and felt in his dressing gown pocket for cigarettes. Instead of reading the account of the attempted abduction and successful escape of the wanted man, Julia turned to the Arts page and scanned the theatre news.

'Good. It's out,' she said, meaning the article on the new theatre programmes for the season just begun. 'Can't change it easily now. First night at the end of January.'

'Were you expecting someone to want to change the plan?'

'I didn't feel too happy about Hansi's manner last night,' she admitted. She turned now to the front page and read the headlines about the war in Korea, about a petition to the President, about a scandal in the building industry. Then she read the real news.

'They don't give the dead man's name. Next-of-kin, I suppose?'

'Yes. His mother is still somewhere about, they have to tell her first. But I know his name if you want it. Ulrich Benda.'

'That reminds me of something,' said Julia and frowned.

'Me too. He was in the same interrogation camp I was in in '46.'

'What a coincidence!'

'A nasty man' said Georgy judicially. 'It's odd how people turn up again and again in one's life.'

'Well, he won't turn up any more,' she said heartlessly, without remembering why she no longer felt any concern at his death.

'I wonder where Tenius is by now?'

'If Thorn's news a week or so ago is correct, in Bozen.'

'Today in Bozen, tomorrow in Trieste, next day on board a Lloyd-Triestino ship bound for Rio.'

'Won't they wait a little, to tidy him up, first?'

'Possibly, but I doubt it. A wig, dark glasses and a recommendation to the ship's doctor of a very sick man needing complete rest and privacy.'

'Name of Schmidt!' Julia ate her egg in silence and with appetite.

'Darling, don't forget to get me those papers to sign for poor old Malczewska. Or do I have to write a letter?'

'I'll find out this morning and let you know. I expect a letter would be a good thing, as well, in any case.'

'Well, you just tell me what to do, and I'll do it.' She thought for a moment and then went on. 'I just hope we're doing the right thing with Malczewska. She really hates us all, you know.'

'I hope and believe she will feel differently when she has some genuine identity. Don't you think so?'

'Well, I can't judge. It must be awful not to be anybody, I see that, not to belong anywhere. Probably you're right.'

'You will see, this afternoon, what a state of nervous distress she is in.' Kerenyi did not discuss his own anger and suspicion the evening before and he told himself that it was unnecessary to worry Julia with his momentary fears. But he felt a quite new unease at hiding from her what was in his mind, a scruple he never felt before with any woman. Indeed, formerly the stronger his feeling for a woman, the more he had always felt entitled to make decisions on her behalf without troubling her for her own opinions. And that Julia seemed ready in this matter to delegate responsibility to him made his unease deeper because he knew that her confidence was founded on the mistaken assumption that he was bound to have told her everything concerning Malczewska. Lali is coming home today, he thought, so Robert will be busy, but I'll have a word with him tomorrow.

'What d'you think of Robert's idea of leaving the Service?' he asked.

'I'm not sure. I don't want Lali to have the penurious life of endless work that my mother had.'

'That is a matter of capital, surely? Your people had no money to invest in the place, to expand it, do something with it.'

'That's true. And it would mean that Nando's future was settled. But it is rather unambitious of Robert, somehow. Don't you feel that?'

'No, I don't. Robert took the defection of Stephenson and the Communist infiltration of British Intelligence very hard, you know. He's such a quiet chap, one can easily ignore his feelings. And, too, we think of ambition being connected with big towns, with public life in some form. Country life has been devalued, but that is our mistake, not its own loss of value. Land has been gradually robbed of its dignity, its prestige, but nowadays transport is so effective, that country life and its proper influence in the world may come back into its own. If Robert made a career of the place, it would give the place back its real dignity—it would cease to be a suburb of your town life, a luxury.'

'I suppose it's been in the air for some months, but I didn't notice it.'

'It must have been. Robert's not the man to make sudden moves, is he . . . ?'

'I've thought about it, it's true, but in the future. For Nando, in case the Kasda place . . . we can't know what will happen in Lower Austria.'

'Lali's mother and a generation ago, your mother—they are the real heroes of our time. Holding things rather helplessly together for the future.'

At the same moment the telephone began to ring, the postman pressed sharply at the doorbell and Frau Lisl could be heard greeting him. They rose from breakfast and the day was started.

The art historians from Munich were about to leave, and this morning's meeting was full of the compliments from all sides, the thanks for help given, usual on such occasions. The careful formalities of the Germans, their pedantic exactitudes, were already wearisome and must now be gone through from the beginning, over again. There was a question, apparently, of the copyright of some of the photographs they proposed to use, and for this reason Hella's presence was perhaps not entirely essential, but at any rate felt by herself to be needed. Looking a little wan, a certain pallor showing through both the summer tan and her superb self-confidence, Hella included herself and was included by the historians, so that not only her right to be there but their implied need of her was established. Up to now Hella had been occupied with other affairs and took no part in the volunteered aid of the Burgtheater in the work of the academics. Now she insinuated with her somewhat bored manner that in spite of much other business she was quite willing to be used by them. It was not until the coffee drinking and handshaking was over that Julia understood that this taking on of protective colour was not all that was planned for the morning. Hella was coming with Julia to the hired rooms of the Ronacher, or rather its extension, where fabrics must be inspected and plots against the costumier carried further, and where a group of the production team was gathered. Nothing at all was said about Hella's abruptly terminated tour in so many words; only a suggestion of scorn in the air gave the hint that Hella could really not be bothered with people who made such ridiculous fusses and that they must get along as best they could without their star performer. Neither was the cancellation of the other Shakespeare production originally planned for that season as much as referred to obliquely.

The stage designer, Florian, usurping even more ground than the despised Peter's competence, was full of ideas encroaching on the producer's territory. Whether he knew it or not, and he may have plucked the notion from the gossip of the last few days, Florian judged with minute exactness how far he could advance his determination to put his imprint on the project in hand. Hansi Ostrovsky showed a slackening of his nervous concentration that morning, and this allowed the latitude he normally held in narrow bounds, to be extended in an elastic web of casualness which could always be withdrawn again if it proved to be widening too far. What caused Hansi's division of concentration was not at first clear, but it was Jochen Thorn, who had once known Hella intimately, who first grasped what the hidden suggestion was going to be from some tiny break in her smooth run of comments and questions. This unnoticeable catch of a mental breath came when the proximity of Cleopatra to her attendants at a number of moments in the play made both a contrast and a harmony in the colours of their robes a question of subtle decision on which they could not easily agree. Anita Silovsky as Charmian made her own opinion clear, but the part of Iras was not yet filled so that there was no one present to offer her balancing or contrary viewpoint, and here came that hardly measurable hesitation from Hella before she gave, as an independent, her view. Thorn looked across the room at Hansi, not believing in his own intuition, and at that very moment Hansi interrupted the movement of his hand in turning over a sheet of sketching paper on the table, and glanced up at Julia, to whom he was speaking. He instantly looked down again at the sketch, completing the movement of turning it over to lay it face down. The only question now remaining in Thorn's mind was why Hansi had agreed to this manoeuvre. The inclusion of an actress of the first rank in a secondary part was not unusual; but Hella did not normally co-operate, if she could help doing so, in such demands of casting.

A few minutes later someone mentioned Walter Harich, whose major new production was to be a drama of the War, a play that later became famous but was then still unknown. Hella laughed and rallied Hansi with having arranged for Harich to get this role—which he was not to produce—as compensation for not getting Shakespeare's Antony. It was quite untrue, Hansi countered, laughing with them all. They all knew very well that the War play was already engaged for a year before, and he had taken no hand at all in its planning. Why this exchange from one unspoken question of casting to another already known, should confirm Thorn in his guess he did not know, but it did.

On their way from the room, Thorn asked Julia what she thought now of the progress of their work, and she replied that she was still undecided about costumes. Adaptations of designs none of them approved were a mistake, and she should tackle Hansi on the subject as soon as she was clear about whether Malczewska could produce ideas more in keeping with Florian's suggestions. Thorn was surprised at Malczewska being seriously proposed as a source of costume design and when Julia admitted having been herself sceptical until the newcomer's creativity convinced her that she was familiar with all branches of theatrical art, Thorn agreed that a new hand could be tried. But, he said, that was not exactly what he had in mind. Julia stopped in the doorway and turned the full force of her gaze on his bold, aquiline face.

'Ah, you mean . . . ? It was like me, in the war? That's what I thought about it. Playing for the highest stakes with great skill.'

'You really are breath-taking sometimes,' he said reluctantly. 'But—since you mention the War—you can hardly compare what you played for with a professional set-back like Hella's?'

'Why not? Everyone puts the stakes at their own value.'

'Let's go on, the others are coming. Tell me something—you brought the subject up, remember. Did you ever think that you could have gone to jail for years?'

'Of course,' she said. 'I was scared blind.'

They walked on and Thorn turned his steps to accompany her on her short way home.

'I'll tell you something else,' she said, her voice held down and vibrating with the controlled vitality which fascinated him. 'In the same position, Hella would have done what I did.'

'You can't be serious! You and Hella are entirely different kinds of women. You couldn't be more different than you are.'

'Ah, but you see, we've each developed after the trend of our experience. I don't believe this dogma about character being fixed in childhood. I know I've changed, and it's what happened to me that changed me. If those things had happened to Hella, she would have been forced into another development, too.'

'But she would never have allowed those things to happen. That's the point.'

'She could no more have helped herself than I could. It could easily have happened to Hella, if her stepfather hadn't died when he did, and if her first husband hadn't gone off to Hollywood. Look —after the first moment, a moment one doesn't *know*, the crime against the State is committed and from that moment on, there's no going back. That's what outsiders don't understand, people who haven't lived with it.'

They were near the house now, and Thorn stood, thinking sombrely.

'You are right,' he said at last. 'That's what we can never explain.'

Julia put out her hand and smiled interrogatively.

'No thanks,' he said, 'I won't come up.' He took her hand and kissed it, even though they were standing in the street.

XXIII

'But why did you arrive in an Army automobile?' Julia asked the question with astonishment. Malczewska glowered in answer, as Julia could see, but said nothing, only turning back towards Kerenyi who entered behind her. It was one of those dull autumnal afternoons when the rooms in big cities are dim, and to turn on lamps and expel the shadowy bulks of a multitude of high houses and piled clouds would only confuse the eye still more with crossing planes of half-lights.

Malczewska sank into an easy chair with a stiff weariness that showed she was in pain, and hauled her useless arm angrily across her thin lap.

'I seem always to be offering you coffee,' said Julia. 'Would you rather have a drink?'

'God, I would,' Malczewska's deep, almost masculine voice grated with irritable depression, and since Kerenyi clearly did not mean to answer Julia's query, she added with an edge on her voice, 'I came in an army car because I'm in protective custody. There's a British sergeant outside your door right now.'

'Oh dear,' said Julia, still more astonished, 'hadn't we better ask him in?'

'I did, idiot angel,' said Georgy. 'He says he's on duty and can't.'

At the extreme childishness of this endearment, Malczewska looked up at Georgy with disgust; evidently such intimacies did not form part of her picture of their private life, and neither did she welcome an implied approach to familiarity with them.

'But protective custody?' The expression had a sinister sound for those who lived through years of tyranny, and Julia's voice encompassed its associations.

'Not in a dungeon! She's staying in a room of her own with a bathroom in a special guest place up at Schönbrunn barracks. Robert says it's where the King's Messengers stay.'

'But why didn't you tell me last night, Georgy? I've practically committed myself to produce some ideas for designs. . . . I thought you were working!' Julia turned from one to the other of them, astonishment giving way to impatience at their uncommunicativeness.

'Robert didn't want you—anyone—to know until the formalities were arranged. He couldn't get the whatever-it-is until this morning.'

'I've done some sketches,' muttered Malczewska, defensive and half injured. 'Hell, I've left my portfolio in the hall!' Before she could even begin to rise, Georgy was out of the door and returned with the black sketching cover. 'I shouldn't think the drawing is any good. I was in such a state I couldn't keep my hand still.'

'That doesn't matter—Peter's staff can redraw them. Oh, show me, Georgy, don't fiddle with that thing!'

'Patience, patience. Don't bully me.' The tape was tangled, tied as it was by Malczewska's awkward single hand. She rose, biting her lip to hide her nervousness, but it was freed and Julia almost pulled the top sheet out of Georgy's grasp in her eagerness. Nothing could have been more flattering to Malczewska than this enthusiasm and impatience, and the strain in the thin, dark face as Julia positively swallowed the drawings whole, one after another, would have been unbearable if either of the others had been looking.

'They're good,' cried Julia jubilantly, 'they really are! Thank goodness—I was so afraid I'd have to sing small after all the fuss I've made. This is splendid, so is this. This one's no use. Here, Georgy, look!' She pushed the sheets at her husband and, still overflowing with delighted, broken-off phrases, Julia caught the stiff, anxious figure in both arms and kissed Malczewska with emphatic gratitude on her lined cheek. Between amazement at the change in Julia and relief at her success, Malczewska was for a moment almost stunned. Then the ugly face twisted painfully, she sat down as if her knees were folding under her and began to cry.

They could not help themselves laughing at this and after a moment Malczewska began to laugh with them, in spite of weeping, and almost choked herself.

'Now I've got them!' sang Julia, and began to spin in waltz time. 'Now we shall see what they say! Florian will be delighted, the others will be in a rage, I can make them do what I want, it's splendid, splendid!'

'I don't understand at all why you're so excited,' said Malczewska. 'Does the costume question make such a difference?'

Julia sank into a chair, still laughing and a little out of breath.

'Not by itself, but it's much more than costumes. You see, Hella wants to cover her nakedness by creeping under the wing of this production. She wants to play Iras. The others won't like that because she's too big for the part. Except Hansi who for some reason of his own, has agreed. If I let myself be persuaded that Hella should get the part, they'll have to let me have my own way over the rest of the production—*and* Hella will have to sign your papers *and* you'll get your foot in the door at the theatre, at any rate as a consultant.'

'But that's a terrible idea, Hella as Iras!' objected Georgy, in a furious tone.

'Not at all. In any case, she'll be fed up with the idea in a week or so when she recovers her nerve and then she'll back out. And if she does play it—why not? She's very good, you know that.'

'It will make trouble,' said Georgy with conviction. 'I feel it in my bones. It will pull you into the Tenius affair.'

'I don't see how it can. But I don't think it will come to anything, this plan. She'll take over in the Nestroy; and then, "Lovely Lulu" is going back to the Thalia so one of Chekov's three gloomy sisters will be clear for her. You'll see . . . but in the meantime, I can get what I want, if I work fast.'

'I still don't see. . . .'

'But of course you do! I was betting on your costume ideas to put a lever under Hansi—evidence that we can make the production visually new—different—not just fall drearily between the two stools of Florian's stage sets which are revolutionary, and the old moth-eaten notions of Shakespearian production. Without some terrific designs to slap on to the table before him, I didn't have a case!'

Malczewska was watching Julia with a still suspicious concentration. 'I suppose you do realise,' she asked, 'that you've completely changed? You seem like a different woman.'

Julia gave her a sharp and laughing look but she did not answer the comment. Instead she took the portfolio from Kerenyi and shuffled several of the designs out of the handful in it. They were all rather bad drawings which would have to be copied by a professional, for Malczewska was no draughtsman.

'Redraw a couple of lines for me, here,' she said. 'They aren't clear as you've done them. And this one I don't like—can you do another one?' She deciphered the scrawl at the foot of the sheet. ' "Charmian, Act V". I'll mark it on the back, shall I?'

'Here, let me have them.' Malczewska pulled herself towards a small table and then looked about her. 'No. I'll need the big table.'

'What a slave-driver you are, Julie,' protested Kerenyi. 'Give the poor thing time to have her drink, at least.'

'No, no, I'll drink it afterwards.' Malczewska was already leaning over the round dining table and muttering to herself as she scanned her work.

In half an hour the designs were substantially improved, so that the exigent Julia was satisfied and Malczewska reluctantly obliged to remember that she was 'awaited without' as she put it, in a Shakespearean joke, by soldiers.

'If only poor Krassny was still at the Interior,' said Julia as the guest was going, 'we should have your papers signed and sealed in a few days. But don't worry. It won't be more than a week or so.'

'As a matter of fact, though the whole thing is being exaggerated, I'm not sorry to be where I am—a private bathroom is a great luxury. I wallow in the hot water for hours on end.'

Julia and Kerenyi noticed with the satisfaction of those who combine their own interests with a service to another, that the prospect of success was at once having a mollifying effect on Malczewska's difficult temperament.

'What did she mean, the whole thing is exaggerated?' Julia asked as soon as they were alone again. 'And why did Robert feel she needed protection?'

'She is suspected by the exile Poles of being not altogether on their side, and they have some rather rough habits,' Kerenyi explained. 'The police, I gathered—of course, they don't say much—know that the SS group was in touch with friends of the Polish exiles through this man, Benda. They met at some squalid little bar in the Leopoldstadt which is watched by the police. It's all rather obscure, but Robert thought that until Malczewska has the protection of a genuine citizenship, she was better off among the brutal and licentious soldiery than among the chivalrous Poles.'

'Very proper caution on Robert's part,' approved Julia.

'And, incidentally, Malczewska was far from thinking care unnecessary last night. You, on the other hand, are being imprudent over Hella. I just hope you get away with it.'

'When I've got what I want, there is still time to reconsider,' pointed out Julia, with the hard practical judgment of the professional dealing with her own intimately understood position.

'Thank God you're on my side,' said Kerenyi laughing. 'I wouldn't care to have you as an enemy. . . .'

'Enemy?' she was sincerely surprised at the word. 'But I have no enemies, no personal ones.'

'That,' he said, 'to be coarse, is what *you* think, my love.'

But all this excitement, as Julia put it to herself, was quite outside her real life, a sordid overspill from the War which belonged to the notorious Leopoldstadt and occasionally flowed far enough over its banks to touch some unfortunate like Malczewska. At some moment one of them would have the disagreeable task of making it clear that citizenship and the entry into a more stable livelihood, if achieved by the aid of herself and Georgy, would bring with it the need for Malczewska to detach herself by an effort of will from her obsession with the past. Bluntly put, as they would not put it in words, Malczewska was going to be obliged to drop her former acquaintances if she wanted to recreate her life.

Stepping into the evening street for the few minutes' walk to the Ronacher, Julia was surprised to find a chill in the dusky air; from high summer it was autumn within a few hours, and so much was it autumn, that the hint of winter already lay in the clouds pressing almost on the rooftops. Very softly, a dim, small rain only just heavier than September dew, began to fall and gradually damped the pavement.

Lali, the next day, repeated this thought. The sun of that summer was so strong and fierce, so sustained, that all the trees were early turning their colours and before it was time to come back to the city the gold and copper of leaves mingled with the brilliant reds of apples on the young fruit trees, and the mourning purple of a heavy plum crop was left visible as the half-dry foliage scattered. This time was a feast for the pigs and geese, competing with much grunting and hissing in the thick grass, already twice scythed, for the rich harvest of fallen fruit. Lali herself resembled the trees, almost as russet brown as the winter pears, glowing with stored sunshine like the apples, she was delighted and relieved to have shed the burden of pregnancy and assured them with the frankness of perfect health that if there were to be any more children these must arrange to be born in winter or spring. Until the other guests arrived, neither Robert nor Lali talked of anything but the country and their life there and it was quite clear that their whole contentment was already firmly bound up in the prospect of returning to country life soon and permanently.

These intimacies ceased at the entry of Hansi Ostrovsky and Monika. Neither country life nor domesticity was part of their lives and the spare anxieties of Hansi's manner soon made it obvious that professional matters were on his mind even to the extent of coming in between his preoccupation with Monika. Not that the conversation turned at once to the theatre; having refused to drink anything but mineral water on the grounds of his touchy liver, Hansi began to talk in wide circles of concert programmes, of the winter collection offered that day by a well-known dressmaker which was of interest to Monika, of the progress being made in the rebuilding of Willy Mundel's house in the Marchfeld. In short, of anything and everything except what was unceasingly in his mind. Should one, he proposed, follow Mundel's example? Perhaps the year-long negotiations of the Austrian Ambassador in Moscow would lead to a result and the four Allies would at some time still only dimly be seen in the future, leave the country; in that still hypothetical case land in eastern Austria would become valuable property once more and it could be a good bargain to buy oneself a little something in that line for the pittance it would cost at this moment? He heard recently as the most vagrant of hints that the whole matter could, eventually, turn on the question of Austria's adhering to neither east nor west, the geographical and topographical situation of the country making it strategically so important. A new 'Swiss' solution was being whispered of, although neither eastern nor western powers were yet even remotely ready to abandon their plans to build Austria into either one or other of the blocks between which the Danube was a handy if inaccurate figurative division.

Hansi was almost visibly disappointed at a failure to draw Kerenyi into this fascinating speculation, for a good reason of which the speaker was unaware. Kerenyi had been one of the first people in Vienna to see the distant possibility of adhering to neither side when the abortive but not abandoned efforts to draw the western parts of Germany into a west-European defence posed the implied question of what was to become of cis-danubian Austria in that case. If men like Kerenyi had failed at that time to maintain a stubborn but unnoticeable silence on this subject, there is little doubt that the occupation of Austria would have lasted for generations rather than for years. The infinitely delicate task of the faithful diplomat in Moscow who was looked upon by the simple as a most sinister fellow, would have been impossible without a conscious conspiracy of discretion in the face of gossip such as Ostrovsky's. As so often in public affairs, Kerenyi was among those obliged not only on this evening, to bear the quips of chatterers who were glad to suggest that the editor did not, after all, know as much as he claimed to.

Faced with this apparent innocence, Hansi turned his remarks to the German millionaire of such recent fortune who lately visited Kerenyi and Julia, and since there was no reason to preserve silence on this topic, they were glad to go into much detail on the subject of Luders, his money and his purpose in coming to Vienna. On the occasion when Hansi and Monika met Berthold Luders, Hella too was present and therefore no mention was made of Tenius; and Hansi now found that his curiosity brought him up against the very subject he did not wish to discuss as if against an unexpected wall across an open street. That he braked his conversation as soon as he could after the first mention of Tenius neither escaped nor surprised Julia, but for her own reasons she was not willing to abandon it just because her guest changed the subject. The former acquaintance of Tenius and Luders made a good story and between Georgy and herself, aided by a number of details from Robert, the narrative was embroidered into a burlesque drama which they all enjoyed except for Hansi who unwittingly introduced it.

Thus offered the chance, Julia carried her own thoughts on the matter of Tenius much further than she had done yet in public. The possibility of a trial in Vienna should he be recaptured loomed large in her and Georgy's minds, she said. That would involve them all in courtroom scenes of an agonisingly painful nature and wide publicity. Hella could certainly not escape and even Georgy and herself might be drawn into providing evidence about the events of October 1941; this latter was less likely than the almost certain demand for Hella's testimony, but if the extremity of contrast between what she, Julia Homburg, would have to say about that time and what Hella would be obliged to admit to, were by luck avoided, there would be a great deal of evidence from others which would show up starkly enough the backdrop to Hella's brilliant career. This was only the worst that could befall; even if a trial were held in Germany and on other charges than the transport from Vienna—

for which the organisational responsibility of Tenius was so easily provable—the consequences for Hella could hardly be less and those for Kerenyi would be professionally, though not personally, greater. And Julia Homburg could then be publicly branded as having married a man accused of betraying anti-Nazis to the secret police in return for his own safety. That the betrayal was a deception and had never happened would be taken as an obvious subsequent excuse which would not be believed either by the outside world or by the millions whose most frequent assertion today—whether true or false—was that *they* had never approved of the National Socialists. Even the detailed account of what did happen at the end of July 1944 between Tenius and Kerenyi, which was being prepared for print now, before it could turn out to be a noose if kept secret, would not be remembered if the story was recapitulated in Court through the hostile questioning of defence counsel and Judge.

In the face of increasing unease from Hansi and distress from Lali and Robert Inglis, Julia continued inexorably to paint a lurid picture of the reports of a future trial as they would be published in the scurrilous illustrated weeklies. As she said, when weakly challenged for overdrawing her portrait, they could ask Barber when he appeared after his evening's work and he would tell them what to expect from the powerful, self-righteous and uninhibited popular press of his own country and of West Germany, not to mention of every other European country. She admitted with a brave show of cynicism that her and Georgy's own feelings about Tenius, his reappearance and later his escape, were radically changed from her first attitude. His escape was a mercy, if one they could not trust to, and recapture would be a disaster for them all. Georgy's monthly review would be driven to the edge of bankruptcy in spite of the financial aid promised by Luders; her own position and still more that of Hella Schneider would be impossible. She supposed they would be obliged to retire in the middle of their careers. Even if Tenius were never heard of again the next few weeks could be expected to produce some wild versions of what had happened and a crop of rumours as to the hand taken in it by anyone who ever had reason to fear a trial. The reports of the last days, as Kerenyi pointed out, were cautious because the police were being careful; as soon as it became clear that Tenius had showed them all a clean pair of heels—if he did so—the storm would start.

The longer Julia spoke of these things and made them in all

their possible danger clear to her own mind, the more she frightened herself with her own prophesies. Begun to secure a difficult point with Hansi, she saw that she had not seriously considered before this that everything she was saying was not only likely but near-certain, if Tenius were to be recaptured. However, practical as she always was, Julia continued to work out her original design, in spite of a growing apprehension that the devils she conjured up were only too real and were far from being the figments of imagination she intended them to be.

The forcing of a colleague who was in such public danger on to a production which, in any case, was a large financial and artistic hazard, was to her mind the greatest folly. If she, Julia, gave in to pressure and accepted Hella Schneider with good grace into the cast of the new project, it was certainly not because she was unaware of the dangers and she wished that to be clearly understood. Her misgivings were, if anything, greater than she said, because they could by no means be certain that Tenius was gone for good: too many different kinds of enemies were looking for him for anyone to take that for granted. And enemies, be it noted, who were scattered all across the globe by the actions of Tenius himself and his kind, so that there was hardly a town in the world where he could be sure of his safety.

With this assertion, Julia neatly removed from Hansi the weapon he was only waiting to use against her structure—the sureness of those who had rescued Tenius from his enemies. It was rare, indeed, for a fugitive helped by the SS brotherhood to be found; but as far as she knew Tenius was the first man to be spirited away whose health would not stand any serious strain.

Julia did not mention any return she might expect for her complaisance over Hella's role in the play; that would have been much too open and was unnecessary for Hansi certainly could not feel any illusions on that score. But she was allowing her worries to dominate the conversation, she said; she wouldn't have talked so much if her anxiety were not so great, but it was time she stopped and let them talk of other things.

Naturally, everyone present knew that Julia had not let her tongue run away with her, that she intended every word she said to serve some purpose which certainly was not to frighten them with horror-stories about Tenius; the only detail which was not yet quite clear was the exact nature of her purpose. Its general meaning was clear enough; it was directed to Hansi Ostrovsky and Hansi was as sure of this as any of the other hearers. One thing only surprised him and that was the detail of Julia's staging the incident in this way in front of witnesses. She had worried them all, including herself, with her gloomy foresight even if she did express it scattered with jokes and cynicisms like sugar on the cake they were by now eating; most of all she worried Hansi whose judgment of worldly matters was far from infallible, and who had allowed Hella to persuade him of the need to cover the theatre in covering one of its members. That was bad, evidently, and made worse by the public evidence that Julia meant business.

Barber now appeared, but Ostrovsky did not take up the suggestion that his expert knowledge should be consulted. Their professional intrigues were no concern of outsiders, and certainly not of newspaper correspondents who were quite active enough without any encouragement. Not that such a farrago of unlikely chances would interest a great foreign paper, but Barber and his colleagues could always relay interesting details to local friends in the surety of getting help from them when it was needed. So far from considering an extension of Julia's chatter to the tall American, Hansi suspected Julia—or Kerenyi, he thought with disfavour—of having invited Barber of a set purpose; to show him that they could use an access to foreign opinion not available to himself. The less Barber knew, the better.

This was a natural but unjust thought. Barber was always welcome to Georg and Julia and their circle. An old enmity was changed with the passing of time and the accumulation of experience on both sides into a genuine and serviceable friendship valued by all of them. He was clearly on terms of confidence with the cool and retiring Robert Inglis and, remembering the occasion of their first meeting, Ostrovsky noted this development with interest. The talk turned to the house in the south and to interests and people unknown to Hansi, but Monika fulfilled the social part required of young girls and asked a thousand questions about children and livestock with an ease that suggested she might have spent years fitting herself to please hosts and fellow guests. And when they returned to the coming winter season, Monika showed the same new determination to please by letting Kerenyi talk. She gathered from every sentence something for her own use, and this willingness to learn was proof of intelligence as well as ambition and did not altogether please her lover, who naturally preferred her to remain dependent on himself.

Dinner was now over. Barber having exercised the prerogative of his uncomfortable trade not to be bound to timekeeping, had arrived in the middle of the meal. Now as the company moved and mingled, two further guests came in, within a few minutes of each other; Anita Silovsky whose part that evening was over before the Interval, and Florian Dellin, the stage designer.

Ostrovsky watched Julia move with Lali Inglis to sit together. Whether because the two women formed a composition together with the chairs in which they sat and the coffee table between them which might have been arranged by a painter seeking colours and forms for a double portrait, or whether Julia's remarks before dinner had produced a slight but noticeable sensation of alienation, Hansi was able for the first time in many years to look at Julia as if at a stranger. To see her not as a familiar friend of such long standing that she had ceased to exist as a separate entity, as part of an intimately felt complexity of his own, but as an almost unknown creature, one whose character he could not take for granted, just as he for a moment did not take for granted her physical being.

The chairs formed low blocks of curved whiteness or near whiteness which merged into the surrounding carpet so that the elegant thin curves of the rococo table legs defined themselves sharply as dark lines and as belonging to another age. On this design were blended a brilliant dark rose in a flowing curve that swung towards a more angular colour mass of green which was Lali's dress. The green was rather dark, dully dark, and merged upward into glowing skin and the mingled strands of hair falling under and over in contrasts of flaxen and near-brown from the sun's month-long action. The animated movement of the young mother and the laughing murmur of her voice as she described with her so personal humourous affection which showed a strange little talent for the telling, comical phrase, a small chronicle of children's doings, formed a shimmer both of sound and sight. Against this shimmer Julia was still, a continuous line of soft and brilliant colour that did not move but was not immobile, being suffused with a concentration of attention. The stillness of the figure created a space about itself, an attribute of personality which lies mysteriously between the physical and the spiritual, and the onlooker found himself wondering with a certain surprise at himself, how he would express this 'presence' if he had to do so. In former times it was the attribute of royal persons or of priests, whose function attached an assured respect to the holder but in the modern world respect of any kind is a suspect concept. Nowadays a highly trained athlete is more likely to possess this strange attribute than an hereditary dignitary, drawing it from disciplined muscular control; and indeed it is occasionally to be seen in perfect animals. But it was unsatisfying and unreal to relegate a phenomenon so rare to mere physical coherence, and Hansi recognised that the ability to form an invisible ban about herself in which she moved so surely that it seemed as if other people and inanimate objects must remove themselves from her path, was founded in Julia's character as much as her physical being. It came not only from harmony of feature and line, but from long schooling and self-discipline and a cohesion of inward and outward qualities which added themselves together under the word power, rather than the word beauty. Yet she was beautiful, and one could not even say she was still beautiful, because the bone and muscular foundations held and would continue to hold all the lines and movements of her body in the harmony of an instinctive confidence. Just as natural grace had been disciplined so that she was incapable of an ugly movement, so nature had with unique luck provided a combination of feature and colour so well fitted together that no part could with the action of time become dominant and upset the balance. What was near miraculous about the face, he decided, was that its symmetry was not insipid; just to look at, it was too good to be real, with its clear lines and bold drawing. Its quality came from the expression of the extraordinary eyes of which the colour grey was a useless hint at description, and from the bold and proud set of the mouth. Yes, thought Hansi somewhat grudgingly, Florian was right about the *A & C* costumes; Peter's ideas were quite wrong and could only obscure the realities of the players and the play.

He looked about him, to say this to Florian, and found him with Monika, both bending forward to look into the depths of the Chinese cabinet.

'You see what I mean?' she said eagerly and her hair fell forward over one cheek as she moved her head. 'It's mysterious, isn't it? In itself mysterious, not just because it's dark and old?'

'It's the way the reflections play, I think,' he said, hardly noticing his companion in his own concentration. 'Wait, it's given me an idea. If the lights are used like this—no, don't move, you're throwing a shadow that I need. Yes, look—the lights blend more as shadows than lights, only just reflected from the polished stone and wood, they move, it's a miniature of . . .' He put out a brown, strong hand and pulled Monika's thin wrist upward. 'You see, even a slight movement alters the play of shadows all over the space, the inside space.'

Florian turned his head and spoke to Ostrovsky, not for the first time without either name or title. He did not release Monika's wrist which he still required for his demonstration.

'Look,' he said excitedly, 'this is just how the Palace should be lighted, by reflections off the wall-masses. . . .'

'Rot,' said Hansi brusquely. 'The walls could have no reflections, they were hewn stone, not polished. . . .'

'What does that matter—I don't mean it naturalistically.'

'We must retain a certain verity to the historical facts. . . .'

'This is important for the music,' said Florian, not even hearing his chief's objection. 'We must work out exactly the movement and blending of reflections to fit the music—you see?'

'And what about fitting the people?' asked Hansi sharply. 'They'll be invisible.'

'No, no, they would move into cross-blending muted spots and drift away again as others speak. Let's see, now, there would be torches . . . ?'

'You mean, all the lighting would be still? That's impossible!'

'Oh, everything is always impossible,' said Florian rudely. 'Why is it impossible? For the same reason Peter's clothes can't be changed! Because that's the way they've always been.'

'If you can find some usable costumes, I'd drop Peter's designs at once,' rejoined Hansi with some heat. 'The ideas you produced yourself are unwearable and you know it. Clothing must have some relationship to the human frame, it can't be completely abstract or expressionist.'

And all the time they were declaiming in the immoderate fashion of those who are totally absorbed by their work, Hansi kept having to push away the memory of himself twenty-five years ago, being just as impatient and inconsiderate to his elders as this boy now was to him. He could see in the stocky figure and the short, pushing nose, the forward cheek-bones and the dark, glittering eyes what he himself, so physically different, had once possessed. A weary resentment filled him that his career had been wasted in the struggles of politics and war; this boy was lucky, that was all, but he thought of his luck as being his own achievement, like all young-sters. We should see how long you'd keep your fire if there were an-other war, he thought bitterly. If it hadn't been for us there would be no theatre for you to make your plaything. It would have gone under in the holocaust, lost like the stones of the Burg itself, a heap of rubble. The thought of the noble structure which he could never believe would stand again—although he knew it would—was like a bodily pain to him and his face twisted as it did with a liver twinge.

'You're being unkind to Hansi,' said Anita. 'You're not half as clever as you think you are, young Florian. Hansi, come and show me. . . .'

'No,' said Hansi slowly, 'I don't feel well. I think I'll get off home. You stay a bit, Kiki, and enjoy yourself.' He turned away, aware of doing precisely the false thing, of making himself pathetic to the hard virility and drive of Florian. 'Him with his hair brushed forward!' he muttered as he moved away to excuse himself. He really did feel tired and weak. It's worn me out, he thought, worn me out. I'm an old man before my time. Monika was making some objection, she would go with him, they would have an early night for once. But he waved her away with a gesture of rejection and she stopped her movement, offended at his public indifference and glad to accept the excuse to stay.

'I'm afraid my tale of doom was a bit too effective,' said Julia to Kerenyi as he came back from seeing Hansi out. 'I didn't mean to upset him like that. . . .'

'I don't think it was you,' answered Robert, following Georgy's eyes to Florian and Monika. And somehow the gathering split into two; everyone but the dark boy and girl sat down together and they remained near the Chinese cabinet talking in low, animated tones about Florian's plans.

' "Ist's halt der Lauf der Welt," ' quoted Georgy in the exact tone-fall of the celebrated musical phrase. 'It's Hansi's own fault. He should have asked her to marry him when he had the chance.'

'We can't all be as clever as you!' Anita said with pretended acid in her voice.

'Georgy was very clever,' said Lali slyly, 'he pretended so well that he didn't want her, Julie almost believed it in the end.'

'All the same, I worried myself,' protested Julia when their laughter died down. 'It's all too dreadfully possible, what I meant to be merely a spine-chilling tale.'

'What is not very likely is that Tenius will be caught. We may contemplate the possibility with impatience or nervousness—or with mixed feelings as I suppose we all do—but it remains a fact that not one person "removed" by this secret organisation has ever been found again.'

Whether Robert meant this comment to be a reflection of some official opinion or not, it was taken to be that by at least two of his hearers. Barber opened his lips to reply or to question the statement and glanced at Kerenyi to see what he thought of it. In the space of this glance, he realised that he could not press Robert Inglis to say more than his military duty would properly allow him to, and with recognition mingled of irritation and discretion he let it pass; but not before the strange expression of Kerenyi's frowning eyes warned him with a less obvious sign than his own tact that there was some factor in the return of Tenius which he did not know about. Barber was not aware of any direct connection from the past between Tenius and Kerenyi, but he was suddenly reminded of the first occasion that he and Kerenyi met. On that evening Barber was determined to force just such an issue as he now felt a premonition of, with Julia, and the result for himself was a bitter lesson in humility. Since then, he had learned much and he now held his tongue, glad that a social rule had saved him from a more serious dereliction of friendship.

Julia too looked at Kerenyi, and recognised self-reproach in the look that Barber could only guess at. She saw that her husband knew he ought to want the recapture of the man who had tortured his friends and who was now a symbol for the insane outbreak that had destroyed their world. He did want it but not wholeheartedly; he wanted it with half his mind and with the other half he wanted peace. Peace to return to living, peace for living with herself. She knew this with a physical impact as if a signed and sealed packet of inestimable worth had been put quietly, weightily, into her hands. The answer to this sensation rose and flowered in her being for the first time in her life; an absolute attachment, loyalty and gratitude which was not demanded of her but had the quality in its absoluteness, of a total freedom. Because it was absolute, then there was no reservation in it, no chance of going back towards anything less than completeness. Into this mysterious freedom of what could only be the reverse of freedom, she felt herself liberated as if into a great, spacious and wonderfully ornamented openness of unlimited variety which was to be her inheritance. She no more tried to put a name to this prospect than to that other experience of being borne up by the waves of the sea on to a far distant and unknown shore. If there were any signposts in this country they were not words.

XXIV

Two days passed before the moment was ripe for Julia to carry out her plot. She came into a rehearsal room and found just the right people present, as she expected, to go through a Schnitzler comedy with 'the new boy' as they still called him. Georgy called him a golden boy, Julia thought, but he's a very conceited one; gilt rather, I'd say.

'Good morning, Julie,' said someone with surprise. 'Didn't expect to see you, this morning.'

'I'm not staying. Just want to ask Hansi about something. How are you feeling now, Hansi?'

Ostrovsky kissed her hand, to thank her for the evening two days before as if it had been, for him, an unmixed pleasure. But his look was nervous.

'Here are the designs Malczewska made for me,' she came direct to the point. 'Have you five minutes to look at them?'

Relieved that this was all, and hoping at the same time that the ideas would be usable and that Peter could be persuaded to use them without too much trouble on his, Hansi's part, he took the portfolio out of Julia's hand and they went to a side table to lay out the contents.

She sounded so casual that he was surprised at the excellence of the ideas.

'She's no draughtsman,' he said. 'But they're quite good. This is very unusual. Ah, this one for the barge? Really, she has talent.'

'Unfortunately, she has, wretched creature,' said Hella, leaning over his shoulder. 'I think you'd be mad to let her get a foot in the door, though Hansi. She's a troublemaker.'

'Hark who's talking!' murmured someone, and there was a slight giggle which Hella ignored.

'Look, Hella, here's Iras—good, isn't it?'

Hella glanced sharply at Julia who gave her a bland smile.

'I like the cross-bands,' agreed Hella. They might have been speaking of the weather.

'What sort of arrangement d'you think. . . .' Hansi began.

'She wants nothing for them. They are a personal favour to me. I think they're good—if Peter will use them.'

'Nothing?' He was startled.

'She wants the prestige, that's all. When she gets her naturalisation papers, she would like to open a small atelier.'

'Naturalisation?' Hella laughed. 'That's something new!'

'There's been a lot of delay because she has no papers of any sort about her origins. I'm surprised you don't know about it, Hella. It's been going on for some months.'

'She said nothing to me,' said Hella. 'But we were hardly on those terms.'

Julia rested one hand on the drawings spread over the tablè, and swung herself upright with a slightly emphasised movement which brought her round to face Hella. Hansi too, stood upright.

'I think we ought to help her with her papers, don't you agree, Hansi? I mean—we were both there in Warsaw, Hella and I. We do know that she was there, that she belonged there. That would make a difference.'

'We?' Hella's voice was defiant enough to sound a little uncertain.

'Georgy and I have decided to support her request. It's a kind of guarantee, I believe. . . .'

'But do you think that wise, Julie? Do you know her so well?' Hansi was feeling his way. 'I mean, just at this moment. . . .'

'But *just* at this moment! Don't you feel that a demonstration of sympathy—for someone not our own, and from Warsaw, too—it wouldn't be a public matter, of course, but it's bound to be known and shows a confidence. . . . That we feel ourselves quite. . . .'

Hella and Julia were both looking at Hansi; there was not a shadow of expression on either of their faces. Julia moved her hand on the table, and the sheets of paper rustled. This sound could be heard but none of the three glanced at anyone else although the room was now still enough for distant traffic sounds to filter through the windows. At the rustle of the stiff paper, Hansi looked down. The uppermost drawing was inscribed in the lower right-hand corner 'Iras, Act V.'

'Yes, you may be right,' said Hansi quietly.

'I have the papers with me,' Julia moved her hand. 'I've signed this oath thing already.'

'Oath?'

'That I knew her during the War in Warsaw.'

Hella's eyes wandered. The window, as she looked, was clouded with a burst of rain flung as if with haste against the glass.

'Damn,' she said. 'I've sent the car away. Well, where is this paper, Julie?'

'At the back of the portfolio. Shall I leave the designs here, then, Hansi?'

'Oh, certainly. Of course. I'm more than glad we can use them. Keep Florian quiet for a day or so.'

'I won't disturb you any longer,' Julia smiled. Hella was reading. Presently, she put out her exquisite hand and Hansi reached for his pen.

'Not that I understand it,' she said, scrawling her signature. 'This official language.'

Julia took up the folder, now empty but for the affidavit, and made to leave the room.

'Would somebody please tell me when we're going to start work?' asked the 'new boy' in an exaggeratedly plaintive tone.

'Doesn't a declaration like that have to be sworn before a Notary?' Hansi hesitated.

'Apparently they don't bother one with that until the case is decided. Georgy thinks in about ten days.'

'But I won't be here,' said Hella blankly. 'I shall be in the country off and on until December.'

'It can be witnessed in Salzburg just as well,' pointed out Julia, referring to the house bought by Hella at the end of the War.

'Oh. Of course.'

The new acquisition to the company was now asserting his rights by chattering loudly to someone on the other side of the room. The three of them stood as if by chance, half turned towards the table with the drawings on it, and none of their faces was visible to the rest of the people present.

'I'm sure we're doing the right thing,' said Julia. 'It costs us nothing and means a great deal to Malczewska. Always better to have people on one's side, don't you agree?' Hansi looked at Hella and they saw the expression of her enchanting face, glowing with her light tan and brilliant fair colouring. For a moment she pressed trembling lips together and her eyes were full of an uncomprehending bitterness, an almost hunted unsureness.

Julia and Hansi moved slightly, as if to look again at the designs. That others were there was essential, to avoid an acrimonious dispute, but the last thing Julia wanted was to humiliate Hella publicly. She wanted now to say something reassuring but nothing she could say would make any difference to Hella's real trouble. It was best to go, and she went, scattering farewells.

At the same moment, in a room rather similar to the rehearsal room, Malczewska sat with men in uniforms, some in khaki and some in the dark green and black of police officers. Clerks brought card index boxes and photographs were shown her, pictures· like those kept of known criminals, with slips of opaque paper across the names printed below the faces. A hard-faced man in olive drab with the winged insignia of a colonel on his shoulders, sent for coffee to ease Malczewska's visible nervousness; from his grim look it was not a gesture to have been expected. Like the conversation in the theatre, it was all very quiet, nobody spoke above a discreet undertone. They all maintained the reserved formality of policemen dealing with a member of the public.

'Ah!' Malczewska caught her breath. 'This one. That's him.'

'You're sure?' asked the American colonel. She looked up at him with a frightened nod. He reached imperiously behind him without looking and a master sergeant put into his hand a sealed envelope. The colonel slit this open with a paper knife from the large table and without rising from his chair, pushed three shiny black and white photographs, one by one, across to the blotter lying before the witness's place. They were very bad photographs, taken obviously under poor light.

'It's the same man.' An untended finger-nail pressed on one figure of a group. 'This one. This is even better—you can see how he moves. You see? He sort of rolls his shoulders when he walks.' This picture had been snapped in a street, and the figure in it was evidently walking along. At the third photograph she shook her head. 'No, that's not him.'

'Good,' said the American briefly, pushed the three sheets back into the envelope, taking no notice of a man in British battledress who now approached Malczewska's elbow and offered her more pictures, of which she identified two.

'What about this?' asked the British officer, and laid yet another group picture before her.

'I can't see him, quite. His head is half turned away. But isn't that, that other man—I've seen his face somewhere . . . This does look like him. . . .' She pointed to the police portraits already identified.

'The other man . . .' she said. 'He's not a Russian.'

'No, he's British. You saw him in the library once or twice, I dare say. He married your librarian—you remember her?'

She shook her head, frowning with anxiety.

'Miss Macdonald, the first librarian.'

'Oh, yes. Yes, I remember her. Did she marry him? She did get married—that's why she left.'

'You don't quite recognise either of them, for certain then?'

'I couldn't swear to it,' she said carefully.

'Look again,' he said, and moved the brilliant light a little.

'Check this again,' said the hard American voice, and the sergeant slid forward one of the three already examined likenesses.

'Isolate a feature,' one of the police officers advised quietly. She moved the two pictures about, slanting her head and squinting to get a different angle. 'The forehead looks the same, where you can see from the side here. . . .' She described a circle with her forefinger, first on one shiny sheet and then on the other. 'I think it may be him, but I don't want to be too certain.'

'How about this?' asked the light, clipped English voice over her head. His thin hand was hairy. He laid down a professional portrait.

'Oh yes, I know him. I've seen him in the papers. That's the defector, some years ago. His name's Torek.'

'You have a good memory,' approved the policeman who had spoken before. They all seemed to be pleased with her in a moderate way. They were all getting up, and Malczewska rose too, but nobody told her she could go.

The Allied officers were leaving and the others shuffled their papers together, speaking to each other in detached phrases. The clerk carried out the card index box.

'May I go now?' she asked uncertainly.

'Of course,' the man looked surprised. A senior police officer spoke sedately. 'You may leave whenever you wish. Your presence here is entirely voluntary.'

Since Malczewska did not at all understand the formalities of police routine this was to her a meaningless, or possibly a sarcastic remark. Her memories of policemen were of a different order. She drifted to the door, and not until the driver of 'her' car greeted her in the chill hall, did she recall that yet another interview with the Aliens Department was due that morning. The meagre, grey man she saw there was also some kind of policeman, but she did not think of him as such, since he wore civilian and shabby clothes and had black cotton bags over his lower sleeves to protect them from the constant rubbing on his desk.

But to her surprise she was not, this morning, kept waiting; she was sent in at once to the dark, narrow office, and the familiar face of the clerk creased into a cautious smile of greeting. He stood up and carefully removed his over-sleeves before opening the far door of his cubby-hole and beckoning her with impressive mien to follow him. This was a bigger room, not quite so dark, and the man behind the desk was attended by an elderly female assistant. He did not wear bags over his sleeves, nor were there packets of midday food to be seen on his window-sill. In fact there were plants along it, in pots. He rose half out of his chair, he actually offered her a hand. Her dossier was there on the tidy desk before him, but he did not open the tapes. He asked her, instead, a question she did not understand about the town of her childhood, and she stammered a description as far as she could remember it. His questions were slow, formal but polite, almost kind. He wanted to know names, and addressed her by her own name; once when he interrupted to correct a misunderstanding, he said, 'Excuse me, *gnaedige Frau.*' She could hardly believe her ears. The questions were all ones gone through often before and gradually it dawned on Malczewska that they were quite perfunctory, a matter of routine. Was it possible that the case had been decided? When he half-rose again to say good morning and the assistant came forward to lead her to the door, she could contain her anxious hope no longer and asked, her voice breaking slightly with strain, if she might assume, perhaps. . . . She would hear officially, he assured her with a slight reproof, he could say nothing yet. But as she drew breath to apologise, he added that he thought they could congratulate her, or would be able to as soon as she had received a summons to a place where she would sign documents and swear an oath of loyalty.

She felt shaky, only half knowing in which direction to turn at the door, which led into the corridor and not through the outer office. The elderly assistant, with the friendliness of one very plain woman for another, pressed her arm familiarly and showed her the sign to the way out.

'I'm so glad,' she said. 'It's a great thing to have friends to help you.'

Malczewska muttered something, she did not know what; she felt almost blind in the gloomy passage and was forced to stop and lean against the wall on the way down the wide, flat stairs. There had been small occasion in her life for the emotion of gratitude and she put no name to what she felt. The astounding speed of her success robbed her of understanding; it was less than a week ago that she sat in her furnished room, in despair of the outcome of frantic efforts to become what she did not even want to be. But I was nothing before, she thought; certainly not Polish. They wouldn't admit I'd been born.

'It was the lucky combination, of everything coming together at the same time,' said Kerenyi when she expressed something of this to him. 'I think I might use your story as one of this series we're doing. Without names, of course. Luders suggests they might be collected eventually, into a book. *Personal Fates of our Times.* You know the sort of thing?'

'Is Luders here again, then?' she was surprised. 'You couldn't use that title. Kitsch.'

'No. He's still waiting for some news of Tenius before he comes. But we talk on the telephone.'

'He's not likely to get any news, if the whole resources of the Allies, the Austrian Police and all the others who want to find him, can't.'

'He's a queer chap, Berthold. Knows a lot of people.' He sounded as if he were hedging. Then he said, 'Like you, after all, my dear. You knew Tenius was to return before we did, isn't that so?'

'But how did you know that?' she asked, defensive. 'From Luders?'

'No. You were upset about it for days before, I recall you said so yourself. I didn't believe at the time that you had—as you said—lain awake for nights because of what the doctors were going to tell you about your arm. You've known for years that the injury is incurable.' He smiled, shaking his head. 'One always knows when something is unchangeable.'

They were sitting in a coffee house and now an elderly man

who could only be a retired civil servant, came to the rack that stood beside their table and selected a newspaper from it, rattling the bamboo frames. Malczewska was prevented by this, for a moment, in the sharp answer she had ready. Instead she said obliquely that she had given her landlady notice and was looking for another room.

'Yes. It'll make a lot of changes,' he said.

'One of the changes will be that I shan't be in a position to let you know if anything is heard of . . . him . . . from my former friends. You realise that?'

'You forget. I have a vested interest in his never being found.'

'You're a queer fellow, Kerenyi. I shall never understand you.'

'Do we ever understand anything?' He pushed the theme aside with levity.

'I still can't get over the speed of the change. Last week they offered me less than no hope at the Aliens Office.'

'It only took a day or so for the police on the one hand to know that you were ready to help them with something of importance to them; and on the other for the Aliens Department to know that Julia and Hella Schneider meant to guarantee your petition. The formalities could wait. It's as simple as that.'

'But why did your wife do it? Why should she be bothered?' She gave him a curious, questioning, an almost shady look.

'If you don't feel satisfied with the explanation Julia gave you, why don't you ask her?'

'She would say no more than she has said. You know that. But it's very strange that you don't seem to know the real reason.'

'My dear girl,' he said, raising his hand to signal the waiter. 'You're being too subtle for me. Julia's motives are always practical. You know that by now.'

'Yes,' she admitted, almost amused, 'very practical. It's good news about the designs being accepted. Suddenly everything goes well for me.'

Only after they had gone their separate ways did it occur to each one of them that he, and she, still did not know what the other understood by this exchange.

XXV

The year gathered weight and fled before those living in it with accelerating force towards its end. All the activity of a fresh season
filled the days for Julia; his own work and the reorganisation of
business affairs filled Kerenyi. The return to the city of the Inglis
family could be felt as having something temporary about it; they
waited in the midst of all their family and social busyness, for the
release from Robert's service commission and, not without a pleasant nostalgia, contemplated leaving the city and becoming country
folk, provincials. Hella was heard from as an echo that bounced
off the Salzburg mountains, to catch the leaden waters of the sea in
Hamburg's tidal river and then, before her return, from the press
and roar of New York. At All Souls there was snow and bitter wind
as usual, but this year the gale carried off the life of an old friend
who lived with Lali's mother in the Kasdahouse in the Russian Zone.
Their last respects to him in the echoing, freezing, neglected church
were made melancholy by more than the end of a ruined life. Lali's
mother showed a stoic hardness, a bitter stubbornness in what
would now be total loneliness.

Julia and Lali did not take their husbands with them but went
together to a funeral of more than one old man in the village adjacent to the Kasda property. There was a furtive and condemned
air about the ceremony, for the Church's rites were frowned on
here. With all the guilt of prosperity the two women tried to persuade Lali's mother to return with them, at least for a visit, but the
survival of the family's land-ownership was by now an obsession and
she could not be prevailed upon to desert the half-ruined house
even for a week. Its survival had become an iron law under which
she was condemned to a sentence that might have no end.

At home, neither spoke of this, except on the return journey, to
each other.

It was many years since Julia had made the customary visits
to the dead at this time of year, but a few days after the funeral
she went out to Nussdorf to her father's granite tombstone and to

the central cemetery, to the mass grave where Franz and Fina were commemorated by a plain stone with no inscription but the dates. She went too, to the enclave in the cemetery and laid white chrysanthemums under the Star of David, unable even to mock herself for her superstition, as she thought of it. This tribute was intended for her father-in-law whose portrait hung in the hall of the apartment he had built. But for the first time for years the Saturday afternoon in March 1938 returned to her mind; the day it all started. She did not know that with Benda the last remaining actor in that event was now dead and that she was the only living witness.

It was as if by visiting the graveyards, she exorcised her ghosts. After disposing of her ill-gotten gains in reality, the substitute votive sacrifice of her small pilgrimage, of which she spoke to nobody, now pronounced her free from some obligation. Julia did not examine this feeling for she accepted it, disingenuously perhaps, as an infrequently carried out duty. The duty Julia thought of, as far as she did think, was to a custom of religion. Thus a real obligation was transferred to a demonstration in itself meaningless to any but a pious believer, and that in turn was transferred from her own need to undertake it to the abstract region of a minor rite, which both sealed the expedition with approval by authority, and safely robbed it of emotion. She was conscious, rather, of having got quietly away with a rather ridiculous outing and the result was a heightened enjoyment of the rest of the day.

The early evening was to be devoted to accompanying the Inglis children to the opening performance of a famous circus which was in Vienna for the first time since the War. The *Grande Cirque de France* was, as always, polyglot and not French except in name; it contained in its membership many performers who originally came from strange places where, as Julia delighted Nando by saying, the wolves say good night to each other. Such people do not care for any very strict form of administration and the circus was therefore obliged to put up its tents somewhere outside the predestined site of circuses, the Prater. It was on a recently cleared bombed space in Meidling, which was a safely 'western' sector of the city where the children had never been.

Julia having claimed the prerogative of a colleague, they were to make an inspection of the living quarters of men and beasts before the show began. The sturdy nursemaid was there to carry Sebastian, Nando strutted self-consciously in his first fur hat. It was black dark and very cold, lazy flakes of snow curled through the air and hissed on the flares of the booths where spun sugar and heart-shaped cakes, flat and hard to bite, with announcements such as '*ich liebe dich*' written in pink and white sugar on them were offered for sale. Drawing the children by promises of yet greater delights past the seductions of electric motor-racing and a merry-go-round with white horses and red cockerels, they reached a board gate in a high fence and were admitted to an inner circle of vibrant excitement and exotic if pungent smells. There were people everywhere in the flickering darkness, all moving fast on errands unknown to the outside world, and shouting in queer tongues to each other. At every angle were high wheels and on these wheels, atop wooden ladders, were tiny houses full of light and heat and strange people in them like those in fairy tales. In one a tremendously tall and broad man with a completely bald head gleaming pinkly and wide, waxed moustaches; in another a beautiful lady in spangled tights with all her legs showing as if she were going swimming, only hard to the touch when she lifted Sebastian, with both muscles and corsets. In a third was a small person hardly taller than Nando who was rather unnerving but proved kind with cream cake, of which he gave them squashy pieces although, as Nando remarked later, you'd have thought he needed it all himself, being so small. A brisk young man with a cockney accent, speaking French, leaned in at the door of this caravan and offered to take them to the cages.

The cages smelled sour and sharp and were of thick metal bars behind which great creatures prowled and grunted, yawned, stretched huge paws like nightmare cats and looked insolently past their visitors with yellow, bored eyes. Next door there were monkeys, being dressed in sailor suits, chattering to themselves very seriously. On the way back through the throng, they were startled when a cluster of great arc lights suddenly turned the whole scene into an incomprehensible landscape like mountains, of sharply-edged blocks of moving colours against an impenetrable and palpable black. A short frail old man with a quiet air of dignity bowed to Julia in a draughty corridor between canvas walls and they had to stop while Julia talked to him. This was the most famous of clowns, but Nando did not believe that and failed later to recognise him, accusing Julia of teasing him. There was a tremendous and exciting noise, chatter, cries of recognition, greetings, the thumping of countless feet on hollow board-walks. Then a triumphal fanfare of trumpets and the crowd subsided gradually in a long, slow rumble and rustle as the procession majestically began.

'Half the world's here,' said Julia, more to herself than to Lali. 'That is, everyone who can remember Grillo from before. People who never go out any more. . . . Kari, how are you?' An elderly man, tall and thin with a great hook of a nose leaned over the low division of the open boxes. 'I didn't know you ever left the country, these days!'

'Yes, he's delightful,' agreed Lali later, as the clowns were tumbling out of the ring. A small boy who looked like one of the public, reaching up to his full height, flipped Grillo's shiny flat black hat from his head and it spun and rolled into the centre of the spot-lighted empty space. The old clown stood there by the exit, alone, wringing his hands, weeping for his hat and pointing to it, his monstrously large white glove flapping off his finger, then looking round slyly at the howling audience. He made a wild swipe at the urchin, lost his balance, trod on the tail of his morning coat, which tore off, and recovered himself. Then with the sweetest smile in the world and with ineffable dignity he wrapped the remaining tail of his coat up over his shoulder and walked off. The crowd rocked and screamed in innocent sadism and Julia wiped the tears from her eyes, still shaking with laughter.

'But I don't see why—just the same. *Everbody's* come to see him. Half Gotha is here. I can see from here a Schwarzenberg, two Pallavicinis, the Hohenlohe Stani with—who's that with him? There's old Princess Werdenberg, there's a whole clutch of Esterhazys two boxes from us. And there's Janko—' She broke off as Kerenyi and Robert entered. 'Oh, darling, you missed this famous clown!'

'No, we were standing in the gangway.' Robert bent over Lali. 'Do you understand the enthusiasm?' she asked him.

'But he's a genius! Look at Nando's face, you can see from that!'

'Yes, he's sweet—but he doesn't do anything the others don't do.'

'He doesn't have to,' said Julia, smiling up at Georgy.

Several persons came and went with greetings, most of whom were leaving now, in the interval, having seen what they came for. Grillo would not reappear tonight. It was intended that they too should leave, before the children became tired. But Nando pleaded with such passion to wait for the horses, just the horses, only the horses, then he would . . . that of course, it was agreed to wait.

Julia leaned out over the edge of the box to say good night to their neighbour, and as the old man straightened up and moved away, another group caught her eye. They stood below, between the barrier and the first row of seats, Hansi pulling up his coat collar and Kiki talking with lively gestures to which Hansi seemed not to be attending. He was frowning slightly, inwardly communing with himself, the very picture of a man weighing some problem. They moved together out into the crowded gangway and started up the flat steps towards the way out. Kiki looked up and waved to someone disappearing out into the night, and Hansi spoke to her inaudibly, and as he spoke he jerked his head towards the doorway above them. Two heavily bundled figures moved between the viewer from the box and Hansi, and when they were gone Julia could see how Hansi argued with Monika, moving head and shoulders sharply to emphasise something, persuade her of something, which clearly had nothing to do with their personal relations. There was none of the smiling or passionate persuasion of a love scene about it, no personal feeling. Hansi was in deadly earnest about something but it was not, for the moment, Kiki. The girl said something, something that evidently made light of his concern, for he bent towards her with an urgent gesture, held up his hands to count off four fingers and then swept one hand again towards the exit. As he did so, he turned and his gaze crossed the boxes above him. He saw the children with their parents, Julia, Kerenyi, and for a moment was quite still in apprehension and surprise.

He was looking directly at her and Julia waved as if she were waiting for him to see them, and indeed she was. Both Hansi and Monika waved back, but they did not come to the box; they went out, still arguing, and disappeared.

'How very strange,' said Kerenyi behind Julia.

'What—strange?' she looked behind her.

'They didn't come by.'

'Probably they have an appointment?' she said. But it was strange. 'I wonder who it was went out before them.'

'Didn't you see? It was Malczewska. She was sitting behind Hansi.'

'Even stranger the way Hansi looked when he saw us!'

Their attention was exigently claimed by Nando and for the

time being they thought no more of it. The brass band began to play, the crowd clapped, stamped its feet and whistled as the horses, gleaming and elegant, tapped into the ring, arching their necks, pointing their narrow hoofs, and tossing their delicate heads crowned by bunches of coloured feathers.

'Oh, Mummy,' screamed Nando, his voice piercing even the music, 'the horses! The horses!'

They were all tired out by the time the children were finally got to bed and were glad to sit for a while with nothing at all to do.

'I shall be sorry when you leave this house,' said Kerenyi. 'It's very familiar.'

'You will still come here,' answered Robert, 'the military are giving it up when we go and your old friend Frau Pantic means to live here again, herself.'

'Can she afford to?' asked Julia, surprised.

'Apparently. She does quite well with films, these days. And she's going back to the Josefstadt next autumn.'

'The Josefstadt? That's where she started out from, all those years ago!'

'That was just what she said when she told us.'

Julia rose and began to walk about the room, touching things here and there, trailing her fingers over the polished, slightly uneven surface of a baroque chest of drawers, peering through the uncovered double windows at an invisible garden. She lifted her hand to shade the lights, but even when she could see there was nothing to see but a slow drift of snow streaks in the black air. Without the shading hand there was an amalgam of yellow lights and the coloured shapes, wavering in the glass, of the room and the people in it. What she saw went back a long way, not memories or pictures but a swirl of presences, the exact bend of a shoulder, the carriage of a head that remained when features were gone out of mind, the moving outlines of figures forming their essential identity, by which they can be recognised at a distance at which faces are a blur. There was too, not to be seen, a slight oppression of the mind, tiny signals of recognisance, a stir of nerve memories so distant that connections were unmanageable. She knew that something had happened. Out of a press of figures, some well and some half remembered, Julia recalled faces and personalities she had known in her childhood, some of them seen again that evening. Many, part of a great and silent army, would never be seen again and this great crowd seemed to stand in silence, somewhere a little way off, watching the living, witnesses of their performance, judges of what those who still possessed the world would make of their gift of life. Among them the almost forgotten look of anxious serious-ness her father always wore in her memory; it must have been he who took her to see the clown Grillo, the first time she went to a circus. And Hansi Ostrovsky presented himself familiarly, with his similarly anxious brow. Just as he had been seen in the flesh that evening. Yes, something had happened about Tenius; Hansi and Monika spoke of him and then saw Malczewska sitting just behind them, too late to hold their tongues. Was her perception of the liv-ing and the dead a premonition that Tenius was gone to join that silent army? Or was it perhaps Hansi whose chronic vague illness was so much part of him, who was about to join it? Fancies, she said to herself.

They were talking of other circus performances, of the first ones they remembered; Robert at Earl's Court, Georgy in Budapest, Lali for some forgotten reason, in Linz, Julia in the Prater.

'But the best show I ever saw was in the summer somewhere, at the back of beyond, where they had a camp and were practis-ing.' Julia sat down again and took a rare cigarette from the green box on the table, an action that connected somewhere in a distant time with her sensation that something had happened.

'Where the wolves say goodnight?' Robert asked and they laughed at the thought of Nando, his pleasure at the old-fashioned expression.

'He'll be saying that for days, you'll see,' said Lali.

'Don't the companies break up for the summer?'

'I believe they do, but this must have been a family, or clan, they were gypsies. It was a long, flat valley. I remember, and there were the caravans and horses, and a high-wire.'

'Darling, I think you dreamed it,' said Georgy.

'D'you think so? Perhaps I did. It's the kind of thing one might have dreamed.'

'It's getting late,' said Kerenyi. 'And you have a rehearsal to morrow.'

'I'm still not sure I understand about the clown.' Lali held a yawn politely back as they went to the door. 'But it was a lovely evening.'

'It may just be that he's old. He goes back so far, for all of us. Lord knows where he came from, but he's always been there, as long as I remember.'

'Oh, yes, that. He must be eighty.'

Julia came briskly into the rehearsal room next morning, slapping her sable hat against the skirt of her coat to scatter the drops of water. The cleaning woman had, as usual, put away her indoor shoes which she left standing in a corner and she was obliged to go and get them before she could tug off her high boots which were then still called Hungarian boots.

'What a fearsome day,' she said pushing up her hair. 'Snow yesterday and sleet this morning. Wasn't the circus splendid? The children did love it, it was almost like seeing it all oneself for the first time.'

Monika entered for the second rehearsal running and Julia automatically noted that she was evidently being adopted into the production. No wonder, then, that Hansi was so cautious about using Malczewska's help, and so relieved that it would not have to appear in the accounts. It was obvious, too, that for the first few minutes Hansi was watching her with something like apprehension.

'Goddam winter,' groaned Thorn and blew his nose. 'It's like five in the morning outside. Be dark all day. Julie—you didn't walk here, surely?'

'You know I always do, that two minutes.'

'You'll get influenza,' he threatened. 'Even in those sexy boots.'

'Jochen! Behave yourself,' said Anita. 'I'll tell on you.'

'Don't be jealous, darling,' he put his arm round her. 'Ah, you're nice and warm. I didn't say Julie was sexy, I said her boots are.'

'I meant you worrying about her health.'

'Oh that. That's pure professionalism,' said Julia. 'I hope.'

'No, it's this erotic poetry. I find it quite upsetting to the self-control.'

'It will soon be automatic,' Mundel comforted him. 'Then you'll get your um—libido—under control again. At least, in public.'

'Willy! Really!' Hansi pretended prudery. 'Mind the child, here.'

They began work and the nonsense ceased. When they stopped for coffee, Hansi broke into his own dissertation of what they were doing wrong to mention something else, after Monika silently showed him a memorandum slip.

'Listen. I've set the Press conference for the theatre critics for Friday and I'd like you all to be there—I've let the others know.' He meant those members of the cast who were not at rehearsal that morning. 'But a lot of Press people have asked to come apart from the usual stage crowd. So be very careful. Keep your wits about you. They may ask questions that have nothing to do with Shakespeare, inquisitive swine.'

'Well, don't make the mistake of shutting them up, if they do,' Mundel warned him. 'We got away with that business easier than I expected. Don't let's spoil it now.'

'There's no reason why any questions should be answered that don't concern this production,' Hansi was stubborn. 'That's a general rule.'

'It may be a general rule, but this isn't a general situation,' Thorn was sharp. 'Willy's quite right. Don't forbid any question at all. We'll deflect their rage, don't worry.'

'Now look here. . . . Wait, Jochen. Hella will be back tomorrow, she'll be at rehearsal all the time from now on. But she doesn't think it wise to advertise the fact, even now. So keep off her.'

'*She* doesn't think it wise—well I'll be damned!' Mundel laughed.

'She won't be at the P.C., will she?' asked Anita.

'Of course not! So, would you mind, Anita, if you don't come either? We'll have just the principals.'

'That makes sense,' agreed Thorn. 'But don't put up any ban, Hansi. You know they won't agree to it and there'll be a row.'

'We stick to the usual rules,' insisted Ostrovsky.

'We'll keep the rules, Hansi,' said Julia, 'but there's no need to mention anything. That will only start them off.'

Hansi was about to say something more, but Thorn interrupted.

'I shall never understand how a man of your talent and experience, Hansi, can be such a booby with the Press. You want the publicity, you can't do without the papers—why don't you learn to handle them!'

'I'd as soon handle a cage full of those lions,' muttered Hansi gloomily.

'But Hansi! They're all right if you just relax a bit.'

'Yes, all very well for you, Julie. You've got a private wire, we all know that.'

'What a monstrous thing to say,' began Mundel indignantly.

'I didn't mean Georgy,' said Hansi hastily, and a little disingenuously. 'I was speaking of that Barber fellow.'

Julia laughed. 'He's not even here!'

'Well, he's always turning up.' Hansi was defensive.

'Of course. That's his job,' argued Thorn.

'It's time we got back to work,' suggested Anita. Thorn looked at her and dropped the subject.

Towards the end of the morning, Florian came in and sat half on a table, watching them with his glowering intensity. His appearance produced a slight tremor in the atmosphere, though not among the actors, who were concentrated on what they were doing. This reminded Thorn of something and he watched Julia covertly for the next few minutes. But there was certainly nothing missing in her consciousness now; indeed, when he touched her forearm with his elbow and indicated Kiki with a small jerk of the head she did not, for a moment, react at all to this outside stimulus.

Kiki was showing Florian something from a folder, but he looked away only impatiently from the players to attend to her with a brief nod. This did not disconcert her for she was only groping through his ambition towards her own. An assistant joined them and they spoke of something to do with lighting before going away together.

Ostrovsky glanced at the door as Monika went out. It was he whose mind was elsewhere, if only momentarily and partially.

The scene ended, the group disintegrated, hunger made itself felt. Mundel, longing for a first drink, disappeared and others followed. Hansi took Julia's arm to expound a difficult moment in the action in which he did not agree with her movement. She listened with her head bent and her eyes narrowed to follow his thought, as if she tried to make out something very small on the scratched linoleum of the floor. Thorn and Anita watched, as Julia felt her way into Hansi's meaning.

They were startled when the door flew open and Malczewska rapidly entered, still in her outer clothes and with a newspaper in her hand.

'He's dead!' she cried. 'In the night.'

Ostrovsky straightened with a jerk and flung round to face the door with as much force as if a shot had sounded behind him rather than a woman's voice.

'Oh! I'm so sorry,' she continued, confused, 'I thought you'd finished.'

'Dead?' shouted Hansi. His eyes took in the newspaper. 'You stupid fool! I told you not to mention. . . .'

'But what's the matter . . . ?' Malczewska seemed stunned.

The three actors all jumped sharply at Hansi's voice, to stare at him, astounded at his tone of harsh fury. Jochen Thorn was about to say something, but Julia moved, laying a hand on his sleeve, and then, still staring with histrionically wide eyes at Hansi she moved to Malczewska and took the newspaper out of her grasp. She dropped her eyes to the headline right across the top and to the photograph under it. When she raised her eyes again in the silence, they looked as if she might have held a revolver instead of a newspaper in her clenched fist.

'Who did you think was dead, Hansi?' she asked in a very soft and reasonable tone. She raised the paper a little and read in the same tone. ' "The greatest clown on earth is gone".' Julia looked at Malczewska and back at Hansi. 'It must have been second sight that made us all go to the circus yesterday! Don't you agree—Hansi?'

'I remember him in Warsaw when I was still only a girl,' mourned Malczewska. Then she gasped, tried to cover a little cry of recognition and covered her mouth with her good hand.

'Perhaps you'd better tell us what this is all about?' suggested Thorn mildly.

'Hansi's going to tell us,' said Julia. 'Aren't you Hansi? I knew there was something, last night. You couldn't have been more obvious if you'd put on false whiskers. . . . You should never try to act, Hansi, it's not your strong point.' She tipped her head to one side and stepped round Ostrovsky as if to examine his head from all angles. 'Whiskers! As a matter of fact, I think a little beard would suit you. Perhaps an imperial? Now that you're a distinguished public figure . . . ?'

'I don't know what you're talking about.' Hansi tried to recover himself. 'I was startled for a moment. That's all. I'm sorry I was so rude.' He turned to Malczewska. 'But you know it's not allowed to interrupt rehearsals.'

'Yes. Yes, I beg your pardon,' stammered Malczewska. 'I thought, when I saw the others going. . . .'

'Now just a moment!' Thorn protested.

At that moment Hansi gave a warning sign and the door handle rattled loosely. Kiki came in, smiling over her shoulder at Florian, and almost collided with the group.

'Jochen,' said Julia coolly. 'I didn't quite get that last bit. Could you say that again. Cleo should lean over and—what?'

'Cleo should lean right over, sinuously, and fix him with a glare; just like you're doing now. That's it, only of course, you need the low couch to get the movement.'

'Yes, we'll get props to put one in for tomorrow,' chattered Hansi.

'You lot still working?' asked Florian. And suspiciously to Malczewska, 'What brings you here?' He saw the paper in Julia's hand and read off the headline. 'Oh, hell. I missed him last night. I say, that'll be a funeral. I must see that!'

Julia gave him the paper and went over to her clothes. She kicked off her shoes and bent down to hold the top of a boot. As she pulled it on she turned her head up to the others. 'Every time I put my shoes on I see this filthy old paint on the walls here. Why on earth don't we get this room decorated, Hansi?'

'I complain, but they say it isn't worth it. We shall only be here another couple of seasons, so they say, until we get the Burg rebuilt.'

Julia stood upright, slightly flushed, her hair falling forward slightly. She gave them a radiant smile.

'God! Just *imagine* the intrigues there'll be for the first performance when we open again in the new house!' She laughed, throwing back her hair and showing her perfect teeth.

'Doesn't she look marvellous when she laughs?' demanded Thorn.

'Don't start that again, Jochen,' Anita said. 'We've had enough sex for one morning.'

'I'm off,' said Julia, pulling on her hat without looking. She reached the door and opened it slightly, peered dramatically past its edge into the corridor, and turned back. She put a finger to her lips, screwed up her eyes and nodded slowly, conspiratorially to them all before she went out.

'What on earth are you playing at here?' asked Florian.

'She's been camping it up all morning,' said Hansi trying to sound amused and resigned. 'I don't know what's got into her.'

'But it's awfully sad about Grillo, isn't it,' said Monika innocently.

'A bit like one of his scenes, really,' said Thorn. 'I think the old boy would have appreciated it.'

As they went out, Ostrovsky muttered to Jochen Thorn. 'I hope you got the message?'

Thorn raised his eyebrows.

'I play along with Julie,' he said. He almost ran out of the building, hoping to catch Julia up and ask her what the whole scene meant; but she was out of sight. He was just about to turn up the side street she would take to walk home and then stopped himself. What you need, my dear boy, he addressed his shadowy form in a shop window silently, is a new mistress.

Julia was in any case not walking up that way, so Thorn could not have overtaken her. She was going to meet Kerenyi at a restaurant to which her normal path would have taken her down a somewhat unsavoury little street, past a low night bar, a cinema and a reeking fried-fish shop. But without ever considering why, she never went down that street; if she did she would have to pass a post office across the doors of which, in her mind's eye, the steel expanding grill was always locked and where, somewhere in another reality, an exhausted, half-wild woman leaned against the wall. In that other, still real, but well-hidden world it was warm, almost hot, too hot for a dirty beaver coat and the air was full of a menacing stink of burned wood and stone dust.

They were sitting in the tiny bar on stools which always make men look ridiculous if one comes up behind them, but both of them had the wit to sit sideways. The soft lights were on as if it were evening.

'What are you drinking?' she asked, smiling at the fat woman who took her coat with reverence. 'Oh, my hat's crooked,' she added as she saw herself in the glass wall behind the bottles. 'How are you, Berthold? Finished all that business?'

'It went awfully fast,' said Georgy, 'I expected it to take all day.' He was still holding her hand, and chafed it now, between his to warm it.

'I,' she said with a grand air, 'have news for you two. They know where he is.'

Both men raised their heads sharply, both started to speak, both stopped. The handsome boy behind the bar gave Julia a glass containing the same mixture that the two men were drinking, without sa, ing anything. 'Where's Louis?' she asked nobody.

'Day off,' said Georgy.

'Do you know where?' asked Berthold, and drank from his flat glass.

'They didn't say. Not they. In fact, nobody said anything but a lot of fooling. Sad about Grillo.'

'Isn't it? But a good way to go.'

The two men looked at each other fleetingly, thinking of ways other men had gone.

'This tastes nice. What's it called?'

'Champagne cocktail,' said Luders, looking astonished.

'Are we celebrating, then? Good, I'm feeling very—mm—very something. . . .'

'Today nothing but champagne. We've just signed the management contract, after all.'

'I should have thought we celebrated that on its fifth anniversary, and not before,' she said. The barman left them alone and Luders spoke quietly.

'Who found out?'

'I can only guess. I think probably *her* lawyers.'

'Ah. Yes, that figures. And you don't think you can find out . . .'

'I may,' she began. Without being aware of a decision, she changed her words. 'It's not likely though. You'd be surprised how secrets are kept if everyone wants them kept.'

'Very true,' said Berthold, and shot his cuff to see his watch face. 'Have some more of this stuff?'

Three new guests entered, so that the space was now filled. They talked of circuses, and the old clown. One of them nudged her neighbour when she recognised Julia, but Julia did not see. Luders and Kerenyi began to invent toasts to drink to, until they had finished the bottle, when they went to table.

'I do wonder sometimes,' said Kerenyi as they unfolded their heavy, cold napkins, 'how one would manage, trying to say things to people whose language is not words?'

Julia gazed at him abstractedly. The waiter suggested *bisque d'homard* and she said no, that would be tinned, so far from the sea, she would have clear soup with bone-marrow. The others agreed and the man went away.

'Funny you should say that,' said Julia to her husband. 'I thought that was your particular thing.'

'It only works with our kind of people, people who know what I mean anyway. That's the difference from writing, where one has to explain everything.'

'Hofmannsthal wrote a play about that. About not saying things. It's very difficult to put over.' She thought with a slight shock, I shall never play that part again, and her face altered subtly. They were alone at the table now, and she tried to explain to the two men what had so oddly happened at the rehearsal. Malczewska must have heard Hansi and Monika at the circus refer to Tenius in some unmistakable fashion, and they then saw her behind them, too late. Hansi warned her not to speak of what she heard and that morning in the rehearsal room, thought she was defying him. In his sudden anger at being, as he thought, disobeyed by this outsider, he betrayed himself to Julia.

'I must find out what they know,' Luders was restless and disturbed.

'Better not,' Julia warned him. 'The less said the better. As you see from this story, someone always hears something they aren't supposed to. What does it matter where he is? He is dead. Or he will die. That is all.'

'We can't be sure of that. People sometimes drag on for twenty years after several seizures.'

'Not after five years in Siberian camps. They pop off at the climacteric.' Kerenyi sounded brutal.

'But have you considered? If Julia is right and Ostrovsky heard through Frau Schneider's lawyers, not only must at least half a dozen people know already, but he may actually still be in the country?'

Kerenyi's head came up sharply, and then his expression relaxed again.

'Not at all. They could have traced him to his point of departure and discovered his destination. There's nothing in Julie's evidence that says anyone has been in touch with him.'

'You could ask Frau Schneider?' Berthold persisted, to Julia.

'If he is alive and still in Austria, she would lie. That gets us nowhere. Besides—I've pushed Hella as far as she will go over Malczewska's papers. It would be a fatal mistake to bully her again.

311

There's a point at which desperation takes over in such situations. And Hella's lifelong success has not made her patient in misfortune.'

'I suppose you are right,' he agreed dubiously. 'But there must be some way. . . .'

'Berthold, don't expect too much. One can't know everything, and it's best not to want to. I don't quite trust your passion for having your facts all orderly and complete.'

'I promise you I won't do anything without getting your consent first. There, that's handsome of me, don't you agree?' Luders pushed his table napkin away from him, holding on to its slippery folds with a firm grip. 'Still, I'd like to know how his hiding-place was found. My own private detectives are the best firm in Hamburg, and they've found no trace. But on the other hand, it may be an oblique hint that Tenius is still in Austria, or possibly in South Tyrol. A north German enquiring would come up against the local obstinacy; mountain people don't like strangers except in their controllable character of tourists.'

Julia looked sideways at him. 'Now you are just spinning tales,' she said.

'Well, we've nothing much else to go on,' Georgy agreed. 'Odd too, it should have come out today, when we've just signed our partnership. And the first of the series in "Tales of Our Times" is in print for this month's issue. My own story, that is.'

'It didn't come out today,' Julia pointed out. 'In fact, Hansi may have known for some time. He's been a bit preoccupied—I thought it was about Kiki, but it may not have been, or not Kiki alone.'

'Was it difficult Kerenyi, writing all the stuff about the past?' Luders changed the subject as the waiters busied themselves round the table. 'Bringing it all back again?'

'Damned hard. I felt much more seriously about it all than I did at the time. At the time, it was just what was going on—you know? In retrospect it's a pretty terrible story, and I scared myself half to death. And all those chaps. . . .'

There was silence, and then Kerenyi said, 'It was Tenius who saved my life, by betraying me, I'm sure of that. The police would have tracked me down to Agram if I'd stayed there.'

'I believed they had, until you came back again,' said Julia.

XXVI

'Certainly there is an alternative,' said Robert. 'And a good one. For me good because I should continue in the same direction, and use the same skills and experience, such as they are, that I have so far managed to acquire. But it has a drawback. When I first began to think about leaving the Service I thought it had two disadvantages, but during the summer I came to the conclusion that my worries about my own stupid little conscience were a form of cowardice. The other disadvantage remains, however. It's that Nando would be forced to repeat the experience of my own childhood and youth and live between worlds. I don't want to be pompous, but I wouldn't burden anybody with that condition, and certainly not my son.'

'You've discussed all this together, then?' Julia asked.

'After the funeral we talked about it,' Lali answered for Robert. 'When I got back. You see, if we knew that our land, the Kasda place, was lost for good, it would be easy.' She turned her bonny look, now solemnly almost childishly frowning on Kerenyi, as if he should interpret what she found so difficult to formulate. 'It's not, you see, a matter of possession, the place. It's that we can't abandon it. It exists, mother exists, the other people who depend on us for help there can't just be forgotten either.'

'If we were sure that we could never again go back there, Lali feels, and Frau von Kasda feels too, then we should shut the past out of our lives.' Robert took the theme up again. 'Then it would not only be useless, as Countess Kasda puts it, but wrong to hang on to it—the thought of it. But we can't know. And, you see, the tenants there who farm the land would be in a very awkward position with the local authorities who have to answer to the Occupation. I can't go there myself, as you know, because of my job. But that doesn't mean I haven't made it my business to keep in touch, and the peasants have returned to a practically feudal attitude to Frau von Kasda and Lali as Nando's mother. They rely on the two women to protect their hold on their—it is for practical purposes theirs—land. It may not make sense in law, but I don't have to tell you that the law is bent into some pretty curious shapes in that part of the country. Property is no longer a possession, it is a social duty to your neighbours. I was amazed last year when the Occupation authority moved out of the Kasda house—there was practically a panic locally because everyone was afraid it meant the removal of a form of protection. It seems to have worked out all right, but only because Frau von Kasda was *there*.'

'Of course, people resent all this bitterly,' said Lali. 'I dare say if the Occupation is ever ended, they will change their attitude at once. But for now, that's the way things are.'

'And, you see, all this makes Nando belong here in a much more real way than he could ever be part of a genuine life in London. He would be bound to feel the division of loyalties—he'd be made to if he didn't—in a way that would absolutely wreck his character.'

'But don't you fear—feel—that you will be divided in yourself if you make a definite decision to stay here forever?' Georgy frowned down at the table, at an unoffending book lying open there, as if the book were to blame for the difficulty of saying things of such intimacy. 'I mean, it's one thing to stay even after your Commission is ended, as if by chance. Quite another to take an active resolve that you can't really go back on, should you want to do so later.'

'I may do. I can't know that in advance. But I don't really see why I should feel any alienation. I remain English. Thousands of British families have lived abroad for generations. Why not me? I think we've all got into a rather over-emotional state of chauvinism. . . . Probably the war, I suppose. I think if I feel anything about belonging anywhere except simply with my family, I feel like a European. Wouldn't that be an acceptable state?'

'If the world leaves you in peace,' said Julia, breaking a long silence.

Robert smiled at her serious face.

'That, after all, applies to us all, and not only here. If we really did start to murder each other again, the end would only be a little sooner than if I were on the other side of the continent. That's a decision, as it were, that's taken for everyone by their parents, when they are born.'

'There isn't going to be another war,' Lali said hastily.

'No, of course not, little one,' Julia was comforting in spite of her own lack of faith in what she said so readily.

'I don't feel pessimistic,' Kerenyi rose and began to make his habitual track up and down the long room. 'Perhaps we're moving into a long period of prosperity. It will be uneasy. But life always has been. Human beings once feared death every day from the Plague, and every night from the forces of the devil. All too real, that part! They didn't stop living, so why should our present fears lame us?' He stopped for a moment, hands in pockets, in front of the Chinese cabinet. 'This thing—which I don't really admire much, by the way, it's not my style—is a sort of guarantee that the past survives. Enough of it for the thread of continuity not to be quite broken. The loop of time, you see. . . .' He turned to look at Julia. 'From the time of our birth, think of the changes. You would hardly have said people could survive them and remain in any relation to those who went just before us. Yet we do, recognisably. We belong to the old world and we live quite comfortably in the new, carrying the past over into the future and infecting the young with the past in every breath we draw.'

'You're right about the cabinet,' said Julia, laughing slightly at the thought. 'That was the only thing I inherited from my old aunt. And I only got that because she'd failed to sell it during the Inflation. Heaven only knows where she got it—I mean, she inherited it of course, but I don't know how it came into her family. For years I thought of it as really a bit of a nuisance. I was astonished when the old man'—she tipped her chin quickly to indicate the portrait—'went into raptures about it. He knew a lot about old things, as you can see from the stuff he bought for this place. All the good things were found by him, and he valued the cabinet especially because it was the one thing inherited, not bought.'

'I imagine he was one of those who bought in the Inflation,' guessed Kerenyi.

She looked up, startled at the thought.

'If he did, I'm sure he offered fair prices,' she said. 'He was the most generous man I ever knew, a real spendthrift. I only knew him for a year or so, but I remember him saying often that one could never really enjoy anything one hadn't paid for. He used to quote the Spanish proverb—at least, he said it was Spanish—"take what you want—and pay". Then he'd put his head on one side with his clever little grin, he was a bit like a squirrel to look at, and say one

315

should always pay the full price, otherwise payment would be ex-
acted in some other way. He was a very wise old man.'

'So I may take it then, that your consent is given,' Robert swiftly
prevented the sarcastic rejoinder he could see coming in Georgy's
expectant smile. 'Lali and I can build on our "back to the land"
movement?'

'You're getting too clever by half, young Robert,' said Kerenyi.
'I was just about to start a splendid argument, then.'

'I know that, you old devil.'

'Speaking of arguments, you never heard any more about
Tenius, did you Robert?'

'Not a word. Somehow, I don't know why, I don't think we
ever shall. Wherever he is, nobody can get at him, because there's
been no divorce petition listed in the courts. Not here, not in Salzburg, nor in Tenius' own home town. So that's that.'

'D'you know what I think?' asked Lali. 'I think he's asked for
asylum in some monastery somewhere.'

They all stared at her, at the unconsidered, but so obvious possibility.

'But he'd have to be handed over by the monks,' objected
Robert.

'No, not if anything he said were in the confessional. Don't you
see?'

'Good God. . . . I wonder if that's the answer?' Julia said at last.

'Was he Catholic?' asked Robert. She shook her head.

'I've no idea,' she said. 'Do you know, Georgy?'

'He could be, I suppose. He came from somewhere near Müns-
ter, didn't he.'

'I must ask Hella if they were married in church,' said Julia.
'Oh. Well, I suppose I can hardly do that. . . .'

'Pity,' said Georgy. They were all obliged to laugh at the regret
in his voice.

The talk drifted back quite naturally to the future lives of Lali
and Robert, but the strange thought that Tenius might be immured
somewhere, perhaps not far away from them, enclosed for ever in
silence, stayed in the air about them. It was an idea very typical
of Lali's mind with its possibility of a merciful self-imprisonment
and this thought of a possible reconciliation by the man's own will
was comforting in its suggestion of repayment, even a very partial
one, without revenge. Both Julia and Kerenyi knew themselves

316

too well to allow any deception as to their own urgent self-interest in such a solution; but the wise do not reject a solution to a painful problem just because it suits practical as well as moral interests. It would be so very much what all of them desired that it began quickly to seem as if it must be so. That Tenius, ill and afraid, might have taken refuge in a place where he could hardly help but ponder on his life, showed a symmetry that is rarely offered in the chances of real life.

Julia went over to a window and pulled back the long curtain to see out.

'Black dark,' she said musingly. 'And it's begun to snow again. Isn't it strange just this year, that it should snow all winter. . . .'

They looked across at her tall figure, darkly posed against the pale, silky folds of the curtain, but she was not looking at them.

'I've never seen such huge snow-flakes. They float in the air like butterflies, like feathers. As if someone tipped up a great big featherbed. It doesn't feel as if it ought to be winter. I've been existing for months in the heat of Egypt and here it is, snowing. . . .'

'Does it dominate you all the time?' Lali asked curiously.

'Oh yes. Until it's been played in front of an audience half a dozen times or so. Then the obsession fades. You will come to the dress rehearsal, won't you? What's today—Friday? Yes, it's just a week today.'

'You never force your moods on other people. It always surprises me over again to think of you living another life that we don't see into.'

'There's not much energy left over for playing up my moods,' replied Julia in the same musing tone. 'Egotism takes up a lot of vitality that is needed for work.' She let the curtain fall into place and came back towards them. 'Strange. This part is terribly important to me. I feel as if it were the most important thing in life, more demanding than real life, and if I fail in it, it will be the end of . . . some old ambition. Yet I feel less strain in it than I ever remember in a major new part.'

They were silent, oppressed by the hitherto inconceivable thought that Julia could fail. Even Georgy was afraid to touch her hand, to say anything, lest he should appear to force himself on her, to try to disengage her chosen and lonely concentration and draw it to himself. She said she felt less strain than ever before, and that must be enough.

317

'Barber and Berthold Luders giving a big party after the opening night is not too popular. We had to help them with their list,' said Lali at last. 'I have a new dress and I'm going to flirt outrageously. They're as rich as Croesus between them, those two.'

'I haven't opened my card yet,' said Julia, laughing now at herself. 'It's one of my few superstitions, not to count on celebrations of first nights before they are over.'

'Why not popular?' asked Robert.

'Several people have said to me they're strangers, why should they give the party. . . . It doesn't stop anybody accepting, though, so that's all right.'

'It adds to the pleasure for most of those invited,' said Georgy. 'They can resent foreigners flaunting their wealth as well as feeling they are imposing on them by taking their hospitality without liking them for it.'

'The fate of generosity,' Julia said idly.

Nerves of communication were quivering with life and they were both of them almost waiting for the guests, however close and affectionate the bonds that bound them, to leave them alone. She was feeling her way towards what Georgy wanted to know, but she failed because the image of Tenius inside uncommunicative high walls, although not of a prison, filled her mind with a magic force; it sometimes happened that an idea would fascinate one level of her mind enough to cover up its real preoccupation. This is a protective device of the artistic temperament that allows work to develop without interference, especially in the crucial moment of time when the project is prepared for appearance, for good or ill, in the actual world for judgment. It was, indeed, the reminder of Tenius that activated anew Kerenyi's curiosity but he was concerned with another aspect of that unsolved and unsatisfactory business. They did not know much about what had happened, as little as they knew of what was happening at that moment to Tenius. How deeply was Malczewska at some former moment involved with the plots circling about the returned prisoner; and how clearly did Julia perceive at that moment past, that at least one threat to their common peace of mind could be eliminated by engaging Malczewska's loyalties through self-interest—this question concerned Kerenyi. Above all, whether Julia was aware of her reasons for intervention. She did not develop trains of thought, but acted out of a comprehension of deeply experienced situations, grouped

318

constellations of related personalities. These were what she sometimes recognised in her phrase of nerve-memories; but she had never said or even implied anything to Kerenyi about this matter that would give away a consciousness of her own motive. There was no important reason why she should help Malczewska and oblige others to help her, except to remove a threat to Georgy's position in his world. For her own position, no matter what she said about it, remained neutral, unassailable as long as she simply stayed outside the orbit of the lowering scandal. When she deliberately involved herself she did so because—there could be no other motive —her own life was so much identified with his that she felt a threat to his reputation as one to her own.

If Julia worked this intricate little puzzle out beforehand in her conscious mind, its value to Kerenyi as evidence was gone; he knew she did not do that for that was not the way her mind worked, but he wanted to know if she now recognised what her purpose with Malczewska had been.

Thinking of all this, it occurred to Kerenyi with an effect of startling suddenness, that in spite of the ever-present watchfulness of various police systems, and in particular those of the eastern countries, no trace of evidence had officially been discovered about Tenius. Some quasi-private agency of which Ostrovsky was able to hear a hint, discovered his hiding-place, and the proximity of knowledge suggested, almost proved, that the successful agent must have been Hella Schneider's lawyers who worked with only very limited means and powers.

The vast apparatus of military espionage, multiplied by four, failed; a civilian with only restricted means, succeeded. This implied clearly that wherever Tenius was, he was under some protection over which none of the Allies had any power. They all assumed until this evening that the escape was achieved by a clandestine brotherhood over which all of the military establishments had power, if they could lay hands on it. But Lali, in her odd little feminine fashion, had thought of another solution and one that lay in an almost absolute sense, outside temporal powers, and indeed, in the secrecy of the confessional to some extent outside its own higher organisation. Lali wanted a possibility that could be reconciled with her own gentleness, her incapacity for hatred. Was it possible that mercy had hit upon the truth where the massive powers of the world had failed even to consider it?

It was a consideration that Kerenyi was peculiarly fitted to enjoy.

Something of this Georgy said to Julia when they were alone, but without mentioning Malczewska. She was rearranging something untidied during the evening, leaning over a sofa with coloured silk cushions. She turned towards him, to consider what he said, a square of brilliant softness held in one hand so that a cyclamen pink was forever the colour of joy.

'It ought to be true; it's so right. Let's hope it is, for then he will never reappear. And I might not have Malczewska and Hella to put pressure on if he turned up again.'

'Your arrogance is really astonishing,' he said with great satisfaction.

'It seems a long way back to the night we returned from Greece,' she answered, as if agreeing with him.

A long evening of turmoil, pent energy expended in a flood, exhaustion of what seemed almost a lifetime of preparation. The theatre, so often criticised, blamed for being too small, was this night cramped to anguish for the players and the pressure on the audience was almost unbearable in the too narrow space. Julia could hear her own voice hitting the far walls and sinking into the over-near, smothering block of humanity; Thorn's harshness seemed to be smiting both herself and the public with blows of sound. The compression that so burdened them was, too, explosive. It was as much relief as pleasure that stampeded the hundreds of people into a tornado of applause. The words of triumph, storm-taking, attack and fury that flew about the corridors, made it sound as if a battle had taken place there, and they felt as if that were the case. It was not a play at all, the voice of a critic could be heard, it more resembled a long rape of the senses, he was worn out.

Thorn leaned against the door post of her dressing room, his face gaunt and hollow with strain and fatigue. The car was waiting.

No, she said, they should all go on; she and Georgy would walk.

He was waiting, almost unfamiliar in the formality of his clothing. She greeted him with an astonished lightening of tension as if she had feared not to find him after such a stormy passage in high seas, at the other side of the evening's journey. They did not speak;

she was too tired out for words and needed a space of movement between the effort and its dispersal into gaiety.

The disapproving dresser pulled straight a thin waterproof cape over furs to keep out the heavily falling snow. Only Julia would think of walking to a party on a night like this, somebody said, boots and all.

The wind was fierce, and they bent into it as it tore up the narrow street, funnelled into rage by ancient walls. The tall lights swung violently to and fro like witches' lanterns, making the shadows fly in the snow-shot darkness.

It was not far across the almost deserted, brilliantly illuminated shopping street, down dark alleys, past a looming curve of palatial façade, under the austere spire of the Augustine church. As they came into the perfect townscape of the square, they stopped and their own footsteps died, his uneven, hers sharp and decided. The lighted windows of their destination stretched away to their right. The square, not big but great in its supreme harmony, surrounded them familiarly, the Emperor Josef riding for ever forward in its centre. They threw their heads back to take it in for the thousandth time. A great burst of tempestuous wind swirled round, flinging the crowding snow upwards in a blown spiral, obscuring the shapes about them into a dreamlike shimmering winter pattern.

Temple Israel

Minneapolis, Minnesota

In Honor of the Bar Mitzvah of
WILLIAM B. DWORSKY
by
Mr. and Mrs. Mischa Dworsky

March 29, 1980